KT-382-068

ALSO BY TOM BALE

All Fall Down
See How They Run
Sins of the Father writing as David Harrison
Skin and Bones
Terror's Reach
Blood Falls
The Catch

C0053 51813

bookouture

Published by Bookouture
An imprint of StoryFire Ltd.
23 Sussex Road, Ickenham, UB10 8PN
United Kingdom
www.bookouture.com

Copyright © Tom Bale, 2017

Tom Bale has asserted his right to be identified
as the author of this work.

All rights reserved. No part of this publication may be reproduced, stored in any retrieval system, or transmitted, in any form or by any means, electronic, mechanical, photocopying, recording or otherwise, without the prior written permission of the publishers.

ISBN: 978-1-78681-207-0
eBook ISBN: 978-1-78681-206-3

This book is a work of fiction. Names, characters, businesses, organizations, places and events other than those clearly in the public domain, are either the product of the author's imagination or are used fictitiously. Any resemblance to actual persons, living or dead, events or locales is entirely coincidental.

For Kate & Dan, Lucy & Tony

CHAPTER ONE

He'd crossed her path before, but today was different. There was a flash of light as the man hurried across the patch of grass at the front of his property; Jen caught the glint of sunlight on metal, the sense of something falling.

For most of August he'd been running later than normal, which made her wonder if his schedule, like hers, was influenced by the school holidays. As usual, he was carrying a couple of his mysterious boxes, cradling them awkwardly in both arms, as if the contents were precious rather than heavy.

On some mornings he took his car, a Nissan X-Trail that was parked at the kerb; on others – like today – he was being collected. A white Subaru waited in the road, engine running. The driver, a middle-aged woman, had already thrust the passenger door open.

Until recently the man had often attempted eye contact, and sometimes a cryptic smile to acknowledge that their routines had coincided yet again. Perhaps he'd secretly hoped she would ask what those boxes contained. But a couple of weeks ago she'd been crossing the road by the hospital when his X-Trail came blasting around the corner and nearly ran her down. Since then she'd made a point of ignoring him, and he must have got the message. Without so much as a glance in her direction, he crouched and manoeuvred himself onto the seat, propping the boxes on his knees.

The car was already moving as he pulled the door shut, the woman accelerating with unnecessary vigour towards the junction with Bristol Gardens. As Jen drew level with the man's property she had to shield her eyes with one hand. The low morning sun had set the windows ablaze: perhaps that was what she'd noticed?

No. After a month of hot weather the scrap of lawn was parched and pale, so it wasn't difficult to see what the man had dropped on the grass.

A set of keys.

Instinct took over. Discarding her sports bag, Jen snatched up the keys and ran.

In a past life, pre motherhood, she had been a dedicated runner and climber; even now, at thirty-four, she was light on her feet and very fast. She made it to the end of the street in seconds, but the Subaru was already too far away.

Checking the road was clear, Jen stepped out and waved to attract the driver's attention. A flash of brake lights gave her hope, only for the car to take a sharp left turn and disappear. Jen stood for a moment with her hands on her hips. Now what?

The grumble of an engine reminded her that she was in the middle of the road; a delivery van rolled towards her, the driver frowning even as he checked out her body. She was dressed for work, which meant trainers, tracksuit bottoms and a baggy T-shirt. Not baggy enough, perhaps.

She jogged back to the house, aware that the keys in her hand now represented a problem. Unless. . .

She rang the doorbell, waited a few seconds, then knocked loudly. She couldn't recall having seen anyone else coming or going, but that wasn't to say the man didn't have a partner or a family. Should she put the keys through the letterbox?

It was almost nine thirty. She had to be at work for ten, and the bus service in Brighton wasn't always reliable. Ideally she needed somebody to open the door, take the keys and let Jen get on with her day.

Retreating across the grass, she squinted at the upper windows. No hint of movement. She turned in a slow circle, hoping someone had seen her predicament and was coming to help. *Mislaid his keys, did he? Don't worry, I'll take them for you.*

Regency Place was a curious but not unattractive mix of terraced houses, new builds and small apartment blocks. Jen's own flat was about ten minutes' walk away, up the hill. This house was one of only three modest two-storey homes, squeezed between a row of lock-up garages and a plot of fenced-off waste ground. Directly opposite was a longer terrace, but it was positioned side-on to the road, so the occupants of the end house had only a limited view across the street. Because of that, Jen thought, they were unlikely to know the people who lived here.

But there were at least two neighbours she could try. She knocked at the house next door, but the sound that came back had a hollow, empty feel to it. Moving to the third property, she made out the frantic skittering of paws on a hard floor. There were signs everywhere: 'WARNING: BEWARE OF THE DOG'. . . 'NO CALLERS'. . . 'ADDRESSED MAIL ONLY'.

A volley of barks followed her knock, and what sounded like a heavy animal threw itself against the front door. Jen backed away, feeling slightly relieved when no one answered.

She returned to where she'd left her sports bag on the lawn and studied the keys in her hand. Three in all, attached to a cheap plastic key ring: a Yale, which seemed to correspond to the front door; a bulkier key for a mortise lock; and a small one that might fit a padlock. She checked the time again – nine thirty-three – and considered her options.

*

Now that she'd found the keys, she could hardly toss them back onto the grass. Somebody else was bound to come along and spot them, and that person might not be as law-abiding as Jen. Nor were there any better places to leave them for the householder to find.

Again she thought of slipping them through the letterbox. But if they were the only set, the man would have to break in to his own house, or hire a locksmith. Jen didn't want to cause him that kind of hassle, even if he did sometimes drive like a maniac.

Hand them in at the police station? That was no doubt the correct thing to do. But the nearest station was a bus ride away, and how long would it take to be seen? These days there were probably all sorts of forms to fill in.

I could take the keys with me and leave him a note? That seemed like a far better solution.

She crouched to open her bag. She usually carried a couple of the weekly timetables from work, listing the various training sessions and fitness classes on offer. She was less certain about a pen, but maybe there'd be something at the bottom of the bag; even just a pencil or crayon used by her seven-year-old son, Charlie.

After rummaging for several seconds, she emptied her spare clothes and toiletries onto the grass and felt around in every corner of the bag. She found a copy of the timetable, but nothing to write with. Returning home to fetch a pen would take fifteen or twenty minutes – time she didn't have.

She turned to scan the street in both directions: no one in sight. She sighed. There was an idea forming, though she wasn't yet sure if she wanted to entertain it.

Then she flinched, and turned towards the house. Had she heard something from inside?

She moved closer to the front door and listened carefully. Did the silence have a different quality to that of the neighbouring property, or was it merely her imagination playing tricks, because she wanted someone to come and take these keys off her hands?

Nine thirty-six – she *really* had to get going. She knocked again, four loud thumps on the door. Glanced up to check the windows, and at the same time registered that there was no box to indicate the presence of a burglar alarm.

Make a decision. . .

When she looked down, the Yale was gripped between her thumb and forefinger. She slipped it into the lock.

CHAPTER TWO

After opening the door a fraction, she hesitated, alert to any sound or vibration from within, then called out: 'Hello? Anyone there?'

All that came back was a faint ticking noise, and the hum and gurgle of a fridge. She opened the door wider and peeked inside. The hallway was narrow, with a flight of stairs to her left, a living room to the right and the kitchen straight ahead.

'Hello?' she called again. 'I found your keys outside. Can you come and get them?'

There was no answer, no movement, no sense of anybody listening. And yet Jen felt a tickle on the back of her neck. She turned quickly, sure that somebody was about to accuse her of intruding. But the street was deserted.

She shook off an irrational twinge of guilt. This wasn't intruding: she was trying to do a good deed. If she went inside, it was only to find a pen so she could write a note.

Okay, maybe there was just a tiny illicit thrill as she stepped over the threshold – because who *didn't* enjoy an opportunity to look around an unfamiliar house?

The hallway had laminate flooring, and as she set her bag down she noticed dust and grime in the corners, bolstering her gut feeling that this man lived alone; housework obviously wasn't high on the agenda.

She was in two minds about shutting the front door, and settled for leaving it ajar. She cleared her throat, and called out once more: 'Is anyone home?'

Gonna be very late for work. With that urgency on her mind, she moved towards the open doorway to her right and found a small living room, bare except for a sofa, a single straight-backed chair and a TV on a metal stand. There was a mirror on the wall but no pictures, no photographs or personal effects. A folded newspaper on the sofa was the only sign of recent occupation.

She made for the kitchen, passing a toilet and a closed door to what she assumed would be the dining room. There was a faint smell of aftershave or body spray in the air, she realised; something woody and masculine and not very subtle.

The kitchen was small, with shiny white units and black marble-effect worktops. The built-in appliances were rarely used, if the dust on the hob was anything to go by. A single coffee mug sat on the worktop, next to a kettle that still had condensation visible through the water-gauge window. A wrapper from a cereal bar lay on the floor: breakfast on the run, consistent with the man's urgency as he left the house.

She couldn't see anything to write with, and wondered if she should just leave the keys outside the front door, perhaps covered by a pot or a bowl. She felt a growing sense of unease, and decided that venturing upstairs would be too intrusive. It was the dining room or nothing.

She gripped the handle, then let it go and knocked instead, chilled by a sudden notion that she would open the door to find an entire family seated at the table in absolute silence, all turning to stare at her.

No one answered, of course, so she opened the door, had a look inside, and gasped.

Her first thought: *Well, this explains the boxes.* And if pushed, perhaps she'd have to concede that her curiosity about them had been a factor in her decision to enter the house.

The room still held a dining table, but it was covered with dozens of figurines, ranging in size from a few inches to perhaps a foot and a half tall, set into heavy resin bases. The figures themselves were constructed from ingenious combinations of steel and copper wire, glass and precious stones and even the sort of everyday nuts and bolts that you might pick up at a DIY shop.

Most of them were representations from classical mythology – the gods and monsters of ancient Greece, the spirits and demons of Celtic folklore. Jen stared at them in fascination. As an outdoor enthusiast from early childhood, she felt a deep affinity for the myths and legends of the Green Man, of Cernunnos the Celtic god of the forest, and saw a lot of merit in the idea of treating the planet as a single precious organism.

She took a step into the room and felt something crunch underfoot. The floor was gritty with fragments of glass and strands of wire. That suggested some work was done in here, although the room wasn't equipped as a studio, and the man projected none of the vitality or enthusiasm that Jen had encountered in the artists she'd met over the years; he usually had the weary, put-upon demeanour of a bureaucrat.

Jen wondered if he was a retailer, and chose to keep some of his stock at home. She had little doubt that this artwork was valuable. Each piece was individually crafted, and must have taken many hours to produce. Perhaps the man was familiar enough with the work to make a few tiny alterations himself.

At the far end of the room there was a shelving unit on which more of the figures were arranged, along with a stack of flat-packed cardboard boxes. There were also scissors and packing tape, and a jar with half a dozen Sharpie pens. A large roll of bubble wrap sat on the floor beside the unit, and resting on that was a spiral notebook. Hallelujah!

Jen moved slowly, anxious not to bump into any of the larger figures. It was tempting to stop and admire them, but she was already going to be late for work, and that would only make things more difficult with Nick.

The notebook was brand new and unused. She tore out a page, took a Sharpie from the jar, but as she crouched slightly to write there was a soft clanging noise. Her foot had nudged a metal waste bin beneath the table.

At first she thought it contained no more than ordinary rubbish – scraps of packing tape, offcuts of cardboard and bubble wrap, an empty bottle of cherry cola – but then she spotted a head poking from the debris.

And she recognised it.

She couldn't resist taking a closer look. Retrieving the figure carefully from the bin, she saw that one of the legs had snapped below the knee, presumably rendering it worthless.

Jen didn't agree. Even with the damage, it was a beautiful, delicate piece of art: a tall, sinuous representation of Elen of the Ways, an antlered goddess of ancient Britain who was said to watch over pathways, both physical and spiritual. Jen had first heard of her a few years ago, while hiking in Northumberland with a group that included a couple of practising Wiccans.

The figurine was about ten inches tall, with antlers carved from what might have been real bone sprouting from her skull. Her glorious red hair was composed of multiple strands of copper wire, and she was clad in a long, flowing cloak made with dozens of dark green beads, each one no larger than a peppercorn. Her face had been shaped from crystal, perhaps rose quartz, and caught the light as Jen turned it in her hand, making it seem almost as though her expression had changed from sombre reflection to something warm and wise.

Jen had never seen such a gorgeous piece, and she resolved to ask the man, when he came to collect his keys, how much these figures sold for and where she could buy them.

But this one's broken, thrown away; you could easily—

She shut that idea down at once, but felt a twinge of disappointment as she placed the goddess gently back in the bin. She scribbled a note, explaining that he'd dropped his keys and could arrange to collect them by calling her mobile number. Then she tore off a couple of strips of packing tape, retrieved her bag from the hall and left the house, struck by the shock of heat and humidity as she stepped outside. For the past few weeks, Brighton had felt more like some sun-drenched resort in the Aegean or the Med than the English Channel, and Jen was loving every minute of it.

After closing the front door, she fixed the note to the upper panel, smoothing out the tape until she was sure it was stuck firmly in place. A car passed while she had her back to the road, but otherwise the street was quiet.

So why the knot of tension in her guts as she turned away, the feeling that she was being not just watched, but *judged*?

She shivered. Hefting the sports bag onto her shoulder, she set off at a jog towards the corner and kept up the pace all the way to the bus stop on Eastern Road, praying for an uncongested route to Portslade. If there were any lingering doubts, they were quickly pushed aside. What she'd done had been the right thing, as well as the easiest solution at the time.

CHAPTER THREE

Work was at the Skyway, a sports centre built on the site of a former engineering works on the border of Hove and Portslade, a short walk – or, today, a breathless run – from the bus stop on New Church Road. There was a well-equipped gym and a twenty-five-metre pool, available to members only, with squash courts, a soft play area and a large mixed-activity hall – for basketball, trampolining and so on – open to the public.

Jen spent most of her time at the centre's newest addition: an indoor bouldering area which offered five hundred square yards of rope-free rock climbing for all ages and abilities. As well as being available for individual tuition, she ran regular classes for small groups, mostly first-timers curious about this relatively unknown form of exercise.

She was twenty minutes late, which wasn't ideal, though the hot weather was having a notable effect on visitor numbers, making it the quietest summer holiday anyone could remember. The first class didn't start till eleven, and there were only a handful of regulars limbering up when she arrived.

Glynn was on the desk this morning. He was a tall, wiry man in his forties, an avid road cyclist who had quickly become obsessive about climbing. He had a ball of putty in each hand, and was squeezing them to build up the strength in his forearms.

'You've got Nick on the warpath.'

'Have I?'

'Just kidding.' Glynn's soft Welsh accent and deadpan manner were perfect for wind-ups, but Jen should have known better. Appraising her carefully, he said, 'You up for a one-to-one?'

'I guess so.' Jen looked around, surprised there was any demand for tuition this early in the day.

'The feller was here a second— Ah, there he is.'

A young man had emerged from the changing rooms, dressed in green shorts, a yellow T-shirt and a pair of Scarpa climbing shoes. Jen turned before he could make eye contact; her wince told Glynn all he needed to know.

'Then again, you could assume command of the cash register while I instruct this novice in the finer points of crimping?'

'Thanks.' Jen grinned. 'Least you can do, after scaring me like that.'

A flurry of customers appeared, and then it was time for the eleven o'clock class. After that, one of the seasonal employees begged for help setting up the soft-play equipment. A couple of regular staff had called in sick, including the woman whose job was to oversee birthday parties.

As a result, Jen was in the sports hall for nearly two hours, corralling a boisterous group of nine-year-olds. The job was often like this, chaotically varied, and Jen rarely spent the whole day in the role that had been assigned to her. Some of her colleagues resented that variety, but in general she welcomed the chance to acquire different skills.

By most people's standards this was an unconventional occupation, though for her it represented a major compromise: not only was it rooted in one geographical location, but the majority of her work took place indoors. There were times when she sorely missed the freedom she'd once had, leading small groups of wealthy tourists on treks across the Serengeti or over the mountains of

Patagonia. And while she had been glad to make the sacrifices that motherhood required, it was proving far more difficult to meet the challenges of life as a single parent, while also accommodating the many demands made by Charlie's dad, Freddie.

Thinking of her ex-husband made her realise that he hadn't been in touch about the arrangements for the final week of the holiday. She sent him a quick text once she'd finished up in the sports hall: *Don't forget you're having Charlie from tomorrow night.*

When she returned to the climbing centre it was almost two o'clock, and Glynn had just finished an intermediate class. There was no sign of the young man from this morning, whose name, she thought, might be Dean. Earlier in the summer she'd given him some tuition in a number of group sessions that had also included his girlfriend – an attractive but surly woman who'd shown little enthusiasm for bouldering and even less for her partner. This sort of climbing tended to be very social, with a lot of discussion about the best way to tackle a problem, and yet the two of them had barely exchanged a word.

Since then he'd come in several times on his own, and she'd caught him gazing wistfully in her direction. Glynn confirmed her worst fears when he said, 'That bloke Dean was asking if you were single.'

'What did you say?'

'Oh, don't worry. Married, I told him.' A wink as he placed his palm above his head. 'Loved up to here.'

'Who is?' a voice cut in. For such a burly man, Nick had a disconcerting ability to appear from nowhere, usually when there wasn't much work being done.

'Me, boss.' Glynn came to Jen's rescue, only to get a signal that one of the climbers needed advice. His knowing look as he trotted away told her: *You can take it from here.*

Nick frowned in his wake. 'He's joking, right? I thought Glynn's been with his wife forever?'

'Fifteen years – and don't look so shocked. Some people can stay in love for that long.'

The lucky few, she thought, while he only shrugged at such a preposterous idea. But she was glad that Nick hadn't picked up on the true subject of the conversation. The centre had had problems in the past with female staff members being propositioned – and even stalked – so he tended to react very firmly to any hint of unwanted attention, and sometimes he could be a bit too heavy-handed.

Nick was thirty-eight, a lifelong fitness fanatic who'd moved here from Australia more than a decade ago. He was short and thickset, with piercing green eyes set into a face that might have been carved from mango wood. His light brown hair was cropped close to disguise a growing bald patch, and he had Aboriginal dotwork tattoos on his biceps. As far as Jen could tell, he wore shorts and muscle vests all year round, the better to display his fabulous physique.

'You okay?' he asked, in a warmer tone. 'I heard you came in late?'

Jen nodded, wondering who had ratted her out. 'Yeah, sorry, I'll make up the time.'

'What's up – more problems with the ex-hole?'

She shook her head, taking half a step back as he edged closer. 'Just bad luck with the buses—'

'Jen! Call for you.' They turned; Clare at the desk was holding up the phone. 'It's Freddie.'

Not great timing. Freddie was usually impossible to track down, and Jen had texted with the expectation that he wouldn't reply for hours, if at all.

Apologising to Nick, she hurried over to take the call. 'Hi, Freddie.'

'Uh, Jen, about tomorrow ...'

'Freddie, this has been agreed all summer.' She heard her voice come out flat, as it always did when they spoke.

'Yeah, I know, but I don't see why you have to get so hung up on, like, *exact* dates.'

Jen opened her mouth to respond, then closed it again. Transferring her frustration to a clenched fist, she said, 'Are you telling me you can't have him? Because he'll be devastated.'

'Nah, that's not what I'm saying, if you'd listen. It's just, Wednesday's not great. It'd be better if I took him from Thursday, or maybe Friday? Friday for a week would be cool.'

Jen sighed. A clenched fist wasn't enough, and now the muscles in her legs were rigid with tension. A few feet away, Nick was pretending to inspect the main noticeboard. Jen knew the glossy printed posters had a reflective sheen, so either he was admiring his own image – a distinct possibility – or he was slyly keeping an eye on her.

'Charlie thinks you're taking him to Cornwall. Is that still the plan?'

Freddie made a surprised little sound in his throat, which she had come to recognise as a signal for incipient dishonesty. 'Something like that, yeah.'

'Well, Friday for a week isn't possible, because he starts back at school next Thursday.'

'So what? It's only a day or two—'

'He can't afford to miss the start of term. Year three is a big deal. What's so urgent that you can't have him tomorrow night?'

'Oh, it's just—' The way he broke off suggested a reluctance to incriminate himself.

'A new conquest, then?'

Silence, until her snort prompted a laugh. 'Jen, c'mon. I can't admit to that – but if I did, we'd be talking seriously, *scorching* hot.'

She glanced round at Nick, the muscles in his shoulders taut from the effort of eavesdropping, and said, 'I've got to go, or I'll be in trouble at work.'

'What, with that guy *Nick*?' He said the name in a taunting sing-song voice. 'Nah. My guess is he'd bend all kinds of rules for you.'

Jen was shaken by the innuendo, but affected boredom. 'Whatever. Please think about tomorrow, and for Charlie's sake try and stick to the schedule we agreed.'

She ended the call, and Nick was immediately at her side, his fingertips brushing against her arm. 'Hope he wasn't giving you a hard time?'

'Just problems with the arrangements for Charlie.'

'So the bastard's going back on his word?'

'Not completely, but. . .' Jen shrugged. Even now, after the infidelities and the lies and the break-up, the failed attempt at mediation and the prospect of the painful, expensive court hearings to come, she was still reluctant to be openly critical of Freddie, particularly to another man who, if she was honest, shared more than a few of her ex-husband's less appealing traits.

Too many men interfering in my life, she thought, *and the only one I want or need is Charlie.*

CHAPTER FOUR

Jen left work at four thirty and was lucky with the buses she needed to get to the Hanover district of Brighton. Anna Morgan's home was in a smart Victorian terrace within easy walking distance of Queens Park, where Charlie had spent so much of his summer holiday with his best friend – Anna's son, Lucas.

The boys were in the back garden, constructing a den from garden chairs and beach towels. When Charlie spotted her on the patio, he dashed across the lawn and thudded into her arms, hugging her as if they'd been apart for weeks rather than twenty-four hours. Jen was touched by his willingness to show such wholehearted affection in front of his friend, though the intensity of his embrace only deepened her guilt that she didn't have enough time to give him. Her own parents had warned her how fast he would grow up, and there wasn't a single day, a single hour she'd ever get back.

'Hiya, bud! Had a good time?'

'Yeah. We went to the beach, and I swam underwater.'

Lucas, who had charged up beside him, rubbed his knuckles into Charlie's dark curls and said, 'I held my breath for two minutes!'

Charlie countered: 'I held my breath for longer!'

'I can do it the longest.' Lucas took a dramatic gulp of air and then clamped his lips together, scrabbling away as Charlie tried to tickle him.

'It was closer to twenty seconds than two minutes,' Anna confided, 'though they both did really well.'

'Oh, they did. And thanks so much for taking them to the beach.'

'Best place to be in this heat. You know, I think this could be the summer that defines their memory of childhood. Endless days of sunshine and carefree living. . .' She paused, examining Jen closely, and said, 'Carefree for them, at least. You, by contrast, look rather …'

'Frazzled?' After telling Charlie to go and fetch his bag, Jen explained that Freddie looked set to renege on his agreement.

'What about Cornwall? Charlie's talked about it non-stop.'

'I don't know. I strongly suggested he put Charlie first, instead of. . .'

'This week's floozy,' Anna finished with a disparaging snort. 'Does that mean no drinks on Thursday? Because we are both badly in need of a night out.'

Jen nodded. 'All we can do is hope.'

Charlie was chattering happily as they left the house, and Jen didn't have the heart to tell him about her conversation with his dad. She'd leave it till tomorrow morning and hope that Freddie's better conscience prevailed.

Earlier this afternoon Nick had sidled up and told her she should insist that Freddie keep to his agreement. 'It's important to get time to yourself. You're overdue a bit of freedom.'

Jen had nodded, though in reality any sense of liberation was quick to evaporate, with Charlie's absence from their dingy flat making her feel lonely and dispirited. But she understood what Nick was hinting at, and deftly changed the subject.

The best part of her working day had been a one-to-one tuition with Oscar, a boy of eleven who had cerebral palsy, epilepsy and learning difficulties. He'd bonded with Jen from their first encounter, and with her help had rapidly overcome his fear of this strange new environment. Now he could spend twenty or thirty minutes on the wall, slowly negotiating the lowest-grade problem. Following a lateral route, he was never more than a couple of feet off the ground, but the sense of achievement when he completed the challenge – the glitter of pride and delight in his eyes – was a joy to behold.

Today his parents, who for the first few sessions had watched with hand-wringing anxiety, had felt confident enough to slip away to the centre's cafe. When the session finished, his mother had spontaneously kissed Jen on the cheek. 'We can't thank you enough. This is having such a positive effect on other areas of his life.'

Embarrassed, Jen said, 'Only doing my job. And I love watching him progress.'

'No, it's more than that,' Oscar's father said. 'The time you take with him, the patience and encouragement, that's going well beyond what we'd expect for our money.'

Recalling the conversation now, as she walked home with Charlie, Jen couldn't help thinking it should be her son who benefitted from this level of attention. Then again, she was hardly unique in having to earn a living while others took care of her child.

And isn't it the truth, a wicked voice whispered in her head, *that full-time motherhood would drive you insane?*

They trekked down the steep hill towards Kemptown in almost thirty-degree heat. Beyond the grand Regency terraces and ugly modern tower blocks, the sea was as flat and blue as a child's drawing. Maybe go for a swim after dinner, she thought.

Then she remembered this morning, and the keys that hadn't yet been collected. She considered whether to walk on and check the note was still in place, but Charlie had been muttering about needing to pee, and now he protested again: 'Mum, I'm bursting!'

'We're nearly home. Why didn't you use the toilet at Anna's?'

'I didn't need to go then.'

She hustled him along the street, the sweat trickling down her spine. Home was a modest, poorly maintained flat in a small block, just eight apartments on four floors. In return for swallowing up nearly nine hundred pounds a month in rent, they had only one bedroom – which she'd given to Charlie – while she slept on a sofa bed in the lounge.

Jen unlocked the main door, and again thought about the man who'd dropped his keys. If he had a shop in a big retail centre like Churchill Square, he might not be home until eight or nine o'clock.

'Faster, Mum!' Darting past her, Charlie ran for the stairs. Jen had made a game out of climbing to the top floor, mostly to quell his complaints about the lack of a lift; now she quickened her pace, but made sure she didn't catch him till the landing.

'I won! I won!'

'So you did.' She placed a finger to her lips, but behind her the door was opening.

Their neighbour, Mrs Martin, was a small but solid woman in her mid eighties, still remarkably active for her age, though a couple of times lately she'd confused Jen for her own daughter, Angela, who must have been sixty if she was a day.

'Hello, Bridie, sorry about the noise.'

'Oh, I like to hear him. Popped out somewhere, did you?'

Jen let Charlie into the flat, then turned, frowning. 'No. I've just got back from work.'

'Really? I could have sworn you were at home today.' She issued a little laugh, but Jen caught the flash of concern in her eyes.

'Don't worry, it's easy to get mixed up.' Jen gestured towards the flat. 'Sorry, I have to check on Charlie. . .'

*

That wasn't strictly true, and Jen felt lousy when it struck her that Bridie might have concocted a reason to engage her in conversation. The poor woman didn't get enough human interaction, so once she started talking it was virtually impossible to get away – and right now Jen just didn't have the energy.

She was fretting over the likelihood that Freddie was going to ruin the final week of Charlie's holiday. The prospect of having to manage his disappointment was grim enough, without the problem of trying to sort out more childcare, when she'd already asked so much of Anna.

Tomorrow, she told herself. I'll invite Bridie in for a cup of tea and properly catch up.

She made for the kitchen, reminding Charlie to wash his hands as she passed the bathroom – lately he'd started taking more care to shut the door. She filled two glasses with water, added ice cubes from the freezer and found a purple straw, aware that it wouldn't be enough to compensate for the essential dullness of the drink.

Sure enough: 'Can't I have Ribena?'

'No. It's bad for you.'

'Juice, then?'

'You had juice at Anna's. Water's better than anything.'

'But it tastes horrible.' He didn't raise his voice, but he opened his mouth again, his tongue moving to form the word 'Dad' – as in, *Dad lets me have juice* – then caught her expression and thought better of it.

They moved into the small, cluttered living room, which after six months still didn't feel like their own place. They'd had to vacate their previous apartment in a hurry when the landlord decided to sell. This one, in Jen's mind, was only a temporary bolthole, though the reality was that they stood no chance of finding somewhere better – *affording* somewhere better – for a very long time.

The problem was that her marital home had actually been owned by Freddie's father, Gerard, so when the relationship ended there was no alternative but for Jen to move out. Her divorce lawyer agreed that she'd had little option, but it had placed her at a disadvantage from the start.

The TV on, Charlie roamed the Freeview channels, wisely saying nothing about the Disney, sport and movie channels available at his father's. *Second best, in every respect*: that was how Jen thought he must regard her, because what seven-year-old didn't rate their parents in terms of the benefits, treats and luxuries they could provide?

Her eyes fluttered closed; maybe a few minutes to zone out, then do the beach before they ate, and on the way down she'd try at the house again. It was always possible that some mischievous kid had come along and removed the note—

A knock on the door made her jump; she must have been on the brink of dozing off. Charlie barely reacted. He'd put on a *Thunderbirds* DVD and there was a daring rescue under way.

Must be Bridie, she thought, hoping her neighbour hadn't got confused about something again.

She prepared an expression of gentle humour as she opened the door, but it was wasted on the police officers who stood before her. Two women: one tall, square and fortyish, the other short, slim and a decade younger. Both a bit hot and flushed in their uniforms; both looking serious, almost sombre.

'Jennifer Lynch?'

Her married name; these days she thought of herself as Jennifer Cornish again. She nodded, thinking, *Charlie's safe, he's with me, but could it be about Dad, Mum, one of my sisters?*

'May we come in?' asked the older one, who had warm brown eyes and a reassuring, almost motherly tone.

Jen took a step back. 'What's this about?'

'It's best if we go inside,' the older one said, and the younger officer, who had that sharp-eyed look of your best friend's bitchy mate, moved forward and spoke in quick, clipped sentences.

'There's been an allegation made against you. We need you to come with us to discuss it. To do that, we have to arrest you. So it's better if we can—'

'Wh-what?' Jen stammered. 'Did you say *arrest*? What do you mean, I haven't done—'

The younger one was nodding impatiently. 'Jennifer Lynch, I am arresting you on suspicion of burglary and criminal damage which occurred today, Monday, 22 August 2016, at 14 Regency Place, Brighton.'

CHAPTER FIVE

What followed wasn't a blur so much as an out-of-body experience. Jen saw the cops from a different vantage point; not up in the corner as the near-death survivors often describe, but slightly off to the side. She felt it would take only a twitch of her eyes and she would be able to see herself, a stricken, unfamiliar figure frozen in the doorway of her flat.

The younger officer started relaying the official caution, so familiar from a thousand TV dramas. Some of the words and phrases seemed to elongate into meaningless sounds, while others struck like fistfuls of sand: *evidence against you. . . later rely on in court.*

Jen had been in danger before, often in the most hostile of environments, but they were emergencies that demanded quick thinking and a predominantly physical response – fight or flight – which wasn't appropriate here. She had suffered shock, too, most dramatically after a fall in the Cairngorms when she'd broken her ankle, hip and collarbone. But all she'd had to do then was try to stay conscious, stay warm, stay alive until help came and she was wrapped up and carried to safety.

In this situation, something was required of her but she didn't know what. Her brain just couldn't compute, and when she heard herself talking she marvelled at how unfamiliar her voice sounded, hearing it from the outside.

'I don't understand what this is about. I'm not a. . . I haven't done what you said, I wouldn't—'

The officers were gesturing for silence. 'It's really best not to say anything at this stage,' the older one said.

'But it's not true. I've got the keys to number 14 – he'd dropped them, you see. I can get them for you now.' She started to turn away but the younger officer moved to intercept her.

'We'll take care of that.'

'Please, Mrs Lynch,' the older one said. 'Let's just get to the station and you'll have an opportunity to put your side of the story, all right?'

Registering their eagerness to shut her up, Jen felt she had to comply. Perhaps it meant a lot more paperwork if she kept trying to explain.

From inside the flat came the sound of an explosion. The younger officer frowned. 'Is anyone else here?'

And with that, Jen was back inside her body, still reeling but horribly clear about her predicament. Charlie shouldn't have to witness this.

I've got to protect him.

It registered now that these police officers were only outwardly calm; there was a wariness about them, a readiness for action that wouldn't have been appropriate in a normal social encounter. What they no doubt understood from bitter experience was that not everyone went quietly – and they didn't yet know whether Jen was going to give them any trouble.

'M-my son, Charlie,' she said, fighting off the urge to let out a sob.

'How old is he?'

A gulp. She was so disorientated, she had to run through her memory to find his year of birth.

'Seven. He's seven.'

'It's just the two of you here?' the older one asked, and when Jen nodded, she said, 'Is there somebody who can look after him?'

'I. . . well. . .' The officer must have spotted how Jen seemed to deflate, her shoulders dropping as though her legs were about to give way, for she reached out and held her by the arm.

'This may take a while, so best if Charlie could stay with someone for the night.'

The younger one said, 'What about his dad, is he around?'

Jen flinched. It was a question that had come to sting. *Charlie's growing up without a father, because I failed to make it work.*

'He, uh, yes, good idea. I'll call him.'

She turned, then stopped, realising that the cops intended to follow her into the living room. 'Charlie? Wh-what should I…?'

With a gentle smile, the older one said, 'We don't want to make this any worse than it needs to be. Just tell him you've been asked to help with an investigation.'

Jen nodded, blinking away sudden tears. The kindness hurt more, somehow, than if they'd simply manhandled her out of the building.

Charlie was still engrossed in his DVD. Jen popped into the lounge, grabbed her phone then shut the door behind her. The older officer stayed close while her colleague took an undisguised interest in the flat, peering into each of the rooms as if to confirm that no one else was lurking.

Jen called Freddie's mobile, which rang half a dozen times and then went to voicemail. She cut the call, dialled again. Same result.

'He's not answering his mobile.'

'Landline?' the older cop suggested.

'He doesn't have one. I can text him.'

At this, the younger officer said, 'Can anyone else lend a hand?'

'The sooner we get this all sorted out, the better for you both,' the older one reminded her.

Jen had already typed a text: *Call me*. About to tap on Send, she hesitated. Did she really want Freddie knowing about this? Even an innocent mix-up could be twisted up and used against her, especially when Freddie's lawyers got to work on it.

Her parents? No, they were a good hour away, and she couldn't bear the humiliation, or her mum's inevitable overreaction: *Were you taking drugs? What have you done, Jennifer?*

'There's a friend, a childminder,' she said, abandoning the text.

Anna answered with a cheerful question: 'What did he forget?'

'He didn't.' Jen felt her face burning as she stammered out a feeble excuse: a family emergency, can't say anymore, so sorry but I have to ask a *huge* favour.

'Of course. Do you need me to come and get him?'

'I'd be really grateful, thank you.'

'No bother. It'll be about half an hour, though. I'm in Sainsbury's, so I'll fetch him on my way home.'

'Yeah, uh, hold on a second.' She pressed the phone to her chest and began to explain, but saw the younger officer's face harden.

'What about one of the neighbours?' the older cop asked. 'Is there anybody you know well enough?'

Good idea. Bridie Martin wasn't the perfect childminder, but Charlie liked her, and if it was only for half an hour. . .

The old woman took a few seconds to come to her door. She was readily agreeing until she spotted the police officers, and then her attitude changed in an instant. 'What's happened? Are you in trouble?'

'Not exactly. I don't really understand, to be honest, but I have to. . . I just have to go. . .'

Bridie's expression was a mix of doubt and disapproval. 'Thirty minutes, is it? You'd better bring the lad over.'

*

They let her find some fresh clothes to put in Charlie's overnight bag. The younger cop left the flat to make a call on her radio, while the older one stayed with Jen, hanging back discreetly when it was time to fetch Charlie.

'Change of plan tonight, I'm afraid, buddy.'

He barely reacted until she switched off the DVD. He seemed to welcome another chance to see Lucas, though he was less enthusiastic about having to wait with Mrs Martin.

'It won't be long till Anna gets here, I promise.'

'But why can't I stay with. . .' Now he turned, and for the first time registered the presence of a police officer in his home. Startled, he gaped at her for a second, sent Jen a doubtful, questioning look, then stared at the cop again.

'Your mum just needs to come and help us with something.' The officer smiled at Charlie. 'I'm sure it won't take long.'

His expression grew wary as he picked up on the discrepancy between the policewoman's friendly smile and his mother's unease. Jen flashed him the *Don't act up now* look that had worked so effectively when the marriage first began to deteriorate. 'Be a good boy, and I'll text Anna later and let you know when I'm home.'

She saw him hitch a breath, then swallow firmly. 'Can you come and get me? Tonight, I mean?'

'Don't you want another sleepover?'

'I'd rather be here.'

'Well. . .' Jen glanced at the cop, whose expression gave nothing away. 'If I'm not too late, I will.'

She hugged him for as long as she dared, and felt a wretched relief when he was delivered to Bridie Martin. At least he wouldn't have to witness the next stage of her ordeal.

The younger cop watched closely as she locked the flat, then took the keys from her. As she was escorted to the stairs, Jen stumbled, weakened by another wave of shock and disbelief. 'I promise, I haven't done anything wrong—'

'It really is best to wait till you're formally interviewed,' the older cop said. With her colleague one pace behind, she took Jen's arm in a grip that was still supportive but now in a subtly different way, and together they descended the stairs and emerged into the bright, golden sunshine of early evening.

The police car was parked at the kerb. A Jeep had to pull in behind it to allow another car to pass. The driver was a woman who had kids at Charlie's school; she'd sometimes nod and smile when they passed in the street. Now she stared, aghast, before quickly looking away.

Jen had been grateful that at least she wasn't handcuffed, but she realised it made little difference. Only one thought came to mind when you saw someone being escorted to a police car.

They're a criminal.

CHAPTER SIX

The journey seemed to take an age, and at every set of traffic lights she became an object of curiosity for other motorists and passing pedestrians. Even with her gaze fixed straight ahead, Jen could feel the heat of their unwanted attention, like sunshine on burned skin.

She was sitting behind the front passenger seat, with the younger officer driving and the older one beside her on the back seat. Jen asked once again what she was supposed to have done, but the officers were unwilling to discuss it. After some strained small talk about Charlie, the older one started bemoaning her husband's ineptitude at DIY.

'Somebody lent him an angle grinder to take up the path at his sister's, and he only went and cut through the internet cable. Kathy went ballistic!'

The younger officer made a noise in her throat; not particularly interested. They were in Hollingbury now, passing the Asda superstore whose car park was still crammed with evening shoppers. 'Beer and barbecues,' the older cop murmured, with a wistful air.

The car turned into the entrance to the police station and stopped at a large green gate. The younger officer entered a code and the gate slid sideways. As they drove through, Jen felt a shiver run through her and had to resist the urge to turn and watch it closing behind them.

She was already a prisoner, and this was only the start.

The driver got out first, opened the door for her colleague and then both of them moved to Jen's side of the car. The older one met Jen's eye and gave a little nod of encouragement. The woman no doubt meant well, but it felt slightly patronising. All Jen had done was sit, stand, walk, breathe – why the congratulation?

Because of all the things you *haven't* done, a small voice spoke up. They're used to dealing with people who scream and fight and rage.

She was taken inside the building, which wouldn't be winning any prizes for architectural style or beauty, and for a couple of minutes they milled around in a waiting area. Two other officers were there with a prisoner of their own, an elderly man who appeared to be doped to the gills. He was singing something under his breath, his eyes rolling as his head swung from side to side.

Then the door opened and they moved through to a large room dominated by a high, semicircular counter, half a dozen custody staff working behind it. The counter was divided by partitions that gave a measure of privacy during the booking-in process. Jen barely registered anything about the other detainees; it was all she could do to quell her sudden panic.

This wasn't a dream. An illusion. It was actually happening. She'd been arrested, and would be placed in a cell.

Locked up.

Jen wrapped her arms around herself and suppressed a shiver. She was led over to the counter and directed to stand on a set of footprints marked out on the floor. They were greeted by one of the custody sergeants, a giant of a man with woolly brown hair and a large mole on his temple. He listened as the younger officer relayed the nature of the offences for which Jen had been arrested. There was talk of burglary, criminal damage – utterly surreal, but Jen was advised not to interrupt.

Next came a series of questions about her health and wellbeing, asked in a surprisingly caring manner. It wasn't unlike being checked into a spa or a hotel, and in fact she'd encountered plenty of desk staff over the years who'd been far less considerate than this. If the police truly believed that Jen had done what they were saying, surely their attitude would be a lot harsher?

With this in mind, she felt comfortable about declining the offer of legal representation. She didn't require a duty solicitor, and wouldn't need to call a lawyer of her own.

'Fine,' the custody sergeant said. 'Just remember you can change your mind at any time, and we'll get it sorted.'

'I will, thank you.' Jen found some strength returning. This was a world she knew only from television dramas, and she clung to the thought that it was a mix-up; nothing more. Soon she would be able to explain what had *really* happened, and no doubt there would be embarrassed laughter, and perhaps some heartfelt apologies, and hopefully the offer of a lift home in time to collect Charlie from Anna's.

The pleasant atmosphere was disrupted by a sudden loud screech. Jen turned to see a woman kicking and writhing as several officers struggled to bring her into the room. She was in her forties, Jen guessed, and painfully thin, with sores on her arms and lumps of something nasty caught in her hair. She was dressed in oversized jogging pants and a grubby T-shirt with a large wet patch on the front.

'Get off me! Get the *fuck* off me, you tossers!' Her voice was slurred, almost unintelligible. Misty, bloodshot eyes struggled to take in her surroundings, then came to focus on Jen. 'What the fuck you staring at, bitch? I'll fucking have you—'

She lurched forward but was hurriedly restrained; then she doubled over and vomited with enough force to splatter some of the staff around her.

At the desk, the giant sergeant observed this commotion with dismay. 'Oh, Mandy,' he tutted, 'why'd you go and do that? Poor Simon here's gonna have to clean it up.'

There was a burst of laughter from his colleagues. 'Not my turn,' one of them declared, as the woman continued to hack and spit onto the floor.

'Oh yes it is,' said another. 'I had to deal with Liam Smaith.'

'Loose Liam.' The sergeant grimaced. 'So this one's yours, Simon.'

'Nope. Kerrie's taking my turn.'

'Since when?'

'Since I let her have my Albion tickets.'

There were cries of mock outrage, which the officer fended off with good-humoured defiance. 'Hey, we're talking 1901 club, not your bog-standard tickets.'

'Yeah, but no one told me we could trade,' someone else objected, and the debate continued as Jen was led away. This kind of banter was so familiar from her own workplace, she felt a pang of regret that she couldn't be a part of it.

The reality of her status hit home when she was searched, photographed, fingerprinted and asked to give a sample of her DNA. She was told that the police officers who'd brought her in would be returning to her flat to undertake what they called a 'Section 18' search of her property. Her clothes and shoes were bagged as evidence, and she was given a cheap pair of joggers and a T-shirt, along with a pair of plimsolls of the sort she hadn't worn since childhood.

Finally she was taken into a long, bare corridor lined with cells. The absence of furnishings and fabrics meant every sound reverberated. Her escort was a heavy, grey-haired woman, keen to tell Jen how much she preferred this job to her previous employment with a large clothing retailer, which treated its staff 'like scum, to be honest'.

Her voice attracted complaints and demands from the occupants of the cells they were passing, and she interrupted her monologue to throw out responses: 'Not too much longer, Karen. . . Nothing I can do about that, Mikhail. . . Settle down, Bob, you're impressing no one with that sort of language.'

They came to a halt outside a vacant cell, and Jen was asked to leave her plimsolls by the door. When the guard ushered her inside, Jen went to move but her legs refused to obey. Although her brain had accepted the necessity of temporary imprisonment, her body was having none of it.

She pictured a team of officers being forced to carry her, kicking and screaming, into the cell. And then she thought of her dad, his quiet disapproval whenever she'd thrown a tantrum as a child; the disappointment in his eyes that had always cracked open her heart.

'How long. . .?'

'I'm sure they'll be talking to you as soon as they can. I'll bring you a meal, if you're peckish. And there's tea, coffee – hot chocolate would be my personal recommendation.'

Jen declined, even though her mouth was as dry as sawdust. The fear of enclosed spaces had never troubled her much, mostly because her lifestyle had enabled her to avoid them. A couple of times she'd forced herself to try caving, but she'd kept moving and never thought too much about her surroundings, and she hadn't been alone.

This, she thought, was more like Tilgate Forest. A solitary ordeal, and one she had brought upon herself.

She had to consciously take command of her foot and lift it through the doorway. A second step, and a third, and then the guard said something cheery but the message was wiped away by the clang of the door and the heavy thunk of the lock engaging.

Jen shut her eyes, fighting the urge to scream. *This can't be happening.*

It took a whole minute before she had her breathing under control, but she could feel the panic waiting, patient and sly, a whispering voice behind the walls.

The cell was bare except for a toilet immediately to the right of the door, and a cot-like bed running along the opposite wall. The thin plastic mattress was bare, though there was a blanket folded up at one end. High above the bed was a window of sorts, a set of glass bricks that allowed in some muted light.

So much for beer and barbecues: right now a sandwich on the sofa with Charlie nestled at her side would have been utter bliss.

Instead, she was locked up, and all because of a good deed. She started to wonder if she'd been too hasty in turning down the offer of a solicitor. She thought ruefully of the firepower that her father-in-law could have brought to bear. Stay on the right side of a man with Gerard Lynch's connections and a problem like this could be whisked away in no time.

Suddenly bereft, she sat down and covered her face with her hands. It was a brief moment of despair, quickly shoved aside. All she had to do was stay calm and wait it out, to keep faith in the knowledge that she wasn't any kind of criminal, and that an honest account of what happened would soon see her released.

CHAPTER SEVEN

Typical. It had been an unusually interesting day, and wouldn't you just know it – the witch was home early.

Russell knew what to do. He had an efficient routine, honed over many months.

Left to his own devices, the house was his playground from around seven thirty in the morning (not that he often got up that early) till six or seven in the evening. His main task during that time was to research employment opportunities, badger the agencies with whom he had registered and apply, apply, apply for whatever jobs were available. The witch knew or at least suspected that he did little else that she would regard as a constructive use of his time, but Russell was nothing if not a sly young fox.

This week he'd been assigned the task of painting a section of the rear wall. A leaking garden tap had stained the render, which was cracked in places and pitted with moss and mould. Grunt work, in other words, and a complete pain in the arse.

Foregoing all the tedious preparation – for which he had no energy after a long and satisfying morning of masturbation – Russell had popped outside at four o'clock, armed with a roller and a tin of masonry paint. Twenty minutes of frenetic effort was enough to represent half a day's worth of diligent painting, and soon he was back at his favourite spot, just to the side of the living room window, shorts round his ankles, a box of tissues and his camera both within easy reach.

*

The time passed in a pleasurable blur, as it always did. Jolted by the sight of Kelly's Dacia, he ducked and crawled away, then rose at a safe distance from the window and hoiked up his shorts. He walked calmly into the kitchen, and when the front door opened he was to be found running water for a refreshing and healthy drink.

He gave a start, as if surprised by her presence. 'Oh! Sorry, I was painting the wall.'

'I can see that. You're covered in it.'

'What?' He looked down and saw a fine mist of paint splattered over his T-shirt. Little blobs of it had caught in the hairs on his forearms.

'Are you going to run that water much longer? We're on a meter.'

'Sorry.' He filled a glass and turned the tap off.

'Stick the kettle on, though. I fancy tea.'

She stepped out of the back door to take a look at his handiwork. Russell ignored her while he filled the kettle, then wandered into the lounge, not wanting to seem too eager for congratulation.

'Russell? Russell!'

No, he thought. He wasn't going to come running whenever she called. He wasn't under the thumb, as some of their friends and family believed. Oh no, *he* was in control of this relationship, but it was a subtle form of control – as befitting a sly young fox.

The witch loomed in the doorway. 'You've only done the bottom half of the wall.'

'Yeah, but it's a start. Like you said, it's sweltering out there, and it's a fiddly job, with the waste pipe, and the tap—'

'You've got paint on everything, Russell. Not just the pipe but the window, the frame. It's on the path—' She gasped, looking over his shoulder, and for a second he wondered if being positioned for so long in one place had left a kind of after-image, and that Kelly could now see him at the window, fully dressed and respectable from the waist up, secretly naked and pleasuring himself as he watched the girlies go past. . .

'What is it?'

Kelly marched towards him, so angry that she might be about to lash out. *Just give me a reason to hit you back*, he thought.

'There's a smear on the curtains.'

He turned, shocked, then saw she meant paint and had to hide his relief. *Wouldn't be the first time*, he thought, and had to suppress a giggle.

'It'll wipe off.'

'Why didn't you clean up when you came inside?'

'I thought I had.'

'And what were you looking at that was so important?'

He shrugged, wondering if her question was as casual as it sounded. 'Can't remember.'

'There's a police car outside that little terrace. Did you see what happened?'

'Doubt it's anything exciting.' He heard the kettle boil and used that as an excuse to get away.

When he returned with her tea, Kelly was scratching at the paint with her thumbnail.

'It's not coming off. And these are dry-clean only,' she moaned.

'I didn't do it on purpose.'

'That's not the point, Russell. You ought to take more care.'

'You're never happy,' he muttered, placing the mug on the glass coffee table. He wasn't going to put it on a coaster, either.

'I would be, if you could manage the simplest of tasks without making a lot of mess that I have to clean up. Or better still, if you found a job and started going to work every day.'

'That's not fair. You know how tough it is at the moment.' Time to add a little wounded indignation. 'I worked so frigging hard out there, in boiling hot weather, and all I get is criticism.'

There was a stare-off, then her gaze flicked towards the coffee table; Russell grabbed a coaster and slipped it under the mug.

Her face softened, and she opened her arms to offer an embrace. Not much he could do but walk into it. Kelly was a couple of years away from forty, and took far more care of her appearance than he did, and yet even the slightest bodily contact repulsed him. Russell couldn't remember when it had started, or why, but it was getting worse and he didn't know what he was going to do about it.

Sex was the biggest problem. These days he preferred imagination, his own hand working to the rhythm of fantasies as outrageous and forbidden as anything you'd find in the darkest reaches of the net.

He squirmed a little, hoping she wouldn't get any ideas, and for a second his loathing was directed inward: *You're a mess. Kelly deserves better than this.*

To his relief, she let him go and regarded him with a humble gaze. 'I'm sorry. It wasn't a great day at work. Mitch kept us in the conference room for nearly two hours, ranting about the projections for the final quarter.'

He tutted. 'Mitch is a cock. You can't be blamed when the projections were unrealistic to start with.'

'Exactly. It's like I said to Lindsay afterwards. . .' And off she went, while Russell's mind drifted back to the far more captivating issue of the police car outside number 14, and the various comings and goings he'd tracked today, starting with the fit blonde.

The *super*-fit blonde. Definitely one of the top five in his summer folder. Top three, maybe.

Nothing Kelly needed to know about that.

CHAPTER EIGHT

Jen didn't have sight of a clock, but it felt like an hour or two had passed before she was taken to be interviewed.

The hardest part of waiting was that it became impossible not to worry herself sick about Charlie. How was he feeling? Had he understood that his mum had been arrested? Worst of all: how might this influence his opinion of her? When it came to law and order, there wasn't a lot of nuance in the mind of a seven-year-old. Cops were there to lock up the bad guys. Jen was locked up. That had to make her a bad guy, didn't it?

Ever since the separation it had become clear that, unintentionally or not, she and Freddie were competing for their son's affection. Jen was frequently stung by the fact that Charlie seemed to adore being with his dad, whose concept of parenting featured an unending stream of gifts and treats and spontaneous fun, whereas he often resented the fact that life with Mum was centred on rules and routine.

The same custody assistant escorted her back to the main room, and maybe it was just paranoia but she didn't seem as friendly this time. Jen felt a spasm of guilt as she set eyes on the two detectives waiting to interview her. Quite irrational – though perhaps a couple of hours in a cell was enough to make anyone believe they'd done something wrong.

She realised she was breathing in short, desperate gasps. Clenching her hand into a fist, she pressed her fingernails into her palm. *Hold it together.*

The detectives explained that she had to be signed out for interview, and took her over to the custody sergeant, who gave her a kindly look. 'Don't be worried now. These two are fully house-trained. And remember you can ask for a solicitor at any stage.'

Jen managed a timid smile. Maybe she should be taking up that offer, but she wanted this over quickly. According to the clock on the back wall, it was almost eight in the evening. With her promise to collect Charlie in mind, she nodded with more confidence than she felt, and confirmed that she did not require legal advice.

Her new custodians introduced themselves as Detective Sergeant Talia Howard and Detective Constable Matthew Reed. Howard was fortyish, wearing a crumpled navy suit over a white shirt; she had an oval face with red spots on her cheeks, and light brown hair spilling from a tortoiseshell claw. Her manner was more energetic than her appearance suggested, as if dog-tired, but ready to pursue this investigation for as long as it took.

Reed was about a decade younger, short and pot-bellied, and had dark hair held in a wave with plenty of gel or wax. He wore black trousers and a pale pink shirt, with the suggestion of a vivid tattoo peeking between the top buttons. A thin but strangely ominous folder was wedged beneath his arm.

The interview room was nothing like the dimly lit, moody spaces she'd seen in TV dramas; it was more like an office, furnished on a tight budget. There was a table with a computer, a TV and DVD player, and recording equipment that included a video camera mounted in the corner of the room.

DC Reed signed onto the computer and began tapping away, the screen hidden from Jen's view. Gesturing at the camera, Howard explained that the interview would be filmed, and afterwards Jen would be told how she could obtain a copy.

Essential viewing for all the family, she thought wryly, and then congratulated herself. At least her sense of humour was intact, just about.

Once the officers had formally identified themselves for the camera, they asked Jen to confirm her name and date of birth. She was reminded that she could have a solicitor present, or failing that, speak to one on the phone.

DS Howard ran through the reasons for her arrest, cautioned her again and explained what the caution meant. She was softly spoken, with a crisp Home Counties accent, whereas Reed had the sort of watered-down Cockney that probably meant he was local to this area. It was he who asked if she understood why she was here this evening.

'Not really. I heard what they said when I was arrested, and it's ridiculous. I've been trying to explain what happened, but everybody said I should wait. . .' Into the silence, she blurted out the question that had occurred to her while she was in the cell. 'How did you find me?'

'We'll come to that,' Howard said. 'To start off, why not give us your account of what happened today?'

It was the invitation Jen had been relishing, but when she spoke next her throat was dry and she had to cough.

'I'd left home around nine fifteen and was on my way to work. Charlie, my son, had stayed over at a friend's, and I must admit I'd got up a bit late. I was heading down Regency Place towards Eastern Road, to get a bus to Portslade. As I approached number 14, I saw the man who lives there coming out, obviously in a hurry. There was a car waiting for him.'

She hesitated, sensing that Reed had a question, but Howard motioned at her to continue.

'After they'd driven away, I noticed something on the grass in front of the house. A set of keys.'

She paused again, expecting some kind of reaction, but their expressions remained impassive. Jen described how she had run to the end of the street and tried to attract the driver's attention. When that failed, she had considered her options and made the decision to go inside the house.

'I found a pen and paper in a sort of storeroom. I wrote a note, leaving my contact details, and taped it to the front door. The owner couldn't have missed it.'

Reed tapped the pen against his teeth. 'And what happened then?'

'That's it. I thought he'd get in touch at some point and come to collect the keys. I work at the Skyway – it's a sports centre in Portslade.'

The detectives nodded, which Jen took to mean they knew of the place. Then she realised it was more than that.

They knew she worked there.

Next came a set of questions about her journey: which bus stop had she waited at, what time had the bus arrived, when did she get to work? As she answered, she was aware of Reed occasionally tapping at the computer.

DS Howard was sitting at the far corner of the desk, adjacent to Jen. Her eyes had barely strayed from Jen's face; it wasn't by any means a harsh or unfriendly gaze, but it was having the desired effect. Jen felt compelled to tell the truth, certain the detective would immediately spot any trace of dishonesty.

Now she said, 'Can you explain what you did next, with the keys?'

'Nothing.' Jen was puzzled. 'I still had them with me when—' She swallowed. 'When I was arrested.'

'So you didn't return to the house at all?' Reed asked.

'No. After work I had to collect Charlie from his friend's, and that was in the opposite direction. I thought about it as we were walking home, but Charlie was bursting for the toilet.'

'That's kids for you,' Reed muttered, and DS Howard gave a wry smile.

'I'd intended to call round there this evening, on the way to the beach. Charlie and I sometimes go for a swim around six, seven o'clock.'

'In the sea?' Howard gave a mock shiver. 'Isn't it too cold?'

'Not this year,' Jen said, and Reed was on her side.

'I went in yesterday and it was fantastic. Nearly as warm as the Med.'

Jen sat back, feeling as though a great burden had been lifted. She'd given her explanation and here they were, the three of them chatting like friends.

'And that's it?' Howard asked. No pressure in her voice.

'That's it. So you can see why it was such a shock to find the police at my door.'

Without comment, Reed mirrored her body language, resting back in his seat and gently touching his palms together on the table. 'This man at number 14, is he known to you?'

'Only by sight. He's quite often leaving the house as I'm walking to the bus stop.'

'So a nodding acquaintance, that type of thing?'

'Not even that, really. . .' Aware that she must seem unfriendly, Jen considered telling them about the time he'd nearly run her over, but thought she might sound petty.

Except that DS Howard had registered the hesitation. 'Are you sure you've never spoken?'

The question was so assertive, it made Jen doubt her own memory for a moment. She frowned, then shook her head.

'No. Never.'

There was a heavy silence. Jen was determined to say nothing more, understanding that this was one of the techniques they employed, in the hope of drawing out a contradiction, an indiscretion.

After a few seconds, Reed took them back to the point when the car had gone, and Jen had to decide what to do. 'You say you tried the neighbouring houses? What about across the street, or further along?'

'The flats opposite are side-on to the road, so I wasn't sure if anyone there would know the man. Leaving the set of keys with any old stranger didn't feel right.'

'But *you*'re a stranger to him,' Reed said. 'That's what you've just told us.'

'I am. But I know that I'm an honest person. Someone along the road might have gone in there and stolen. . .' She trailed off, aware that she was painting herself into a corner. These police officers had no more reason to believe in *her* trustworthiness than Jen did in any of the man's neighbours.

Reed looked dubious. 'I'm still not sure why you had to go inside the house.'

'Like I said, if I'd put the keys through the letterbox and they were the only set, he'd have had to get a locksmith out. I didn't have a pen and paper on me.'

'But you live just up the street?' Howard chipped in.

'There wasn't time to go back. I did what I thought was the best thing at that moment. If I'd had any idea I would end up here. . .'

Reed grunted. 'After pinning this note to the door—'

'Taped,' Jen corrected him. 'I used some of the packing tape in the. . . the room full of artwork.'

'Okay, you taped the note. And did you lock the front door after you?'

'I didn't have to use the key. The door locked when I shut it.'

'Ah, right. I'm with you.' Reed nodded, as though this detail was significant in some way. 'So, the artwork. . . what did you make of it?'

Jen frowned. 'I don't see what that has to do with anything.'

'Humour us,' he suggested, with a cheeky grin.

'Well, I thought it looked wonderful. Beautiful craftsmanship, and some really interesting subject matter.'

'Valuable?' Howard asked.

'I would think so.' She felt a rush of heat to her face as she saw where they were leading. 'I didn't take anything, I wouldn't dream of—'

She broke off, not just because Reed was now opening that folder of his, but because she recalled how she had been tempted, just for a second; tempted to take something that wasn't hers.

Wetting his thumb, the detective constable slid out two sheets of paper. Howard, as ever, was looking directly at Jen, her expression now regretful.

'We've been given a very different account,' she said. 'The allegation from the tenant at number 14 is that you entered the house without his permission and caused damage to that artwork, which has a total retail value of approximately seven thousand pounds.'

As she finished off, Reed turned the papers over. There were two A4 photographs: one a wide shot of the room, the other a close-up of the dining table. In both, it was clear to see that practically every single piece had been destroyed. Someone had gone on the rampage, snapping and smashing and stamping until all that remained was a heap of unrecognisable fragments.

Jen gaped at the images. 'That wasn't me. W-why would I do that?'

Howard regarded her sadly, while Reed shrugged, and said, 'You tell us.'

CHAPTER NINE

Jen swallowed. She was experiencing another dislocation, looking across at herself, stammering and trembling with the shock.

'No. This is just. . . crazy. The room wasn't like this when I left it.'

'And yet you locked the door behind you,' Reed reminded her. 'That's what you've just told us.'

Feeling like she'd been tricked, Jen said, 'Other people might have keys. You said he's a tenant – what about the landlord?'

'She's in Spain.'

'Okay. A letting agent, then?'

Howard tutted. 'It's not impossible, but given that you've admitted going inside this morning, you'll appreciate that we have to treat you as the likeliest suspect.'

'You asked how we identified you.' Reed took a silver disc from the folder and slotted it into the DVD player. 'Well, the tenant had some concerns about a recent houseguest, so he took the precaution of setting up a hidden camera. We'd like you to take a look at this.'

Still stunned by the sight of the damage, Jen said nothing as the TV was switched on, and a small video file was played on the DVD.

The camera had been positioned in the hall, probably somewhere above the front door. There was a time code in the bottom right-hand corner of the image, beginning at 09:36. The top corner of the door swung into sight, and then Jen appeared, only her head and shoulders visible as she leaned over. Putting her bag down, she realised.

Viewed like this, her actions looked horribly suspicious. She was like a pantomime burglar, peeking into the living room, then creeping along the hall and out of sight. After a few seconds she reappeared, hesitated outside the dining room and knocked first – she recalled her sinister vision of the room being occupied – before opening the door.

The camera caught only a sliver of her on the threshold, but it was enough to show that she had paused before entering the room. In reality she'd been taken aback by the sight of the artwork, but to these detectives it might look as though she was preparing to attack.

'This doesn't mean anything. I've freely admitted that I went into the house.' She indicated the TV screen. 'Does it show me leaving? Because I was in there for hardly any time at all. It wasn't long enough to do all that damage.'

'I'm not so sure about that.' Reed pressed fast forward and the image remained the same, though the numbers sped up. Jen waited, expecting to see herself emerge within a matter of seconds, but nothing happened.

She glanced at the detective, who watched impassively. A moment later he jabbed at the remote, and Jen saw herself crossing the hall. Reed hit pause again.

'You were actually in there nearly four minutes,' he said. 'More than enough time to smash up a load of fragile ornaments.'

'But I didn't.' The words emerged as a weary groan. 'I'm not a vandal.' She gestured again at the screen. 'Are there any other cameras? Anything in the storeroom?'

'Nope. Just this.'

'It makes no difference, then. It doesn't show me damaging anything.'

'True. But it shows you entering the room and staying inside for four minutes.'

'And I've explained why!' It was the first time she'd raised her voice, and she saw the detectives look at her with a new interest. 'I had to find a pen and paper, and then I was writing the note.'

'Yes,' said Howard drily. 'The note.'

'I stuck it to the door,' Jen insisted, fired up by the scepticism in the detective's tone. 'If he's been home today, he'll have seen the note.'

'That isn't what he told us,' Reed said. 'Nothing about a note. Nothing about dropping any keys.'

'Maybe he didn't realise?'

Howard shook her head. 'He says he was given two sets when he took out the rental. One for his girlfriend, which is what he's using now. . .' A glance at her colleague, who dealt the next blow:

'And the set he reported missing, yesterday afternoon.'

'Yesterday?' Jen repeated, dumbly.

'They vanished while he was at the gym, sometime around 4 p.m. on Sunday.'

Howard added, 'The Skyway gym, to be precise.'

'Hold on.' Once again, Jen's voice was too thick with emotion to risk saying anything more. She turned away from them, covering her face with her hands. It was the worst sort of body language, but she didn't care about that right now. She had to create at least the illusion of privacy for a moment, until she could absorb the impact of this new and terrible shock.

'Sure you wouldn't like something to drink?' Howard asked softly.

'Please. Some water would be good.'

Reed fetched a Styrofoam cup of water and both officers waited patiently while Jen took a few sips. Then she wiped her face with her hands and took a large, calming breath.

'You're saying he notified the police that he'd lost his keys?'

'Yesterday afternoon,' Reed confirmed, glancing at his computer screen. 'He phoned John Street station at. . . 17:47.'

'But he can't have. Or it can't be the same set of keys.' Jen paused, determined not to sound distraught. 'He dropped them on the grass, I swear to you. I ran after the car as it was driving away, but they didn't notice.' She gasped, remembering something. 'A delivery driver saw me, standing in the middle of the road.'

'Any details?' Howard asked. 'Do you know which company?'

Jen tried to picture the van's livery, but got nothing. Desperate to find a flaw, something she could dispute, she said, 'If he genuinely lost his keys, why didn't he get the locks changed?'

Reed suppressed a snort. 'We're talking about less than a day later. Plus it's a rented property.'

'These things have to be done via the agents,' Howard pointed out.

'I know that. I rent myself. But if I was in that position, I wouldn't go out and leave the house unattended.'

Reed said, 'He thought it was a low risk, because when the keys went missing there wasn't anything to identify his address.'

'Though I daresay the staff at the Skyway have access to the membership records?' Howard phrased it as a question, but Jen could see from her face that she already knew the answer. *Yes, they did.*

'I wasn't working yesterday, so I couldn't have accessed the system.'

But you popped in during the afternoon, a voice in her head spoke up. It was just for a few minutes, returning an Xbox game that one of her colleagues had lent to Charlie. And the centre's CCTV had probably picked her up.

She breathed loudly through her nose, and in a new spirit of defiance, she thought: *I'm not telling them that. They can go to hell.*

In a slow, deliberate voice, Reed said, 'The tenant's name is a Mr Alex Wilson. Can I ask you again whether Mr Wilson is known to you?'

'I've told you. Only by sight.'

'A nodding acquaintance?' asked Howard. 'Nothing more than that.'

'Exactly.' Jen let out a frustrated sigh. 'Why, has he claimed that he knows me?'

'Is there any reason why he should?'

Jen shook her head, determined to let them answer her question for once. Reed stared at his screen for a few seconds.

'He's denying that he knows you to speak to. When he discovered the damage, he reviewed the footage from his camera and realised he'd seen you walking past in the mornings. He also thought he knew you from the Skyway. He checked their website and found a picture of you on the page for the climbing centre.'

'So, if we're both saying the same thing, why do you keep asking if I know him?'

'An action like this,' Reed said, 'we've got to wonder if it isn't a domestic issue.'

'You're not serious?'

Howard ignored the sarcasm. 'Do you know Mr Wilson's girlfriend?'

'I didn't realise he had one. There was a woman driving the car he got into this morning, but I didn't see her clearly. I've never seen anyone come out of the house.'

'And you're not in a relationship with him? You've never been in a relationship with him at any time in the past?'

'*No*. This is farcical. I mean, even if I had, I'm not in the habit of destroying people's property.'

Howard pursed her lips, while Reed leaned over to study the photographs once more. He said, 'This is serious stuff, Jen. The value of the damaged artwork means that a conviction could result in a prison sentence. Right now, the evidence against you is looking pretty persuasive.'

'And that's just for the criminal damage,' Howard added. 'There's also an allegation of theft. Mr Wilson reported the loss of one of the pieces, worth approximately four hundred pounds.'

Reed consulted the computer. 'A figurine of the, uh, Celtic goddess, it says here. Elen of the Ways.'

'*What?*' Jen's exclamation was instinctive, but she knew at once that she'd given something away. *Elen* was the broken piece of artwork that she'd noticed in the waste bin. The one she'd picked up and admired, and been tempted to—

She felt a rush of heat to her face. Reed was leaning forward over his desk. 'Anything you can tell us about that?'

Jen shook her head, lips clamped together like a child sworn to silence. A knock on the door brought some welcome respite.

Howard was closest, but it was Reed who stood up – a consequence of his lower rank, presumably. He opened the door in such a way that Jen couldn't see who was outside. After a murmur of conversation, something was handed over and the door closed.

Jen took a deep breath, preparing to fight off whatever ludicrous accusation was coming next, but then Reed turned and placed an evidence bag on the desk. Through the clear plastic she could see the figurine: the horned goddess, Elen.

'You're aware that a search was being carried out at your home,' Reed said. 'Well, what I'm showing you now is Exhibit WAF/2. It was found this evening, hidden in a chest of drawers in your bedroom.'

CHAPTER TEN

With a better atmosphere between them, Russell went outside and did some more painting, taking it slowly this time, partly to avoid the witch's company while there was any danger of her getting amorous. He'd sorted himself out three times today, and things down there were feeling a little. . . chafed.

Kelly had talked of going to the gym, but after fretting so much about the curtain she ended up taking it down and soaking it in various solutions to remove the paint. She was making another attempt when the doorbell rang.

'I'll go,' she called, as though it were some great hardship.

'Thanks!' he had to call back, or else she'd take offence. She was a woman who required constant praise, along with confirmation that she was the one who worked hardest, who took on the biggest chores and responsibilities and who suffered and sacrificed and achieved far more than he did.

Which was undoubtedly true, but how bloody tiresome to keep bringing it up?

He ran the roller out to arm's length, then placed it carefully in the tray and took a step towards the back door. A visitor at this time of the evening was an anomaly.

Leaning into the kitchen, he listened hard and made out Kelly's voice, an exclamation of surprise and then something downbeat: a denial. The other voice was female, too; sounded quite serious, but also young.

Russell liked young.

Intrigued, he stepped inside and heard the witch saying, '. . . here all day. You ought to speak to him.'

A little flare of panic: the police? *Why*?

But he had it under control at once.

This wasn't about him. It couldn't be.

He waited until the summons came, then shouted 'Okay!' and made a couple of stamping noises on the kitchen floor. He noticed a blob of paint on the back of his hand and swiped it across his cheek, then mussed his hair for extra effect: man at work.

He was sweating lightly, which was about right. Heart beating fast, from excitement, but also a reaction to the danger. Encounters with the police were best avoided; he imagined it was a job where you developed an instinct for deviance, so there was always a slight chance they'd 'see' something in him, demand to come in and search, seize the computers—

Stop it. He smiled but it felt too wide, so he toned it down, only to crank it back up when he set eyes on the cop.

She was on her own, slim and dark, couldn't have been more than twenty-five. That ugly shapeless uniform, of course, but his expert gaze lingered on her chest, then the face: a bit narrow, the nose too long, but good blowjob lips.

And flinty blue eyes, running an appraisal of their own.

With a goofy grin, he said, 'Sorry. Painting the house.'

'Oh God, you're still covered in it.' Kelly's exasperation had a comical edge that was purely for the cop's benefit. *We're both acting*, he thought, *in our different ways.*

'How can I help? What's happened?'

'I was explaining to your wife, there was a break-in along the street, around nine thirty this morning. I wondered if you might have seen anything?' She was holding a clipboard, a pen poised above it.

'Nine thirty?' He pretended to think. 'No, I was out in the back garden by then. I didn't hear anything suspicious, either – no windows breaking or anything like that.'

'The, uh, intruder may have had keys.'

'Oh, I see.'

He thought it best not to show too much interest, but Kelly said, 'That's a bit unusual, isn't it? How did he get hold of the keys?'

'The suspect is female, actually. How she gained possession of the keys is something we're trying to find out.'

The witch reacted with: 'Very fishy,' so Russell felt brave enough to raise his eyebrows and grimace. 'Uh oh. Relationship gone wrong, maybe?'

'That's a possibility, I suppose. But you're sure you didn't see anything this morning?'

'Not a thing.' He'd eased in front of Kelly, so she couldn't see his flirtatious smile. 'Sorry I can't be of more help to you.'

'That's fine.' The cop didn't seem to notice the smile. 'I'll let you get back to your painting.'

When they closed the door, Kelly headed straight to the lounge window. She wouldn't see much, Russell knew. He was three inches taller than her, and even he had to lean and stretch for a full view of number 14.

'Did they take our details?' he asked.

'Only the basics. Why?'

'No reason.'

'I wonder what it's all about,' she said, still on tiptoe. 'Sounds to me like they know who she is.'

'Yeah. Certainly not your normal profile for a burglar – a young woman.'

The witch turned, gave him a sharp look. 'Who said she was young?'

Russell quickly laughed off his mistake. 'It's got to be, hasn't it? An old biddy is even less likely.'

Still that probing gaze. Finally, she let him off the hook. 'No, you're right,' she said, and expelled a strangely burdened sigh. 'Most criminals are men.'

He grunted his agreement, then stalked back outside, asking himself: *Just what the* fuck *does she mean by that?*

CHAPTER ELEVEN

Afterwards Jen would wonder if it could have been a coincidence – the knock on the door, just as they'd raised the issue of theft. She knew from the TV shows that other officers might be monitoring the interview, so perhaps they'd waited, deliberately, for the moment when production of the figurine would have maximum effect.

The accusation floored her. Without thinking, she blurted, 'You must have put it there.'

Reed shook his head, scornfully, while Howard, in a crisp voice, said, 'The officers I work with are not in the habit of planting evidence.'

'No. I'm sorry.' Jen felt ashamed of her reaction. 'But *someone* put it there.' She swallowed; almost a gulp. 'I *swear* on my life that I didn't take it.'

Silence. Jen felt beads of sweat breaking out on her forehead. She wasn't sure where to go from here. Swear on Charlie's life – could she bring herself to do that?

Because there were more than a few treacherous thoughts in her head. Such as: what if she'd had a blackout, or was suffering from some kind of breakdown?

She'd admired the figurine. Coveted it, even.

Was it possible that she had stolen it?

*

Stricken by the idea that she couldn't trust her own memory – her own *sanity* – she slumped in her seat and stifled a sob. Her fighting spirit was already seeking answers.

'May I see the tape again, please? When I crossed the hall, all I had in my hand was the note.'

Reed shifted awkwardly in his seat, which Jen took as a signal in her favour: the first indication that the detectives were operating on anything less than solid ground.

'The angle's not great,' he admitted, 'so it's inconclusive.'

He brought up the video, fast-forwarding through the minutes that Jen was in the dining room. When she emerged, he slowed to normal speed and even paused a couple of times, catching her in mid stride as she headed towards the front door.

He was right. The camera's position meant her right arm was obscured, though Jen thought she glimpsed her hand, and a collection of white pixels that must have been the note.

'Could you run it in slow motion?' she asked. 'You can just about see the paper in my right hand, and there's nothing else.'

Patiently, Reed complied with her request, and the three of them studied the procession of images with fierce concentration.

'Not an ideal view,' Howard finally conceded, 'but it's quite possible that you concealed it under your right arm, then slipped it into your bag.'

Jen gaped at her. 'Why would I do that? I didn't know the camera was there.'

To that, there was only silence. Reed returned to the start and ran the footage again. Jen couldn't help noticing the furtive, hesitant way she moved: to these officers the woman on screen must appear sneaky and dishonest.

She realised she was shaking her head, as if denying it to herself. Was that the behaviour of a wholly innocent person?

*

She remembered an occasion when Charlie was a baby, and not sleeping well; Jen had walked out of a department store without paying for a packet of babygrows. Fortunately, the staff had accepted that it was forgetfulness rather than shoplifting, but she'd been mortified.

Then a more positive memory, a straw to clutch at: 'A few weeks ago I was in a cafe,' she told them. 'The woman at the next table walked out, leaving her handbag on the floor, wide open, with her purse just sitting there. It would have been the easiest thing in the world to take it, but I handed it to the staff. The next time I was in, the manager told me how grateful the woman was.'

DS Howard affected a look of puzzlement. 'I'm not sure what this has to do with—'

'I'm saying: *this isn't me*.' She nodded at the evidence bag. 'I don't steal. I don't vandalise property. Mr Wilson dropped the keys on the grass, and I picked them up and wrote him a note. I was trying to be helpful. . .' And there she was forced to stop, because her vision was blurred with tears and she knew she was about to lose control.

Reed produced a tissue and passed it over. Jen nodded her thanks, blew her nose, and said, 'It's easily verified. Just get in touch with the cafe.'

'That isn't strictly relevant to this case,' Howard said, 'but we're happy to take the details.'

Reed scribbled a note, while Howard picked at her nails and looked eager to move on. Jen could see that this example of her honesty wasn't likely to make any difference, but she was clinging to it more for her own benefit.

I'm not a criminal. I wouldn't steal something and then blank it out. . . would I?

The stress of the divorce had certainly taken its toll on her emotional wellbeing, but it had been going on for more than a year, and she hadn't exhibited any strange behaviour up till now. Why would she suddenly turn into a thief?

'I just did what I thought was best,' she said. 'I wish now that I'd handed them in at a police station, but I was going to be late for work. I thought leaving a note would be just as good.'

As if she hadn't spoken, Howard said, 'This sort of artwork is something that interests you, isn't it? Celtic mythology. Gods and goddesses.'

Jen stared at her, then looked away. 'Not particularly.'

'Oh?' The detective had heard the lie. She glanced at her colleague, who took out another sheet of paper.

'This is from your Facebook page, about eleven months ago.'

Jen leaned forward to take a look, gripping the table as if she feared her connection to the world was about to break. It was a printed screenshot from a blog post that one of Jen's friends had shared on social media. The blog was devoted to Pagan deities, and had included images of the male and female horned gods, Cernunnos and Elen. They were paintings rather than statues, but the representation of Elen was strikingly similar to the figurine on the table before her.

Jen stared at the sheet of paper. She wasn't a regular on Facebook, but posts like this cropped up all the time and occasionally she commented or shared something just to demonstrate that she was still alive; a lot of people seemed to think it odd if you weren't constantly parading your life for the world to see.

But this. . . this innocent click on someone else's post felt like the final condemnation, sealing her fate.

She looked up, and it was clear in their faces: she could deny it all she liked but it wasn't going to help. Only one option left to her now.

'I'd like a solicitor, please.'

CHAPTER TWELVE

The interview was suspended at once. Reed left the room, then returned for a whispered conversation with Howard, leaning across the table with his back to Jen, before explaining that she could be represented by either a duty solicitor or somebody of her own choice – but not right now.

'It's almost 10 p.m.,' Howard said. 'I suggest you get some rest and we'll resume in the morning.'

'I've got to stay here?'

The detective nodded. 'We're allowed to hold you for twenty-four hours, I'm afraid.'

Jen was mute. At the back of her mind she'd known it might come to this, and yet to hear it confirmed was much harder to bear. There would be no collecting Charlie tonight: instead she would be sleeping here, in a tiny horrible cell.

With the formal interview over, the detectives seemed to relax. Discussing her options for legal assistance, Reed sounded genuinely concerned for her wellbeing, and approved of Jen's suggestion that she would speak to the solicitor handling her divorce and see if she could recommend a specialist in criminal law.

'Good idea. And once that's sorted, you'll want to get your head down. An experience like this is incredibly draining.'

Until he'd said it, Jen hadn't appreciated just how exhausted she felt. But the evidence was there when she got up from her chair and stumbled, her legs struggling to keep her upright.

Then it was back to the main area, which now had the rowdy atmosphere of a football terrace. Five or six young men were being booked in, presumably for fighting – they were all hopelessly drunk and hurling abuse at the staff. One of them spotted Jen and leered, shouting, 'Oy, you're fucking fit! Hope I'm sharing your cell.'

'That's enough,' the custody officer growled, and Reed swiftly led her out of their sight.

The conversation with her divorce lawyer threatened to be painful, but Yvonne Cartwright was a shrewd woman who quickly spotted the potential for distress. After listening to a brief summary of the day's events, she assured Jen that 'just the right man' would be there for her in the morning.

By ten thirty she was back in her cell. The custody assistant persuaded her to accept a meal, and brought her a microwaved shepherd's pie, along with a drink of hot chocolate. Jen didn't think she was the least bit hungry, but she found herself greedily devouring the entire meal and felt quite a lot better for it afterwards.

She steeled herself to sit on the toilet, reminding herself that this was luxury compared to the many times she'd had to use a hole in the ground, then lay down on the thin mattress and covered herself with the blanket. By turning towards the wall, she hoped to fool herself into believing she was in a normal room, rather than confined to this small, unwelcoming space.

Over the years she'd slept in tents and caves, on bare earth and painfully hard floors, in hotels and hostels infested with bedbugs and roaches (and sometimes with their human equivalents). She'd slept in searing heat and icy cold conditions – she'd even slept on the deck of a ship in a terrifying thunderstorm – but never in a cell. Never as a prisoner.

The closest experience was probably on a ferry crossing in the Philippines, where her cabin had been smaller, hotter and much dirtier than this, thick with the stench of rotting food and diesel fumes; she'd gone down with food poisoning and barely moved for fifteen hours, hugging a bucket like a lifebelt. At least this room wasn't pitching up and down. . .

But sleep didn't seem feasible. Even if she was able to silence the turmoil in her head, there was nothing she could do about the commotion from the other cells. The young men kept up a barrage of screams and shouts; one of them was repeatedly stamping his foot against the door, while another seemed to be headbutting the wall.

Jen recalled a visit to a zoo where Charlie had expressed his concern at the sight of animals in cages. 'Doesn't it make them unhappy?' he'd asked, and when she tried to explain that often they were treated better here than in the wild, he had said, 'It's still not fair, though. Because the animals don't get to choose.'

And now that's me, she thought. *Someone decided I had to be put in a cage, and I didn't get to choose.*

She felt heartbroken for Charlie. In terms of the battle for his future, the implications were almost too awful to contemplate.

The break-up of her marriage – and its impact on her son – was an all-pervading source of anxiety. For the most part he seemed to have adjusted well to the separation, but the failure to agree on sensible residency arrangements threatened to undo the progress they'd made. Jen did all she could to shield him from the knowledge of the ugly, bitter disputes that continually erupted between her and Freddie, or between her lawyers and his.

Freddie, she suspected, made slightly less effort, though even he seemed to recognise that there should be boundaries set for Charlie's benefit. But Freddie's father saw things differently, and it was he, as the ultimate paymaster, who seemed intent on making the divorce as grisly and expensive as possible.

Depending on what happened tomorrow, Jen would probably have to come clean about the allegations against her. She liked to think Freddie would take no pleasure from her predicament, though Gerard was sure to feel vindicated. He'd had the lowest of opinions of her from the start, for many reasons – one of them being that she disagreed with almost every aspect of his worldview. And since broadcasting his trenchant, bigoted views had made him a multimillionaire and media darling, he hadn't taken kindly to such bold opposition from within the family.

He was also a fervent advocate of 'traditional families' – despite being on his third marriage – and felt that a wife belonged at home, attending to her husband's needs. He'd been outraged by Jen's intention to carry on travelling the world, especially once she had a baby to consider. Freddie had wavered in his support, sometimes enthusiastic about the adventures they would have when Charlie was a bit older, but rarely brave enough to say so in front of his father.

The police clearly suspected that she and this Alex Wilson had been having an affair, and she'd destroyed the artwork in an act of spite. It was the sort of story that thrilled the tabloids – the spurned lover cutting her man's clothes to shreds or wrecking his car – and for that reason it would be easily believed, not least by Gerard Lynch.

That reminded her of Freddie's insinuation that there was something between Jen and her boss, Nick. She'd never really mentioned him to Freddie, and it couldn't have come from Charlie: her son had met Nick only a handful of times, usually on the desperate days when childcare was unavailable and Jen had no choice but to bring him along to work. Maybe he'd said it just to goad her, but it was a good example of Freddie's hypocrisy. He still got touchy at any hint of another man taking an interest in her, even while boasting about his own conquests.

As the night wore on, the cells around her grew quieter, but sleep wouldn't come. The knowledge of her imprisonment was an agony; no matter how uncomfortable she became, she could not get up and leave this room. At times she was close to panic: what if there was a fire, and no one let her out?

She tried to construct a fantasy that she was at home with Charlie, going through the normal bedtime routine. Often, instead of reading a story, he wanted to hear about one of her adventures. Norway was the winter favourite: how she'd camped on the edge of a glacier, which in the depths of the night would creak and groan like some great alien beast, restless in its slumber. Or she would describe the vast summer plains of the Serengeti, swarming with wildlife. Charlie was obsessed with giraffes, in particular, and desperate to see them in their natural habitat.

Jen had always promised that one day she would take him on the sort of adventures she used to have, but to keep telling him that now would make her a liar and a fraud. After this, she might lose him forever.

Thoroughly despondent, she tried to break this chain of thought. It felt like the odds were stacked against her, but for Charlie's sake she had to stay strong, think logically, fight her corner.

So *think*. The damage seemed real enough, and it must have happened today. Either she'd done it herself, and somehow blanked the memory of it, or. . .

Someone else had done it. And they hadn't stopped at vandalism – they'd planted the stolen object in her flat. But the idea that she was being framed seemed just as bizarre, just as hard to accept, as the suggestion of a blackout.

Insanity or paranoia, she thought miserably. It wasn't much of a choice.

CHAPTER THIRTEEN

Jen slept a little, but sleep was not her friend. It was a feverish few hours of wretched unconsciousness, fractured by dreams of Tilgate Forest. The one consolation was that she woke with a measure of relief. *I'm only here, in a police cell; it's warm and well lit, and the monsters can't be real.*

The cells around her were blissfully silent, the young men sleeping off the booze that had derailed their evening. A new custody assistant looked in on her, and they chatted for a few minutes, Jen feeling ridiculously grateful for some human interaction. Her stomach was raw from the tension of the previous day, but she agreed to breakfast: cornflakes in a Styrofoam bowl, and water to drink.

Her whole body ached, so she ran through a few yoga moves: a pretty standard routine, though doing it in here made it feel like some corny montage from a prison movie. Afterwards she felt only marginally better. Normally the reward for a bad night's sleep in a hostile environment was a glorious vista, or the thrill of the exploration that lay ahead – a desert to cross, a mountain to climb. Here there were only the drab four walls, the echo of clanging doors, the fetid smell of male bodies discharging all manner of waste. As the custody assistant glumly reported, 'Night on the tiles, and with a lot of 'em it's coming out of both ends.'

But there was progress, as well. At eight o'clock Jen was taken to see the custody sergeant, a different one from yesterday, who authorised her move to a private room for a meeting with her solicitor.

Tim Allenby was about forty-five, tall and thin, a natural clotheshorse in a light grey Ted Baker suit, with foppish blond hair and attractive features marred only by the acne scars that pitted his cheeks. After shaking hands, he met her gaze and said, 'I'm afraid I must be brutally honest. It doesn't look good.'

Jen nodded. 'I sort of had that impression myself.'

He ran through his briefing from DS Howard, who he'd known for years. 'She's diligent, and fair – and very thorough,' he said, as if by way of a warning.

There were only a couple of embellishments that Jen could add, such as the recent demonstration of her good character. Allenby sucked his teeth as he considered it.

'I'm not sure that would carry much weight with a jury. Stealing a purse from an unattended bag is very much the act of an opportunist. This situation feels rather more premeditated.'

'But it wasn't!' Jen exclaimed. 'I didn't do it.'

He studied her carefully. 'And you're not acquainted with this Alex Wilson?'

'Only what I told them – sometimes he crosses my path as I'm walking to work.'

'And the landlord, the building's owner?'

'No idea who that is.'

'Very well.' He sighed. 'The accusation that somebody planted the figurine in your flat presents quite a challenge. Upstanding juries can react very negatively to claims of police corruption.'

'I'm not saying the pol—'

'DS Howard said that you did.'

Jen felt herself blushing. 'Only in the heat of the moment. The thing is, if it wasn't them. . .'

'Who was it? Exactly. I take it you saw no evidence of an intrusion when you got home?'

Reluctantly, Jen shook her head. 'Not a thing.'

'Good locks on your doors?'

'Just the one. Though I'm in a rented flat, so there could be any number of people with keys.'

'Ever had reasons for concern in that respect?'

'No,' she admitted. 'Though I've only been there for six months.'

Allenby thought it over, then delivered his conclusion. 'On the bare bones of the case I'm surprised, frankly, that they haven't charged you by now. It suggests to me that they're not a hundred per cent sure – and I know Tania won't go to the CPS until she has a rock-solid case.'

'Glad to hear it. What do you think she's waiting for?'

'Could be more enquiries at your place of work. I'm concerned by the allegation that Wilson lost his keys at the Skyway, though I understand they've confirmed that you weren't at work on Sunday?'

She winced. 'That's true – though I did have to pop in during the afternoon.'

'You were there on Sunday? DS Howard didn't say—'

'Because I didn't tell her.' She registered the solicitor's expression, one eyebrow sceptically arched, as if he'd lost any lingering faith that she was being straight with him.

Jen ran through the reason for her visit, and stressed that she went nowhere near the changing rooms where the men's lockers were located. And Charlie had been with her, of course.

'Let's hope it doesn't come to putting a seven-year-old in the witness box,' Allenby remarked. 'The CCTV coverage – think very carefully about where you went, and what the cameras would have seen.'

*

Jen closed her eyes, trying to visualise the layout of the sports complex. 'The CCTV's quite limited, and half the time the cameras are playing up. They cover the main reception, and a couple of other desks that handle payments. The cafe, one or two corridors, the sports halls.'

'And is it possible to reach the men's lockers without being seen on camera?'

'I guess you could probably find a way via the boiler room, but you'd need at least one key that isn't normally issued to staff like me.'

'And do you know where those keys are kept?'

With a sigh, she nodded.

'And can *that* location be reached without being seen?'

Another nod. 'I'm screwed, aren't I?'

'Well, if they find you on the centre's CCTV, even if it's only in the reception area. . .' He massaged his temples with his fingertips. 'It's unfortunate that I wasn't present for yesterday's interview.'

This seemed like such a huge understatement that Jen couldn't see any point in responding. After thirty seconds of silence, Allenby spoke again, his smile a kind of tactful grimace.

'Bear in mind that a full admission now, and a guilty plea in court, might see a greatly reduced sentence—'

'But I didn't do it.'

'Even a non-custodial sentence,' he continued gently, 'especially as your record until now is unblemished. Is there any possibility that the victim would speak up in your favour?'

She couldn't help glaring. 'This isn't a lovers' tiff. I've never said a word to the man.'

'All right. But if they find evidence of a connection between you and Mr Wilson, that will be the clincher.'

'There *isn't* a connection,' Jen stressed, infuriated that he didn't seem to be listening.

'So we're sticking with your account? Nothing to alter, and the only omission is that you dropped into the Skyway yesterday afternoon?'

Jen nodded. 'I know it probably looks obvious that I did it – it almost looks like that to *me*. But unless I've had a complete mental breakdown, there has to be another explanation.'

'Is there any history of mental illness? Blackouts? Psychotic episodes?'

'Nothing.'

'Right, okay. I've already suggested that Tania would be wise to look into some anomalies.' He granted Jen an encouraging smile, as if he'd been waiting for the right moment to lift her mood. 'This hidden camera, for a start. If Wilson had a problem with the lodger, why only the one camera in the hall? Why not in the room with the valuable artwork?'

Warming to the energy in his voice, Jen said, 'I suppose it does sound a bit iffy.'

'It does, though we also have to bear in mind that human beings are intrinsically peculiar, so the purpose of the camera may never become clear.'

'Something I thought of last night – what about the pen I picked up? It'll have my fingerprints on it.'

'That helps them as much as it does you. It puts you in the room where the damage occurred.'

'The pad, then. If there was an impression of my writing on the sheet below, it would prove I left a note.'

He agreed to ask about it, then told her that enquiries with nearby residents had drawn a blank. 'I want them to push this angle a bit harder. Somebody might have seen you picking something up from the lawn and not appreciated the significance.'

'There didn't seem to be anyone around. I was looking for a neighbour who might have been able to take the keys.'

'Doesn't rule out someone watching from a window.' He sucked his teeth again. 'Once you got into work, did you tell anybody about finding the keys? Did you mention it to your son, or to his friend's mother when you went to collect him?'

'It just didn't seem that important.' She sighed. 'Would the police be prepared to talk to the other residents of my building, in case they saw anything suspicious?'

'Regarding an intruder? It's doubtful, unless we can give them a good reason.'

'So in the worst case scenario, what's likely to happen?'

'I think they'll charge you,' he said bluntly. 'And because of the value, and the apparent degree of premeditation, it'll go to the magistrates' court for a plea.' His eyebrows went up: a question.

'Not guilty,' she said.

'Then it'll be referred to the crown court, which is preferable, on the whole. Better to take your chances with a jury than a lot of stuffed-shirt magistrates.'

He ran through the issue of costs, and reassured her that she should qualify for legal aid. He seemed content to finish there, but Jen had another question: 'And if it goes against me, at the crown court?'

Allenby leaned back and folded his long arms across his chest. 'You're of previous good character, you have a dependent child, a steady job. . . With a fair wind and a top-notch legal representative' – he winked – 'you might swing a suspended sentence and a large fine, though at this stage it would be prudent to make contingencies for six to twelve.'

There was a strange black flash in her mind; the first apocalyptic shudder of her world coming apart. 'Six to twelve. . .?'

'Months.'

'In prison?'

'I'm afraid so.'

Jen said nothing more, but she was sure the horror showed in her eyes.

Six to twelve months. In terms of what it would mean for Charlie – and for her role as his mother – it might as well be the rest of her life.

CHAPTER FOURTEEN

After that, the morning passed in a daze. By eleven o'clock she found herself stepping outside into another glorious summer's day, a free woman once again.

For now.

Shielding her eyes against the blazing sunshine, she descended the hill into Hollingbury, stopping at a patch of open ground next to Carden Avenue. There was a children's playground on the far side of a football pitch, but only a handful of people in sight. The grass was baked hard and Jen found a spot where she was unlikely to be noticed. She sat down, covered her face with her hands and sobbed until her palms were wet with tears.

Part of her reaction was down to relief, a way of exorcising the painful emotions that had built up during her night in the cell. But it was also one of horror at what lay ahead.

Six to twelve months, away from Charlie, away from her family. And then a lifetime to bear the taint of criminality.

She'd been let out on police bail, pending further enquiries, with a date to return in two months, though DS Howard had advised that they might be in touch a lot sooner. A number of conditions were attached to her release: she was forbidden from making contact with Alex Wilson, and nor could she enter Regency Place from the south or go anywhere near number 14.

That meant taking a different route to the bus stop for work, which was simple enough. But how would she explain it to Charlie when they were heading to the beach or the shops? *Hey, buddy, let's take a detour so Mummy doesn't end up in jail. . .*

On their return to the interview room, Allenby's presence seemed to provoke a more adversarial mood. Jen had agreed to the suggestion that her solicitor should read a short statement, confirming the version of events she'd previously given and informing the detectives that she had made a brief visit to the sports centre on Sunday afternoon.

It was clear from their reaction that they hadn't yet unearthed this information. The questions that followed were persistent to the point of tedium, and Jen felt it agonising to have to confine her answer to a single phrase, repeated over and over again.

'No comment.'

'You're in the process of divorcing,' Reed said, in a sudden departure from a series of questions about the layout of the Skyway. 'Never an easy time, especially if there's a child involved. Custody issues to sort out. What sort of man is your ex?'

Jen glanced at her solicitor, as if to say, *Surely this can't hurt. . .?* He answered with a warning look: *Better not to get drawn in.*

'No comment.'

Reed gave Allenby a cold smile. 'Freddie Lynch, that's his name, right? And he's, what, a musician or something?'

'No comment.'

'And he's the son of Gerard Lynch, I just found out.' A note of admiration in Reed's voice. 'Must be interesting, having a famous father-in-law. My dad always asks for his new book at Christmas, even though he reads the column every week.' He snorted. 'How nice is that, getting paid twice for the same bit of work? And Gerard's very big on law and order, from what I've seen.'

Jen struggled to keep her expression neutral. 'No comment.'

'Seems to me that if you did something which you now regret, you'd be scared to admit it for fear of embarrassing the family, and maybe damaging Gerard's career—'

'No comment.' This time it was said through gritted teeth, and the detectives were quick to pick up on the difference in tone.

'He's a polarising figure,' Howard said, 'so his opponents are likely to use it against him. But I suspect you're a lot more worried about admitting to a relationship that might impact on your divorce.'

'I'm not—' Jen began, then swallowed. 'No comment.'

'This is a fishing expedition,' Allenby said. 'My client's made a statement, and she has nothing more to say. I think we've all got better things to do with our time, haven't we?'

The interview had ended soon after this contribution. Now, as Jen picked herself up and walked to the nearest bus stop, she realised that she had to take Allenby's advice and get her own life back on track.

Her mobile phone had been returned, but it was switched off. She powered it up, and found several texts: two from Nick, wanting to know why she wasn't at work, and one from Anna: *Hope you're ok. Let me know when you can x*

Jen spent a few seconds thinking herself into the role of 'unwell woman', then called Nick and claimed to have come down with a stomach bug. She'd been up half the night vomiting.

'Why didn't you call earlier? I could have got somebody to cover.'

'Sorry. I was just wiped out.'

He made a disgruntled noise. 'Hope it's only a twenty-four hour thing?'

'Me too. I'll let you know.'

'D'you need anything? I could come round tonight.'

'No, better not,' she said hastily. 'Might be contagious.'

A bus was trundling towards her. She got off the phone and jumped aboard. Although she was desperate to be reunited with Charlie, the police had kept her clothes and shoes as evidence, and she didn't want her son to see her in this drab grey tracksuit. It also made sense to check the apartment, in case the search had left it in chaos.

Resting her head against the cool glass, she gazed out of the window, glad to be on a bus rather than in a police car. If it had been in her nature to wallow in misery, the poverty evident in London Road was a sobering reminder that many lives were on a downward spiral in this vibrant city.

She changed buses at the Old Steine and disembarked, out of habit, on the corner of Bristol Gardens. Then she remembered the terms of the bail and had to take a ten-minute detour to enter Regency Place from a side road, Henley Gardens, some fifty or sixty yards north of number 14.

She stopped at the corner, unwilling to turn and head for home. She stared at the house where Alex Wilson lived, wondering who he was and why this had happened. There were no cars parked outside, no windows open, and she found herself taking a few steps in that direction, almost drawn by the fact that it was now forbidden. *Always the rebel*, as her dad liked to point out, though she would argue that she just wanted to understand—

A cough made her jump. She turned to find a man ambling towards her from a house on the opposite corner of the junction. He was perhaps late thirties, medium height and fleshy, with thinning brown hair and narrow eyes hidden by the shadow of a heavy brow. He wore grey jogging shorts, spotted with white paint, and a rugby shirt with yellow stripes. He was fiddling with the drawstring on his shorts as he stopped alongside her, gesturing with his other hand towards the terrace.

'There were police out there most of yesterday. Going door to door as well.'

Jen merely nodded. Why was he telling her this?

'I live just there.' He jerked a thumb over his shoulder, and used the distraction to sneak a look at her chest. 'I've seen you walking past sometimes, with a little boy?' He sounded vague, but the intensity of his gaze suggested he was anything but uncertain.

Even though he made her uncomfortable, Jen couldn't help experiencing a spark of hope. 'What about yesterday morning?'

'Yesterday morning?' Again, there was something calculated about the way he pondered. His tongue was visible when he spoke, and added a slushy sibilance to his voice. 'I think I might have done – around nine-ish?'

'Nearer to half past. The guy who lives at number 14 came out and got into a white Subaru. Did you see that?'

'Not sure if I did. But that's the house the police were interested in. Apparently there was a break-in—'

'Where did you see me, exactly?' Jen, in her impatience, was almost gabbling as she indicated the opposite pavement. 'My route took me along here. I was on my own, carrying a sports bag. When I got to number 14, you might have seen me picking something up off the grass. . .?'

The man was frowning; she sensed that her interruption had displeased him. With another, less furtive appraisal of her body, he asked, 'What did you pick up?'

'The man dropped his keys. I noticed them as I walked past, and didn't want to leave them there—'

'The police said it was a break-in, but the suspect might have had keys.' It was his turn to interrupt, and he seemed to take pleasure in relaying this information, his lip curling slightly. 'A young woman, they said. So I assume it was you?'

*

Now on the back foot, Jen reluctantly admitted that it was. The man looked intrigued rather than disapproving; he introduced himself as Russell Pearce and offered what turned out to be a moist and overly firm handshake. Surreptitiously wiping her hand on her leg, Jen decided that she had little to lose and possibly something to gain, so she gave her name and briefly described her actions yesterday morning, then explained how the police had turned up at her flat and presented her with a completely different version of events.

'They think you smashed up his possessions? Why would you do that?'

'Exactly. It would be really useful if you can remember what you saw – not just me, but if there were other comings or goings at the house.'

'I was decorating round the back most of the day, but still. I can see how much this means to you.' He fingered the stubble on his chin. 'Perhaps there's a way we can sort this out.'

'Like what?'

She took a half-step back and his palms came up, anxious not to lose her. 'If it'll help, I could go to the police, and tell them I saw you.'

'But if it was only when I walked past here. . .'

'I'll go a bit further than that. Like I say, I really want to help.' He fished a phone out of his back pocket and checked the screen. 'I work from home, so I can arrange my time pretty much as I please. Why don't we grab a coffee, or a drink, maybe?'

'I can't. Sorry.'

'Just to talk it through. Make sure I know how to deal with any awkward questions.'

Jen shook her head. 'I haven't lied to the police, and I wouldn't dream of asking anyone to lie on my behalf, either.'

'But I'm happy to do you a favour. . .'

'No. We could both end up in prison.'

Her tone wasn't particularly sharp, but he flinched as if she had spat in her face. A flash of anger was replaced by an unconvincing smile.

'It sounds to me like you're in a heap of trouble, Jen, and here I am, doing everything I can to help.'

'I know that. I just don't want to make things any worse.' She started to move. 'But thanks for the offer.'

'Think it over. You know where to find me.' He frowned, and added quickly, 'I'm often busy in the evenings, but drop by during the day. Weekdays are good.'

You're married, she thought, as she watched him marching back to his home. It was right on the corner, the perfect location to monitor activity in the street. *A total sleazeball*, she thought. And yet she couldn't quite shake off the sense that she'd been a bit too hasty in turning down his proposal.

CHAPTER FIFTEEN

After the second knock, Anna's muffled cry of 'Just coming!' sounded a little stressed. Jen understood why when her friend opened the door with a toddler under one arm: both she and the little girl had white powder dusted all over their faces.

'Oh, Anna,' Jen tutted. 'Didn't I say – no more cocaine parties!'

It won a belly laugh, but even that wasn't enough to dislodge the concern in Anna's eyes. 'We're icing some buns. The boys decided the two of us should become snowmen – in August.'

'I'm so sorry. I forgot you had Keira today.'

'It's fine. They all get on well.' She ushered Jen inside. 'You look like you could do with a coffee, and maybe a coconut bun – if the boys haven't guzzled them all.'

'I wan' bun!' Keira shouted. By now Jen could hear the clatter of spoons and voices from the kitchen. On the way over she'd pictured Charlie running into her arms, just as he had yesterday afternoon, but perhaps he didn't realise she was here.

She reached the doorway and saw the boys kneeling on chairs at one of the worktops, giggling as they competed to scrape icing sugar from a mixing bowl. Then Charlie registered her presence and fell silent, turning to gaze at her with a grave, almost shameful expression.

Jen felt her stomach lurch, but did her best to keep the sorrow from her voice. 'Hiya, buddy. Sorry I couldn't get back here last night. The, er, thing took longer to sort out.'

Charlie just nodded curtly and turned back to the worktop, clashing elbows with Lucas as they jabbed their spoons into the bowl.

'Not so wild,' Anna chided them, before murmuring to Jen, 'He's a bit upset. Let's get a coffee, and I'll explain.'

Jen had been longing to hold Charlie, but now she approached hesitantly, fearing rejection. She put her hands on his shoulders and he squirmed slightly, but didn't throw her off. She settled for kissing the top of his head, and whispering, 'I'm back now. It's all right.'

The response was a disinterested grunt. Anna saved her embarrassment by announcing that the mixing bowl had to go in the dishwasher. As she took it from them, Jen felt her phone buzz.

It was a text from her divorce lawyer, suggesting she drop by for a chat. Deciding not to reply straight away, she helped Anna clean up, then they sent the boys into the garden. Keira sat in a highchair, munching on a carrot stick while Anna made coffee and described how Charlie had woken her in the middle of the night.

'I heard him crying and thought it was just a bad dream. But he'd wet the bed.'

Jen covered her mouth with her hand. It was a problem that had surfaced when she and Freddie first separated, and continued intermittently for a few months, but as far as she knew it hadn't happened for nearly a year.

'I didn't make a big deal of it,' Anna said. 'And Lucas sleeps like a zombie. Once I'd changed the bedding and given Charlie a hug – which I told him was from you – he went back off quite quickly.'

As Jen thanked her, Anna remained sombre, lips pursed. 'I'm afraid that's not all. When I fetched him last night, your neighbour was a bit sniffy. She said the police had come round and you'd gone off with them. I didn't want to pry, but while I was comforting Charlie in the night, he mentioned that you might have been. . . arrested?' She gave a fluttery laugh, as if it must be a mistake.

Jen had to nod. 'I can hardly believe it myself, but it's true.'

It took her about twenty minutes to recount the whole story, though she found herself unable to admit to the report of the keys going missing from the Skyway. That detail, she felt sure, would see her condemned even by someone who knew her well.

Anna listened mostly in silence, and then admitted that she was utterly baffled. 'I'm lost for words.'

'You don't think I've had a blackout and did it without remembering?'

'I very much doubt it.' She leaned towards Keira, who was bored with the carrot and trying to escape the highchair. 'I wonder if the man came home, saw your note and realised it was a chance to stick in an insurance claim.'

'So he smashed up his own artwork?'

'Perhaps it wasn't selling. Claiming on the insurance is a much faster way to turn property into cash.'

It was a feasible idea, up to a point. 'But what about the figurine they found at my flat?'

'That they *say* they found at your flat. How much do you trust the cops?'

Jen had to smile. Anna had previously told her about a wild period in her late teens when she'd picked up a couple of cautions for possessing class B substances, an experience that had formed a somewhat jaundiced view of the authorities.

'They didn't give me any reason to suspect them.' Jen sighed, then told Anna about the text from her solicitor. 'God knows what she'll say.'

'And Freddie.' Anna grimaced. 'Will you tell him?'

'I suppose I'll have to.' She opened the back door and called to Charlie. 'Time to go!'

Their farewell was hampered by Keira, writhing against Anna's shoulder as she fought off the need for a nap. With Charlie waiting sullenly at the front door, Anna whispered, 'He'll be okay. Just keep me updated – and let me know if you can still do Thursday night.'

Once they were away from the house, Jen offered her hand and felt profoundly relieved when, after a couple of seconds, Charlie's fingers curled around hers.

'We've just got to pop into town before we go home.'

He groaned. 'Do we have to?'

'It's only for a quick chat with Yvonne. Hey, how about if we grab a McDonald's afterwards?'

He stared at her in astonishment. 'You never let me have McDonald's.'

'Yes, I do. Occasionally. Anyway, I think you're due a treat, for being so good at Anna's.'

He said nothing, and she guessed that he was dwelling on the bedwetting. Then, after a minute or so of silence, he asked, 'Are you in a lot of trouble?'

The arrival of a bus gave her time to get her thoughts in order. They sat at the back, opening some windows to lessen the stifling heat. And then, doing her utmost to sound normal, Jen explained that a good deed had somehow been misinterpreted, but would soon be recognised for what it was.

Charlie listened to the end, his bottom lip protruding, then he thrust his head against her chest and sobbed. 'I thought you'd gone to prison, and I wouldn't see you again.'

His raw anguish speared her heart, and it took every ounce of self-control not to break down. Drawing him into a tight embrace, Jen gave what comfort she could, but the thought of being forcibly separated from him was unbearable.

It *was* a good deed, she insisted to herself. So how could it mean that she stood to lose everything?

The solicitors occupied two floors of a modern office building in Middle Street, a short walk from the seafront. The office next door was home to a visual effects company, which had recently expanded after winning an academy award. One of the partners, an acquaintance of Freddie's, had suffered a terrifying home invasion that led to the abduction of his wife and daughter. Jen tried to draw strength from the knowledge that the family had faced a far greater ordeal than her own, and they had come through it.

So will I, she told herself. *So will Charlie.*

Yvonne Cartwright was in her forties, a tall, plump black woman with unruly hair, a Croydon accent and the cheekiest smile Jen had ever seen. She had a fondness for charcoal suits, generally half a size too small, and bright purple eye shadow. Stepping into the reception area, she greeted Charlie with genuine fondness but sent Jen a quick worried glance. Clearly this wasn't going to be a child-appropriate conversation.

'Will you be okay to wait out here?' Jen asked him.

'Do I have to?' Charlie looked with disdain at the low table on which half a dozen glossy magazines were fanned out. The likes of *Sussex Life* and *Latest Homes* were never going to capture a seven-year-old's attention.

Jen passed him her phone. 'You can play *Lego City*. But nothing else.'

'Where are you going?'

She indicated the first of several offices in a short corridor, and Yvonne said, 'I'll leave the door open. Come in if you need anything.'

Jen followed the solicitor into the office, and confided in a whisper that Charlie was still very unsettled by yesterday's incident.

'I'm not surprised. My jaw hit the ground when you rang.' Yvonne took her seat behind a desk piled high with documents, reports and folders. 'Old-fashioned chaos,' she'd explained when they first met. 'It brings out the best in me.'

And she was probably right. Certainly Jen couldn't dispute the effectiveness with which Yvonne had countered the initial attacks in what Freddie's representatives had made clear was going to be a long and vicious fight.

Now, though, she began with an update. After months of arguing over the terms of a possible shared residency, Freddie's lawyers had announced that an increase in their client's private income – courtesy of Pa – enabled him to give Charlie far more time and attention than Jen could provide, and as such they were proposing that Freddie should be the resident parent.

'Not so much shifting the goalposts as bashing them down and using them for firewood,' Yvonne commented.

'But it's about more than money. I'm far better placed to give Charlie a stable routine. Freddie's supposed to be a busy professional musician, remember?'

'They're saying it's predominantly local session work, with only a minimum of evening gigs, and usually just at weekends.'

'But even that's not true. Freddie's lucky if he plays for money half a dozen times a year. He's in love with the *idea* of being a musician, because it justifies the lifestyle, the partying, the women. And that's no environment for Charlie.'

Yvonne nodded curtly. 'By contrast, they're arguing that your shift work is far too intrusive. It's bollocks, you and I both know that. But it won't be easy to refute, even without the horror story I got from Tim this morning.'

A pause. After a heavy sigh, Jen said, 'I didn't do it, Yvonne. I *can't* have.'

The solicitor narrowed her eyes at this odd turn of phrase, but Jen had no better way of expressing her tiny, lingering doubt.

She ran through Anna's theory of an insurance scam, but had to concede that it didn't account for the item they found in her flat.

'No, it doesn't.' Yvonne lowered her voice. 'And as it stands right now, I think you're gonna be found guilty.'

Her confirmation of Allenby's grim prognosis hit Jen like a physical blow. 'Six to twelve months, according to Tim.'

'Perhaps less. From our point of view, even a *week* is a disaster. With that in mind, I'm duty-bound to suggest you consider going for a settlement, even if it means making concessions that—'

'I won't do that. It's not right for Charlie.'

Yvonne held up a hand. 'Hear me out. You have to be aware that whatever ground we surrender now, it could be nothing compared to what they get once you have a conviction to your name.'

'No, I'm sorry. I don't mean to sound nasty, but Freddie's still a child himself at heart. He has no routines, no discipline, and if you strapped him to a lie detector he'd probably admit that he doesn't really *want* full parental responsibility. It's more about that bloody father of his being determined to win at all—'

Yvonne's sideways glance alerted her to the mistake she'd made. Jen looked over her shoulder, and there was Charlie in the doorway, his gaze burning into her, the hurt all over his face.

CHAPTER SIXTEEN

'All right, buddy?' Jen tried to keep her voice normal: there was always a chance that he hadn't picked up on the conversation.

'Can we go soon? I'm hungry.' He sniffed, and she saw he was on the brink of tears. Of course he'd heard. And he was embarrassed, backing away even as she assured him that they wouldn't be long. 'Five minutes at most, and then we'll get lunch.'

She turned back to find Yvonne studying her. 'How have you been sleeping?' the solicitor asked quietly.

A shrug. 'Not great.'

'You have to take care of yourself. The stress of a divorce can cause serious illness – even somebody as fit and healthy as you isn't immune.'

Jen thought of the woman who'd shouted at her in the custody suite, the vomit stains all down her front; how easy it would be to lose control, to become weepy and confused and even violent.

'Do you think I did it?' she asked abruptly.

Yvonne had a smooth line in evasion. 'What a solicitor thinks isn't relevant, as you know. What matters is getting the best possible outcome for you and Charlie, and that's what Tim and I are here to do.'

Jen chose the branch of McDonald's in the Churchill Square shopping centre, but swiftly regretted the decision. The food hall on the top floor appeared to be the exclusive territory of noisy teenagers, making Jen feel almost as oppressed as she had last night in the cell. Charlie seemed unaffected, though – and this was his treat, after all.

She had said sorry about the conversation he'd overheard, and now she apologised again. 'I know it sounded like I was being really mean about your dad, and that was wrong of me.'

'He thinks you hate him,' Charlie said, in a matter-of-fact tone. 'I heard him on the phone to someone. He said, "I loved her like crazy but I couldn't live with the bitch".'

He cringed as the b-word came out, unsure whether the rules against bad language applied to quotes from other people, but Jen only frowned.

'Did Daddy know you were listening?'

'Um. . .' Now awkward, Charlie decided that the burger required his full attention.

Jen took a sip of water. 'I don't hate your dad, I really don't. But there are a lot of things about his lifestyle that worry me – especially if you were living with him for most of the time.'

Charlie pondered wisely, funnelled a couple of French fries into his mouth and said, 'I'd keep being late for school. Dad never does anything when he says he will.'

Jen tried to be diplomatic, though there was no way she could plausibly disagree. This week's proposed trip to Cornwall was a good example: she'd heard nothing more from Freddie, and Charlie had stopped asking about it.

They were both subdued on the journey home. Charlie made no comment when they got off the bus a stop early and followed an alternative route to the flat. Nor did he seem to register how quietly Jen opened the front door, anxious to avoid an encounter with Bridie Martin.

Having popped home earlier to shower and change clothes, she knew that the police had left few traces of their presence.

Now, with Charlie watching TV, Jen examined the front door more closely. Somebody must have gained entry to the flat to plant the figurine, and yet there was no sign of any damage; just various nicks and scratches around the keyhole consistent with years of wear and tear.

She joined Charlie on the sofa, grateful for a chance to cuddle up and relax. But within a few minutes he was complaining that it was too hot in the flat. 'And it's boring.'

Jen shut her eyes, sent a prayer for some energy to the gods of parenting and sprang to her feet.

'Beach?'

Jen was distracted as they turned the corner into Henley Gardens; passing Russell Pearce's house, it felt like she was being watched, though she couldn't see him at the windows.

Then Charlie tugged at her arm. 'This way's quicker!' When she wouldn't change direction he broke free and ran back into Regency Place.

'Charlie, stop!' She chased after him, but that just turned it into a game. 'We're not going that way.'

'Why not?'

'Because I said so.' An answer she'd once sworn she would never give. But Charlie was laughing, putting everything into outrunning her, only faltering when he heard the snarl in her voice: 'Come here now or you can forget the beach!'

'But Mu-um. . .' He slowed to a trudge, jerking his shoulders in disgust, then came stomping back.

Behind him, across the street, there was a man walking towards the X-Trail, parked outside number 14. It was Alex Wilson. Without looking in her direction, he moved towards the back of the vehicle, tapping away at his phone.

Jen gasped. Was she close enough to be in breach of her bail terms?

Then came defiance: *To hell with it. I haven't done anything wrong. I ought to be demanding an explanation from him.*

Charlie grumbled: 'I wanna go this way. I'm tired.'

'It won't be much further, and we can get an ice cream.'

She grabbed his hand and hurried him away. Good sense had prevailed: it would have been disastrous to confront the man in front of Charlie. But she wondered how long she'd be able to resist the urge to approach the house.

It was just after three o'clock when they got to the beach. The hottest part of the day in an exceptionally hot spell of weather, and the sea was blissfully cool and refreshing. Jen stayed in for twenty minutes or so, helping Charlie improve his freestyle technique. He was already a proficient swimmer for his age, and one of the coaches at the Skyway rated him highly, joking that she might never get a lie-in again. The juniors who were serious about their sport were in the pool at 6 a.m.

Some of the kids splashing around in the shallows were from Charlie's school. Before long he was playing with them, and Jen climbed out, dried off and checked her phone. She had two missed calls from Freddie.

She felt a tremor of unease as she rang him, in case word of her arrest had already filtered back, but Freddie's tone was easy-going, even diffident.

'I changed a few things, so I'm fine to have Charlie tomorrow night.'

'Oh.' Jen had to stop herself from thanking him – all he'd done was revert to the original plan. 'Are you still going to Cornwall?'

'Ah, no.'

'Freddie, he'll be really disapp—'

'It's because I can take him to Greece instead.'

'Greece?' Jen was stunned.

'Yeah. A villa on Crete. He'll love it.'

'Whose villa?'

'What? Just a friend.'

Jen heard the lie but decided not to call it out. 'How long for?'

'A few days, that's all.' She started to interrupt but he spoke over her: 'I know what you said about school – back for Friday, yeah?'

'No, *Thursday*. He needs to be home with me on Wednesday, to have time to prepare.'

'It's fucking primary school, Jen. He's not off to uni.'

She was stung by the scorn but made an effort to stay calm. She was still trying to process the bombshell of a foreign trip. In other circumstances she might have refused to agree until her solicitor had been consulted, but right now she had other considerations.

'Look, can I ask a favour? Could I borrow one of your cars while you're away?' Freddie currently had an Audi SUV and a Porsche 911, even though his fondness for a drink at lunchtime meant he went almost everywhere by taxi.

After an incredulous silence, he said, 'We're in the middle of a divorce.'

'I know. But I've just agreed to let you take Charlie abroad, and in return—'

'Sorry, Jen, I can't do that. I'll pick him up tomorrow night, say around six? Make sure he's packed for a Greek island, yeah?'

The call ended, and only then did Jen realise that she was crying. To make it worse, Charlie was crunching up the bank of stones towards her.

'What's wrong?'

'Nothing. I'm fine, honestly.'

He knelt down on the towel and put his arms around her, his body chilled by the sea, his hair dripping water onto her face as he leaned in to kiss her cheek, and not for the first time Jen felt that she might be the real child in this relationship, and Charlie the adult.

'Try not to worry, Mum. It'll be all right.'

CHAPTER SEVENTEEN

On Wednesday Jen made a snap decision to call in sick again. She did it early, knowing Nick wouldn't be there yet. She wasn't proud of her behaviour, but this was her first such absence in nearly three years at the Skyway, and these were exceptional circumstances. Not only was she still traumatised by her arrest, but she was about to lose Charlie for nearly a week. . . and soon she might lose him altogether.

She wasn't at all comfortable with the idea of Freddie taking him abroad, and wondered now if the trip to Cornwall had only ever been a ruse. It was hard to shake off the feeling that she'd been outmanoeuvred, though if she was honest she'd have to say that Freddie was neither smart nor devious enough to play that sort of game.

The superficial nature of his personality had prompted mixed feelings from the start, but his good looks and easy charm had overcome her reservations. Jen had never encountered a man with such a carefree attitude to life. His shameless devotion to taking pleasure wherever he could find it made for an exhilarating contrast with her own deeply ingrained belief that nothing worth having came easy. In the words of a friend of hers upon first meeting him, Freddie had just the right degree of intelligence to understand the world and have fun, but perhaps not so much that he couldn't be manipulated when the need arose. . .

And that sort of assessment, she thought, was just one of the reasons his dad had both feared and hated her from the start.

The fact was, she had little choice but to let Charlie go. During a long period of anxious wakefulness in the early hours, she'd come to the conclusion that no one was going to rescue her from her current predicament. Somehow, she would have to do it herself – and for that she needed some time on her own.

It was a measure of Freddie's unreliability that she still wasn't confident enough to tell Charlie he was off to Crete. The disappointment would be too much to bear if it fell through. But she got started on packing a suitcase with plenty of summer clothes, while he ate toast and Marmite, and they discussed what to do. Jen was determined to wrestle the maximum enjoyment from this final day with her son.

'Can we go bowling at the Marina?' he asked.

'Really?' It was hard not to baulk at the cost, though Jen reminded herself that she'd be spending less on food while Charlie was away. Quite often she lived on little more than pulses and fruit.

'Let's have a swim first, then bowling. Though I'll warn you now, we're not having junk food two days running. We'll take a picnic.'

He was happy with that, and said, 'Can Lucas come?'

'Good idea.'

Anna was surprised by the change of plan – she was scheduled to have Charlie today – but admitted that a few hours without Lucas wouldn't be unwelcome. 'I've got lots of errands to run, and he hates being cooped up in the car.'

'That's perfect, then. Uh, talking of cars, is there any chance I could borrow yours at some point in the next few days, if I need to?'

'Of course. Just say when.' A hesitation. 'Is this anything to do with. . .?'

'Yes and no,' Jen replied. Which was perfectly honest, since she hadn't yet formulated any sort of plan.

*

They collected Lucas and went to Hove, where the beaches were quieter, and at low tide offered up patches of sand for small boys to dig and mould and fight on, to kick and dive-bomb and use as a grave in which to bury their willing victim (Jen).

After the picnic, they caught a bus to Brighton Marina and went bowling, then mooched around the arcade games. Charlie normally knew better than to pester for money – even at his tender age he understood that Jen didn't have a fraction of the resources available to Freddie – but his friend's presence perhaps added to the pressure.

Jen gave in and let them go on a couple of games, though Charlie still got whiny when it was time to leave. She nearly told him about Greece, only to think better of it. She'd texted Freddie to confirm what time he was getting Charlie tonight, and he hadn't replied.

On the bus to Kemptown the three of them were tired, probably a bit dehydrated, and increasingly fractious. Slipping onto autopilot, Jen disembarked at their usual stop before realising her error.

It was already a much longer walk to take Lucas home, and she couldn't face adding what would seem to the boys like an utterly pointless detour. *We'll hurry past number 14 on the other side of the street*, she told herself. *That can't do any harm.*

Regency Place was quiet. The only car parked outside the terrace was a white Citroën. Jen kept her head down and walked briskly, urging the boys to match her pace. When she heard a door opening, she tensed, expecting a cry of recognition. For the sake of saving a few minutes' walk, she might be arrested and hauled back to a cell. . .

She risked a look: a teenage girl was slouching towards the Citroën, while a middle-aged woman shut the door of number 12.

Jen turned her head away from them, just as Charlie complained that his legs ached.

'You're both doing really well.' Just a second or two till they were safely past. 'Let's pretend we're explorers, okay? In the jungles of Sumatra, which is an island in Indonesia, there are tigers, and rhino, but also poachers armed with guns, so we'll have to defend ourselves—'

'I've got an Uzi!' Charlie declared, instantly drawn into the fantasy.

'Me too!' Lucas cried, and both boys lifted their hands and sprayed automatic fire into the surrounding gardens.

Over their sound effects, she caught the growl of an engine. She turned, and saw the X-Trail coming up behind the Citroën, which was waiting to pull away from the kerb.

Jen sped up, praying she hadn't been noticed. The boys ran ahead, engrossed in their imaginary slaughter. Risking a glance back, she saw Alex Wilson staring coldly in her direction. Would he know the precise terms of her bail?

They needed to take Henley Gardens to go west and then north to Hanover. Crossing the side road, there was an unmistakable flash of movement from a window at the corner house. Russell Pearce.

Jen looked back one more time, just before the X-Trail slipped from view. Alex Wilson was still watching her.

Who are you? she wondered.

Who are you to me?

CHAPTER EIGHTEEN

Freddie didn't get in touch until ten to six, by which time Jen had practically given up on him, though as a precaution she'd finished packing and made Charlie an early tea. Her heart fell when she saw Freddie's name in the display.

'Who is it this time?'

'What?'

'You ignored my texts, so I take it there's been another lovely distraction, and as usual I'm the one—'

'Hey! I'm parked up outside.' He sounded amused. 'Bring him down, will you? I've got a surprise for you.'

Fuming at the way she'd been lured into an overreaction, she switched off the TV and said, 'All set to go? Your dad's here.'

Charlie was slumped on the floor, his back against the sofa. He nodded without enthusiasm.

Jen knelt to face him. 'You're going to have a great time. I think he's got something really special arranged.'

'In Cornwall?'

'No. He'll tell you.'

She drew him to his feet, but his expression remained serious. 'You'll be all right, won't you?'

'Me?' The word almost caught in her throat. 'Hey, of course I will. And it's only a few days till you're back here.'

He nodded. 'I love you,' he said, and then, while she was holding him close: 'Be careful, Mummy.'

*

In manoeuvring the suitcase through the front door, she bumped it against the frame; a second later her neighbour appeared. 'Ah, I wondered if you'd been trying to avoid me.'

'Oh – hi, Bridie! No, why would I?' Jen offered a sickly grin, saw Bridie register Charlie's presence and took advantage of her hesitation. 'Can't stop. Perhaps have a chat later?'

'I think we should. It quite shook me up on Monday, the sight of. . .'

'We'll talk soon, I promise.' Jen hustled Charlie into the stairwell, plagued by a fear that Bridie would find the energy to follow her out of the building and mention the police in front of Freddie.

She would have to tell him, she knew that. But she wanted to do it on her own terms.

The suitcase was bulky, but her progress was hampered more by Charlie, who slouched listlessly from step to step. Jen wondered if the lack of urgency was for her benefit – not wanting her to see how excited he was. But when they reached the lobby, he grabbed her T-shirt and asked for another hug. 'I'll miss you.'

The sorrow in his voice carved up her insides. This was on another level from the usual difficult adjustment he had to make, going from one parent to another. She'd long worried that it must be making him feel schizophrenic, having to adapt to two such different lifestyles and personalities.

'You'll be fine. And don't you worry about me for a second.'

Freddie was waiting by the entrance, wearing a prepared smile that gave no clue to his mood. His eyes, as befitted a wannabe rock musician, were hidden by his trademark Ray-Ban sunglasses.

'Hey.' He opened his right hand to show her a smart key. 'For the Q5.'

'I can borrow it?' Jen took the key and mumbled her thanks. She was about to ask what had prompted the change of heart when her attention was caught by a Mercedes SUV drawing up behind the Audi.

'Grandpa!' A yell from Charlie as Gerard Lynch climbed out and marched round to the pavement, crouching to beckon the boy into his arms.

'Hello there, Chip!' he roared, using the nickname that seemed to have been designed to annoy both Jen and Freddie.

Charlie, his grandfather had declared when the boy was little more than a few months old, was the *real* chip off the old block: 'He's got my eyes, my spirit, my character – you just wait and see.'

Jen thought of this when Gerard glanced at her over Charlie's shoulder, a triumphant glint in his eye. *Look at this bond we have.* Squeezing the boy until he didn't know whether to giggle or gasp. *You think you can break this?*

She turned away, and caught Freddie looking defensive. 'If you're having my car, I had to get a lift back,' he explained.

Gerard finally released Charlie. 'What about your daddy, Chip? Hey, has he told you where you're going?'

Charlie looked uncertain, perhaps because the three adults present were united only in their desire to put on a charade for his benefit. It was bitterly unfair, Jen thought, presenting him with conflicting loyalties when his natural instincts were so straightforward, so pure: to love them all.

'Pa's staying tonight and giving us a lift to the airport tomorrow,' Freddie confided. He broke off to greet Charlie, and that was Gerard's cue to join them.

Lynch senior was taller than his son – a little over six feet – with a once muscular frame swollen by years of sumptuous living. In his favoured summer outfit of mustard-coloured slacks and a white silk shirt, there was no hiding a considerable spare tyre. On some occasions, however, it all but vanished, leading Jen to suspect that he wore a corset for TV appearances, book signings and the like.

His hair was long and scruffy, and much darker than was realistic for a man in his mid sixties, though he would stridently insist it was natural. Jen had once mischievously suggested that there might be some Romany influence in his DNA. To a man who thought gypsies belonged in concentration camps – and had pretty much said so in the *Mail*, the *Express* and the *Telegraph* – there were few things that could be more insulting.

He had a narrow face dominated by a crooked nose; his eyes were small and dark and deep-set, with black pouches that several cosmetic procedures had failed to improve. His teeth were yellow, with prominent incisors, and he revealed too much of his gums when he bared them. His smile was a gruesome sight: hungry and mocking, it rarely contained even a trace of warmth.

He looked her up and down, and sniffed disapprovingly. 'Nice of Freddie to lend you the car.'

'Yes.' For Charlie's sake, she wasn't going to rise to it. She heard the boy's sudden exclamation – 'Greece!' – and for the first time this evening his face lit up with real pleasure.

'Just wait till you see the villa, Chip,' Gerard said. 'A real home away from home.'

Jen frowned. 'Are you going with them?'

'Not this time. Too busy.'

She looked from Gerard to Freddie. 'Hold on, so whose. . .?'

'It's my place.' Gerard showed his teeth. 'Bought it nearly a year ago, and the damn builders have only just got their sorry arses off the site. Five bedrooms, three bathrooms. . .' He turned his attention to Charlie. 'A huge swimming pool, Chip – and a games room, with table tennis and pool, and there's a drum kit. How about that? Now, jump in Grandpa's car. We need to get going.'

After a final hug and kiss, Charlie headed to the car. Freddie picked up the suitcase and went to follow, then said, 'Got the passport?'

'Here.' Jen reached into her pocket, only for Gerard to put his hand out for it.

'Do Charlie the world of good, getting him away from this cesspit.' It wasn't clear whether he meant Jen's flat, the street, or the whole city. Gerard had no time for Brighton, decrying it in print as a sinful hotbed of gay perversion.

She was speechless, reeling from the news of the villa in Greece, and the fact that she'd just surrendered Charlie's passport to a man who bore her nothing but ill will.

'Enjoy your time alone.' Grinning sarcastically, Gerard raised one arm and waggled the passport in farewell. 'Make the most of your freedom, Jennifer.'

CHAPTER NINETEEN

That night she got drunk, not in a pleasant, social, accidental way, but steadily, with determination and effort. There was a decent bottle of Sauvignon that Nick had bought her as thanks for helping out during a crisis at work, and a good deal remained of the Grey Goose that her parents had given her at Christmas. Taken together, with only a couple of slices of toast to eat, it was more than enough to induce the unconsciousness she craved.

Through the evening she obsessed over her father-in-law's parting words, which hinted that he knew of the arrest and was gloating about her fate. Gerard had always envisaged a union for his son with somebody whose money and connections complemented his own. Having paid for Freddie to go on a six-week expedition from Santiago to Rio – part of a rehabilitation process after kicking a gambling addiction – he hadn't reacted well to the news that his son had fallen for a penniless tour guide.

While frenzied and passionate in the beginning, their fundamentally opposing personalities might have seen the relationship burn out within a year had Jen not accidentally fallen pregnant. She'd expected a commitment-phobe like Freddie to run a mile at the news, but instead he had insisted that this was 'a sign' – not only that he and Jen were destined to be together, but that it was time for him to knuckle down to a more conventional way of life.

He blamed his lack of boundaries on the fact that his mother had died of cancer when he was seventeen. Gerard had by then been married to his second wife – who Freddie despised – and they had two young daughters. Now Freddie had a chance to make a family of his own.

They had married in secret, with Jen reluctantly agreeing not to tell her own parents. Though diplomatic about it, they approved of Freddie only slightly more than Gerard did of Jen. After a low-key ceremony at a register office in London, the newlyweds escaped to Hawaii for a month, where Freddie burned through the last of his mother's trust fund and set about gingerly negotiating a peace deal with his father.

An uneasy truce was established, and Gerard had reacted with delight to the arrival of a grandson. By then his second marriage was in meltdown, and it soon became clear that Gerard would be seeing little of his daughters as they grew up. It still puzzled Jen that he had meekly conceded custody of the girls – who nowadays spent more time at boarding school than they did with either of their parents – whereas he seemed enraged by the idea of Freddie losing Charlie.

Then again, she knew Gerard to be highly irrational, as well as spiteful. But he was nothing if not well connected, and there was every chance that news of her arrest had found its way to him via his network of contacts in the worlds of politics, media and the law.

Either that, or she was being paranoid. After all, hadn't Nick made a similar comment on Monday?

In sleep, all her fears were unleashed: she was a criminal, doomed to suffer a criminal's fate; she had lost her mind, and more blackouts would follow. But the slippery black vein that snaked through every nightmare was the terror of losing Charlie – losing not just his physical presence but his love, his trust in her.

She woke with a start at some time around four, disorientated because she was in a proper bed rather than on the sofa. Then she felt her temples contract and her throat swell; she only just had time to throw herself off the bed before she vomited.

It made a revolting mess on a carpet already stained by previous tenants, but at least Charlie's bed had been spared. Jen mopped up the worst of it with an old towel, rinsed her mouth and then forced herself to sip some water before staggering back to bed, where she collapsed and promptly passed out again.

More dreams. She was in Tilgate Forest, somehow as both her fourteen-year-old self and simultaneously her present age, with an adult's perspective on her childish bid to escape from the world.

She'd grown up in a small town in Surrey, an outdoorsy, tomboyish kid with plenty of friends but no real soulmates, given to solitude and undoubtedly a bit quirky, if not downright weird. How many teenage girls had a poster of Ranulph Fiennes on the wall, alongside George Michael and Take That?

Raised in a loving, prosperous family, Jen was the eldest of three girls, though sometimes she'd felt excluded by her sisters, who were six years younger, and twins. There had been little sign of adolescent rebellion until, in the late summer of 1996, a growing sense of alienation had compelled her to run away from home.

Her destination, Tilgate Forest, was a place she already knew well. She was experienced at camping, having been a Brownie from the age of seven, and then a Girl Guide. She planned her move carefully, taking a tent and enough high-energy foods for three or four days. The weather forecast was favourable, though on the first night the temperature dropped much lower than she'd anticipated, making it impossible to sleep. But what had really turned her adventure into an ordeal was the power of her imagination.

Deep in the forest, where full daylight never reached, the feather-light rustling of dry leaves could be a mere breath of wind or some harmless squirrel, but more likely it was confirmation that she was being stalked. Wrapped in a lightweight sleeping bag, curled up in the hollow of a dead tree trunk, she somehow managed to survive three long nights, convinced that she was about to be attacked by dogs, wolves, bears, rapists – even vampires and zombies.

In all the years since, even during a couple of bad falls while free climbing, even with hypothermia in the mountains of Norway or dysentery in Tanzania, she had never felt as certain that she would die as she had been in Tilgate Forest. Hour after hour she'd wept silent tears, shivering so violently it might have knocked her heart out of rhythm.

But I came through it, didn't I? Shouldn't that be the point—

She was trying to explain to somebody who refused to listen when a piledriver started up. Jen opened her eyes and the sound morphed into a thumping on the front door. A familiar voice called her name.

Nick.

She wiped her mouth and found it crusted with saliva – at least she hoped it was only saliva. She managed to cry, hoarsely, 'Just coming!' Then sat up, but felt the room shift violently and had to lie down again, staring at the ceiling as she willed the carousel to stop.

Eventually she made it to the door, having pulled on a full-length robe and wrapped a towel around her hair, hiding as much of herself as possible. A glimpse in the mirror made her want to cry, and Nick's reaction confirmed it.

'Bloody hell, Jen, you weren't kidding, were you?'

Confused for a second, she remembered that she was supposed to be off sick. Nick thought she looked like this because of a stomach bug.

'Was the main door unlocked?'

'Your neighbour buzzed me in. She asked if I was a cop.'

'You?' Jen snorted, inadvertently blowing snot from her nose. She wiped it away with her arm, lost her balance and nearly hit her head on the doorframe. *Still drunk.*

Nick pushed the door shut and moved towards her. Jen cringed, aware that she probably stank of booze and vomit, but he showed no sign of revulsion as he took her into his arms.

'I'm worried about you, Jen. That prick Freddie better not be giving you more grief?'

'No, it's nothing,' she mumbled, fighting the temptation to bury her face in his chest.

'I'm not buying that. Tell me.'

His arms were comfortingly strong, his torso a slab of muscle. He smelt ridiculously good, too. Jen didn't trust herself to speak. Nick's hands had started to move, one slipping lower, the other trailing up her spine and along her neck. . .

She pushed herself backwards, out of his grip. 'I can't do this. I look disgusting.'

'Nothing a shower wouldn't fix.'

'No. I feel really dreadful. And it's wrong.'

He sighed. 'I don't get what the problem is? We're both single—'

'But I'm not, yet. Not officially.'

'That doesn't stop him screwing everything in sight.'

'I know, but anything I do will be used against me, because that's what they're like, Freddie and his dad—'

'You can't let them control you like this.' His tone was sour, even petulant. 'Or is it easier just to blame them if you're not really interested?'

'What?'

'Well, come on. You can't say you haven't been sending mixed messages.'

Jen shut her eyes, pressing her fingertips to her forehead: the pain was drilling through her skull. It stung that there was an element of truth in his words. Although she liked Nick, she hadn't yet decided whether she liked him enough for anything to happen.

They'd come close a couple of times, most recently on a staff night out; at the end of the evening they'd been kissing in the dark corner of a pub when one of their colleagues nearly caught them, reminding Jen of the added complications of a relationship with her boss.

'Nick, I'm sorry. It was good of you to come round, but I need to get some rest.'

'I'm not here just to see how you are. You were meant to be at work and didn't show up.' He sniffed. 'And call me a cynic, but I think you look hungover, more than ill.'

She met his gaze, unashamed. 'If you want the truth, today I am. I got so pissed that I threw up in the night.'

'But you hardly drink. Who were you with?'

'No one.' She couldn't help rolling her eyes at his assumption. 'I know this is short notice, but can I have a few days off? I'm not in any fit state to work at the moment.'

'We're already short-staffed.'

'I wouldn't ask if it wasn't important. It's only today and tomorrow, and then I'm off anyway. Please, Nick.'

She could see him weighing up the advantage of having her in his debt. Eventually, with a sigh, he said, 'I guess I can ask Paula to do some more hours.'

'Thank you. I'll stay in touch, and perhaps catch up properly at the weekend?'

He nodded reluctantly, aware that he was being asked to leave. 'So Charlie's away – I bet you'll be glad of the freedom?'

She flinched. 'What are you talking about?'

'Getting some time to yourself—'

'It's not a chore to be with my son. I miss him like crazy when he's with his dad. I don't see why everyone keeps going on about freedom. . .'

'Okay, okay.' Nick had both hands up to placate her. 'I didn't mean to upset you.'

She winced – raising her voice had sent the headache up a notch – and eyed him suspiciously. 'Do you know a man called Alex Wilson?'

'Name doesn't mean anything. Who is he?'

'Forget it.'

'Jen, if someone's giving you hassle, I wanna be here for you.' He looked ready to embrace her again.

'It's fine.' She gave a conciliatory smile, and ushered him out of the flat, aware that her behaviour must seem truly alarming.

Nick wasn't her enemy. What was she thinking?

CHAPTER TWENTY

After showering and brushing her teeth, Jen felt human once again. Maybe not well enough to scrub the carpet, but ready to risk a mug of sweet tea and some toast.

She decided that it was bound to fuel her paranoia, the fear that Freddie had whisked their son away and might not bring him back. The knowledge that Gerard had acquired a property in Greece was another reason to be afraid.

So what next? The question, only half-serious, floated in her mind as she picked up her phone. She had a brief message from Freddie, assuring her that Charlie had slept well and sent his love; he promised to let her know when they landed in Crete. There were also a couple of texts from Anna: Were they still on for tonight?

In one sense she was gratified: she'd been worrying that her friend might cool towards her as a result of her arrest. As well as the childcare, Anna had been a great source of moral support over the past year or so, and Jen couldn't afford to lose her friendship – even if, right now, she couldn't imagine anything worse than a night on the town.

Back to that question: what next? She had no proof, that was the trouble. No proof that anyone was acting maliciously against her. No proof of her own innocence.

She had to get some evidence, one way or the other, but how?

The answer was obvious, really.

Confront Alex Wilson.

*

She phoned Anna, and heard the hubbub of children in the background. 'I hope you're not gonna cancel on me,' Anna warned, with a laugh. 'I'm *craving* some grown-up company.'

'No, I can make it. I might not be up to drinking, though.'

'You have to. I'm the sober one – your wingman.'

'I won't be needing a wingman.'

'Don't be negative. You're too gorgeous to be on your own, and it's my mission to find you the perfect partner for life – or, failing that, a decent shag.'

Laughing, Jen could only agree that Anna would collect her at seven thirty.

'And dress up, girl. Any glimpse of sportswear and I'll put you over my knee.'

'We're not going anywhere posh?'

'Up to you. But it's got to be lively. With a decent menu.'

Hoping she might have regained an appetite by then, Jen drank some more water and took a couple of ibuprofen. Then she cleaned the carpet, struggling against waves of nausea at the sour smell of regurgitated vodka.

She left the windows wide open while she showered again, but made sure they were shut and locked before leaving the flat. Couldn't be too careful.

The air felt slightly cooler, making it a warm and very pleasant English summer's day. She wondered about the temperature in Crete, and whether Freddie could be trusted to remember the importance of a hat for Charlie, and regular applications of sun cream.

It was now mid morning. At a nearby block of flats, a team of three men were putting up a scaffold. As Jen passed, one of them whistled, and another barked at him: 'Keep your bloody eyes on the job!'

She continued down the hill, towards the point where she would, in effect, be breaking the law. There were no cars parked outside number 14, and no activity near the house, but Jen's heart was beating hard.

She knew she mustn't appear furtive, so she lifted her chin and walked briskly over the dried-out grass, rapped confidently on the front door and heard the sound echo through the house. No one there. She peered closely at the door, but the tape she'd used for the note didn't seem to have left any mark.

After half a minute she rang the doorbell, without much hope, then glanced over her shoulder. And sighed.

Russell Pearce was hurrying towards her, dressed in what looked like the same outfit he'd worn on Tuesday – jogging shorts and a rugby shirt – but with the addition of long white socks and brown crocs. He raised a hand in greeting, and said, 'He's gone.'

'What?'

'The guy who lived there. He left yesterday.'

'You mean he's moved out?'

'Yep. He must have been renting it furnished, because there wasn't a van or anything.'

Mystified, Jen shook her head. 'I don't believe it.'

'Always was a bit odd, if you ask me. Some days I'd see him go out in the morning with one of those boxes, only to return after twenty minutes and take the box back inside.'

He shrugged at the absurdity, but Jen was still trying to process his previous revelation. 'How do you know he moved out?'

'Oh, he had these bin bags with duvets and pillows. . .' He faltered, then said, 'I've been taking a closer interest, in light of what happened to you.'

Jen turned to stare at the door. 'Was his girlfriend with him?'

'I wasn't aware that he had one.'

Conscious of his ravenous gaze, she crossed her arms and shivered. 'The police said he used his girlfriend's keys because his had gone missing the day before the break-in.'

A grunt from Pearce. 'To be honest, I thought he might be gay. The only regular visitor I saw was a young Pak— uh, Asian bloke. The type that really love themselves, you know? Flash suits and perfect hair, and this fuck-off silver watch you could see from a mile away.' He sniffed, disparagingly, and sidled a little closer.

Jen said, 'I suppose it's irrelevant, now he's moved out.' She started to turn away, only for him to paw at her shoulder.

'Hold on. What about my offer?'

'It's very kind, but I can't ask you to lie.'

'I'm not. I wouldn't be.' He dropped his gaze. 'I didn't want to admit it before, in case it made me look a bit. . . dodgy. The thing is, I *did* see you on Monday.' He gestured at the lawn. 'You bent over, like you were picking something up.'

'Honestly?' Despite his manner, she felt a rush of optimism – but it lasted only a second. 'Haven't you already spoken to the police?'

'I'll say I've just realised the significance. I doubt if the officer even filed a report.' He took out his phone and asked for her number. 'Let me text you my full name and address, and please feel free to pass it on to the cops, or your solicitors, or whoever. Anything to help.'

Against her better judgment, Jen gave him her number and Pearce sent her a text to confirm he'd got it right. He grinned as her phone bleeped, and murmured, 'Gotcha.'

'I think I'd better talk it over with my solicitor,' she warned.

'Good idea.' He walked alongside her, clearly not wanting her to go. 'So, er, what does your husband make of all this?'

Too weary to lie, she said, 'We're separated.' And then could have lip-synced his corny response: 'Really? He must be mad.'

She gave a disdainful shrug. 'Thanks. I'll see what my solicitor says.'

CHAPTER TWENTY-ONE

'How certain are you that he's telling the truth?'

'Not a hundred per cent, to be honest.'

Allenby was doodling something on a pad; he didn't look up as he asked, 'I mean, are there any possible ulterior motives? Something the prosecution could embarrass us with?'

'Oh, I'm pretty sure he'd offer to say anything if I agreed to sleep with him.'

That caught his attention. 'I assume that's not a likely—'

Jen recoiled so violently that her chair shifted on its casters. Allenby dropped the pen and said, 'I'll take that as an emphatic no.'

She was back in the Middle Street building. In contrast to Yvonne Cartwright, Allenby kept his office in an immaculate state, all his files and folders shut away in glass-fronted cabinets. There were several photo frames on his desk, but positioned in such a way that Jen couldn't see what they contained. On a narrow shelf behind him there was a line of small objects that she thought might be Pokémon sliders, a toy craze she vaguely remembered from fifteen or twenty years ago.

'I'm not comfortable that Pearce told the police he didn't see anything, and yet now he's claiming he did. He'd be mincemeat in the witness box.' Allenby intertwined his fingers and pressed them against his chin. 'Let's keep him in reserve if we get *truly* desperate.'

'Are we likely to?' Jen shot back, and when no answer was forthcoming, she sat forward. 'Don't you think we should be looking at Alex Wilson, and why he's suddenly moved out?'

'I'm not sure how relevant that is.'

'Isn't it a coincidence – only two days after claiming I'd burgled the place?'

'Push him on it, and he may claim that Monday's incident is what provoked the desire to leave.'

Jen sighed. That hadn't occurred to her. 'What about the "girlfriend", then?'

'Just because Mr Pearce hasn't seen her, it hardly means her existence can be called into question, particularly as we have doubts about his credibility.'

Jen had no option but to nod. Go on insisting and he was likely to view her as unhinged.

Allenby's next report was that the police had failed to record the presence of a notepad in the storeroom. 'So that's no longer an avenue we can explore. But if I can engineer a suspicion that Mr Wilson isn't what he purports to be, I will gladly do so.'

Jen's mood was flat as she left the solicitors. Physically, she wasn't feeling too good, either. The headache was creeping back, along with an intermittent queasiness.

She bought a carton of fruit juice and a banana from a supermarket in North Street, and sat on one of the long benches in New Road, a pedestrian thoroughfare on the edge of Pavilion Gardens. Was there anything else she could do, or was she better off going home?

An idea occurred to her, which involved the risk of personal humiliation, as well as another encounter with Nick. She decided it was worth trying, and returned to North Street to catch a bus to Portslade. On her limited income, her one lifeline was the annual bus ticket bought through a scheme at work, the cost deducted monthly from her wages.

It wasn't a particularly long journey, but in the heat she found herself unable to keep her eyes open. She kept jerking awake, her head lolling like a daytime drunk. Was this her destiny, to become an embittered spinster and ex-jailbird who couldn't control her drinking, shunned by her grown-up son and his family?

At the Skyway she got lucky. A few of the staff, including Nick, weren't yet back from lunch. In the main reception area, someone was taking a new member through the health and fitness questionnaire, leaving just one person at the desk. Nina was an unassuming young woman who'd only recently been hired and barely knew Jen.

'Hi, Nina. Mind if I check something on the database? I can't seem to access it from the climbing centre.'

'Sure.' She moved aside, and as Jen stepped behind the counter she spotted an e-cigarette lying beside a coffee mug.

'Actually, I can spare five minutes if you want to get some fresh air.'

Nina's eyes lit up. 'Do you mind? I need to call my boyfriend.' She grabbed the e-cig and was gone. And if she'd noticed that Jen was wearing denim shorts and black T-shirt, rather than her normal sports gear, she obviously hadn't thought anything of it.

She'd also left herself logged onto the system. Jen got to work, and within thirty seconds had confirmed that Alex Wilson was a registered member of the gym. He'd joined in late May, three months ago, and taken only the most basic membership.

The Skyway used swipe cards, so it was possible to see how often he'd attended. There was a rash of visits at the start, quickly falling to just once or twice a week, which was nothing out of the ordinary. Most people joined with good intentions and then lost the discipline as other, everyday demands took priority over fitness.

With the desk to herself, she opened up the centre's incident log, which was an intranet file updated from a handwritten book kept in the manager's office. Jen found an entry from last Sunday, recorded at 4.20 p.m. Loss of house keys, possibly from the main locker room. No damage found to the locker. No witness corroboration. No relevant CCTV available. A thorough search had failed to yield any clues, so the complainant had been advised to check at home in case he was mistaken, or failing that, report the loss to the police.

Which tied in with what the detectives had told her, though Jen would have expected the complainant – Alex Wilson – to have made a bit more fuss than this. Nothing in the report indicated that he'd demanded to see a manager, or threatened them with a claim for compensation: the usual response nowadays to any kind of problem.

She imagined taking that argument to the police, or even to Allenby, and being told: 'Perhaps he's just a reasonable guy?'

It was another dead end. Sighing, Jen waited for Nina to return, chatted for a minute and then left the building feeling more despondent than ever.

In fact, this was worse than a dead end. If the whole thing was a set-up, how on earth could Wilson have known that Jen would notice the keys and go inside the house?

He couldn't have.

So how had he been able to report the keys missing the day before?

That seemed impossible, and yet she'd just seen solid evidence that supported his version of events. Which meant the only logical explanation was the one she'd been trying so hard to dismiss. She must have blanked out taking the keys on Sunday, and blanked out the destruction of the artwork the following day, while dreaming up a flaky alternative scenario which nobody – including her lawyers – thought was remotely plausible. . .

No, she told herself, *that isn't me*. She could see herself picking up the keys from the lawn, writing the note and sticking it to the door. She couldn't have invented those memories.

'Then how do I explain it?' she whispered aloud. *How do I prove my innocence, when all this evidence says I'm guilty?*

She took a bus to Queens Park and walked to her flat on a route that avoided both number 14 and Russell Pearce's house. Running it through in her mind, she had to accept that on the basis of the known facts – supported by police reports and CCTV – a jury was almost certain to prefer the prosecution's version of events over hers.

In that case, the only option was to find stronger evidence in her favour, or else adjust to the reality of a prison sentence. Her chances of surviving were probably better if she spent time preparing for it, as she would for any other major challenge: look at her diet and fitness, work on meditation techniques – and brush up on her self-defence skills.

All well and good in theory, but for one fundamental flaw.

Charlie. She couldn't bear the thought of him having to visit her in prison, and yet incarceration without contact would destroy her utterly.

As she reached home, there was a niggling feeling that she'd failed to pick up on the significance of something Russell Pearce had said, but she knew it would never come to her if she approached it directly. In any case, the vibe she'd got from Pearce was that he shouldn't be trusted on anything.

By late afternoon the effects of her hangover had mostly worn off, but she still didn't feel much like a night out. She was cheered by a brief phone call from Charlie, using his dad's phone. They had arrived safely in Crete and Charlie was almost gabbling in his enthusiasm for the villa.

'It's so amazing, there's a massive swimming pool, and it's got a slide! There's table tennis which Dad's gonna teach me, and some proper arcade games, and I can hit the drums as loud as I want cos the nearest house is so far away!'

'Take lots of pictures and get your dad to email them to me.'

'I will. Love you, Mum.'

'I love you, too. Have a brilliant time.'

After he rang off, the flat seemed morbidly quiet. Anna's right, she thought. A night out will do me good, and so what if she keeps trying to hook me up with suitable new boyfriends? It was largely her own fault for giving her friend the impression that no one was interested, when the truth was rather more complicated than that.

Nick, for instance. And then there was—

She sat up in shock, recalling what Pearce had said.

No.

It couldn't be.

CHAPTER TWENTY-TWO

Anna rolled up in her Volvo estate, ten minutes late because Lucas had insisted on one more chapter of *James and the Giant Peach*. 'He says Daddy doesn't read it as well as I do.'

'Can't argue with that.' Jen settled in the passenger seat, then registered Anna's scrutiny.

'Well, well. For somebody who sounded mighty reluctant to go out, you've scrubbed up rather nicely.'

Jen managed a smile, though she was nervous about her reasons for making so much effort. She was wearing a black lace body-con dress and strappy sandals with a three-inch heel. She had applied a little make-up – lips and eyes, and a hint of blusher on her cheeks – and her blonde hair had been pinned in a deliberately tousled up-do: it was against her nature to look immaculate.

Anna, who was dark-skinned and curvy, let out an appreciative whistle. 'Wow! That stomach of yours is flat even when you're sitting down.'

'I'm breathing in. Anyway, what about you – got a licence for that cleavage, have you?'

Anna looked down. 'Mm, sorry. Road testing a new bra, and it's not so much balcony as forklift truck.' She gave her boobs a comical squeeze. 'If you think it's too obvious I'll take it off.'

Jen grinned. 'That seems to be all the rage at the moment, going braless. I saw a guy at the gym literally fly off a treadmill because of the distraction.'

'I wouldn't dare go untethered,' Anna said. 'Whereas you'd look stunning.'

'Stop it! You're far more attractive than me.'

'Oh, don't you be starting that again. This is Freddie's work, doing you down.'

'Actually, it's more of a family trait. My dad would rather hack off his own foot than boast about something.'

'Well, modesty has its place, but not right now, when you're about to get back in the game.'

'I can't. The situation's too delicate.'

'I think that's become your fallback. What about Nick?'

Shocked, Jen could only bluster: 'Wh-what about Nick? Why would you...?'

'Save it. I know you've got the hots for each other.'

Jen shook her head. 'You should have let me drive. I still feel a bit ill.'

'Changing the subject!' Anna clicked her tongue, and was abruptly serious. 'By the way, if you want to talk about Monday, or anything else. . .'

'I don't think so. But thanks.'

'All right. So where are we going?'

'Actually, I wondered about Breakaway.'

'That's a bar, isn't it? Near Hove town hall?'

Jen nodded. 'The food's good, and it's lively – just what you wanted.'

'Okay. What made you come up with that?'

A shrug, to mask her dishonesty. 'I was there a few weeks ago with a couple of girls from work.'

'Anyone pull?'

Jen laughed. 'No, but it was a possibility.'

'For one of them, or you?'

'My lips are sealed.'

'Well, well. Breakaway it is, then.'

*

The bar/restaurant occupied the ground floor of a large Victorian mansion block on the corner of First Avenue and Church Road. It was a large space with a central serving area, squared off with counters on all four sides. The walls were lined with booths, and there was a small stage and dance floor for their live music and comedy nights.

At a little before eight, the place was still quiet. Jen counted about twenty patrons, mostly an after-work crowd, plus a few mellow souls who appeared to have come straight from the beach.

'Looking for someone?'

'Not really.' Jen pretended not to notice Anna's wry smile. An attentive waiter rescued her with the offer of drinks, and seemed disappointed that the order was for two Diet Cokes and a jug of tap water.

'Living it large,' Anna quipped, and that led to a discussion about healthy diets. In the course of their relationship, Anna's partner had become a vegetarian, then a vegan, and now he was talking of ditching his high-flying job in corporate acquisitions and retraining as a nutritional therapist. 'I'm practically teetotal these days, because when I drink I want a cigarette, and when I smoke I fancy a joint. But imagine – no *bacon*, Jen. No chicken, no fish, no *cheese*.'

'What does that actually leave?'

'Grass and twigs, I think. I'm protected at the moment, because I've insisted that Lucas eats a balanced diet until he's old enough to decide for himself. But once he's grown up, I might as well just buy a hutch and call myself Bugsy.'

Liberated by her partner's absence, Anna ordered deep fried camembert followed by pork belly. Jen had bruschetta and then sea bass. As they ate, they kept the conversation fairly neutral – not too much about the kids, because Anna knew how much Jen pined for Charlie when he was away.

The bar started to get busier around nine. Thanks to a well-positioned mirror, Jen could keep tabs on quite a large section of the room. Anna caught her at it more than once; she said nothing but quietly smirked, as if she knew exactly what was going on.

But you don't, Jen thought sadly. *You really don't.*

Then, as they were finishing the main course and debating the wickedness of dessert – mitigated if they had one to share – and Jen had all but dismissed the foolish hunch that had prompted her to nominate this venue over any other. . . there he was.

He'd come in alone, dressed in a dark suit with a white shirt; no tie. At the bar he waited with his hands in his pockets, his stance casual, no apparent interest in who else was present. Just as he lifted his hand to pay for his drink, her view was obscured by somebody moving to the bar.

By then, he'd sensed that he was being watched, though he pretended he hadn't. Playing it cool – which was logical, after last time.

Anna began to lose the thread of a somewhat catty anecdote about her mother's new boyfriend, then broke off mid sentence. 'What is it?'

'Nothing.'

'You look tense.'

Jen glanced in the mirror and saw he was heading away from the bar; a moment of eye contact with her reflection and he gave a little double-take, then turned in their direction.

She sat up straighter. *Tense* didn't begin to cover how she was feeling. She heard Anna emit a tiny gasp of pleasure as she registered what was going on, but Jen's heart was pounding from something very different to attraction. She looked him up and down, saw he had a bottle of Peroni in his right hand, but his left was still thrust into a pocket.

Damn.

'Hi there – Jen? Nice to see you again.'

'You, too.' With quick thinking, Jen offered her hand to shake. The man had to switch the beer to his left hand, and as the cuffs of his shirt and jacket rode up, she was able to see his wrist.

No watch.

He shook hands, but also leaned over and kissed her cheek. As he straightened up, Anna was rising from her seat.

'This is my friend, Anna.'

'Pleased to meet you. I'm Sam.' A slight smile to acknowledge the possibility that Jen hadn't remembered his name. Then he tutted. 'You didn't call me.'

'Been busy, you know how it is.'

'Shame. You've still got my card, though?'

Jen managed a flirtatious smile. 'I think I mislaid it.'

He grinned back, a lot of light in those gorgeous brown eyes. 'Mislaid into the nearest bin, I bet. You must get given so many.'

'Oh, hundreds,' she said, in a mock weary tone. 'Let me have another one, and maybe I'll be more careful this time.'

'I hope so, or else I'll have to keep coming back here to find you.'

'I'll make sure she does,' Anna cut in, which was his cue to turn the charm on her.

'Then I'll be forever in your debt. Thank you.'

Jen braced herself for a spiel, but Sam left it at that, simply reaching into his jacket and bringing out a business card, which he set down upon the table. No cheesy comments, no sleazy attempt to brush against her – significant points in his favour, or might have been...

It was as he retracted his hand that she saw the watch, big and brash and chunky; not on his left arm but his right. That's a *fuck-off* watch right there, Jen thought, and felt an icicle of pure fear plunging into her heart – a reaction she had to hide, at least for the few seconds it took Sam to wish them both a fine evening.

Then he sauntered away, and Jen felt sure that Anna, vibrating with curiosity, couldn't fail to ask why she looked so stunned, so disturbed. But she didn't.

'Oh. My. God. You *lucky* cow!'

CHAPTER TWENTY-THREE

Jen bought herself some time by turning to watch Sam stroll away. She wanted to see if he was meeting up with anyone, though not for the reasons Anna would have assumed.

Her friend hissed a warning: 'Don't be too obvious.'

Jen snorted. 'Did you really just say that, after months of urging me to jump on any half-decent bit of male flesh?'

'Your friend Sam is rather more than "half-decent". Now tell me everything!'

'It's no big deal. Last time I was in here, with the girls from work, we got talking at the bar and he offered to buy me a drink. In fact, he offered to buy all three of us a drink. I said no, and he backed off, but asked if he could give me his card. The others were urging me to take it, so I did.'

'Good grief, Jennifer. Why didn't you call him?'

'I keep telling you, I can't afford to be in a relationship until the divorce is complete. Freddie's girlfriends are one thing – it's like everyone expects men to shag around. But anyone new coming into my life and his lawyers will make out it's party night for paedos, and suddenly I'm not trusted to have Charlie anymore.'

'No, no, you're exaggerating. Whatever the risks, you make an exception for a guy like that.' Anna gestured at the bar in exasperation. 'It's so blinking obvious how keen you are. You can't stop looking at him.'

Jen was fighting the urge to stare. Sam had moved to the far side of the bar, only a sliver of his right arm and shoulder visible.

Tracking him, she felt sick with confusion, but somehow to Anna it came across as uncontrollable lust.

The waiter sidled up, and Jen changed her mind about dessert. 'What the hell, let's have a banoffee pie to share.'

Anna grinned. 'Two spoons, or three?'

The bar was now so crowded that the dessert was served promptly – the table was wanted for a second sitting. In the melee Sam was almost impossible to spot, and the price for seeking him out was a good-natured lecture from Anna on the rules of the mating game.

'I know it's corny, and disgustingly sexist, but he has to respect you. On the other hand, foul this up and I'm gonna get his number and shag him myself.' Anna pursed her lips. 'He's a meat eater, don't you think? And that's not a euphem—' She let out a yelp as Jen leapt up, her chair scraping on the polished wood floor.

'Get the bill, will you? I won't be a minute.'

Sam was heading for the exit. Just the one beer and then he was leaving – suspicious, or had someone let him down?

As she squeezed through the crowd, she used Russell Pearce's description to justify what might otherwise seem like an act of lunacy. A young Asian man, sufficiently well-groomed to be regarded as gay – which said more about Pearce's preconceptions than anything else. The chunky chrome watch seemed to confirm it, or was that just more delusion on Jen's part?

At the door, she glanced back. Anna was lost from sight and wouldn't know she'd left the bar. That made it a little more hazardous, perhaps.

But Sam was nowhere to be seen. Church Road was well lit and busy with traffic; unless he'd ducked into a doorway he ought to be visible. First Avenue was a different matter: it was an extra-wide residential street that offered parking spaces on each side, as well as a double row down the centre. The pavements were punctuated with trees that threw deep shadows across the cars.

It was a tree that had concealed him, as Jen discovered when she ran a few yards, wobbling a little because the heels made a drastic change to her usual trainers. Sam was alone, head down, walking purposefully with a phone in his hand.

When he suddenly cut left, into the road, Jen ducked behind a parked car. She heard the soft thunk of a door opening, a louder one as it shut. Stooping to remain below the roofline of the parked vehicles, she crept closer until she caught sight of a sleek BMW saloon with two figures inside.

One was Sam Dhillon.

The other was Alex Wilson.

In her shock, she almost gave herself away. Stumbling backwards, Jen rested against a van, one hand clutching her belly, breathing as if she'd just been winded by a fall.

She heard the loud click of heels and found three young women tottering in her direction, all Kardashianed to the point where their own mothers would struggle to recognise them. 'You all right, babes?' one asked, and when Jen assured them that she was, they moved on, exchanging whispers that led to a burst of giggles.

Jen didn't care what they'd said, but she suspected their appearance would divert the attention of the men in the BMW. Ducking low, she headed back towards the bar, only checking behind her once she was sheltered by one of the trees. She could just about see the BMW. Sam was looking at the driver, whose head seemed to be cocked slightly, as if he was on the phone.

Was it Alex Wilson? Already she was starting to doubt her own judgment. From this distance, at night, with other parked cars in the way, surely it was impossible to confirm the identity of a man she didn't particularly know in the first place?

She hurried on, only to hear an engine purr into life. The BMW was facing Church Road, so they'd be coming her way.

Crouching down, Jen slipped off her heels and dashed back to the corner and into the bar, apologising as she shouldered past a group of people on their way out. A couple of them made rude remarks, but she ignored them, loitering by the big glass doors as the BMW reached the junction, waited a few seconds for the road to clear, then pulled out.

Jen guessed it would go right, but in fact it performed an illegal U-turn and headed back into First Avenue, heading for the seafront. That meant there was a chance. . .

She found Anna chatting to the waiter as he tore off the receipt from a portable card machine. Sensing her approach, Anna looked up and frowned at Jen's agitated manner, and the shoes in her hand.

'We need to go. Quickly.'

Not waiting for a response, Jen ran out and crossed First Avenue. Fortunately, Anna's car was parked facing the coast. Up ahead she could see brake lights flashing in the darkness at the end of the street. She was counting on the A259 being busy enough to delay the BMW for a while.

Anna caught up with her at the car. 'Have you lost your mind?'

Jen indicated the driver's seat. 'Please hurry. It's really important.'

'But you can't—'

'Give me a minute and I'll explain. Please.'

Grumbling to herself, Anna unlocked and got in. Jen dropped into her seat, grabbed the belt and checked over her shoulder. 'You're clear to pull out. Go.'

Anna backed up sharply enough to send the parking sensors into a frenzy, then lurched out of the space. 'Where, exactly?'

'We need to follow a black BMW, only it's got a bit of a head start.'

'So who's in it – your new friend?' Catching a nod from Jen, she said, 'Then why don't you phone him?'

'It's not about Sam. It's who he's with.'

'Ahh.' Anna thought she understood. 'Don't tell me it's one of the girls from your work?'

'Nothing like that. This is about Monday.'

They were coming up to the junction; no other cars ahead of them. Jen hadn't seen which way the BMW had turned, but left seemed the likelier option.

Anna hit the brakes and for a moment they both stared forlornly at the coast road, traffic zipping past in both directions. Beyond the road lay Hove Lawns, sprinkled in the darkness with the glitter of mobile phones and the flicker of several barbecues. At Jen's command, they took a left turn and drove east, towards the city centre.

The speed limit here was thirty, but Jen urged her friend to overtake the obedient drivers and catch up with a mass of traffic now stationary at a set of red lights. She leaned forward, one hand on the dash, squinting to lessen the glare of oncoming headlights as she tried to identify a particular vehicle from the dual lines of traffic ahead.

From here to the Old Steine there were a number of junctions in quick succession, most of them controlled by traffic lights. With a bit of aggressive driving it should be possible to make up some of the distance between them, but that depended on Anna's cooperation.

'I'm really sorry,' Jen said quietly. 'I can imagine how crazy this must seem. But it could mean the difference between life carrying on as normal for me, or being sent to prison.'

CHAPTER TWENTY-FOUR

While Jen did her best to explain, she was also puzzling over the BMW's route. Why do a U-turn to get to the coast when they could have turned right into Church Road and reached the centre that way?

It had to be that their destination was on the seafront – either that or they were heading for a distant part of Brighton that was more easily accessible via the A259. Like Kemptown. Like Regency Place.

Had Russell Pearce got it wrong about Wilson moving out?

Anna, thankfully, was responding to the challenge and driving like a demon. At one point she veered into the opposite carriageway to overtake a particularly slow driver who was hogging the outside lane.

'Don't get us killed,' Jen muttered.

'Make up your mind.' Anna nodded at the inside lane. 'Isn't that a BMW?'

'Yes, it is. Shit.' The car was in a line of eight or nine vehicles waiting to pull away from lights that had just turned green. The outside lane had responded more quickly, which meant Anna was coming up fast on the BMW. Four or five car lengths and they would draw alongside.

'Slow down,' Jen said.

'I'm trying, but I have to keep moving – otherwise it'll be noticed.' Her point was emphasised by the impatient flash of headlights from the car behind.

The inside lane sped up, only to slow again for a car turning left at the junction. Then a blinking light caught Jen's attention. The BMW was indicating left.

'Can you get over?'

'Not really.'

Jen checked to her left – solid traffic – but when she looked back the BMW was already pulling off the road, veering into a lay-by or slip road just ahead of the junction: Jen realised it was the entrance to a hotel.

'Carry on!' she yelled, and Anna gave a bark of sarcastic laughter.

'Jesus, you're a crap navigator.'

Anna saw the lights changing and hit the accelerator, zipping through as they turned to red. Now there was a space, since the car travelling next to them had stopped for the lights.

'We need to pull over.'

'Okay.' Anna changed lanes, then deftly swerved into a lay-by. She'd barely come to a stop when Jen opened the door.

'I'll be five minutes.'

'Jen, please, it could be dangerous.'

Anna tried to clutch her arm but Jen pulled free, her attention already switching to the junction they'd just passed. The green light for pedestrians was still lit so she ran towards the crossing, saw the light wink out but by then she was committed, sprinting across the road as a small van tried to anticipate the lights, edging forward and almost taking her out.

Jen dodged sideways and leapt for the pavement, grateful for her decision to stay sober tonight. She felt clear-headed, fast and agile; pumped up with adrenaline and ready for anything. . . not that she had a plan, beyond seeing where the two men had gone, and hopefully determining whether the driver was Alex Wilson.

That part turned out to be easy. The front corner of the BMW crept into view, and Jen quickly turned to a restaurant with a handful of tables outside, pretending to inspect the menu while the car nudged its way back into the flow of traffic. It rolled past, and Jen chose her moment to snatch a look at the driver's face.

Definitely Alex Wilson.

She weaved around the tables and took a right into the access road, racing up the steps to the hotel entrance. Ignoring the revolving door, she pushed through the glass door next to it and slowed, knowing that she mustn't attract too much attention, blundering barefoot and dishevelled into the lobby.

Fortunately the hotel was quiet. Most of the sofas placed around the room were unoccupied, and a couple of staff at the reception desk were deep in conversation with a guest. There was a bar to her left, and a sign for lifts and stairs pointing straight ahead.

Jen couldn't see Sam in the bar, and her instinct told her that he'd make for the lifts. She crossed the lobby and turned into an alcove that housed two elevators and a door to the stairs. One of the elevators was stationary on the ground floor, the other was rising from two to three. . . and then it stopped.

Could she get there in time? The stairwell was deserted, the dusty concrete steps functional and rarely used. Jen took them the way she might race up a scree-covered slope, her feet never making contact for more than a fraction of a second.

She dimly heard the clunk of the lift door closing. Another five, ten seconds and she was on the third floor, pausing a moment to listen before easing the heavy fire door open. A long corridor stretched away to her left, empty and dark, while to her right there was another fire door and then what looked like a short dead-end corridor.

Jen went that way, wincing as the door creaked. The dead end was actually a sharp right turn into another hallway with a dozen or so rooms. She peered round the corner and saw Sam Dhillon coming to a stop about halfway along. He slotted a key card into the reader, and went into the room.

The presence of a fire extinguisher on the wall helped Jen to mark his position. As soon as the door shut she crept forward and made a note of his room number, then turned and hurried back, stepping lightly so he wouldn't hear the vibrations through the floor.

It was possible that this little adventure would turn out to be worthless, but right now Jen felt more energised than she had all week. After blundering in the dark for so long, now at least she knew something that they didn't.

The big question remained: who exactly were *they*?

At the car, she found Anna in a frantic state. 'Oh thank God, I didn't know whether to come after you, or call the police, or what. . .'

'You worry too much. Let's go.'

'Uh uh. I want to know what you've got yourself mixed up in.'

'If I knew, I'd tell you. I mean it.'

'So what just happened?'

'I wanted to see where he was going, that's all. I didn't speak to him, and he didn't see me.'

'And I take it you won't be setting up a date?'

Jen shook her head, even as she thought, *Now you mention it. . .*

On the short drive back to Kemptown, she tried to explain her theory that she was being set up. As to motive, she had absolutely no idea, and as Anna said, 'Someone like you doesn't have enemies.'

'Mm. I can think of one or two.'

'Freddie, do you mean? God, I hope not, but I suppose you've got to ask him.'

At the flat, Anna declined the offer of coffee. 'Keira's being dropped off at seven thirty.' She also refused to take any money for the meal. 'This is on me, I insist. You just be careful, all right?'

'Yes, Mum.' Jen could laugh off her concern as they kissed goodbye, but when she climbed the stairs to her flat, the fears began to crowd in.

A few weeks ago, Sam Dhillon had tried to chat her up in a bar. Now she knew he was an associate of the man whose property she was accused of damaging. How could that be anything but an indication of a conspiracy against her?

Once in the flat, with the security bolt slid home, she put the kettle on and took out her phone, then found the card Sam had given her. As with the first one, it said simply, *Sam Dhillon, Consultant*, and listed a mobile phone number. No website or address, and no clue as to what he might be consulted on.

It's fake. Created just to lure me in.

She grinned: now that did sound paranoid. But before this bold mood could desert her, she keyed in his number and made the call.

'Hello?' His voice wasn't as warm as in the bar; he sounded cautious, even slightly irritated.

'Oh, hi. This is. . . it's Jen, from earlier.' She didn't have to fake the nervousness, though she allowed her voice to slur very slightly, as if the call was the product of some Dutch courage.

'Jen? Hello! I'll be honest and say I didn't expect you to get in touch this soon – if at all.'

She tried to laugh. 'Well, no time like the present. I, er, wondered about meeting for coffee. Are you around tomorrow morning?'

'Tomorrow? Um, let me see. . .'

She cut in: 'I don't have a lot of time free, so I was thinking quite early. Ten o'clock?' Too much later and her plan might not work.

'Well, okay.' He sounded disconcerted. 'Where did you have in mind?'

'There's a cafe in Hove Museum, on New Church Road. Do you know it?'

'I can find it. Ten tomorrow?'

'I'm looking forward to it.'

She went to end the call but heard him say, 'Can I ask what changed your mind?'

Jen shut her eyes for a second, then forced herself to grin, knowing he would hear it in her voice.

'My friend. She thought I was mad to ignore you last time, and said if I didn't call you, she'd ask you out herself.'

Like all the best lies, it had its basis in truth, and she could hear Sam chuckling as she cut the connection.

Tomorrow, she thought, with a tingle of excitement.

The hunt was on.

CHAPTER TWENTY-FIVE

On Friday morning she was on the seafront more than an hour before their proposed meeting. Ideally she needed to see Dhillon leave the hotel, though if he had other things to do and had already gone out, she was screwed.

It was another sunny day, but the wind was sharper: the perfect excuse for Jen to wear jeans and a thin fleece over her T-shirt; she also had a plain black baseball cap in her pocket, and a pair of sunglasses.

At the aquarium she crossed onto the promenade and jogged along the lower level until she reached the steps by the children's paddling pool. Donning the cap and glasses, she climbed the steps to the pavement and found that one of the city's historic Victorian shelters offered plenty of concealment, as well as a good view of the hotel entrance.

Sam Dhillon emerged at about twenty to ten, by which point she'd watched Brighton's newest landmark, the i360, transform itself from chimney to tourist attraction and back to chimney, and her brain felt deadened by the constant drone of traffic and squawk of seagulls.

Now, with a jolt of energy, she stood up and watched Dhillon make for the cab that had turned into the access road. He was in a different suit, and carrying a slim leather satchel that might contain something essential to his career, but equally could be a clever prop, to persuade her that he was a thriving, in-demand consultant.

The fact that he'd taken a cab was a nuisance. She hadn't wanted to suggest a rendezvous too far away, in case it struck him as suspicious, but Hove Museum now felt alarmingly close. If he changed his mind he could be back here within minutes.

Once the taxi was out of sight, Jen crossed the road and strode into the hotel, removing her sunglasses but not the cap. She went straight to the elevators and ascended to the third floor, using the few seconds of privacy to rub her eyes until they watered.

The left-hand corridor was empty but the distant whine of a vacuum cleaner brought a smile. Jen pushed through the fire door, turned the corner and saw light spilling from a doorway at the far end of the corridor. At room 318 she paused and listened, then lifted her phone and started to speak as she ambled towards the open door.

'No, you must have taken them both. Darling, I'm serious. What am I meant to do?' Plenty of suppressed emotion in her voice, as if tears weren't too far away. 'I know you can't come back, but I need to pick up the. . .' Tailing off as she reached the doorway and saw the cleaner, who caught the movement and cut off the vacuum cleaner.

'Hold on,' Jen said into the phone, 'I've found somebody who might be able to help.' She offered a hopeful smile to the cleaner, a stocky woman of about thirty, whose hair was the same dark blonde as Jen's, except the tips were dyed bright pink.

'I've just realised my husband has taken both of the key cards. It's room 318, Sam Dhillon. I'm meeting him later but I really need to pop in and pick up some, er, Tampax?' She said this with a grimace, judging from the woman's face that she might not be following the conversation.

'Okay.' The woman had a musical voice, and an Eastern European accent. 'But rule is, you must go to desk—'

'Well, I need to get to the toilet as well. Urgently. So just this once, do you think you could open up for me?'

She let the woman study her for a moment, and then: 'Okay. But say nothing?'

'Not a word. Thank you so much.'

If Dhillon does have a partner, I'm in big trouble, Jen thought. But it was too late to worry about that: she stood by gratefully as the cleaner used her pass to open the door.

A second later she was in the room, which thankfully was empty. For the sake of her cover story, she turned on the bathroom light and then shut the door, calling out her thanks once again.

The room was a modest size, with a small double bed. There was an open suitcase on a stand, half full of underwear and T-shirts. Seven or eight formal shirts hung in the wardrobe, alongside two more suits. There was a toilet bag in the bathroom, and two bottles of expensive aftershave.

The bedside table held a book, a large work of non-fiction about modern Russia, and an iPhone charger. There was a writing desk against the opposite wall, and that too had a cable trailing across it, probably for a laptop or tablet.

Fighting despair, she surveyed the room. She'd taken a huge risk, and for what? There was nothing here that could help her. She hadn't even thought to bring gloves, which now seemed like a very poor decision. With a criminal case pending against her, just what kind of mess would she be in if someone caught her in here?

She fetched a strip of toilet paper and wiped everything she'd touched, then used it to open the wardrobe again. This time she noticed a small electronic safe on the top of three otherwise empty shelves. Self-programmable, so unless she could miraculously guess the code he'd chosen, it was impossible to open.

But there had to be something, didn't there? Some small clue as to Dhillon's true motives. Unless he—

Her phone buzzed. A text from Sam: *I'm here.*

*

Three minutes to ten: he was keen. With nervous, clumsy fingers, she texted back: *Running a bit late, shouldn't be much longer x*

In desperation she knelt and looked under the bed, and even tried lifting the mattress. Nothing. Soon the cleaner might question why she hadn't come out.

She inspected the suitcase, trying not to alter the position of the clothes; though it looked haphazard, he might notice if something was moved. There was nothing concealed within the case, and nothing beneath it.

The only object she hadn't touched was the book. Still using the toilet paper as a makeshift barrier, she picked it up and spotted a sliver of paper tucked between the pages: a sheet of A4, folded into four.

As she put the book down, her phone buzzed again. She wanted to ignore it, but what if Sam was cancelling the date?

Hope you're not standing me up! Well, that didn't require an immediate response, so she unfolded the paper. It seemed to be a partial printout from a website, with a footer that said 'Page 3 of 3'. All it contained was a couple of paragraphs that appeared to be describing a successful case study or project. There was a name mentioned – Jonathan Oldroyd – as well as a company: SilverSquare.

On the lower half of the sheet, somebody had been doodling with a pen, lots of swirls and boxes but also a few cryptic notes. There were two sets of initials: *BC*, *PK* and *DG*, *YG*, then another set in a box on its own, *DD*, along with what might have been a date, *24.9.16*, accompanied by half a dozen exclamation marks. Then a scrawled phrase – *KMI?* – followed by *n/a*.

It made no sense to Jen, but it was the only thing that seemed remotely interesting, so she laid it flat on the desk and lined up her phone. A photograph would be a lot quicker than trying to copy the text.

Very James Bond, she thought wryly, but when the phone started to ring she almost threw it in the air – not very cool for a secret agent.

It was Dhillon.

'Sam?'

'Hi, Jen. I don't want to seem pushy, but I've got a few things on—'

'You have to go?'

'No, no. I want to see you. But is there a problem?'

'Kind of. Having quite a hectic morning.' She swallowed nervously, suddenly convinced that some unique quality to the background silence would alert him to her location. 'Give me five, maybe ten minutes.'

'Okay.' Something about the way he ended the call made her think he wasn't buying it.

Would he come back here?

Fighting against panic, she took a couple of pictures of the sheet of paper, and had to hope they'd be clear enough to read – there wasn't time to check. With visions of another night in a police cell, she folded the paper and put the book back, then checked that everything was as she had found it. She stuffed the scrap of toilet paper in her pocket and made for the door.

She heard the rumble of a cleaner's trolley and waited until it had passed, her heart thumping so hard it was making her dizzy. Then opened the door and peered out. All clear.

She hurried along the corridor and took the stairs to the lobby: the thought of the elevator made her claustrophobic. Hat and sunglasses on, and so what if that looked a bit odd? Better that no one got a proper look at her face.

She told herself to relax as she headed for the exit. There was very little chance of Dhillon returning this quickly. Of course, she had to be on the lookout for Alex Wilson as well. . .

She'd registered that someone was climbing the steps outside but dismissed him as the wrong size and shape as either Dhillon or Wilson. It was only as the revolving door began to move that something tugged at her memory: she knew this man from somewhere.

Raising her phone like a shield, she half turned, then caught a glimpse of his face. There was a split second of unacknowledged eye contact before they both looked away.

That was Dean, wasn't it? The man who'd started coming to the climbing wall without his girlfriend. Awkward to see him here, but not disastrous.

She glanced back, preparing to chuckle at the coincidence, then saw that he hadn't emerged from the door. Instead he'd carried on round and was now hurrying down the steps, away from the hotel.

CHAPTER TWENTY-SIX

Jen's nerves were stretched tighter than ever. Could it be a coincidence? If Dean worked at the hotel, or had some other legitimate reason to visit, why would he turn and do a runner?

She descended the steps to find that he had vanished, presumably along one of the side streets that ran towards Western Road. Jen went the opposite way, across the coast road and down to the lower promenade, where she broke into a run. The exercise helped to calm her down, and the speed made her feel less exposed. Anybody trying to follow would be easy to spot on foot.

She thought about going to the police – but what reason would she give for being at the hotel? The original tip from Russell Pearce had only come about because she'd been standing outside number 14, in breach of her bail conditions.

Who could she rely on for help and support? Not Anna: the poor woman was already doing more than her fair share, and last night had clearly freaked her out.

Family, she thought. It had to be Dad.

She ran as far as Concorde 2, a concert venue where in happier times she and Freddie had enjoyed many noisy, carefree nights. Up the steps to Marine Parade, checking to see if she was being watched, then into Kemptown.

It was tempting to stop at a cafe, just for the chance to sit and think somewhere other than at home. But money was always a factor: she had to conserve every penny. Who knew what this situation was going to mean in terms of her finances? The Skyway might dump her, even without a conviction.

There was no answer on the landline, so she tried Dad's mobile. He greeted her with his usual warmth. She could hear the murmur of cricket commentary in the background, and what might have been the whoosh of a kettle.

'At the allotment?'

'Getting set for the day's toil – just as soon as I've finished a contemplative cup of tea.'

She snorted. 'You'll end up dozing in the shed. How's Mum?'

'She's in Copenhagen. Only three days, but then she flies from there to San Francisco – I think.'

'Wow. I hope you're remembering to eat?'

'Oh, the choccy digestives are calling to me as we speak. So how are things with you and the little lad?'

'Not too bad.' He'd hear in her voice that it wasn't true, so she said quickly, 'Dad, can I come and see you? I'd really value a chat.'

'Of course.' He sounded taken aback. 'Or do you want me to come down? The trains are diabolical.'

'It's okay, I've got the use of a car. I'll be there in a couple of hours.'

'Lovely. Though I can't guarantee there'll be any biscuits left.'

It was a brave attempt at humour, given how tense he sounded. Jen admired him for not asking any difficult questions; he simply wished her a safe journey.

She made the detour round to Henley Gardens. No sign of Russell Pearce, but even the thought of him made her skin crawl.

There was no activity outside number 14, and no cars that she recognised. In fact, her little street was so peaceful on this sunny Friday morning that it was hard to believe she had become engulfed in madness.

Then came heavy footsteps, the sluggish tread of a reluctant runner. She turned, and there was Pearce, today in yellow flip-flops, the usual jogging shorts and a long-sleeved white shirt with all but the last two buttons open. His chest was pale, plump and hairless.

'Jen, wait up.' He wasn't looking at her, but at his phone, holding it at an odd angle and squinting at the screen as if puzzled by something. 'I haven't heard from you.'

She frowned, fighting the impulse to march away. 'Were you supposed to?'

'Well, yes. Your solicitors. . .'

'I only saw them yesterday. I don't think they're sure yet what approach is best.'

Displeased, he said, 'And what about you?'

She shook her head, crossing her arms tightly as he moved closer. The phone was still against his chest, held in a pincer-like grip.

'I don't know. There's a lot going on.'

'I'm well aware of that, Jen. And maybe you ought to think about the value of what I'm offering?'

Confused, she said, 'I've already—'

'Hasn't it occurred to you that I could take a whole other route with this? Imagine if I told the police I saw you going in, acting suspiciously, and that you came out with something you'd taken from the house.' He nodded solemnly. 'Think what it would be worth, not to have me saying all that?'

'I won't be blackmailed, Russell.'

'Hey, this isn't blackmail – I wouldn't do that to you.' With a wounded tone, he said, 'I'd much rather tell them I saw you finding the keys. I'll say I've just seen you, and it jogged my memory. But I've got to know that it's going to be. . . appreciated. That's only fair, isn't it?'

Jen wasn't sure she could trust herself to speak. It was a long time since she'd been as tempted to punch somebody as she was right now. But adding a conviction for assault to her present troubles was hardly a prudent choice.

Instead, pretending to go along with it, she said, 'So what sort of "appreciation" do you have in mind?'

He brightened. 'Well, why don't we start by going for that drink, find out what we're both into?'

As he winked, Jen had to uncurl her hands and wipe the choreography from her mind: a kick to the groin, then a swift left-right. . . Because this was the man who had put her on to Sam Dhillon. The man who could still, in the right circumstances, keep her out of prison.

'I don't know if that's wise, Russell,' she said, demurely. 'I mean, what would your wife say about this?'

He blinked rapidly, trying to maintain his composure. Jen hadn't known for sure that he was married, but his reaction left her in no doubt.

'Who says she has to know? Life's for living, that's how I see it.' He tried a grin. 'Any chance for some fun, you should take it.'

'I'll bear that in mind,' Jen said coldly, and walked away.

CHAPTER TWENTY-SEVEN

Uppity bitch. The ingratitude made him seethe. Treating him like he was worthless.

I ought to teach her a lesson, Russell thought. And maybe he would.

Back home, he went straight to the computer, uploading the footage to his digital secret compartment. Had to keep the phone clean; that was a cardinal rule.

Today it proved a godsend. He was at his desk, at work with the editing programme – playing around with the images and simultaneously playing in other ways – when the witch came home.

At frigging lunchtime.

He cleaned up, closed Photoshop and locked the folder back in its hidey-hole, then brought up a virginal Word document and half a dozen employment-related web pages.

Pulling up his shorts, he met Kelly in the hall, his stomach plummeting as his first fear – *Is she trying to catch me at something?* – was superseded by a second: *What if she's been fired?*

'Is everything okay?'

'Why wouldn't it be? You look petrified.'

'Just wasn't expecting. . .'

'I wanted to surprise you.' At her sly smile, he thought, *Here it comes*. But she gestured over her shoulder. 'Lovely weather, it's

Friday, I've got loads of hours in credit, so I thought. . . why not have a half day?'

She opened her eyes wide, as if expecting something from him; after a moment her face fell. 'You don't look very pleased.'

'No, no.' He saw the danger of an afternoon with the witch in one of her strops. 'I had two more rejections today.' This, at least, wasn't a lie. 'I'd planned to get under way on a new CV. Start it again from scratch.'

'Ah, hun.' Her expression was no doubt supposed to be fond and sympathetic, but came across as pitying. 'You've worked hard this week. Take the afternoon off and let's kick back a bit – walk along the seafront, maybe a cocktail at the Grand?'

'Mm,' he managed, before she wrapped him in an embrace that aimed at more than affection. A hand grasped one of his buttocks in a way that, if he did it to somebody else without warning, would be classed as a sexual assault.

'The weekend starts here!' she declared, sounding so cheerful that he wondered if it was guilt. The idea that she was screwing someone else was a frequent preoccupation, and he could never work out why it made him so anxious. If she walked out, was it really possible that he would miss her?

Of course he would, because money was a consideration – especially now, when he had none of his own and was in no real hurry to go out and earn some. It was a reminder that he ought to be counting his blessings: a roof over his head, three square meals and all the rest of it, as well as getting practically every day to himself.

Her lips grazed his ear, her teeth nipping at his lobe. 'I'm off to hop in the shower, and put on something silky. Why don't you join me in the bedroom in ten minutes?'

He swallowed. 'Lovely. Can't wait.'

*

Ten minutes. Just time to hurry back to his computer and the sanctuary of those secret files. He browsed his newest, favourite folder, constructing a fantasy that was guaranteed to get him hard and hopefully see him through the next half hour or so.

A fantasy of *her*. A scenario that went much further than any that had gone before, and felt all the more potent because he knew it wouldn't – it couldn't – be *only* a fantasy. For all his attempts to control the urges that made his life a misery, he knew that one day he was going to succumb to the next stage. It felt as inevitable as the tide.

A none-too-subtle thump came from overhead. Time for one final contemplation of the image on the screen.

Lovely Jennifer would do the business for him, no question about that.

CHAPTER TWENTY-EIGHT

Freddie had upgraded both his cars since he and Jen had separated, which he'd as good as admitted had been his father's way of rewarding him for having jettisoned 'that bloody woman' from the family.

The Audi had by far the highest spec of any vehicle she'd ever driven. Ironically, what she struggled with was the sheer ease of piloting a car that wanted to do everything for her. But once she'd settled in, the drive was fabulously – and dangerously – smooth. A couple of times on the M23 she swept past what seemed like irresponsibly sluggish motorists, only to realise they were doing around eighty, while she was pushing a hundred.

It had always amused her that Freddie worshipped cars, whereas Jen thought driving was deadly dull unless there was a challenge involved. Stick her in a beaten-up 4x4 and send her across tundra or over a sand dune and her blood would be pumping.

Still, today's journey was about the destination, the chance to talk through her problems and perhaps even hit on some solutions.

The satnav unerringly delivered her to the allotments on the southern edge of Dorking, by which time she'd sorted the script for her opening remarks. She needed to lay out the situation without causing her father too much alarm or confusion. But all that preparation was for nothing when Dad stood up from his runner beans, saw the distress on her face and pulled her into a hug, whereupon she let out a muffled howl of pain and said, 'I've been arrested, Dad. They're gonna send me to prison.'

It was a moot point, but she doubted if she'd have taken the same approach if her mother had been present. Their relationship had been prickly since Jen's early adolescence, when her mum, then a cautious, homely woman who worked part-time for a fashion retailer, had found herself at a loss to understand her eldest daughter's love of extremes, of wilderness and adventure, and her complete disregard for make-up and clothes and celebrity culture.

That lack of insight went both ways, particularly when the twins finished their A levels and her mum abruptly threw herself into what became an all-encompassing, jet-setting career as a senior buyer for a different retail chain. This was in stark contrast to Jen's dad. Ian Cornish had joined a telecoms firm at the age of seventeen and worked there for nearly four decades, happily plodding towards the earliest possible retirement. He'd bowed out three years ago, at the age of fifty-five, and was now as deeply content with a life of gardening, badminton and social drinking as Faith was with boardrooms, trade shows and executive lounges.

The set-up meant her parents were often apart, which seemed to suit them both. It certainly suited Jen right now: whereas her mum would have panicked and screeched and invariably said the wrong thing, Dad knew just what to do.

He said nothing. He let her unleash all the pent-up emotion, and only when she'd cried it out did he lead her into his shed to brew up a mug of sweet tea and produce a generous supply of biscuits – 'Of course I didn't eat them all!' – and then lower the volume of the cricket commentary as he waited for her to explain.

'Monday morning, I was walking to the bus stop. . .'

*

She told him everything, up to and including the moment last night when she'd seen Sam Dhillon get into a car driven by Alex Wilson. Her father listened carefully, sipping his tea and urging Jen to drink hers.

'Before I saw the two of them together, I was close to believing that I'd lost my mind,' she told him. 'That maybe I had done it, and then blanked it out.'

'If you had a problem as severe as that, I'm sure it would have manifested itself in other ways, and I daresay Charlie would have alerted me to it.'

'I'm glad to hear that.' Jen had stood firm on refusing Charlie's pleas for a mobile phone, but had recently allowed him to start emailing his grandparents, hoping it would help with his literacy.

'He sent me a brief message on Wednesday about an unexpected holiday in Crete with his dad.'

She nodded. 'A super-luxurious villa owned by you-know-who. He was really excited.'

'Oh? All he said to me was how much he'd miss his mum. He didn't like the idea of being so far away from you. I told him not to think about the distance, because it's only a couple of hours on a plane.' He gave her an encouraging smile. 'At least he's safely removed from all this.'

'Geographically, yes. But I keep coming back to the fact that Charlie is the only thing I have that's precious – the only thing that someone might want to take from me.'

He looked at her askance. 'You suspect this is Freddie's doing?'

'It's hard to believe he'd hurt me like this, but his dad. . .' Jen spread her hands. 'If it's not a conspiracy to discredit me, what else could it be?'

'That's what it looks like, I agree.'

'And to be going to all this trouble – renting a house, hotel rooms. . .'

'It would be quite an undertaking,' Ian agreed. 'Though Mr Lynch senior isn't exactly short of cash.' His face lit up in response to a brief commotion on the radio. 'We've taken a wicket!' he exclaimed, then: 'Sorry.'

'It's fine. I feel awful to burden you with all this.'

'It would hurt a lot more if you kept it from me.'

She nodded, soberly, and took a mouthful of tea. 'Anyway, I called Sam Dhillon last night and arranged to meet him for coffee this morning.'

'What happened?'

'I didn't turn up.' She described how she'd followed Dhillon to a hotel, and then planned an incursion to unearth some kind of clue as to her enemy's identity and purpose.

Although he tutted, her dad sounded only mildly cross. 'I suppose I can't blame you, in the circumstances, but was it really likely to yield a result?'

'I just felt I had to do something.' She took out her phone, and tried to show him the document she'd photographed, but it was hard to make sense of the scribbles, and her dad's thick fingers weren't up to the task of moving or expanding the image.

'Bloody touch screens,' he muttered. 'Let's go home and print a copy on good old-fashioned paper.'

CHAPTER TWENTY-NINE

He'd walked to the allotment, so he drove back with Jen. A petrolhead himself, he pointedly refrained from commenting on the luxury of her ex-husband's car. Jen thought they both needed a break from discussing her troubles, so she asked about her sisters, guilty that she hadn't been in touch with either of them for several weeks.

'Marcie's fine, not that she ever tells us much.' A grunt. 'You girls all have a secretive streak.'

'Independent,' Jen corrected him. 'What about Kat?'

'Mm. Between you and me, I don't think she and Julia will be together much longer.'

'That's a shame. They seemed so perfect for each other.'

'I think so, too. Though I suspect your mum is still trying to convince herself that dating women is just a phase, to be passed over in favour of finding a man and having babies galore. . .'

'I dunno why that's so important to her.' Jen snorted. 'Especially after the mess I made of it.'

'Well, it did give us – and you – a beloved little boy.'

'Oh God, yes. But you know what I mean – life's not a fairy tale. Surely she's worked that out by now?'

'No, because for your mother, it is.' He wore a big grin, and Jen was already groaning in anticipation of the punchline: 'After all, she's married to me.'

*

The house was a detached redbrick villa close to the local tennis club. It had never been Jen's home because her parents, at her mum's insistence, seemed to move house more often than most people change their cars. As well as being larger than the last one, this property had a generous garden at the rear, which called into question the need for an allotment.

'Old habits, I suppose,' Ian said. 'Allotments have always been my sanctuary, which as the only man living among four women, felt quite important to me. Nowadays I don't really need that, any more than Faith needs all these bedrooms and bathrooms, and yet here we are.'

He suggested they sit in the back garden, but Jen got no further than the kitchen, where she discovered a new addition to the family: a tiny black kitten, who was being haughtily ignored by Wisty, their six-year-old short-haired tabby.

'Gorgeous, isn't she? We got her last week, from one of the neighbours.'

'Is Wisty all right with that?'

'I think he's a bit scornful, watching Sprite clamber all over us. What Wisty knows is that the food will be there every day, regardless of how little you ingratiate yourself.'

Jen knelt down and offered her forefinger, the kitten leaping up to paw at it before frantically chasing her tail.

Her dad said, 'We thought we'd keep it as a surprise for Charlie, until the next time he visits. Is that all right?'

'Of course. He'll adore her.' *And pester for a pet himself*, Jen thought.

Her attention was caught by a sheet of newspaper beneath the litter tray. She fished it out and saw a familiar savage grin. 'You don't buy this, do you?'

'That evil shit-rag? God, no. But they always have a copy at the pub, so I make a habit of removing Gerard's column from the Thursday edition and using it for the cats to piss on. All it's good for, if you ask me.'

Jen's phone was already hooked up to the Wi-Fi, and after a minor tussle with technology they managed to send the photos to print. Ian poured two glasses of his favourite organic lemonade, added plenty of ice, and they sat at the rustic picnic bench on the lawn, shaded by an old willow that was the centrepiece of the garden.

Ian examined the printout and agreed with her assessment of its content. 'From a website. SilverSquare. Have you looked them up?'

'They're product designers based in London, a small set-up, I think, but successful – that's the impression they're trying to give, at least.' Anticipating his next question, she said, 'There are quite a few staff profiles, but they don't include Wilson or Dhillon.'

'Or this chap, Dean?'

'No. So either they're lower level staff, or they're connected to the company in some other way.'

'Or not connected at all. These doodles are the sort of thing you do while you're on the phone, in between jotting down notes. Maybe this is just a piece of scrap paper he picked up from somewhere.'

'True.' Glumly, Jen said, 'So it's one step forward, two steps back.'

'Not necessarily. This could well be a piece of the puzzle, but we won't know until we get a hint of the overall picture.'

She pointed to the handwritten scribbles. 'I'm assuming some of these are initials, but what do you make of "DD"? And don't say bra size.'

He smirked. 'Putting it next to that date, I'm thinking due diligence. It's a process you go through before buying a business, to be sure you know exactly what you're getting.'

'Like a survey on a house?'

'A bit like that. So perhaps this is saying the due diligence is starting on the twenty-fourth of September, or has to be completed by then.' He leaned forward, chewing his lip. 'And in that context, "KMI" could mean key man insurance – a policy that companies take out as protection against losing their vital personnel. The question of key staff will figure highly in the due diligence procedure, because the new owners will want to know just how much its success depends on the knowledge or talents of its main people, and whether they're going or staying.'

Jen digested this information. 'All very fascinating, but nothing here seems to relate to what's happening to me.'

'Not really, no.' Sighing, he crossed his arms. 'I will say this. Please think carefully about digging any further into what these men are doing, because the minute you become a threat to them. . .'

He left the rest of the warning unspoken, perhaps because he knew Jen was unlikely to heed it. Then he said, 'Have you considered making enquiries with the artist?'

'What? No. How would I?'

'Search online? Browse a few galleries in Brighton? The work sounds quite distinctive – and valuable – so I think we can assume that Wilson or his cronies didn't make it. If it came from a genuine artist, that person might at least be able to tell you how they got involved.'

She nodded, encouraged by his suggestion. 'It's better than doing nothing.'

'And safer than going after the men directly.' He gestured at the ceiling. 'You know, you're welcome to stay here for a few days. There's plenty of room.'

'Thanks. But it would feel too much like running away.'

He snorted. 'Exactly what I thought you'd say.'

'Sorry. I don't want you worrying yourself sick.'

'Oh, I won't,' he said breezily. 'I've not worried seriously about you since Tilgate Forest.'

'Really?' It came out in an odd tone, and she realised she was trying not to sound hurt.

He scrambled to explain: 'Not while you were missing, that was a living hell—'

'Dad, I know. Please don't.'

'But when you were found, none the worse for wear and still brilliantly defiant about your reasons for running off, I just knew you were one of life's survivors, someone who'd find a way to deal with whatever was thrown at you.' He touched his fist against her arm, like a sporting salute. 'I hope I can claim some of the credit for that – as well as some of the blame.'

'Why blame?'

He looked at her, confused. 'Some girls at school had been picking on you. Because you were a tomboy, basically. They were calling you a lesbian – which I've always thought is ironic, given that Kat at the same age could have put Barbie to shame for hair and make-up. The power of stereotypes, I suppose.'

'And that's why I ran away?' Jen was stunned. 'I thought it was. . . Well, me and Mum. We were always at each other's throats.'

'That was *after* you ran away. Until then, you were pretty much the apple of her eye. Afterwards, she didn't really know how to be a mother to you. She thought she'd failed, and I'm not sure she's ever got over that.'

'Oh, Dad. . .'

'My biggest fear was that you'd done away with yourself. When the news came through that you were safe, it was the single most joyous moment of my life. More than your birth, or when your sisters came into the world. More than becoming a granddad.'

He gazed into her eyes. 'It never once occurred to me to be angry, I promise you. It never has, and it never will.'

Tears had blurred his vision. With a mumbled apology, he gathered her in his arms. Jen rested her head on his shoulder, glorying in the safe, familiar smell of him, and was taken back to the moment of her discovery. She was found by a group of local volunteers who'd been combing the woods around Crawley throughout the hours of daylight. The wretchedness she felt now was only a shadow of what she'd experienced at the time; made worse by the kindness and sensitivity she'd been shown.

Snuffling, she said, 'You moved house because of that.'

'I daresay we would have anyway. You know what your mum's like.'

Not really, Jen thought. And this wasn't a good time to be reminded of the fallibility of memory.

Her father dug out a huge and slightly off-white handkerchief, blew his nose and said, 'Right, that's enough of the sloppy emotional stuff. How are you doing, money-wise?'

'You always ask me, and I always—'

'Fight me, I know.' He pressed a roll of notes into her hand – a hundred pounds – and spoke over her protests. 'Expenses money. Now take it.'

'But I'm thirty-four. I shouldn't still need handouts from my parents.'

'It's not a handout, it's a gift. Do you really think you won't want to help Charlie just because he's grown up? Believe me, you'll always do as much as you can for your children.'

He walked her out to the car, having first scooped an overly inquisitive kitten off the floor. She curled around his hand, paws scratching at his arm. 'Not a word to Charlie about Sprite, if you don't mind.'

'Agreed.'

'Oh, and I might have said I don't worry, but that's not strictly accurate. This neighbour you mentioned, Russell Pearce? Be very careful there. I do not like the sound of that man.'

'I'll be on my guard.'

'And if you change your mind and want refuge, or if you need me to lend a hand, one phone call and I'm there.'

'I know. Thanks, Dad.' *But I won't*, she added silently.

And she drove away, wrestling with a question that had often troubled her over the years. Did it make her strong, that she nearly always rejected offers of help? Or did it make her weak?

CHAPTER THIRTY

She drove home in a funk, stunned by the idea that she'd completely misremembered the defining event of her adolescence. And as a result, she would have to reappraise her entire relationship with her mother.

But she soon returned to brooding about the present. Sam Dhillon hadn't got in touch, which suggested that he already knew why she hadn't turned up. Had Dean reported seeing her at the hotel? If so, the gang would know that Jen was on to them – and as her dad had pointed out, that could have serious repercussions.

In Brighton, she was cutting through the busy streets around Ditchling Road when the car behind her took a left turn, revealing that the vehicle behind that was a black BMW. Despite the clear stretch of road that had opened up, it made no move to get closer.

Then another car pulled out in front of it, and Jen made it through a set of traffic lights but the BMW didn't. Her heart was racing just the same.

Was it them?

She thought she saw it again on Lewes Road, but couldn't be certain. Reaching home, she locked the Audi and ran to the building. Once in the lobby, she turned back and waited, peering through the front door.

A motorcycle roared past, then a delivery van. . . and then a black BMW. The driver was a middle-aged woman, possibly the same one who'd collected Alex Wilson on Monday morning, but once again Jen couldn't say for sure.

Which was no doubt their intention. Gliding past like this, following her at a distance, it was the perfect way to make her feel unsettled, scared, without giving her anything she could take to the police.

Or perhaps it was a completely innocent vehicle that had sent her imagination into overdrive?

Once in the flat, with the door locked and bolted, there was a temptation to pour what remained of the vodka. But booze hadn't helped her on Wednesday night, and it wouldn't help her now. She had coffee instead, and sent Freddie a text, asking if she could see Charlie on Skype this evening.

There was a message from Anna, wanting to know she was safe. Jen assured her that everything was fine, then browsed online for the artwork, as her dad had suggested. That drew a blank, so she looked up SilverSquare and found a number of news articles, most of them focusing on the company's rapid growth and potential for future success. According to one broadsheet commentator, there was a strong probability of a takeover by a much larger rival, which would provide a lucrative payday for the founder and MD, a former soldier called Jonathan Oldroyd.

She checked the initials scribbled on the paper, and saw that *PK* could be Paul Keegan, who was the creative director. And there was a *BC*: the finance director, Barry Collins. The other initials didn't correspond to anyone listed on the website, and since they were kept separate on the page, she wondered if they related to associates of Sam Dhillon. *DG*: could that be Dean?

She trawled her memory for his surname, but wasn't sure if it had ever registered; apart from the initial questionnaire at the climbing centre, he wouldn't have been required to provide any more paperwork, and although he'd signed in and out of each session, Jen had never had any reason to check his name.

It couldn't be ruled out that Dhillon had doodled on a random sheet of paper, but her instincts told her this document held some kind of significance. And if they already knew that she was fighting back, she didn't have much to lose by contacting SilverSquare.

She found an email address for the MD, Oldroyd, and sent a brief message, apologising for the mysterious nature of her enquiry and asking if the business had any connections to an Alex Wilson or a Sam Dhillon. After deliberating over the potential risks, she took the decision to attach a copy of the photographed document.

It felt like the longest of long shots – and there was a good chance that her email would be seen as coming from a crank, and immediately deleted – but at least this felt better than doing nothing.

By seven thirty there was still no reply from Freddie. Checking the time difference with Crete, she realised that Charlie might well be in bed, even allowing for the customary lack of rules when he stayed with his dad.

She'd been tempted to pop out for an evening swim, but the wind looked to have strengthened, and there was some cloud in the sky. This, she told herself, was the only reason for staying home – not the fear that a black BMW would follow her to the beach.

Even while cursing her own lack of willpower, she sent Freddie an email, suggesting they Skype tomorrow instead, and asking whether Charlie was eating healthily and not getting too much sun. She was cooking herself an omelette using leftovers from the fridge when it occurred to her that Freddie might have gone quiet because Charlie had told him about her encounter with the police.

Jen had ruled out trying to coach her son to say nothing. As well as being grossly unfair on him, it would almost certainly have backfired. On several occasions Charlie had let slip something about one of his dad's girlfriends when it was clear he'd been sworn to silence. But the next time she spoke to Freddie, she might have to brace herself for some difficult questions.

And how Gerard will crow, when it all comes out. . .

Since talking to her dad, she'd been retreating from the idea that Freddie or his father was responsible for trying to frame her. It wasn't a question of evidence, or even a gut feeling; just a yearning desire to believe that no blood relation of Charlie's could stoop so low.

Freddie emailed back an hour later, claiming the phone signal was too weak to call or text, and they were also having problems with the Wi-Fi. He would have been happy to Skype but Charlie was now fast asleep after a long day exploring the Lasithi Plateau in a dune buggy.

At this, Jen started to fume, until she read on: *Don't worry, I made sure he was SAFE! And C sends big love to his mama xx-xx*

That sign-off was what Freddie had used with her in the early days – the best days – and Jen, for a moment, felt absurdly moved. It was probably there by accident, a little leftover muscle memory, but still.

With a rare warm glow, she went back to him, reiterating that it would be great to Skype tomorrow. Freddie's reply was immediate, and blunt: *Can't tomorrow. Off on boat trip early till late. Maybe Sunday?*

So much for lingering affection. It was difficult not to respond in kind: *Make sure Charlie takes his travel sickness medicine. And don't forget that he MUST be home Wednesday afternoon at the very latest!*

She wanted to remind her ex-husband that the real world of duty and responsibility hadn't gone away, but she regretted it at once. Sometimes even *she* got bored laying down the rules.

She interpreted the silence that followed as a sulk. Finally, another email: *You didn't tell me he's wetting the fucking bed again.* Her reply was a desperate plea to show understanding, not snap or do anything to increase the stress Charlie would be experiencing. It came as no surprise that Freddie didn't answer.

And that should have been it. She was tired, couldn't take any enjoyment from TV or concentrate on the book she was reading. But instead of going to sleep, she drew her legs up on the sofa, placed the laptop on her knees and scrolled through Facebook until she found – just as she knew she would, because she always did – something that upset her.

Why couldn't she learn?

The picture had been taken by a girl called Ella. No one Jen knew. But her profile was completely public, and she'd tagged Freddie, who had ignored countless warnings by Jen to tighten up his online security.

She suspected it was deliberate: he wanted her to see his many conquests. Though Jen didn't have to go looking, did she?

It was a selfie, Freddie's lightly sunburned cheek pressed to Ella's tender baby face. She looked about seventeen, though the profile information suggested she was twenty-two, a graduate who now worked as a promoter at a seafront bar in Brighton. Still too young, if Jen wanted to take a severe view – which at this time of the night, in this mood, she most certainly did.

Ella had rich dark hair and big blue eyes and a slightly lolling mouth, which in Jen's view made her look a bit stupid. Freddie no doubt saw it differently. The picture had been taken earlier that day, perhaps at the villa; in the background there were marble floors and cane furniture, plump cushions and a few toy cars.

And Charlie.

He was only partially visible, sitting some way behind them. An iPad rested in his lap, and he looked to be hunched over it, a pose that spoke to Jen of profound isolation and unhappiness. Even while she cautioned herself not to read too much into it, she felt her heart breaking. This was the future for Charlie, once Jen was behind bars: the poor boy neglected while Freddie threw back the tequila and smoked weed and fucked teenagers. And there wouldn't be a thing that Jen could do to protect her son.

She knew she was probably overreacting, so she took her sorry self off to bed and promised that tomorrow would be a saner, fresher start. No more negativity. No more paranoia.

The artwork, she was thinking as she fell asleep. Find the artist. *Let Elen be your guide.*

CHAPTER THIRTY-ONE

Saturday was bright but blustery, with fluffy clouds scudding across the sky and the sea pitching luminous green rollers towards the shore. The new, non-paranoid Jen survived a brisk walk into the city and saw nothing that gave her cause for alarm. No BMW or X-Trail or Subaru. No suspicious characters trailing after her.

She spent the morning on a trawl through the gift shops, galleries and antique stores of Brighton. Her quest took her from St James Street across to North Laine, up to Western Road and into Hove, then back to the tourist-crammed Lanes and finally out to the shore and the smart new retail space in the refurbished arches close to the i360. In some places she was in and out within seconds; other times she lingered, lost in the pleasure of idle browsing and all too eager to forget that her search had a serious purpose.

Where possible she chatted to the staff. Some were artists themselves; most were experts as well as warm enthusiasts for their trade, but none seemed to be familiar with the type of figurine she was talking about.

It was going to be another dead end, just like the search of Sam Dhillon's hotel room. That, and the fact that the MD of SilverSquare hadn't replied to her email, caused her spirits to sag.

And it wasn't just that. Despite this boat trip, she'd clung to the hope that Charlie would find a way to get in touch, but she'd had nothing from him. The single bright spot was a lovely message from her father, pledging his love and support.

There were also a couple of texts from Nick, wanting to know if she felt better, and dropping a not too subtle hint that he was available later if she wanted to 'hook up'.

Then: a breakthrough of sorts. In a tiny, cavern-like space underneath the coast road, a thin, stooped man with bright white hair thought he knew the sort of thing she was describing. 'That style, anyway, if not the subject matter.' He couldn't recall the identity of the artist, 'but I do have an acquaintance who might know. Give me your number and I shall have a word.'

Jen, always reluctant to pass her number to strangers, decided that the circumstances demanded it. Leaving the gallery, she realised it was almost three o'clock, and she'd had nothing to eat all day. She found a cafe on the promenade, ordered a panini and while waiting for it to arrive, once again fell prey to the lure of Facebook.

A new update from Ella. A selfie-stick job, or perhaps taken by somebody else. Freddie? She was lying on the deck of what might have been a private yacht, wearing the skimpiest of bikini bottoms, with only a golden brown forearm to cover her boobs from the world.

You'd better not be topless in front of my son. Jen realised she was gritting her teeth. It was hard enough keeping Charlie away from the overt sexualisation on TV, from ghastly online porn, without having to worry about one of Freddie's starlets parading themselves in front of a seven-year-old.

The tears came without warning. She recognised that she was grieving, in a fashion, for the fact that she was losing Charlie, bit by bit: losing him to Freddie, losing him to the big bad world in which he would one day have to find his own space. A grim reminder, also, that she had lost Freddie, and despite all the damage inflicted by the divorce, it still hurt to see him with other women.

She felt like a screw-up. Even her own mother had no idea how to relate to her. Had they really got on fine before Tilgate?

Her recollection was that the twins had gobbled up every scrap of Mum's time and attention, leaving practically nothing for Jen.

And be honest, you ran away to hurt your sisters, too. You wanted to punish them all, for not understanding you. . .

Disgusted with herself – so much for no more negativity – she glanced up and there he was: Alex Wilson, leering at her through the cafe's picture window.

Jen flinched. Rocked back in her seat and nearly overbalanced. She glanced round, wondering if she would need to ask for help or find an escape route, and when she looked back he had gone.

A woman with a buggy strolled past, then an elderly couple. The cafe's other customers were still chatting, eating, reading: life on a lazy Saturday.

Had she imagined it?

She felt bile rising. Her appetite forgotten, she hurried out and scanned the holiday crowds, but of course Wilson had vanished. All part of the plan to mess with her head.

The knowledge that they were out there, watching, following, made her feel like a caged animal. As she crossed the road and walked briskly along East Street, she became aware that her chest felt constricted. Her whole body broke out in a cold sweat and her vision went crazed, the world shifting beneath her, all sound dulled to a maddening insect drone.

She stumbled, groping for the welcoming shadows of a doorway between two shops, only to collapse onto the cold concrete step. The street was seething with people, their bodies strobing the sunlight as they flashed past. Jen was vaguely aware of muttered comments, snorts of laughter or pity, and then someone was shouldering his way through.

Wilson had followed; he was coming for her—

'Hey, you okay?' A stranger crouched before her, gently touching her arm. His voice was deep and comforting, and he carried with him a rich peaty smell that brought to mind a forest floor. *He's the Green Man.*

Jen rubbed her eyes, blinked a few times and saw he was a young homeless guy, his possessions bundled up in a doorway opposite. A small black dog was sitting on his bedroll, observing her with a steadfast gaze.

'I'm okay. Just a dizzy spell.'

'Sure?' He helped her to sit up, and after watching to see that she wasn't about to pass out again, hurried into the shop next door and returned with a glass of cold water. 'They know me there. They're good people.'

And so are you, she thought. It made a welcome change from all the suspicion and paranoia. *There are good people in the world. . .*

Thanking him, she drank gratefully. He stood by as she got to her feet, then he must have sensed the sudden awkwardness, a hand moving reflexively to her pocket. You wouldn't normally offer money to somebody who'd helped you in the street, but knowing he was homeless. . .

'Now take care, all right?' he said, and was gone before she could say a word.

She walked slowly to her bus stop in North Street, resolving to come past another time and drop some money into his hat. While waiting for the bus, she received a text from the white-haired gent at the gallery. His friend thought the artist was a woman called Kitty something, no other details, but a gallery in the town of Rye had exhibited her work and might know more. He'd provided the gallery's name and a website address. *Best of luck!* the message ended.

This isn't over, she thought. *I'm not beaten yet.*

CHAPTER THIRTY-TWO

The drive to Rye was a slow one – fifty miles on single-lane roads choked with holidaymakers and Sunday drivers. Jen wasn't in any great hurry, but she could have done without so much time to think.

Yesterday's collapse had left its mark. She'd experienced something close to a panic attack once or twice before, but never with such intensity. The lack of food and water probably hadn't helped, but it emphasised the damage this was doing, to live in a permanent state of fear and confusion. How much longer before it broke her?

A dull, unhappy evening had segued into a night of troubled sleep. In the worst of her nightmares she'd been back in the forest, hiding from a malevolent search party led by Alex Wilson and Sam Dhillon. Behind them, skulking in the shadows, was a man who seemed to be the sort of strange amalgam that only happens in dreams: *DeanRussellNick*. When they passed her hiding place, she had felt relief – but then she heard Charlie's screams. It was her son they wanted, and when she tried to pursue them her legs became as heavy as stone and the tree branches fell across her path like bars.

You'll never see him again.

She'd woken in a cold sweat, and was out of bed soon after six. She forced herself to go for a run, then took a quick swim in the sea. There was a spike of panic when, from the water, she saw a man who resembled Alex Wilson, strolling along the beach in her direction. But it turned out to be a false alarm.

Back at the flat, she was intercepted by Bridie Martin. 'I had the police round Friday, asking about you. They wouldn't tell me why, but I said you didn't strike me as the criminal type. Of course, I don't know you that well, do I?'

'No,' Jen wryly agreed.

'But I was home all day on Monday, when it happened – whatever it was. They asked if I'd seen you, and I said you'd come home in the evening, normal time, with Charlie. But I'd also heard you earlier in the day, when you came back and then left again.'

Jen frowned, recalling Bridie's confusion on Monday. 'But I didn't, Bridie. I was at work.'

'Who was it, then?'

'I don't know. Are you sure you didn't see anyone coming in or out of the building?'

'Only whatshername, from the ground floor.' She fretted for a moment. 'I suppose it could have been Simon? Though he still hasn't looked at my radiator, and that's three times I've called them.'

Simon was the maintenance man, employed by the managing agents. He'd have good reason to sneak into the building without being harangued by Bridie, though Jen thought it more likely that it had been an intruder, planting the figurine for the police to find. If Bridie had spotted him, it might have helped to clear Jen's name.

But mentioning that now would only scare the wits out of her neighbour. She agreed that it was probably Simon, and they parted on friendly terms.

By the time she left for Rye there was still no word from Charlie. Even Ella hadn't posted on social media since yesterday morning. Now, every glimpse of the sea on her journey east brought forth lurid and irrational fears: the boat had capsized or been swept off course in a sudden storm; a devastating fire on board had caused it to sink. If it was a private yacht, how long before anybody raised the alarm?

You'll never see him again.

It was her first visit to Rye, and nothing about the outskirts of the town explained why it was supposedly a magnet for tourists. The traffic around the modest ring road was snarled up, the fine weather drawing dozens of pedestrians in an almost continuous stream across the road. Freddie's trusty satnav took her to a busy car park in Rope Walk, where she eased the Audi into one of the last remaining spaces.

The gallery was located on the High Street, about halfway up the hill on which the historic town was situated. She'd decided to visit in person after browsing the website. Although she had found a phone number, her call had gone straight to a recorded message, informing callers of the opening hours.

The other factor that had prompted her decision to visit was an image on the website of a wire and glass figurine – a sinuous representation of a deer. The artist's name wasn't included, but Jen felt sure it was the same person who had created the pieces in Alex Wilson's home.

As she walked up the hill, she checked her phone. She'd texted Freddie and had nothing. She was about to try again when a new message popped up, from a number that wasn't in her address book.

Have you thought about my proposal? It's more than fair. Could be a lot of fun too! R xx

She puzzled over it for a moment before it clicked: Russell Pearce. With a shudder of revulsion, she went to delete the text, then decided to keep it for now, in case he gave her any more trouble. There was no way she would be replying, let alone taking up his offer. Creep.

*

Despite its advertised opening hours, the gallery was shut. Jen peered through the glass at the gloomy interior, and immediately spotted another piece of artwork in the distinctive style: this one of a pair of hares fighting. She felt that she was agonisingly close to a breakthrough, but only if the gallery opened for business. If it didn't, her journey had been wasted.

She took herself off for a walk, and while exploring the cobbled streets of the old citadel, she swiftly revised her opinion of Rye. It was a beautiful town in a beautiful location, and somehow the older part, even while mobbed by tourists, managed to retain a winning charm and a wonderfully laid-back atmosphere.

She browsed a few of the gift shops and was back at the gallery by eleven thirty. This time there were lights on inside, and the door was unlocked. The gallery had looked quite small, but it actually extended across several rooms, with the furthest leading out to a courtyard at the rear.

In the central room Jen found a desk with a till, staffed by a plump, well-coiffed woman in a yellow pashmina, completing the sale of a small watercolour. Once that was done, Jen asked about the sculpture of the hares, and was content at first to be mistaken for a prospective buyer. 'I've not seen anything like this before,' she said. 'Is the artist local?'

'She is, yes – St Mary's Bay. The work is popular, but it's so time consuming to produce, she stands no chance of earning a living from it.'

Her name was Kitty Webster, and according to the gallery assistant she'd been on the brink of giving up a couple of years ago. 'We'd held an exhibition for her, but it's the sort of thing the critics simply sneer at. It's a scandal.' She pursed her lips. 'This country produces such fabulous art, so much incredible talent in every town and village, and yet what gets all the attention and money? A pitiful unmade bed, and a cow cut in half. Disgusting.'

Jen had only a hazy idea of what she was alluding to, but she made the right noises in sympathy. Kitty Webster, it turned out, had eventually been persuaded not to quit, though her artwork was relegated to little more than a hobby.

'The poor girl works for a bank in Ashford, which must be utterly soul-destroying.'

Jen tutted as required. 'I'd like to find out more about her work. Does she have a website, a Facebook page?'

'I know there was once a very basic site, but I think she let the domain name expire.'

'And what about commissions? I have a real love of Celtic figurines, the ancient deities. Do you think she'd be interested in making anything like that?'

'It's not her normal subject matter, but who knows?' She hunted for a pen. 'Let me take your details and I can find out.'

'Ah. I don't suppose I could get in touch with her, if you have the number? Only I've come quite a long way.'

'Oh. Whereabouts?'

'Godalming,' Jen said quickly, figuring that Brighton might not be regarded as distant enough to warrant the kind of indiscretion she was seeking. 'If I rang her now and she was prepared to see me, I could go straight over there. St Mary's Bay, was it?'

The woman nodded, still unsure. 'I'll call her myself.'

She took her phone into a small back room. Jen wondered if the woman would even make the call, or just return and claim that Webster wasn't interested.

It was a wait of nearly five minutes, during which time anybody could have walked in and robbed the place blind. She guessed Rye wasn't that sort of town.

Then the woman was back. 'I can give you her number. She's also happy for you to pay her a visit.' Seeing Jen's surprise, she smiled. 'I didn't expect her to agree to it. She's quite shy. But I told her you have a sweet face.'

Jen grinned to mask the guilt. In the scheme of things this was only a minor deception, which she could justify to herself on the basis of what was at stake, but she took no pleasure in the lie she'd had to tell.

'Very kind of you,' she said.

CHAPTER THIRTY-THREE

The text was a reckless move. He'd been longing to do it, ever since he got her number. What was a more precious route into somebody's life than through their mobile phone? Knowing you could whisper into their ear at any time of the day or night. . .

He'd held off for as long as he could bear, and then this morning he succumbed, giddy from an unexpected spell of freedom. The witch had taken herself off to help with some kind of family crisis in Sevenoaks involving her brother, who was a twat, and his wife, who wasn't hot enough to engage Russell's interest for more than a few seconds at a time.

And now, his prize: a glorious Sunday to himself. He'd lain in bed for most of the morning, laptop purring on the mattress beside him, his photographic handiwork fuelling his fantasies until he couldn't stop himself from reaching out to her.

Almost an hour now, and she hadn't replied. No one ignored a text for that long – not if they had any respect for the sender. Okay, maybe there was an outside chance that the phone was out of battery, or she was tied up in some way—

Tied up. Huh. His thoughts were on a loop, back to sex every couple of minutes. There were times when he seriously contemplated whether this was an addiction, a sickness; perhaps he should see himself as a victim, entitled to help and support. . .

Some chance of that. He shut the laptop and picked up his phone. One more text, and if she didn't answer he'd go round and see her.

As his fingers prodded the keys, a voice of caution tried to intervene. Jen knew he was married. She knew where he lived. Armed with just those two facts, she could cause mayhem. And yet. . .

The thrill it gave him, to operate with such a tiny margin of error, was indescribable. He revelled in how much he could hide from Kelly, how far he could push her tolerance, her credulity. Every day he sustained his secret life, every day he flirted with danger.

Which was fine, except for the constant battle against his worst impulses. Because he didn't just want to *flirt* with danger: he wanted to tear off its clothes and screw it senseless.

He looked at his phone so often, it became like an OCD. Again and again: no reply. A perfectly fair, friendly enquiry – and still she was treating him like dirt.

He imagined her in the flat, maybe lying in bed, reading his message and. . . what? Supposing she did want to respond, but was worried about his wife? Some women were really uptight about all that female solidarity shit.

And she wasn't on great terms with her ex-husband, he'd gathered that much from his trawl round Facebook. Her security settings were tight, though he was able to find pictures and posts on other profiles where she was tagged or had made a comment, and from that he'd gleaned a surprising amount of information. The ex clearly fancied himself, so maybe he'd been playing around, and as a result any suggestion of infidelity turned her off.

That wasn't to say she didn't fancy him. All Russell had to do was clear a path.

You could go round there now. He knew her kid was away in Greece: here was his big opportunity.

He read over the second text, making sure he approved of its content.

Assume u saw my message? Have the decency to answer, will you? I'm offering to save your life. Gotta be worth a lot, hasn't it – and you will ENJOY IT, I guarantee that ;) ;)

There: perfectly reasonable. He'd give her twenty minutes.

He thought about a shower but decided it wasn't necessary – he'd had one yesterday morning. There was some of last night's lasagne left, so he ate that, cold, for brunch. He dressed with some care: a clean pair of jeans and one of his old work shirts. Important to make the right impression.

No one paid him any attention on the short walk up the hill. He'd idly followed her along the street a couple of months ago, so he knew the block where she lived, and last week he'd found her name on the set of buzzers by the entrance. Flat 7 – top floor, he guessed, given the size of the building.

He also knew the main door was sometimes left ajar, as it was today. The gods were smiling on him: no less than he deserved. He took the stairs to the top floor and knocked, quietly, so as not to alert the neighbour across the hall.

No answer. He knocked again, then pressed his ear to the door. He couldn't hear anybody inside, though he pushed against the door, just on the off chance that the lock wasn't properly engaged.

'Yes?'

He wheeled round and discovered that a squat, elderly woman had opened her front door and was squinting suspiciously at him, her chin almost resting on the security chain.

'Oh, hello there. I'm. . . a police officer.' He saw her eyes narrow, sceptically, and added, 'Detective Sergeant Doors.'

Stupid name: the first thing that popped into his head, though if pressed he would spell it D-a-w-e-s.

'You know she's in trouble?' he said, jabbing a thumb at the apartment behind him.

'I had that impression, yes.'

'She broke into a house along the road. Criminal damage.' With the old biddy lapping it up, he relaxed into the role. 'I was hoping to gather some background detail. How long has she been separated from her husband?'

'Ooh, I'm not sure. A while before she moved in here.'

He gave her a suitably professional nod. 'And is there anyone on the scene now?' He got a blank look. 'A new boyfriend?'

'Well, I. . .' She faltered. 'If you're a detective, then you'll have a warrant card?'

'Yes, of course.' He made as if to reach into his back pocket, but it was a bluff, and once his hand was behind his back he didn't know what to do next.

The woman issued a scornful laugh. 'I don't think you're a policeman. What are you doing here?'

She was staring at him the way a crow would stare at carrion. Russell focused his own gaze on the silver chain stretched across the doorway. If he threw himself against the door he suspected it would give way, and even if the impact didn't kill the old woman, it wouldn't take much to wring her neck. . .

All this whipping through his mind in a split second, before a reversion to sanity. 'All right.' He tried out his most winning smile. 'I've had a couple of dates with Jenny. She's been coming on strong, but then this happened – the arrest – and it's kind of freaked me—'

'I've seen you before.' The woman spoke over him as though he counted for nothing, just like Kelly did. 'You live along Henley Gardens. I don't believe you're her boyfriend. What are you really up to?'

'Nothing. Christ, you're a nosy old cow!' He stormed away, pushed through the fire door and thudded down the stairs. Now he was truly screwed: she was bound to speak to people – Jen, for definite – and she might even know Kelly by sight.

Shit. Would she go to the police?

Once outside, he started to recover his equilibrium. Okay, so he'd sort of pretended to be a cop, but he hadn't gone anywhere with it, hadn't tried to talk his way into her home or anything like that. What reason would she have to take it further?

She wouldn't need a reason. It was just what women did. And right on cue, here was his phone chiming. A text from the witch.

Hi hun, hope you're behaving! Not as bad as I thought here, thank god, tho Shaz is very weepy. Should be able to come home soon xxx

He frowned. *Hope you're behaving*: what the hell was that about? He felt a tickle of fear. Sometimes he wondered if she was spying on him. It was the easiest thing in the world these days: little hidden cameras and microphones, keylogger programs on the computer. She always acted clueless about technology, but what if that was a bluff? Or what if her lover had the IT skills?

'Bitches,' he growled. 'The whole fucking lot of them.'

Sneering. Mocking him. Well, he wasn't going to take it any more.

CHAPTER THIRTY-FOUR

St Mary's Bay was a small seaside town about fifteen miles east of Rye, in the neighbouring county of Kent. It meant another slow journey on single-lane roads, twisting back and forth across the grassy flatlands of Romney Marsh, past a wind farm whose giant blades were turning even on this calm summer's day.

The artist lived along a dirt track north of the town, on land that might once have been part of a farm. The main building was a large, sprawling bungalow, but Jen had been told to look for an annexe on the right-hand side, partially obscured by a mass of wild rhododendron. The annexe had its own address, The Studio, evidenced by a sign in the form of a large sculpture of an owl, fashioned from wire and glass.

The front door opened before Jen reached it. Kitty Webster was younger than Jen had expected – mid twenties at most. She was a slender, attractive woman with long, dark hair tied back in a ponytail. She wore glasses with narrow silver frames, a large denim shirt and black leggings. Her voice was soft and melodious, her movements smooth and measured.

Greetings were exchanged as the woman beckoned her inside. The annexe's living room served primarily as a studio, but there was a sofa and TV unit squashed at the far end.

'Nice place.' Jen nodded towards the bungalow. 'Neighbours a bit close, though. Do you get on okay?'

'Most of the time. They're my mum and dad.'

'Ah. That works out well, then.'

'It's fab. I'm as independent as I want to be, but I can still ask Mum to do my ironing.'

Jen chuckled, immediately warming to this woman; then felt bad about it. 'Look, I'd better come clean. I'm afraid I can't afford to buy anything from you.'

'Oh.' The woman took a moment to appraise her. 'So why are you here?'

'It's about some artwork I believe you might have made. Celtic figures, deities – there was a beautiful one of Elen of the Ways. . .'

Webster was nodding. 'Those are mine. I'm glad you like them.'

'And the man who sells them for you, Alex Wilson—'

'He doesn't sell them,' she cut in, confused. 'He commissioned me to make them, that's all.'

'Commissioned them? How many – and what period of time are we talking about?'

'It was about thirty, and all in a single order.' Kitty blew out a sigh at the memory. 'Hardest I've ever had to work, but I wasn't going to complain. I bought a car from the proceeds.'

'When was this? And how did he find you?'

She shrugged. 'I think he saw something at the gallery. He first got in touch around March, April? I had the work completed by June, and since then there hasn't been a word from him.' A laugh. 'Never known anything like it before, and probably never will again.'

Jen was speechless for a few seconds, trying to make sense of this news. 'So the subject matter, did you come up with it, or did Wilson?'

'Oh, he chose it all. I had very detailed guidelines. One piece in particular had to be exactly right—'

'Elen of the Ways?'

Kitty almost did a double take. 'How did you know?'

'Lucky guess. Why was that one so important, did he say?'

'No. But he made it easy by giving me a nice clear image. I think I still have it, actually.' She drifted across to a battered pine dresser, which evidently served as storage for tools and working materials. After rooting around in a drawer, she came back with a folded sheet of paper and handed it to Jen.

It was the picture she'd liked on Facebook.

Jen tried to stifle her shock, so as not to alarm the woman, but it was impossible not to let something show.

'Are you all right?'

'Fine.' She smiled, but Kitty wasn't convinced. She slipped away to a small kitchenette and returned with a glass of water. Jen felt embarrassed; for the second time this weekend, she was being nursed by a stranger.

'What's this about?' Kitty asked. 'Is Mr Wilson a friend of yours?'

'Not a friend. He's. . . well, someone I know.'

She took a minute to sip the water and try to process what she'd learned. *They must have planned this so carefully: months of preparation, all designed to frame me for a crime. . .*

And now she was faced with revealing that this woman's artwork, so lovingly created, had been nothing more than expendable props. No, that felt too cruel.

'Can I ask – did he leave you an address, for an invoice or delivery?'

Kitty was shaking her head. 'Once we'd spoken on the phone he came here and paid a cash deposit – half the cost up front, no argument. I was, like, *whoa!*' She smiled. 'Then cash for the rest when he collected it.'

'I see.' Jen sighed: another dead end. 'I know you must be wondering what this is about, but to be honest I wouldn't really know where to begin explaining. I'm just very sorry for raising your hopes of a commission.'

'It's no big deal. I'm more worried about you.'

Jen smiled gratefully. 'You don't need to be. I'm all over the place at the moment.'

The generality sent a clear message, and it was one the artist seemed to accept. They chatted a little about the difficulties of establishing a reputation. Kitty said, 'I care too much just to churn these out, and because of that it'll only ever be a fun hobby.'

'The woman at the gallery said you're working for a bank?'

'Yeah, I love it!' She saw that Jen looked taken aback, and grinned. 'The call centre's such a buzzing place. We have a great laugh.' She regarded a work in progress on the large central table, which appeared to be the hindquarters of a squirrel. 'When I tried doing this full time, day after day on my own, it nearly drove me bonkers. I realised I'm just not cut out for that kind of life.'

This willingness to turn away from her talent made Jen feel sad, even though she appreciated what Kitty was saying. Offering more profuse apologies, she left the house and drove away with her thoughts in turmoil.

The existence of a conspiracy to frame her now seemed beyond doubt, but would the police agree? Running through what she'd learned over the past few days, she had to conclude that it was no slam dunk. If anything, she risked having the spotlight turned back on her, and if it came out that she'd searched Dhillon's hotel room she'd be in even more trouble.

The town of Rye had just come back into view, a bulge in the landscape, when her phone started to bleep; she must have lost her signal in the wilds of Kent. She pulled in at the next lay-by to check her messages.

The first was from Freddie, reporting that Charlie had had a fantastic time on the boat yesterday; they were at the villa today and might be able to Skype later. Jen was pleased to hear it, though her enthusiasm was tempered by the knowledge that she'd have to ask Freddie about all this.

Not *ask*. Confront.

The other text was from Russell Pearce, and it sent a shiver along her spine: *Assume u saw my message? Have the decency to answer, will you? I'm offering to save your life. Gotta be worth a lot, hasn't it – and you will ENJOY IT, I guarantee that ;) ;)*

Jen was tempted to respond straight away, telling him to piss off or she'd report him for stalking. But mindful of her dad's warning, she decided to leave it for now.

Driving home, her mood swung between rage, despair and weary resignation. On closer analysis, what she'd learned was of no help at all. In fact, Kitty's testimony might actually bolster the police's suspicion of a relationship between Jen and Alex Wilson. *He commissioned that artwork especially for you, and then you destroyed it in a fit of temper.*

By the time she reached Brighton it was almost four in the afternoon. After a couple of hours in the air-conditioned chill of the car, the outside temperature came as a shock. Her body felt grimy with dried-on sweat, and her throat was parched. Dehydration could partly explain why she felt so tired and dispirited, she thought. But only partly.

There were plenty of other reasons, such as that creep Russell Pearce. As she walked towards her building she had a strong sensation of being watched. She turned quickly but there was no one in sight.

She made it to the top landing, heard movement beyond Bridie Martin's door and raced inside her flat. After gulping down a glass of water, she stepped into the shower and tried to unwind.

She had to give some thought to the Skype call, and how best to handle a difficult conversation without upsetting Charlie.

Her phone buzzed as she was drying off. Russell Pearce again.

Here's a taste of what you're missing.

And there was a picture attached.

CHAPTER THIRTY-FIVE

It was one of those things you do, and then instantly regret. Sort of.

Russell had no qualms about whether the image would be unwelcome or distressing; the worry was that he was incriminating himself, offering her material she could use against him. Far from wise – and yet sometimes he felt compelled the push the boundaries.

It's an illness, remember? One for which I may or may not seek treatment. . .

The image wasn't anything pornographic – not that Jen was likely to go to the cops, given the power he had over her. He'd used the timer function on his phone's camera, and captured a neat close-up of his upper thighs and groin (with only an unfortunate hint of sucked-in belly at the top of the frame). He was wearing a pair of white Calvin Klein briefs that he'd stopped wearing years ago, when they became far too tight.

He had a full erection, of course.

The thrill was heightened by the fact that the witch was back home, chirpy as hell and busy making them a pie for dinner. He sent the picture, and imagined Jen being out with friends, perhaps in a bar or lying on a beach – yes, the beach. Her friends would see her reaction – the bemused smile, a tiny gasp – and demand to know what it was.

Nothing, she'd tell them, and then she would roll onto her front, shield the phone with her hand and study the picture carefully, trying to hide her arousal from her companions. This message would get a response, no doubt about that.

He was still in the bedroom, working on that fantasy, when the doorbell rang.

No one answered at first. There was a Dacia on the drive, and Jen thought she could hear music inside. Lionel Richie. Somebody was home, possibly the wife – Jen still had the feeling she was being watched, though maybe he was spying on her from one of the bedroom windows.

Then a click, and the door was opened by a woman who looked nothing like Jen had expected. She was probably late thirties, tall and quite shapely, with an expensive, well-cut summer dress that cleverly minimised a few lumps and bumps. Her hair, nails and make-up all pointed to a beauty regime of considerable dedication. Even the few dabs of pastry on her hands could have been applied on purpose to achieve the desired effect: domestic goddess at work.

The woman smiled, a little cautiously. 'Hello?'

'Are you Russell Pearce's wife?'

She nodded, and even while Jen was thinking, *But he's a slob*, the woman's expression turned cold. 'Who are you, and what do you want?'

'What I want is for your husband to leave me alone.'

The woman started to splutter. 'Leave you alone? Wh-what are you—'

Jen thrust her phone forward. 'He just sent me this. He keeps texting, harassing me. You can tell him I wouldn't sleep with him if I had a gun to my head, and I don't care what he threatens to do. One more message and I'll report him to the police.'

The woman wore a vicious scowl, but her mouth was opening and closing, finding no words. Jen had come here with the intention of confronting Russell himself, but she'd said her piece and couldn't see any good reason to stick around.

As she turned away, something wet struck her hair and dripped onto her temple. Jen gasped. Pearce's wife had spat at her, and was now gripping the door, ready to slam it if Jen tried to retaliate.

'Get off my property, you lying whore!' she screamed. 'He'd never go near a skank like you!'

Russell listened from the top of the stairs. His legs were jelly; he had to cling to the banister for support. Hadn't he known it might go disastrously wrong? He should have listened to that inner voice, got himself under control before it was too late.

But ever the optimist, he waited till Kelly shut the door, then feigned surprise. 'What was all that about?'

With a murderous glare, she snarled, 'That's what you're going to tell me. Right now.'

'It was Jennifer, wasn't it?' He glanced casually out of the landing window, wanting to make sure the bitch was walking away.

'You sent her a bloody dick pic. Who is she?'

'It's all right. Calm down.' Russell felt that if he could survive the initial blast, he might just be able to finesse his way out of this. 'I didn't tell you about her, because I didn't want to worry you.'

'Oh?' Arms folded, eyebrow cocked, a stance that said, *This had better be good. . .*

'The other day I'd popped out to the shop. On the way back I saw a woman standing outside number 14, where the burglary was. I asked if she'd seen anything, and she just came out and told me.'

He paused. *Drag it out. Make her ask.*

'Told you what?'

'She admitted to it. Well, not in so many words. It's some kind of domestic issue – remember the policewoman said the intruder had keys?'

Kelly's nod was an encouraging sign. She was buying into it.

'Anyway, I think they'd split up, and he'd accused her of trashing his place. It seemed pretty clear that she must have done it, but she started begging for help. Gave me this sob story about her kid – she's a single parent.' He wore a look of disapproval, knowing Kelly would share it. 'She asked me to tell the police I'd seen some bloke acting suspiciously—'

'But you'd already spoken to them.'

'I told her that, but she kept on and on at me. I ended up agreeing to think about it, just to get away. But then she wanted my phone number.' He sighed, allowing it to become a wince. 'I think she's a bit unstable.'

'That doesn't explain the picture.'

'I know. Call it a moment of madness. She kept trying to flirt, sending me images of herself. . . I wish now that I hadn't deleted them. In the end I relented and did one for her, but not naked the way she asked. I suspect she was setting me up for this sort of blackmail, so thank God it's out in the open now.'

Kelly deliberated for an unnervingly long time. Russell sidled down the stairs, stopping halfway. Close enough to look into her eyes, but still out of striking range.

'I want to believe you,' she said at last. 'But after what happened with that girl, Susie. . .'

'*Nothing* happened with Susie.'

'So you say, but you still had to leave Amex. If not for that, you wouldn't have changed jobs and been made redundant.'

He groaned, flapping a hand. 'That was all a horrible mistake, I don't want to go raking over it again.'

'I'm sure you don't. Neither do I.' Something in the kitchen started bleeping; he thought it might bring him respite, but she ignored it. 'What did she mean about you threatening her?'

'I genuinely have no idea. You saw what she's like. Unstable.'

Silence. He met his wife's gaze and held it, determined not to flinch. He was in control here; not her. Not the witch.

And if she refuses to accept my explanation, he thought, *I won't be responsible for whatever happens next.*

CHAPTER THIRTY-SIX

The Skype call took place at six o'clock – eight in Crete. By that time in the UK Charlie would have been warned to start winding down for bed, but not with his dad. It sounded like they'd be heading out to the nearest town, where there was a choice of tavernas and one in particular whose proprietor had taken a shine to Charlie.

'Fantastic!' Jen said, and she tried to mean it. *They're on holiday. A few late nights won't hurt him. There are bigger things to worry about.*

She decided not to ask about the supposedly unreliable Wi-Fi, or the presence of Ella. There was no sign of the girl, and neither Charlie nor his dad had mentioned her.

After a stilted beginning, Freddie announced that he had to check on something outside and left Charlie to speak to her on his own. Jen was grateful for this act of discretion, which enabled her to have a much more normal conversation with her son.

Charlie, though, remained subdued, and reluctant to elaborate on any of his answers. Almost everything was 'good' – not 'great' or 'amazing' or 'fantastic', which was out of character for a boy who could fizz with excitement over the contents of the sandwich he'd had for lunch.

'Charlie, listen. Just between you and me, are you sure you're all right?'

He nodded, mumbling something like, 'It's too nice here.'

'What do you mean, "too nice"?'

'It isn't fair – cos you're not here to enjoy it with me, and I keep getting bad dreams where you've been put in jail, and then. . . and then I have accidents.' Ashamed, he turned his face away from her.

'Oh, darling, you mustn't worry about that. I promise you, Daddy's not cross with you, and I'm sure it'll stop soon.'

He didn't look convinced, and Jen was aware that she hadn't offered any reassurance on the much bigger issue of whether his mother was going to be locked up. But if she denied the possibility and then later received a prison sentence, it would destroy his trust in her.

'Try not to worry. I'm missing you, of course, but I had a nice weekend. I saw Granddad Ian, and he and Nanny send their love. And we all want you to have a wonderful time out there, okay?'

He nodded dutifully, but still not persuaded. Now for the horrible part: 'Could you ask Daddy to come in? I need a quick talk with him, just the two of us, okay?'

Charlie seemed to recoil. Such a request was generally a signal for conflict between the two people he loved most.

'It's fine,' she added hastily. 'There won't be an argument. It's just yucky grown-up stuff.'

Without another word, he got up and slouched out of shot, and Jen felt her stomach clench with sorrow. But she had to question Freddie, and it had to be done in private.

She heard the slap of bare feet on marble. Freddie's hairy legs came into view and he dropped onto the sofa, wiped his face with both hands and gazed blearily at the camera, like a contestant on *Big Brother* preparing to unleash a grievance.

'Is Charlie out of earshot?' she asked.

'Yes.'

'Definitely? Can you make sure?'

'He is. What's this about, Jen?'

'I need to ask you something. I don't want you making a joke of it, or trying to fob me off. It's serious.'

'Yeah, all right. Go for it.'

'Are you trying to destroy me?'

'What?' A laugh burst from him, even while his face creased with a mix of shock and anger. 'We're getting divorced, and we don't agree on a lot of stuff, but what the fuck—'

'I'm being framed for a crime. I can't see why anyone would do that, other than maybe you or your dad, looking to discredit me in the eyes of the court.'

'I can't believe what I'm hearing. Jen, this is the twenty-first century. What you're describing is like something out of the maf—' He broke off, and Jen moved closer to her screen, wondering if this was it: an admission of some kind. But then he too leaned forward, and said, 'Hold on, have the police got involved?'

She shifted uncomfortably. 'Yes. Why?'

'Charlie said something that didn't make sense. I chose not to push it, so he wouldn't get upset. And out of respect for you,' he added sourly. 'So what happened?'

'They're accusing me of burglary and criminal damage. It's complete bullshit, but someone planted evidence.'

'Bloody hell,' he muttered. 'I'm not gonna do that to you, am I? Hey – is that why he's wetting the bed again?'

Jen took a deep breath. 'It might be.'

'Shit.' Sounding genuinely concerned, he said, 'What's going to happen, do you know?'

'Not yet. I'm waiting to hear if I'll be charged.'

'And if you are?'

'It'll be in the hands of a jury. For a guilty verdict, it's possibly a fine or a suspended sentence – if I'm really lucky.'

'And if not?' He looked up, gazed into her eyes from a couple of thousand miles away, read the answer in her face and shook his head in disgust. 'Oh, Jesus.'

CHAPTER THIRTY-SEVEN

That night Jen slept better than she had expected. When she woke on Monday morning, her overriding emotion was one of confusion. Who was doing this to her, and how could she find them?

Freddie's reaction had restored her faith in his basic decency. If only he could break away from his father's pernicious influence, there might still be a chance to resolve their differences with another attempt at mediation. . .

Except you're going to jail, remember? No point agreeing on the finer obligations of your child's living arrangements when you might not be around to fulfil them.

While still in bed, she checked her phone. Following the run-in with his wife, there had been no more contact from Russell Pearce. She had texts from Nick, and from Anna; she replied to Anna's but left Nick's for now.

And there was an email from Jonathan Oldroyd at SilverSquare. The tone was almost accusatory, wanting to know who she was and where she had got that document. It had been sent at just after three in the morning, and yet he'd supplied a mobile number and asked her to call any time from eight o'clock.

First she took a shower, grabbed some breakfast and considered what to do with her day. The weather was fabulous and it was a public holiday, a combination that meant anywhere worth going would be jammed with people. Perhaps she'd be better off heading to the Skyway and offering her services for a few hours – Nick would no doubt be glad of the extra help.

When she called Oldroyd, he shouted a greeting over the roar of traffic and explained that he was on his way to the office. 'On a bank holiday?' she queried.

'It's my own business, so the calendar's irrelevant.' He'd just flown back from a meeting in Los Angeles, hence the late email. 'I was deeply troubled by the notations on that document, so I apologise if my response was overly aggressive.'

'Do you know what they mean?'

'I believe I do, yes.' He had a deep voice, and the authoritative burr of a moneyed background. 'Look, I don't suppose you're anywhere near London? This isn't a subject to discuss over the phone.'

'I'm in Brighton. Why can't we talk on the phone?'

'Because, to be blunt, you could be anybody. And I can't afford to reveal anything that might get back to my competitors.'

He asked if her background was in product design, and Jen gave a snort. 'I work at a sports centre.'

'Ah. What about those guys you named in the email?'

'I don't actually know who they are. I was hoping you could help me with that.'

'Mysteries abound,' he drawled. 'I'd come to see you, but there are meetings that I have to attend.'

'It's fine,' Jen said. 'What time are you free?'

She decided against getting caught up in the capital's traffic, and went by train instead, grateful for the money her dad had given her. There were plenty of seats, perhaps because the fine weather was sending everybody in the opposite direction. The mid morning tube from Victoria was a different matter, and when she emerged onto Kensington High Street the stifling heat and crush of humanity reminded her why she loved living on the coast.

SilverSquare had an office in Drayson Mews, just a couple of minutes' walk from the station. Jen was buzzed in at the front door and climbed the twisting stairs to a small lobby, where Jonathan Oldroyd was waiting to greet her.

She already knew he was in his early forties, a decorated officer in the Grenadier Guards with a squarish face, clear blue eyes and greying hair. He was sporting a neat beard that hadn't been present on the website photo, and leaning on a walking stick. After introducing himself, he took a limping step towards a door that had been propped open with a fire extinguisher.

'You'll have to forgive me. Leg's playing up.' He explained that on long-haul flights his knee became so painful that he had to remove his prosthetic, but swelling of the residual limb made it difficult to fit back on. He launched into a description of an infected stump, then stopped abruptly, and grinned. 'I have a smooth line in small talk, as you can tell.'

Jen followed him through an open-plan office with a dozen or so desks, about half of which were occupied. The majority of the staff seemed to be in their twenties or thirties, all dressed in casual clothes – including board shorts – and most too intent on their work to spare them a glance.

Oldroyd took her to a small meeting room with a round table and four chairs. A coffee machine and a water cooler sat against the wall, and she gratefully accepted an offer of cold water.

There was an iPad on the table, which he moved aside. Beneath it lay a copy of the document she had sent him. Sitting with his right leg stretched out to the side, he tapped the paper and said, 'If you don't mind, could we start with this, and how it came into your possession?'

She had already formed the opinion that this man was trustworthy, so she began with the frank admission that she was being framed.

In an attempt to clear her name, she'd followed one of the men whom she believed was responsible for her plight, and had managed to photograph a document in his possession.

'I don't know for sure that he or his associate wrote those notes, but if I can find out what it means, it might give me a clue as to who they are.' She set out her theory that one pair of initials could relate to staff at SilverSquare. Oldroyd thought the same, though the other pair didn't correspond to anyone he employed.

'I also wondered if "DD" means due diligence?'

'It does. The twenty-fourth of September is the agreed completion date.' His lips compressed into a tight white line as he looked her in the eye. 'Which is a closely guarded secret, known only to the directors here, and a handful of the senior staff and their representatives at the company who are in talks to acquire our business.'

Jen whistled. 'That's why you were so cross in the email.'

'Yes – apologies for that. But how this Mr Dhillon came by the information, I would dearly love to know.' He tapped the paper again. 'And the reference to key man insurance – very troubling.'

He asked how, exactly, she was being framed, so she gave him the whole story. Oldroyd listened attentively, occasionally flexing his right thigh and adjusting the prosthetic. By the time she'd finished his face was grave, and she had the distinct impression that he'd reached a conclusion about something. She was expecting any number of questions, but not the one he asked.

'How much do you know about corporate espionage?'

CHAPTER THIRTY-EIGHT

By way of background, he explained that it had become all too commonplace for businesses to spy on their rivals, employing specialist firms whose staff were often drawn from the security services, military and police.

'I've heard people in the UK deluding themselves that it's only a problem with Russians, Chinese, some of the Middle East, but I don't subscribe to that. In today's world, you're hunting for anything that can give you a competitive advantage – and for many, it doesn't matter how dubious or downright illegal it is.'

His concern had been prompted by an earlier approach, from one of the biggest players in their sector, which had been rejected. 'Their philosophy and ethics were completely at odds with ours. They're a bunch of raptors, basically. Now we're set for a merger – okay, a takeover, in effect – by one of *their* closest competitors. A lot of analysts think that acquiring our expertise will give them the edge over the raptors. It's been worrying me from the start that these buggers would love to sabotage the deal, if they could.'

'Have they tried?'

'I've not seen any evidence – until this.' He pointed to one pair of initials. 'I've had my IT guys looking through our systems. I'm confident that we're about as watertight as you can ever be, in terms of hackers and the like, but this document indicates that some sort of operation is under way, to be completed before the twenty-fourth.'

'So you think Dhillon and Wilson might work in corporate espionage?'

He nodded. 'Obviously you're an individual rather than a business, but their MO with you looks to be the same – as is the objective, I imagine? Somebody sees you as competition, and they want you out of the way.'

Jen thought about it. 'That answers the question about why they would be doing these things to me, when I've never done anything to harm them. I can't say Wilson looks much like a spy, though.'

He gave a dry chuckle. 'In real life they don't tend to resemble Daniel Craig. This chap probably shifted paper around for twenty years, then saw a chance to make a lot more money, and all he had to do was check his conscience at the door.'

'But I still have the problem of who hired them.' She'd already referred to her messy divorce, and now described how Freddie had seemed genuinely shocked by the news of her arrest. 'But I'm still bothered by something my father-in-law said.'

Oldroyd grunted. 'This is Freddie's old man? What does he do?'

'He's a journalist and broadcaster.' Jen answered reluctantly, unsure whether it was wise to be quite so candid. 'Gerard Lynch.'

Oldroyd rocked back and nearly fell off his chair. 'You mean the professional loudmouth?'

'The one and only.'

'And is he as big a twazzock in real life? I can only tolerate him on *Have I Got News For You* because Merton and Hislop take the piss out of him.'

'He claims they're all best buddies off camera, but I don't believe that. Though he's always bragging that *Private Eye* wouldn't dare take a pop at him.'

Oldroyd's wistful smile faded. 'That newspaper column of his? They were handing the paper out on a flight I took a while back, and he was spouting the usual tosh about politics, and Europe, and immigration. What stuck with me is how he insisted that winning is everything. Forget fairness, rules, morality – just win. Win at all costs. And if that truly is his overriding philosophy. . .' He nodded at the document. 'You certainly can't rule him out.'

Before they could discuss it further, a thickset Chinese man in a 'Ready Player One' T-shirt tapped on the open door and said, 'Jon. Something you need to see.'

With an apology, Oldroyd grabbed his stick, planted his left foot and heaved himself upright. He made it seem natural that his motion caused him to turn away from the door, but Jen caught his face creasing with pain and realised the manoeuvre was intended to hide that reaction from his colleague.

In his absence, Jen sent her dad a quick hello and a reminder – *Eat healthily, or at least just eat!* – then opened the Kindle app on her phone and read a couple of per cent of a thriller that someone at work had recommended.

Ten or fifteen minutes passed. She read through a cliffhanger chapter end and coasted onto a plateau, but the drama in her own life was scratching away at her concentration.

From where she was sitting, she had a limited view of the office. She could hear the insect-like chatter of skilful fingers on expensive keyboards, the hum of the CPU fans; occasionally a laugh or murmur of conversation.

Bored, and growing restless, she topped up her water and gazed idly at a notice board next to the drinks machines. Along with some health and safety stuff, and flyers for pizza delivery and an upcoming comedy gig, there were a handful of photos taken from a work night out. Shot glasses featured prominently. Oldroyd and the Chinese man seemed to be letting their hair down as much as their younger staff, some of whom looked to be shedding clothes and inhibitions as the night wore on.

Hearing the clonk of the walking stick, she darted for her seat, as if Oldroyd might accuse her of spying if he caught her standing up. Coldness flooded her body. It felt like another panic attack coming on, a fight or flight response. But she didn't have anything to fear from Oldroyd. . . did she?

He came in, moving faster than before, as though the discomfort was no longer relevant. The Chinese man followed, along with a tall black woman who was whispering anxiously into her phone. She ended the call just as Oldroyd introduced her as Cara, and the man as Keng. 'They're our IT whizz-kids, and what they tell me is that we have a big, big problem.'

The background: SilverSquare's business was naturally subject to an immense amount of secrecy. Most of their work came from multinational firms who tasked them with creating prototypes of new products. Because of the vulnerabilities inherent in network computers, their policy was to use standalone devices for their design work – that is, not connected to the internet in any way whatsoever. They used iPads, Macbooks and the like for everything else, but sterile computers – or CAD workstations, as Oldroyd called them – for design.

'Paul Keegan is our creative director, someone who absolutely would be identified as a "key man" by anybody who targeted our business.' Oldroyd glanced at his colleagues. 'And we've just found a cache of child porn on his computer.'

'A computer with no internet access?' Jen wanted to be sure she understood.

'That's right,' Keng said. 'It's a large collection of images and videos, but they weren't amassed over time, as you might expect. Looks more like they were gathered and placed in a particular software program, then somehow loaded onto the computer—'

'Via a flash drive,' Cara said.

'The program is a Trojan,' Keng continued. 'We haven't yet completed the analysis—'

'I have,' Cara said.

'But it seems to be designed to give the impression that certain files are being accessed, usually early in the morning or late in the day—'

'No, there's a trigger.'

With a wry smile, Oldroyd explained the conflict: 'I always set the two of them to look into problems individually at first. A spot of competition brings out the best in people.'

Grinning, Cara swiped her tongue across her teeth. 'It's the sudoku-type game that Maisie worked on a couple of years ago. Whenever he stops to play that, the log will record that he also spent some time viewing the, uh, material.'

'Which, from the one or two things I just saw, is truly appalling,' Oldroyd said with feeling.

'But he doesn't actually view it?'

'No,' Cara answered confidently. 'I sit close enough to see his screen. So do a couple of others.'

'But would a court accept that?' Keng put in. 'Or would they be swayed by the police's forensic expert? Usually some poor guy under huge pressure of work, and therefore inclined to go for the evidence at face value.'

Cara shrugged. 'To make it worse, I think there's an end date, when the program will load the images into a public folder, before converting itself into an innocuous software enhancement.'

'A kind of logic bomb,' Keng said. 'And when it explodes, it takes the user's career with it.'

'Some time before the twenty-fourth of September,' Oldroyd said. 'But the computer has sophisticated encryption to prevent unauthorised access, so this thing had to have been introduced during working hours, while Paul was logged on.'

Keng said, 'Outside chance, a cleaner, or a contractor. But most likely. . .'

'An employee,' Jen said, her gaze turning to the notice board. She realised now that her sense of panic had been triggered by something in those photos, but she wasn't sure what.

She got up and peered closely at the pictures, and it happened again: an association with her own workplace. *The climbing wall. . .*

'Jennifer?' Oldroyd sounded baffled by her fascination with the images.

Then she saw it: a group shot of seven people, arm in arm, hair wet with perspiration, eyes shut or out of focus. . . and beside them the eighth person, who'd clearly been dragged into the group but was wriggling free, turning away and almost hidden from sight at the moment the image was captured.

It was the woman who'd come to the Skyway with Dean.

CHAPTER THIRTY-NINE

Jen removed the photograph and brought it back to the table. 'This woman here was at the climbing centre where I work, along with a man called Dean, who I think is connected to Wilson and Dhillon.'

Oldroyd peered at the picture. 'I'm not absolutely sure who that is. Cara?'

The IT specialist studied it carefully. 'The angle's not great – looks like she was trying to avoid being photographed. Her name's Yasmin, and she started around April or May. An admin assistant. After a couple of months she said her boyfriend had got a job in New Zealand and she'd decided to go with him.'

'So she was employed on a permanent contract?' Oldroyd queried. He explained to Jen: 'We keep temporary staff to a minimum, to avoid just this sort of risk.'

'She must have survived the initial vetting,' Cara said. 'But then it's a relatively low level role.'

'And no alarm bells when she upped and left?' Oldroyd sounded exasperated.

Keng scratched his chin. 'Jon, I don't think there are many organisations more vigilant than us. The truth is, you can never be a hundred per cent secure.'

Still glowering, Oldroyd sent them off to continue the task of identifying and minimising the fallout from this discovery, then said to Jen, 'I don't see that they have to know the details of your own problem.'

'I appreciate that. Thanks.'

'In view of the nature of what's been found, we'll have little option but to involve the police – and of course that means explaining how we were alerted to the matter.'

Jen hadn't thought that far ahead, but she immediately agreed. If that led to some awkward questions, so be it.

Oldroyd wanted to know if there was anything else she could tell him about the woman.

'Not really. She only came to the climbing centre a few times. But that's still too much of a coincidence for me.'

'And me.' They agreed to keep each other updated, and then he led her back to the stairs, held the door with his elbow and gave her a farewell peck on the cheek.

'You've shown a lot of courage in choosing to pursue this, but please take a word of warning from somebody who knows. Never underestimate your enemy's capacity for cruelty.'

Good advice, Jen thought as she walked back to the tube station on Kensington High Street. If she were to abide by it, she'd probably jump on a train to Brighton and hole up in her flat until either Wilson or the police made their next move.

Could she do that?

She studied the network map. The underground was hot, noisy, crowded and unwelcoming: for those reasons alone it was tempting to flee the city – and yet, knowing he was only a couple of miles away. . .

Jen took the Circle line to Edgware Road, then switched to the Hammersmith line and emerged at Euston Square, blinking owlishly in the harsh sunlight. Someone walked past munching on a burger, and her stomach gave an envious growl. She made a detour to a Sainsbury's Local, bought a sandwich and ate it as she walked the short distance to Gordon Square.

Gerard's London home was in a row of Grade II-listed Georgian properties, a seven-bedroom mansion over six floors. It looked like the natural residence of the wealthy upper classes, though Gerard didn't quite fit the bill in that respect. His family hailed from Manchester, his father a working-class success story – jobbing builder to millionaire property developer after twenty years of hard graft, aggressive self-promotion and suspiciously good fortune, almost certainly the result of regular backhanders.

Both of Gerard's grandfathers had worked down the mines, and Gerard wasn't averse to appropriating their hardship as if it were his own experience, even though he'd been privately educated at great expense and had never dirtied his hands with anything more perilous than newspaper ink.

She had no idea if he was home today, and couldn't quite decide if she wanted him to be or not. She gave a start when his voice barked through the intercom: 'Yes?'

'It's Jen Cornish,' she said, and she could almost feel a reciprocal shockwave vibrating through the tiny speaker.

A second or two of silence, and then: 'Wait there.'

Jen stood rigidly, hands curled into fists. She took several deep breaths, like a swimmer about to dive into murky water. There was so much resting on the next few minutes – and a lot of it depended on what she said, on how forcefully she could direct the conversation.

When she heard the door unlocking, she couldn't prevent a quick, fearful glance over her shoulder, as if she might not be seeing daylight again for a while. Or maybe that she wouldn't be quite the same person when she came out.

Gerard opened the door himself – presumably the housekeeper had the day off. He was dressed in what looked like tartan pyjama trousers and a thin V-neck sweater with nothing underneath it. White hairs sprouted over the edge of the sweater, and a St Christopher's pendant rested between his moobs.

'Why are you here?' He bared his fangs at her, making no move to invite her inside.

'I need to talk to you.'

'About?'

She studied him closely – surely he would know what she meant, if he was implicated? – but his heavy-lidded disdain gave nothing away. With a sigh, he simply turned and padded, barefoot, along the hall. Taking that as a signal to follow, Jen stepped over the threshold and shut the door behind her.

'Is Deborah here?' She'd been wondering if this was going to be her opportunity to meet Gerard's third wife. They'd married last year after a brief but very public romance, which came to light when the paparazzi caught him with his tongue down her throat on a Caribbean beach. At that time she had still been married to her first husband, a minor TV personality who ended up in the Priory, broken by the media's delight in his humiliation. Jen suspected that Gerard had tipped off the photographers himself.

'She's at the loch,' he muttered, by which he meant a beautiful cottage in the Scottish Highlands, just one of his four homes around the world – or five, now, with the villa in Crete. 'She's happier in Scotland, and I'm happier when she's there and I'm anywhere but.'

This was just the sort of callous plain-speaking that his fans cherished, but to Jen it was vile. She'd seen all too often how he used it to wound those closest to him, and it confirmed Freddie's view that this latest marriage was a dreadful mistake.

She had a sudden fear for her own parents. Was Dad being stoic about her mum's frequent business trips, or did he secretly prefer being on his own? She would hate to think their marriage could be as devoid of love or meaning as most of Gerard's relationships.

*

She had little appetite for small talk with the man, so she came straight to the point. 'How important is it to you that Freddie wins the divorce?'

The question contained a test – it shouldn't be viewed in such crude terms as winning or losing – but Gerard merely let the question hang while he reached for the humidor on his desk, selected a cigar and snipped off the end.

Finally, his answer: 'I care about my son, and my grandson.'

In other words, *Not you.*

Jen said, 'I don't think so. If you cared about Charlie, you wouldn't be setting attack-dog lawyers on his mum—'

'I adore that boy, and he certainly won't be given reason to doubt it as he grows up. As for my lawyers, I leave the tactical decisions to them.'

'How much have they cost you, up to now?'

'I can afford it.' He sneered as he lit the cigar. 'I could afford a hundred times as much, and it would still be money well spent to be rid of you.'

'What a gentleman.' She was feeling sick, and the pungent aroma of the cigar wasn't helping. 'And what else are you paying for?'

He paused, his open mouth full of smoke, his brow creased beneath the improbably brown hair. 'Mm?'

'You've just admitted there's an unlimited fighting fund. So how else have you used your fortune to try and destroy me?'

He gave her a scathing look. 'I think you've been out in the sun too long. Are you seeing somebody?'

Now she was confused. 'No. And what's that got to—'

'I don't mean who you're fucking. I mean a shrink. A psychiatrist.'

'Very funny. The way you've dodged my question, I'll take it the answer is yes.'

'I don't know what you're talking about. Now, if you're finished? I have better things to do than listen to the paranoid delusions of a mentally challenged gym bunny.'

She knew she'd get nowhere if she took the bait, but it was so difficult. She'd seen him like this on TV debates, goading his fellow panellists with unwarranted attacks on their integrity or sanity.

'Did you hire Alex Wilson?'

'Who's that, a boyfriend of yours?'

'I think you know who I'm talking about.'

'Not a Scooby, my dear.' He blew out smoke, his lips a rosebud pout, and squinted scornfully at her. 'I still don't get what Freddie saw in you. Fine, shag the tour guide when you're stuck on a mountain and the only alternative is the herdsman's prettiest goat – though personally I'd fuck the goat over you any time – but bringing back the bimbo. . . Tsk tsk. Though I suppose by then you had your greedy little claws around his thinking tackle.'

Gerard was still cackling when her phone burst into life: an incoming call from Tim Allenby. Glad of a reason to interrupt the revolting conversation, Jen stood up and turned away from Gerard before answering. 'Hi, what's up?'

'Sorry to disturb you. I've just had an urgent message from Talia Howard.'

Jen felt her stomach drop. Probably a mistake to take the call. 'Oh, yes?' she said neutrally.

'It's nothing to do with your case – at least, I hope not.' He sounded flustered. 'A body has been discovered, just around the corner from you. A woman was murdered, and the husband's gone missing. Naturally he's the prime suspect, and DS Howard appears to have discovered a connection between the two of you.'

'What? I don't understand. . .'

'Sorry to deliver such a shock. It's Russell Pearce.'

CHAPTER FORTY

'Russell Pearce?' Jen noticed an antique chaise longue against the wall; she collapsed onto it and sat with her head bowed, one hand cupping her forehead, Gerard utterly forgotten. 'They think he killed her? Are you sure?'

A memory of the woman's face as she snarled and spat. *Get off my property, you lying whore!*

'There's a lot of forensic business to conduct, but it looks that way. The body was only discovered a few hours ago. And Pearce has definitely absconded – the car's gone, he's taken clothes and whatnot.'

'And they want to speak to me?'

'Yes. Talia wouldn't go into detail, but something was found that gives them cause for concern.'

'I see.' She wondered if it was Pearce's phone – the texts, the picture he'd sent her. But wouldn't he have taken his phone? 'Uh, when?'

'ASAP is the impression I was given.'

'I'm in London at the moment, but I could do it this afternoon, say around four o'clock?'

'Excellent. I'll let them know and send you Talia's number.' He took a breath. 'In the meantime, please do take care. By the sound of it, what he did to his wife was not pretty at all.'

She ended the call and wiped her face with her hand. She could feel Gerard's gaze, and had the distinct impression that he was almost as perturbed as she was.

'Who's Russell Pearce?'

'No one.'

'Screwing him too, are you?' He wagged a finger at her. 'If I get word that your promiscuity is having an effect on Charlie—'

'Don't be disgusting. I would never do anything of the sort.'

'Better not. You'd be surprised how much Chip confides in his number-one grandpa. So bear that in mind. . . for the time you have left.'

The comment took her breath away. She gripped her phone as if prepared to use it as a weapon. 'What do you mean by that?'

A light shrug, as he puffed on the cigar. 'You're not going to win this battle, Jen. The sooner you accept that, the better for everyone.'

'No. He needs his mother. Freddie is a good dad, and he loves Charlie to bits – I'd never dispute that. But he lives like a playboy. There's no discipline, no structure, no sense of commitment or hard work.' Studying Gerard's expression as she spoke, she had a flash of insight: *He'll never admit it, but he agrees with me.*

'If you're talking about setting examples, he can look to me for that.' He gestured proudly at the room around them, and it took her a moment to comprehend: he was referring to Charlie.

Gerard intended to be the boy's role model.

Horrified, she said, 'Don't give me that. You inherited this house from your father. I know your readers swallow the idea that you're this great self-made man, but it's a sham. The fact is, you were rich from Daddy's money long before you were famous, and the wealth you've acquired since then has come from whipping up hatred of people who can't answer back, people whose lives are already desperate enough, without you encouraging even more persecution. It's the very last thing anyone should be proud of, and you sure as hell aren't going to warp my son to fit into your nasty little mould.'

By now she was on her feet, bouncing on her toes from the adrenaline rush. Christ, it felt good to unleash on a man who had been the cause of so much misery over the years.

Gerard soaked it up, at first incredulous, then amused, finally red-faced and fit to explode.

'Go ahead, deride my fame all you want. Deride my wealth, too, if it soothes your little liberal conscience – though I don't recall too many complaints when you were living in a house bought and paid for by me.' He shook his head as she went to object. 'But the power I have, I earned that for myself, lovey. It's *real*, and it's *mine*, and it *matters*.'

His roving eye caught something, and he calmed a little, beckoning her towards the bookshelves. 'Let me show you what I mean.'

Thrown by the change of tone, Jen approached warily. Alongside the political memoirs and copies of his own work, there were various framed photographs including several of Charlie at different ages, which caused a painful squeeze of her heart. One prominent image, she noticed with distaste, was a shot of his third wife posing topless in the manner of a Page Three girl. Deborah Lynch was nearly thirty years younger than Gerard, and undoubtedly in fine shape, but Jen didn't care for the very obvious breast enhancements, or the fact that Gerard wanted such an image on public display.

The photograph he plucked from the shelf was a portrait of Gerard with his new wife, taken on a spacious hotel terrace with a glittering ocean in the background. Mexico, possibly, where Gerard had flown over a hundred guests for his wedding – not including Jen, of course, and Freddie had only attended under sufferance.

Deborah was draped in a flowing white gown, her cleavage like treacle-coated footballs propped beneath her chin. She was sitting on Gerard's lap, his arms tight around her waist. He was grinning wolfishly, while Deborah's head was thrown back, her mouth forming a tiny circle as if about to laugh or gasp. Various guests could be seen around them, standing or sitting at tables laden with champagne and orange juice.

Gerard pressed a nicotine-stained fingertip against the glass and said, 'That's at breakfast, the morning after the wedding. I'm wearing shorts and a bathrobe, can you see?'

Jen shrugged: *So what?*

'That, my dear, was for ease of access.' He turned and leered, causing Jen to retreat a step or two. 'We were first out on the terrace, and got settled at our table. I'd popped a couple of blue pills.' He chuckled at the memory. 'I told Deb she wasn't to move or give anything away. If she wriggled, I pinched her. Trouble is, the excitement got too much – she had to pretend she was choking on a mouthful of croissant.'

Another horrible, hungry laugh, and then he pressed his tongue against the tip of a yellow incisor. 'Twenty minutes we stayed like that. Shooting the breeze, entertaining our guests – who, for the record, included a cabinet minister, three backbench MPs, a BBC governor, two newspaper editors and a chief constable. All of them out on the terrace, looking me in the eye while I enjoyed my conjugal rights.'

Jen didn't know what to say. She continued to back away but he followed, thrusting the frame into her face.

'Think on that, girl. Twenty minutes holding court with the great and the good, and Deb's sitting happily on my cock.' He sucked at the saliva leaking from his mouth, then jabbed the cigar at her face. '*That*'s what I can get away with, and don't you ever forget it.'

He was panting noisily, mouth open, with a kind of mistiness to his gaze that suggested he wasn't completely in touch with reality. There was a sexual edge to his aggression which hadn't been so blatant before, perhaps because she'd never been here without having Freddie present. Jen felt her body react to the threat, energy coursing to her muscles, ready to fight back. 'So you're admitting it, then?'

'I'm admitting nothing.' He looked her up and down and seemed to shudder, very slightly, as if registering how savagely she would respond if he were to try anything. 'Whatever trouble you're in, it serves you right. Now get out of my sight.'

Jen was only too happy to oblige. But first she pointed at him, struggling to keep her hand steady. 'If it was you that framed me, I'm going to find out. And I'll fight for Charlie till my dying breath.'

Marching out, she opened the front door, slammed it shut and then rested back against it for a second, taking a welcome gulp of untainted air. But there was barely a moment to recover from the shock of that encounter before she had to consider the terrifying news from Tim Allenby.

If Russell Pearce had murdered his wife, was it Jen who had lit the fuse?

CHAPTER FORTY-ONE

She was back in Brighton by three thirty, and made it to the police station by ten to four. The venue this time was the main station in John Street. She'd been told to ask for DS Howard, who offered a slightly terse greeting and then escorted her to an interview room, where she was introduced to Detective Inspector Victoria Booth from the Surrey and Sussex Major Crime Team. Booth was a bulky middle-aged woman with dark curly hair, dimpled cheeks and the voice of a forty-a-day smoker.

'I'm not a great one for coincidences,' she told Jen. 'And to see two crimes within a couple of hundred yards of each other, to which you are, to date, the only identifiable link. . . well, that strikes me as unusual, to say the least.'

DS Howard said, 'I should make it clear that we don't consider you to be a suspect for the murder – if we did, we'd have asked Mr Allenby to attend – but could you describe your movements yesterday?'

Jen had been tense enough up to this point; now she felt a little faint. Beneath the table, she pressed her hands together, the palms damp with sweat.

'I was up around seven,' she said. 'Had a run, a swim in the sea. Then I drove to Rye, where I wandered round the shops, went to a cafe. . .'

Howard frowned. 'I had the impression you didn't drive?'

'No, I do. I borrowed a car – and don't worry, it's got "any driver" insurance.' She flashed a grin, and when DS Howard motioned at her to continue, said a silent thanks that she hadn't been questioned in detail about her visit to Rye.

'During the day I had several text messages from Russell Pearce. I don't know him – or at least I didn't, other than by sight—'

'Same as with Alex Wilson?' Howard cut in, which Jen thought was slightly malicious.

'Not really, no. He came up to me in the street, one day last week, and said he'd heard about the break-in. I ended up admitting that I'd been accused of a crime, because I had the impression that he keeps a close eye on activity in the neighbourhood. I thought he might have been able to help me, perhaps if he'd seen someone behaving suspiciously. . .'

'Well, we know he spent a lot of time spying on passers-by,' said Booth, and the two detectives exchanged a regretful glance.

Jen went on: 'He hadn't seen anything, but said he'd be willing to make a false statement in my defence.'

Howard: 'In return for. . .?'

'I think you can guess. He only hinted at first, but then he started to come on stronger. Stupidly I'd given him my phone number.' They seemed surprised by this news, which Jen found puzzling. Wouldn't they already know?

'And you declined his offer?' Booth asked.

'Absolutely. I told him I didn't want anybody to lie for me.'

'How did he react?'

'Not well. Yesterday the texts became more frequent, culminating in a picture of his lower body – in his underwear, thankfully.' She frowned. 'I assume you've looked at his phone by now?'

Howard shook her head. 'We don't have the phone, and we're still waiting on data from the mobile provider to give us the numbers he called.'

'Then how did you know I was connected to him?'

'The pictures,' DI Booth said flatly. 'The pictures and the video.'

*

In yet another grim echo of the previous week, Jen had the experience of feeling sick to her stomach as she watched herself on their TV screen. The footage was shaky and often focused on her body, rather than her face. She recalled now the odd way in which Pearce had been holding his phone on Friday. There were snippets of dialogue, but after filming their encounter he must have edited it until the conversation made no sense, removing any suggestion that he had offered to commit perjury for her.

She sat there, numb with shock, as they went on to show her a selection of photographs, mostly taken at long range, of her and a number of other women walking past the house. Some dated back months, and Charlie was visible in a few of them.

Jen shivered. 'I feel. . . unclean. Violated.'

DI Booth nodded. 'That's exactly what this is. A violation.'

'And these are only a fraction of the total,' Howard added. 'He captured dozens, if not hundreds of different women, and a lot of these photographs seem to have been taken at various work places over the years.'

'But what's he getting out of it? There's nothing erotic about them, surely?'

'Who knows, with men?' Howard muttered, and Booth said, 'These are the starting point. He doctored many of them, using Photoshop to merge the faces with images of naked women taken from porn sites.'

Jen shut her eyes. 'Don't say he posted them online?'

'Not as far as we can tell. They seem to have been purely for his own. . .' The three of them grimaced in unison, and Jen waved away the need for Booth to complete her sentence.

Taking a deep breath, she said, 'I'd better tell you what else happened yesterday.' She described how she'd gone to the house, only for his wife to answer the door. 'She was friendly enough at first, until I explained why I was there. Then she started screaming, calling me a whore, and spat at me as I was leaving.'

'One of their neighbours heard that exchange,' Howard said. 'He wasn't able to identify you, but what he told us tallies with your account.'

Jen nodded curtly, stung by the implication that anything she said had to be verified. She confirmed that she went straight home and was alone that night, and since then she'd had no more texts from Pearce.

'Do you know when it happened?' she asked.

'We're not able to go into detail on that,' Howard said, stiffly.

Booth was a little more forthcoming: 'The body was discovered this morning by a delivery driver.'

'And what about Russell? Where do you think he's gone?'

'No idea. There's a major search under way, and of course we're trying to trace the car, as well as any use of his phone or bank cards.'

Jen said, 'I could text him, if you wanted, in the hope of drawing him out?'

Booth smiled. 'Thank you, but the phone's switched off. I bet he knows we can track the signal, even if he doesn't use it.'

'Can you?' Jen asked in surprise. 'If technology's that clever, I wish you could find out who really destroyed Alex Wilson's artwork.'

Howard gave her a chilly smile. 'That's a subject for another time.'

'I mean it. Did you ever find out why Wilson had all that stuff? I don't think he is a retailer, or even associated with the arts at all. In fact. . .' Jen hesitated, then decided to press on. 'I suspect he works for a firm that carries out industrial espionage.'

Booth nodded, as if humouring a lunatic. 'I think we're done here for now. We'll need to take a full statement later, and somebody will be in touch about that.'

'It's not a crime to collect art,' Howard said quietly.

Jen's temper flared. 'But he wasn't a collector! Do you know he's moved out of that house – only a couple of days after it happened? Doesn't that strike you as strange?'

'Breaching the terms of police bail is a serious issue,' Howard said sternly. 'I'm going to give you the benefit of the doubt that it hasn't happened.'

DI Booth looked bemused. 'Even more serious is the possibility that Russell Pearce has developed a fixation on you. From experience, I'd say he won't remain a fugitive for long, but until he's found, you need to be vigilant. We'll have a strong presence in the area for the next few days, and regular patrols for a while after that.'

Howard nodded. 'If he gets in touch, or you have any concerns, call me immediately, day or night.'

I don't think so, Jen thought, then realised she was being petulant. These detectives were clearly concerned that Pearce might try something – in which case, she needed to be just as worried.

CHAPTER FORTY-TWO

Jen walked home from the police station, trying to keep a watchful eye on her surroundings while also heavily preoccupied.

From her visit to Jonathan Oldroyd she had more circumstantial evidence that these people worked as a team, with a mission to bring chaos and destroy innocent lives. Then there was Russell Pearce, a man she'd dismissed too readily as a creep, never dreaming he might be capable of murder.

And finally, her father-in-law, whose illustration of his own depravity had convinced her that he was capable of anything.

To her mind, he'd as good as admitted he was responsible for her persecution, but 'as good as' wasn't something she could take to the police. And his reference to the guest list at his wedding – the cabinet ministers and the rest of them – was all too easy to interpret as a warning: *These are my people*. They'll always take *my* side, not yours.

She'd warned him that she would find out if he was involved, but wasn't that just bravado? She didn't have a clue how to go about it.

As she came into sight of her building, she caught movement by the entrance: someone sitting or crouching on the step. She felt her heart race, DI Booth's warning still ringing in her ears.

The figure rose, his face hidden by a splash of colour. Flowers?

It was Nick, a bouquet in one hand, offering a tentative smile. She scowled, hurrying towards him. 'What are you doing here?'

He flinched at her abrupt tone. 'Just passing.'

'I've been out all day.'

'Yeah, well, I figured you'd be home eventually.'

'Nick, how long have you been waiting?'

He shrugged, and checked his Fitbit. 'About an hour. Nice evening for it, enjoying the fresh air.'

Jen wasn't buying the casual act. She studied him carefully. 'What's going on?'

'Funny question to ask me – you're the one that's acting weird.'

'It doesn't make sense, hanging round here like a lovesick schoolboy. What's the idea? Have you been trying to scare me, so I'd run to you for help?'

Nick took a couple of backward steps, as if buffeted by her accusations. His face was bright red.

'Christ, Jen. Talking about help, maybe you ought to be seeing a shrink?' He raised the flowers like a shield, perhaps because of the tears in his eyes. 'I came round because you didn't reply to my text, and last time we spoke you were really stressed out. And yeah, I wanted to help – is that a crime? I like you a lot, Jen. . . and I thought you liked me.'

He meant it. She could see that from his manner. No way would a man like Nick weep in front of her if he wasn't sincere.

'All right,' she said. 'That was unfair of me. I do have some problems at the moment, but they're private. I have to deal with them myself.'

He stared at her in bewilderment as she tested the front door: locked, for once. 'Why don't I come in, and at least just. . . give you a bit of company?'

'That's not a good idea.'

'Jen, you're a free agent. It's time to forget what other people think.'

'You wouldn't say that if you'd heard my father-in-law this afternoon.'

'What's he got to do with it? You don't wanna be going anywhere near that wanker.'

'Look, I meant what I said about their double standards. They're not beyond digging into *your* life, either. Trying to suggest you pose a danger to Charlie.'

Wounded by the comment, his demeanour changed in an instant. 'If I'm honest, Jen, I'm getting a bit sick of all this. Skiving off work. Treating me like shit. And all this flaky stuff about your ex, it's like you can't get him off your mind.'

She was hurt, but decided they were probably quits when it came to spiteful remarks. Instead of retaliating, she found her key and opened the door. But Nick wasn't finished.

'There's rumours at work that the cops were asking about you. Stolen keys or something? I didn't say anything because I was waiting for you to tell me yourself. Is it true?'

Jen let out a bitter laugh, which must have sounded deranged. Nick had the look of a little boy, taunted beyond patience. With a growl of frustration he threw down the bouquet, kicked it across the path and stomped away.

She would have to make peace with him at some stage. She felt bad about the way she'd been deceiving him over the past week, but what did become clear as she tramped up the stairs was that she couldn't truly believe he was conspiring against her. That, at least, had to count as a positive.

Over a comfort meal of cheese on toast, she pondered the merits of speaking to Freddie again and decided she had little to lose. She didn't know exactly when he would be bringing Charlie home – if it was before she finished work on Wednesday, she'd either have to ask Anna to help, or have Charlie dropped off at the Skyway.

She waited until well past his bedtime, then messaged Freddie. But they were still out, he said, eating supper at their favourite taverna. Just you and Charlie, she wondered, or was Ella there as well?

Skype me once he's asleep, she messaged back. *V important – about your dad x*

Hopefully that would do the trick, though equally he might check in with Gerard before he called, to get some background and presumably be coached on what to say. That, or he simply wouldn't reply at all. . .

But Freddie did get in touch, at midnight Greek time, and he called on her mobile, when she'd asked him to Skype. 'Dodgy Wi-Fi,' he explained.

And easier to lie if I can't see your face, she thought. 'Has Charlie only just gone to bed?'

'What? Uh, no, I had other. . . other things. . .' As he tailed off, she recognised that tone of dreamy detachment.

'You're high.'

'I'm on holiday.'

'You agreed you wouldn't take anything when you had Charlie. It's dangerous.'

'Hey, did I say I was? Don't put mouth in my words. . . I mean, don't—'

'I'm not stupid, Freddie.'

He giggled. 'You sure?'

'Listen to me. How much do you know about your dad's plan?'

'Plan? What, like a pension plan?'

'The plan to put me in prison. I was arrested, remember, for a crime I didn't commit, and I think that was down to your father.'

'N-no, that's garbage.'

'Are you saying you didn't know?'

'I'm saying, it's garbage. If you're in trouble, it's nothing to do with Pa.'

'He hates my guts, and he's determined to get control of Charlie's future – but for himself, not for you. His plan is to skip a generation and raise Charlie to be his successor.'

'Nooo,' Freddie whined. 'Don't say things like that. He was the one that said I should lend you the car. He'd hardly do that if he's, like, *Mr Evil*, would he?' A short laugh was interrupted by a belch. 'And-and he said he didn't see why you couldn't come over and visit us sometimes, so that's a friendly. . .'

'What?'

He'd let something slip: that was clear from the way he immediately rode back on it. 'Ah, forget that. I'm, like, I'm probably talking bollocks, yeah? Why don't I call you tomorr—'

'I want to know, Freddie. What do you mean by "come over and visit". In Crete?'

He made his groan of despair sound like a symphony. 'Aww, don't go and spoil things.'

'Tell me.'

'It's. . . the villa's amazing, so chilled. Pa's offering me a new start, says we can home school Charlie, bring in a tutor—'

'Hold on, let me get this straight. Your father wants Charlie to live in Greece?'

'And me,' Freddie protested. 'That's why I don't believe what you said. You're just trying to. . . I dunno, turn the knife, or is it screw? What's the thing you turn?'

Incensed, Jen barely heard the confusion or self-pity. 'Gerard wants Charlie to grow up in another country, and I don't get a say?'

'Britain's fucked up, Jen. It's got no future.'

'That's not what your dad's been telling the world, since winning the referendum. And why would he want to live in Greece? He calls them a bunch of lazy welfare scroungers.'

'But that's the thing. It's so dirt poor, yeah, everyone's desperate – they'll work for peanuts. He's gonna have an army of servants, says we could live like kings! Don't you think that sounds good, eh? Me as. . . as Prince Freddie!'

His laughter sounded almost delirious. Jen saw now why Gerard had seemed so smug: he had it all worked out.

'Listen to me, please,' she implored him. 'You're not your father. You're a kinder, better person than he is, and you don't have to obey his every command. Think of Charlie. He needs both of us in his life. His mum and his dad.'

'Hey, don't get upset. There's no need—'

'Please, Freddie. Do the right thing and bring him home.'

'Ah, Jen, Jen. . . I try so hard to think the best of you, remembering, like, how much fun you used to be, and then. . . you do this. You ruin everything.'

A little burst of static which might have been a sniff or a sob, and he went on: 'And that's why Pa's right, and you're wrong, you know? Charlie'll be much better off with us – with me and his grandpa. You're a loser, Jen. You've got to accept it. You lost.'

CHAPTER FORTY-THREE

Gerard had been writing an eight-hundred-word weekly column for the past twelve years. It rarely took him more than an hour to produce, and sometimes as little as ten minutes. A certain irony there, given how often he railed against various sections of society that he deemed to be lazy and overpaid: politicians, civil servants, doctors, teachers and, on occasion, bankers and City speculators. At other times – for fun, and to see if he could get away with it – he would insist that the traders who made and lost fortunes betting with other people's money were performing a vital role in society: they were the rebels, the swashbuckling, anti-government outliers.

In his view, it all came down to value for money – and value, in this context, definitely included entertainment value. This enabled him to take wildly opposing positions, sometimes in the space of a week or two. So he'd rage about high public spending as it related to an issue such as welfare payments to one-legged dyslexic refugees, then insist that ill-prepared councils should magic up the funds needed to keep the streets clear on the one or two days per decade that it snowed too badly for his SUV.

By way of a safeguard, he felt sure that his typical reader had a brief attention span and, regrettably, a rather low IQ. Gerard had the populist's skill of appearing to write from the viewpoint of the aspirational working class – the plumber, hairdresser, taxi driver – though in reality he went to great lengths to avoid such people.

He liked to think they wouldn't begrudge him the three hundred grand a year for reinforcing their prejudices in a way that made them smile. *Nice work if you can get it, and good luck to you, mate!* Double props for siphoning the cash through a network of private companies in order to shave off most of the tax liability. *Those tossers in Westminster only go and bloody waste it, don't they?*

The column came easiest when he was angry, so he usually worked himself into a state of righteous indignation. It was like the opposite of meditation (which everybody who read his stuff knew was a scam). Somewhat perversely, given the millions in the bank, the collection of luxury homes and cars, and a woman or three available whenever he desired an alternative to the current Mrs Lynch, he could still be roused to anger by a wide variety of issues: traffic signs, restaurant staff, TV announcers, speed bumps, washing instructions, power tools, Belgium. . . In fact, he could get apoplectic just listing the fuckers.

Today's was easy to pump out: a dig at the tendency of women to poke their noses into matters which don't concern them, and then get all het up when they find something unpleasant. He wrote it with Jennifer Cornish's face before his eyes, her voice ringing in his ears.

By midday he'd caught up on emails, set out the bare bones of a deliciously scurrilous article for Breitbart and had a justified whinge at his agent about the lack of support from his French publishers. He buzzed the kitchen to let Siobhan know she could start preparing his lunch: cold meats, brie and a wedge of focaccia, washed down with a glass of Prosecco.

Then his phone rang: Freddie. He'd been calling at least once a day with some peevish question or complaint about the villa. *The internet's too slow. . . I can't figure out the electric blinds. . . I don't like how the pool guy looks at me.*

'Pa, I need some money.'

'What do you mean?'

'To pay the cabbie. I'm thirty quid short.'

'You're having me on?' A second later the intercom buzzed – *bip bip beeeep*, the way Charlie always did it. Then creaks in the hallway as the housekeeper bustled past, so he knew he wasn't imagining it.

At the door, Charlie was greeting Siobhan with a hug. Gerard ruffled the boy's hair and nodded vaguely at some request or other. 'In a minute, Chip.'

He was focused on Freddie, who was standing by as the driver unloaded his suitcases. 'What's going on?'

'Hey.' Freddie put his hand out for the cash, and Gerard got a clear look at the state he was in: *tired and emotional*, as they said in the trade. The taxi driver was an inhibiting presence, so Gerard kept his back to the street and ushered Charlie inside.

'This is a surprise,' he said flatly, and had to add, in response to the boy's curious look, 'A nice surprise.'

'Daddy wanted to come home.' He yawned. 'We had to get up *sooo* early!'

With the taxi moving away, Gerard turned and advanced on Freddie, who cringed and let go of the suitcase he'd just picked up.

'What have you been taking?' he hissed. 'You look strung out, for Christ's sake.'

'I'm not. I didn't sleep last night, not one minute.' Freddie's lip wobbled and his voice went high with tension. 'I spoke to Jen, and it better not be true.'

'Of course it's not true.' Gerard took the other case, turned clumsily and bumped it against Freddie's leg. He gave a yelp, and Charlie laughed, dodging the suitcase himself as Gerard tried to swing past.

'Mind out, Chip. We need to get indoors.'

'Can we go to the park?'

'Not now, no.'

Clutching his shin, Freddie said, 'That fucking hurt.'

'Don't be a sissy, and don't swear in front of the boy.'

'Daddy said we could go to the park. I wanna play football.'

Gerard scowled, and noticed Siobhan backing away from the chaos, aware that he was on a short fuse. 'Make yourself useful,' he snapped, 'and take this little bruiser to the park.'

A whine from Charlie: 'I want to go with you, Grandpa.'

'I can't now. I need to talk to Freddie.'

'But he promised, he promised if I was good on the plane. . .'

Now he was bawling, and it struck Gerard how much the boy was coming to resemble his mother: the same eyes, the same shape to the face, and a certain girlish quality that suddenly repulsed him.

'*Shut up*!' Gerard shouted. 'Either go to the park with Siobhan or don't bloody go at all!'

Charlie shrank back, cowering. Freddie murmured a rebuke, but it was Siobhan who saved the day. 'I'm about to make some lunch. Will you come and help me?'

She led him down the stairs to the basement kitchen. Gerard strode into the study and gestured at the chair on the other side of the desk, but Freddie defied him, wandering to the window and gazing down at the tiny patch of lawn.

'How can you say it's not true when I haven't even told you what she said?'

'Because she came here yesterday, spouting a lot of nonsense.'

'You know she's been arrested? She claims you set her up.'

'Nonsense,' Gerard repeated. 'She's in a lot of trouble, hence all these wild accusations.'

'But she's not a criminal. God knows she's driven me crazy at times, but I can't see her doing something that would get her locked up.'

Gerard regarded his son with a level gaze. 'What are you saying, Freddie? That you believe her over me?'

'I want a straight answer.'

'And I've given you a straight answer.' He threw out a hand in frustration. 'We could have done this on the phone. You didn't have to abandon the whole holiday—'

'I needed to look you in the eye.' Freddie's voice was trembling again. 'It didn't seem fair to stay out there.'

'This isn't about being fair! It's about whether you kowtow to that bitch, or whether you stand up and *fight* for what's rightfully yours.' He waited, panting from the effort of conveying his passion, conscious that his wet fish of a son was liable to dismiss it as histrionics.

Sure enough, all he got was a weak and watery, 'I dunno. . .'

'Well, I do. And since possession is nine tenths of the law, I suggest you get your sorry arse back where you came from, pronto, and lie low till this is all settled.'

'I can't, Pa. He's starting in year three on Thursday.'

'And I've told you, a few more days or weeks won't make any difference. The tutor'll bring him up to speed well in time for Eton.' Gerard grinned at the shock on his son's face. 'Yeah, yeah, it's only an aspiration at this stage, but who knows? If that useless pig-fucker can go all the way, I'm sure my grandson can do it too.'

'But I agreed with Jen. And the lawyers'll say—'

'Forget about that, I'll sort it. You just need to put yourself and the boy back on a plane, and sit tight at the villa till you hear from me.'

Freddie was shaking his head: not quite buying it, but unwilling to rebel. 'And what do I tell Jen?'

'Don't speak to her. There's nothing she can do about it, not where she's heading.'

He expected more bleating, but Freddie only stared at him. 'You did do it,' he said softly. 'You set her up.'

Gerard had already turned to his computer, intending to look up flights to Crete. A knock on the door reminded him of the need to make amends with Charlie: maybe find time to kick a football about in the park before he sent them to the airport.

Siobhan put her head round the door and surveyed the room. 'Is he hiding with you?'

Freddie was hunched over, covering his face with his hands as if ashamed to be seen. Crying like a girl, Gerard realised.

'Hiding?' he asked.

'Charlie wanted to play hide and seek, but I can't find him. Did he not come in here?'

Freddie's hands fell away, eyes wide and bloodshot. Gerard shook his head at Siobhan. 'Have you looked upstairs?'

'Everywhere.' She sounded scared. 'I left this room till last, because I could see you wanted privacy.'

'What about the garden?'

'No. I've checked. He's vanished, sir. He's gone.'

CHAPTER FORTY-FOUR

On Tuesday morning, Jen requested an urgent meeting with Yvonne Cartwright. She wanted to know where she stood if Freddie refused to bring Charlie back from Greece.

Blessedly she had slept without dreaming, but the fear upon waking was as acute as ever, with Freddie's taunt still ringing in her ears: *You're a loser, Jen*. Traumatic though it was, she might have to accept the truth in that comment.

While she showered and dressed, she attempted to picture Charlie living a healthy, happy life in Greece, and had to concede that it wasn't out of the question – certainly once he'd adjusted to the reality of growing up without his mother. For his sake, she had to hope it would be a swift transition.

But for herself, whether she went to prison or not, the thought of trying to build a new life on her own, trying to endure a daily existence when the centre of her world had been ripped away from her. . . it was impossible to visualise.

If only she hadn't agreed to the holiday, or handed over Charlie's passport without at least getting something in writing. But when Freddie had sprung the idea on her, she'd been too preoccupied by her arrest to recognise the dangers. In that moment it seemed she had been robbed, quite unwittingly, of all control over her son's future.

The earliest Yvonne could see her was midday. Rather than sit around fretting, Jen decided to get some shopping done. She felt slightly nervous as she emerged from the building, but assured herself that Russell Pearce was long gone. Alex Wilson and his cronies seemed to have backed off, and why wouldn't they? From their point of view, it was mission accomplished.

The car ahead of her on the steep downhill ramp into the Marina was an old Honda saloon. It had joined the ramp from the opposite direction, beating the lights by the underpass and slotting in front of Jen at a comfortable distance. Once round the corner it accelerated downhill. Seeing that the two-lane road was clear all the way to the roundabout at the foot of the ramp, Jen matched the Honda's speed.

And then it braked.

Jen automatically touched her own brakes, expecting the Honda to speed up again, but the red lights stayed on, tyres screeching as the driver braked harder than ever. Jen tried to respond in time but she was too close, and taken by surprise. She felt the tiniest of bumps as she came to a halt, not even enough to trigger the airbags or cause any sort of jolt to the Honda. *A near miss*, she thought with relief.

The Honda driver was opening his door, while a woman in the passenger seat turned to stare over her shoulder. Jen released her seat belt, checked the outside lane was clear, then got out.

'The fuck you doing?' the man shouted.

'Me? You're the one that stopped for no reason.'

As he examined the rear of his car, the passenger door opened. The woman who climbed out was fiftyish and scrawny, with an orange complexion and studs in her nose and lip. The man was a similar age, short and wide and brutish. He was twisting a signet ring on his finger and muttering something abusive.

'You're meant to keep a safe distance,' the woman snarled, and started prodding at the phone in her hand.

'You gonna call the police, love?' the man said.

Jen crouched to look at the cars. 'There's no damage.'

'Can't say without a proper inspection.' The man was uncomfortably close, his knee almost touching her shoulder. Jen stood up and backed away. A car rolled towards them, the driver's head on a stalk.

'Anyway, there's injuries to think about.' The woman put a hand on the back of her neck, and sucked in a breath.

'Yeah. Could be whiplash.' The man turned on Jen. 'Hope you're insured?'

'Yes, I am.' But her heart was thumping now. Freddie had said something about his policy covering other drivers, but he was notoriously uninformed about such matters.

'Well? Who are they?'

'I don't have the details with me.' She sighed, then realised she had to stand her ground. 'The cars barely touched. There's no way it could have injured anyone—'

'You a doctor, are you?' the woman sneered. 'An orthopaedic surgeon?'

'Might be. It's a pricey motor, so either she's earning a packet – or her old fella is, and she pays him back in other ways.'

They both sniggered. A couple more vehicles crawled past in the outside lane. Jen heard grumbling through an open window, and said, 'We're causing an obstruction. We need to move.'

'*If* it'll start again. We've had cars shunted before that ended up being write-offs.'

'That's crazy. There isn't so much as a scratch, look.' She wiped her finger along the dirt-encrusted rear of the Honda. 'This is a scam. You braked for no reason to cause an accident, and then claim on my insurance.'

The man was shaking his head, but grinning. 'You're guilty, love. No doubt about it.'

'*Guilty*?' Something snapped inside her. 'Did you say I'm guilty?'

'Yeah.' The woman snorted. 'Rich bitch.'

Jen staggered slightly. She pointed an accusing finger at the man before her. 'You're working with them, aren't you – Alex Wilson? Sam Dhillon? Well, I know what you're up to and I won't let you destroy me, so pass that message on and get the fuck out of my life!'

She hadn't realised she was yelling, or that she'd advanced on the man so furiously that he'd backed away. He looked astonished, but Jen should have been paying more attention to his companion.

With a vicious smirk, the woman was filming Jen on her phone, even moving in for a closer shot as Jen wheeled round and got into her car.

'Looney tunes, love,' she said, and the man, recovering his composure, shouted, 'You're supposed to exchange details. We'll report this to the police!'

'Yeah, you do that.' Jen slammed the door, backed up without thinking to check the mirrors, then carved into the outside lane and roared past the Honda. The woman was still filming.

A car behind blasted its horn, the driver tailgating her all the way to the roundabout. Was that because she'd cut him up, or was he in on it, too?

Abandoning all thoughts of shopping, she went around the roundabout and back onto the exit ramp, accelerating hard until she was content that the car behind wasn't following. Once out of the Marina, she took a few random turns in Kemptown, hoping to throw off any other pursuers, then drove on to the city centre and parked in one of the large multi-storey car parks for Churchill Square.

Her heart rate still hadn't returned to normal as she switched off the engine and buried her face in her hands. *What have I done?*

She sat there for a long time, wrestling with the doubts. Maybe the people in the Honda weren't anything to do with Alex Wilson.

Perhaps it was a coincidence: a couple of lowlifes who spotted a woman alone in a valuable car and saw a chance to make some money from a fraudulent claim.

Or maybe the driver genuinely had overreacted to something in the road, and Jen simply hadn't been paying enough attention. If they were innocent, and decided to take this further, Jen knew she was in big trouble.

Eventually she stirred, walked up to the shopping centre and used the public toilets to clean up and make herself look a bit more presentable. Even then, there was a glint in her eye that told of something not quite right: a woman on the verge of a breakdown. Feeling light-headed, she bought a bottle of Coke in WHSmith, worried she might flake out if she didn't keep her sugar levels up. She didn't want a repeat of Saturday.

At the solicitors, the receptionist gave her an uneasy smile. 'I think Yvonne's still with someone.'

'I'm fine to wait.'

Jen chose a magazine at random and left it open on her lap, a useful prop while she dipped her head and looked inward instead. She fought off images of Charlie, playing right here in the waiting room last week. More and more it felt like she'd betrayed him, by what she'd done or had failed to do—

'Oh, Jen.'

Tim Allenby emerged from the hallway, a heavy folder under one arm. He looked slightly perturbed, perhaps thinking he'd forgotten about a meeting, so she said, 'I'm here to see Yvonne.'

'That's a coincidence, but quite useful, I suppose.'

The doubt evident in that phrase didn't bode well, Jen thought. She cleared her throat. 'Actually, there's something I need to tell you.'

'Yes, same here.' He checked his watch, then nodded. 'Pop on back.'

*

In his office, he waved her to a seat and said, 'I won't leave you in suspense. It's not good news, I'm afraid.'

Jen sat down and pressed her hands together on her lap. 'Okay.'

'I just had a call from DS Howard. They'd like you to attend at Hollingbury, tomorrow morning at eleven, where you'll be charged with theft and burglary.'

Jen gaped at him. 'But I only saw her yesterday, when they asked me about Russell Pearce. She didn't give any hint. . .'

'No. Talia was apologetic about that. It seems the decision has come from on high, so she had no more advance warning than anybody else.' He opened his hands. 'I expect the officers on your case are now assisting with the murder investigation – this unfortunate neighbour of yours – so it's a matter of clearing the decks.'

Jen snorted. 'The minor stuff.'

'From their point of view,' he conceded. 'To us – to you in particular, of course – it's a lot more significant than that.'

'Just slightly.' She lifted a trembling hand then let it fall away, the purpose of the gesture forgotten. 'There's no possibility of a mistake? The appointment wouldn't be to tell me they're *not* going ahead with it?'

'I'm sorry. She was very clear. They intend to charge you.'

CHAPTER FORTY-FIVE

Gerard's first reaction: cold hard panic. It had two components, and each one had to be brutally suppressed. There was fear for Charlie, his only grandchild and a boy who probably meant more to him than Freddie had ever done. Then the greater fear: for himself.

Seen through the lens of self-preservation, the two people present now were not his sulky underachieving son and his Irish spinster housekeeper: they were potential witnesses whose reactions and expectations had to be skilfully managed.

All this took less than a second to compute. His quick mind had leapt straight to the worst-case scenario, from which he could work his way back to the soothing possibility that Charlie was simply crouching by the steps outside or hiding in the doorway of the next house along.

'He won't have gone far. Come on.'

Freddie ran for the door, yelling Charlie's name as he dashed into the street. Gerard concealed his disapproval; even this little public spectacle could be harmful. The fucking *Grauniad* would give anything to make him look stupid.

But he played along, after snatching a bushman hat from the hall. Freddie went one way, Gerard the other, and he sent Siobhan across the road to the gardens in the centre of the square. That was the most obvious location. Plenty of grass to run around on, trees and benches to hide behind.

Gerard reached the corner of Endsleigh Place and scanned in both directions. No sign of Charlie, or anyone carrying a small boy; no one reacting to any kind of struggle. Conclusion: he wasn't here.

He trotted back, regarding it as beneath his dignity to run. Freddie was at the opposite corner, and nearly got mown down when he drifted into the road for a clearer view. Car horns prompted a few pedestrians to turn and stare, as did the sound of Freddie bellowing his son's name.

If they hadn't been in the centre of London, strangers would no doubt have come to their aid, or at least asked what was wrong. Gerard was glad of the public indifference, but didn't want to push his luck.

He drew level with his own front door and met Siobhan returning from the gardens. 'I can't see him,' she moaned, the tears rolling down her cheeks. 'I really don't think he'd go that far.'

'Me neither,' Gerard said. 'Let's search the house again. Maybe he crept from one hiding place to another – down the back stairs, for instance?'

This suggestion was a godsend, offering her some much-needed hope, and more importantly getting her back inside. Gerard didn't believe a word of it, of course, but that wasn't relevant. Siobhan was persuaded: one down, one to go. . .

Gerard beckoned to Freddie, who came at a run and immediately started ranting: 'Why are you just standing there? We have to get help, raise the alarm.'

'Not till we've searched the house again. Imagine if he's inside a wardrobe, and then I'm the butt of jokes on *Mock the Week*.'

'Fuck your image, Pa. My son is missing!'

'If he'd gone outside to hide, we'd have seen him, wouldn't we?'

Freddie was almost doubled over, panting for breath and exuding an air of barely suppressed hysteria that was drawing attention from the tourists and students who infested this area in fine weather.

'What if he's been abducted?'

'Within a minute or two of stepping outside?' Gerard gave a scornful laugh, conveniently ignoring the many times he'd warned in print that a paedophile did indeed lurk on every street corner. 'He hasn't been abducted, I promise you that.'

'How can you be sure?'

'Wisdom. Experience. Let's go in and help Siobhan with a proper search.'

He was unaccustomed to physical contact with his son, but slapped a hand on Freddie's shoulder and guided him through the doorway. Siobhan was stomping around on one of the upper floors, calling for Charlie in a distraught voice.

'Listen,' Gerard said quietly after shutting the front door. 'If he isn't here, there's another possibility that we have to consider.'

Freddie gave him a raking, distrustful glance. 'What?'

'Jen. Maybe Charlie got a message to her somehow, and she came up here and snatched him.'

Incredulous, Freddie said, 'She wouldn't do that.'

'Christ, you're gullible. She's capable of anything, especially now she's desperate.' He blocked another objection, growling, 'We'll discuss it in a minute. Now search the ground floor and the basement.'

He hurried upstairs and had a good look in the bedrooms and bathrooms on the second and third floors, then intercepted Siobhan as she hurried down from the top of the house. Sobbing now, she said, 'He's not here, sir. I'm so sorry. Will we get the police involved?'

Gerard raised a hand, smiling gently. 'It's fine.'

A gasp. 'You've found him?'

'In a manner of speaking.' He produced his phone. 'I've just spoken to Jen. The dispute over custody is heating up, and it turns out she'd instructed Charlie to sneak out and join her. They're on their way to Victoria station right now.'

'Oh, but that's so cruel.' Siobhan pulled a tissue from her sleeve and blew her nose. 'Nearly gave me a heart attack, they did.'

'I know, and you can bet our legal team will raise this with the judge.' He placed a calming hand on her elbow; nowhere more intimate, because he found her unappealing. 'I want you to take the rest of the day off. Get yourself home and have a large gin and tonic.'

He didn't wait for her response, because his plan required her to be gone before she had the chance to compare notes with Freddie. He bounded downstairs, feeling strangely energised, and found his son in the kitchen, peering into the shadows of a rarely used larder.

'I think I know what happened.' That got his attention: once again Freddie looked almost capable of violence. 'Go and wait in my study. Siobhan mustn't hear this – for your sake, as much as anything.'

'Why not?'

Gerard heard movement on the landing above them. He and Freddie went up and let the housekeeper say her farewells. As they returned to the study, he found himself concluding that 'worst case' was now the only scenario in town. He suppressed a yawn – caused by tension, but Freddie was unlikely to see it that way.

'What did you tell her?'

'That he ran off with Jen.'

'Bullshit.'

'It might not be.'

'You don't believe that.' When Gerard said nothing, he lifted his phone. 'I'll call her right now and we can find out.'

'No.'

'Why not?'

'Because if she doesn't have him, she's liable to panic.' He could see Freddie had guessed the answer; he just wanted his father to say it.

'And she'll call the cops. Which is exactly what *we* should be doing.'

'We can't, Freddie.'

'I don't want to hear it. Every second we waste—'

'We'll go to prison,' Gerard said quietly. 'Both of us.'

'You know who's taken Charlie?'

Gerard went to shrug but opted for a nod. 'I have a fairly good idea.'

Freddie's reaction was as decisive as it was unexpected. 'In that case, you can tell the cops when they get here.' He started tapping on the phone, hunching his shoulders as if putting up a barrier.

'Don't be so stupid.' Gerard grabbed the first thing that came to hand – a heavy marble paperweight – and hurled it at his son. It struck Freddie on the jaw, and he tumbled out of his chair with a cry of pain. A spray of blood hit the carpet.

Gerard dived for the phone, getting there just as Freddie scrabbled to retrieve it. They tussled for a moment, then Gerard shouldered his son aside and stood up, victorious. As he turned the phone off, Freddie cringed away from him, crying through a mouthful of blood. 'Have you gone insane?'

'No police.' Gerard shoved the phone in his pocket and stood over Freddie, his demeanour as threatening as he could make it. 'Charlie will be fine, I promise you. But we have to sort this out ourselves.'

CHAPTER FORTY-SIX

Jen was still dealing with the shock when Yvonne Cartwright joined them. After listening to Tim's update, she grasped Jen's hands in hers. 'I won't pretend this is anything but bad news, and yes, it's potentially a setback in our attempts to secure a good arrangement for Charlie. But you've also got to try and be positive, if you can.'

Jen could only nod glumly. There had been times in her life when an inspirational pep talk had renewed her will to overcome obstacles, and she'd given such talks herself on occasion. The adventure tours had invariably included one or two participants who had to be coaxed to stay the course. But right now she wasn't sure that any amount of encouragement could overcome the twin agonies of prison and losing Charlie.

Yvonne was keen to stress the many variables that could determine the final outcome. 'At our end, we'll delay and obfuscate as much as we can. A short custodial sentence, if that's the worse we're looking at. . .?'

A glance at Tim, who made a seesaw gesture with his hand. 'I'd hope no more than six months served, at a maximum.'

'There we are, then. Hopefully we can string out the negotiations beyond that time, and perhaps we'll get a judge who's sympathetic to your circumstances.'

'The verdict itself is not a given,' Tim reminded them. 'Firstly, I think you'll make a terrific witness, Jen. Aside from that, all sorts of things can go wrong for the prosecution – evidence disappearing or wrongly labelled, witnesses who fail to turn up or crumble under cross-examination. They carry the burden of proof, remember.'

Yvonne patted her arm. 'And how is Charlie? He's with his dad this week, yes?'

Jen nodded. She felt sick. 'They're in Crete.'

'What?' Yvonne almost shouted. 'When did that get arranged?'

'Last week. Freddie had been talking about a few days in Cornwall. When he sprang it on me, I'd just been arrested, my emotions were all over the place and stupidly I agreed.' She shuddered, thinking of Gerard and his vile taunts. 'He's promised to bring Charlie back by tomorrow.'

'I wish you'd told me about this.' Yvonne exchanged a worried glance with her colleague. 'I'll speak to his solicitors and make sure he knows to stick to the agreement.'

'But if they decide to stay in Greece. . .?'

'I won't lie to you. We'd be at one hell of a disadvantage.'

'They played me for a fool,' Jen murmured, her voice cracking with emotion. 'And I'm afraid that's not all.'

She described the minor collision at the Marina, and the altercation that followed. She felt herself blushing as she admitted to the accusations she'd made: that the couple were part of a conspiracy that included Alex Wilson, and a man who had asked her out in a bar.

She explained about Sam Dhillon's connection to Wilson, and how it had led her to Jonathan Oldroyd. The more detail she gave, the more she expected disbelief, but Tim seemed to perk up as she recounted the infiltration at SilverSquare.

'Much of that should be verifiable, especially if the police get involved. We might at least have circumstantial evidence of a connection between the various players, enough to damage Wilson's credibility as a witness.'

'Except cases involving forensic examination of computers can take an age to come to court,' Yvonne pointed out, 'and they're a bugger to prosecute.'

Tim shrugged. 'This is all about creating doubt. It's worth a try.'

They mulled that over for a moment, before Jen returned to this morning's incident. 'What if this couple aren't involved, and they go to the police?'

'It could mean a failure to stop and give your details,' Tim said. 'That's potentially six points on your licence, as well as a fine. But I suspect it's the civil action they're interested in. It certainly bears the hallmarks of a personal injury scam.'

Yvonne was more worried that Jen had been caught on film. 'If they put it on social media and somebody happens to identify you, it could make life very unpleasant. I dread to think how a judge might react to footage of you committing road rage.'

They talked it through some more, Jen's emotions a churned-up mess, and then Tim said he had to be at a meeting. Yvonne suggested they move to her office, where she made some notes of the conversation and once again urged Jen not to feel too despondent.

'You look shattered. Are you working?' When Jen shook her head, she said, 'Then get yourself home and try to rest. Like I said, I'll try to put the fear of God into Freddie's solicitors. What time is his plane due in tomorrow?'

'I'll have to check.' She sniffed. 'Hopefully not till the afternoon, if I've got to go to the police station at eleven.'

They agreed to catch up later, then Yvonne gave her a hug and Jen hurried out, feeling like an emotional basket case. The bright sunshine, the noise and bustle and holiday cheerfulness all around her was painfully at odds with her own dark foreboding.

Taking a ten-pound note from her pocket, she walked the length of North Street, searching for the homeless man who'd helped her on Saturday, but he was nowhere to be seen. Back at the car, she checked her phone, longing for a message from Charlie.

There were no texts, but she had an email with an odd header, in capital letters: *YOUR BOY*. The sender was using a Hotmail address with an anonymous name: *bestfriend808*.

A junk message, had to be. She dropped her phone on the passenger seat and started the engine.

Then hesitated. After the past week, nothing could be dismissed so easily.

She opened the email, which was brief enough to read in a single glance.

Dear Jen,
Please don't worry. Charlie is safe with me.
Your friend.

CHAPTER FORTY-SEVEN

With a measure of calm in place, Gerard sat Freddie on a chair and examined the wound. There was a laceration on his chin, and another extending from his lip to his cheek, neither of them deep enough to require stitches. A large bruise was forming on his jaw, and he reported, in a quavering voice, that a couple of his teeth felt loose.

'They'll firm up again,' Gerard told him. 'I, uh, I shouldn't have thrown that so hard.' It was the closest he intended to come to an apology; keeping his manner brisk even while he escorted his son to the nearest bathroom to clean and dress the wounds.

He encouraged Freddie to swallow three ibuprofen and several mouthfuls of good brandy. Whereas booze tended to make Gerard loud and belligerent, he knew that his son was a mellow and soft-hearted drunk.

Mellow *and* malleable, he hoped.

'Couple more of these, and then a lie down,' he said, taking a swig from the bottle himself.

'And what good's that gonna do Charlie?' Freddie let out a sudden anguished whine: 'He's all I've got!'

'That's quite offensive, Freddie. Why do you think I'm doing this, if not because I care about you and the boy?'

Freddie grunted. 'So tell me, what *are* you doing? And how are we gonna find Charlie?'

'What's happened today is linked to Jen, I'm convinced of that. Think about it: Charlie is a smart kid. Very smart. I don't see him just wandering off with a stranger, do you?'

Freddie shook his head morosely. 'I hope not. But he's also very trusting. If someone was friendly, and said the right things. . .'

'As it happens, that fits my theory – because if it wasn't Jen who came for him, it could be somebody working on her behalf.'

'But why? And how would she even know he was here? She thinks I'm still in Greece.'

Gerard pondered. 'I may be able to check out her involvement, without tipping her off—'

'How?' Freddie snapped. Then he groaned. 'You're spying on her?'

'In a manner of speaking.'

'What, by the people who set her up to get arrested?'

'Freddie, will you settle down. It helps no one to start flinging accusations around. All I'll say is that I took some bold decisions to secure the future that you and Charlie deserve.'

'Yeah, but I didn't ask you to, and all that's happened is we're in the shit and Charlie. . . Charlie is. . .'

Overcome, he started blubbing like a two-year-old. Gerard wanted to order him to toughen up, but the situation called for something more diplomatic. Grasping his son's shoulders, he said, 'Go and rest for an hour. By then I should have some answers.'

'And if you don't?' Freddie mumbled something about the police, which Gerard pretended to treat seriously.

'If I don't, I'll take it up a level. That's a promise.'

*

As a precaution, he gathered up the landline phones. He was tempted to lock Freddie into the first-floor bedroom, but maybe that was a step too far. Instead, when he returned to his office on the ground floor, he left the door wide open so he'd hear the moment Freddie got up.

Sipping at a small brandy, he devoted all his concentration to this one grave issue. Charlie wasn't the kind of lad to run away, but if by some chance he had, his nerve would eventually fail him, at which point he'd know to head for the nearest police officer or responsible-looking adult.

That was fine. If the cops turned up with a contrite little boy, Gerard would exude charm and gratitude, sign a few copies of his latest book and all would be well.

The far more likely option was that he'd gone off with somebody, and whoever took him must have had some way of gaining Charlie's trust. How?

Because they were already known to him? Perhaps a friend – or *boy*friend – of Jen's?

The timing puzzled him. It had to be an opportunist act, since no one had known he was coming here – Christ, Gerard himself hadn't known till Freddie turned up on the doorstep. So. . .

'The bastards were already watching me,' he whispered.

It was agreed that communication would be kept to a minimum. The operation had been running for over six months, and in that time they'd spoken on only a handful of occasions. But he'd already had to make a call the day before, in the aftermath of Jen's sudden visit.

He used a cheap, anonymous mobile phone, reserved for this bit of business and nothing else. Hugo Hamilton answered as though he was expecting the call, which raised another red flag in Gerard's mind.

'Your unwanted visitor yesterday?' Hamilton drawled. 'I'm afraid she may have made a connection between Alex Wilson and one of our other staff. Somehow she identified the hotel where he was staying and lured him out. Sam later talked to a chambermaid, and it seems that she tricked her way into the room.'

'What the fuck. . .?'

'Mm. Quite the daredevil, which is not something you mentioned in the brief.'

'She's a frigging ex-tour guide who now shows dimwits how to climb a plastic wall!'

Hamilton made a dismissive noise in his throat. 'Well, fortunately there was nothing of use to her in the room. But it means that Sam has been burned, so our hopes rest with the chap who's been tasked with the slow seduction.'

'Which has achieved bugger all, so far,' Gerard fumed. 'What about that other name I gave you, Russell Pearce? Why did the police want to talk to her about him?'

'That, I haven't been able to ascertain. But he's nothing to do with us, I can assure you.'

'For God's sake, you ought to know how this man features in her life. Are your people still tracking her?'

'Uh, periodically. We know she went to Kent on Sunday, possibly in search of the artist who made the—'

Gerard exploded: 'How much closer is she going to get? This is not what I fucking paid for!'

'Calm down. She won't have got anything useful. At this stage it's simply not viable to be on her twenty-four hours a day.'

'Sheer bloody incompetence,' Gerard muttered. 'Right, I need you to find out where she is now. Can you do that, at least?'

Hamilton called back shortly afterwards. 'She's been to her solicitors in Brighton. Is that what you wanted to know?'

'And she doesn't have Charlie with her?'

'I thought he's with your boy, in Greece?'

'Nice try, Hugo. The trouble is, I recall a conversation we had, long before I required your services. In such a delicate line of work, you told me, your activity is all about giving one party the upper hand over another. But that also means, as a by-product, giving *them* the upper hand over *you*.'

'What of it?' Hugo's tone of dry amusement sounded decidedly forced.

'To counteract that, you proudly described how you make a point of digging into the secrets of the party who hired you, just in case the relationship goes sour.'

'Well, yes, but I see no reason for that to happen here.'

'So you're not keeping a watch on me?'

'What? No.' A minuscule hesitation, but a pertinent one.

'Look, enough of this hogwash. Charlie's missing. Freddie brought him back here this morning. Within ten or fifteen minutes he'd sneaked out of the house and vanished.'

Silence, and then a haughty sniff. 'Gerard, my dear chap, we are not in the practice of abducting children.'

'Do I have your word on that?'

'Of course. Good grief. . .' Then he asked, warily, 'Have you notified the police?'

'Not yet – and in the circumstances I'm reluctant to do so, for obvious reasons. The problem is that Freddie's going out of his mind. There's only so much reassurance I can offer, and it isn't going to satisfy him for long.'

'No, I see. Leave it with me and I'll make some enquiries.'

Which, to Gerard, sounded like a tacit acknowledgement that he'd been right all along. Hugo *had* assigned people to keep an eye on him. Unsettled by the conversation, he gulped the last of the brandy and considered whether Hamilton was now a busted flush – or worse still, holding back on him.

The next call was to an even older, shadier acquaintance – shadier in terms of his past career, rather than his current lofty position in the House of Lords.

Gerard outlined the situation. His contact felt that Hugo's people were 'competent enough' and trustworthy 'up to a point'. Alarmed by these qualified terms, Gerard said he was anxious to establish exactly where he stood.

'My impression is that his crew are white collar. I need someone who'll get answers in any way necessary, and won't baulk at difficult situations. I also have to know if Hugo is minded to betray me.'

With a grunt of comprehension, he was told: 'As it happens, I know just the chap to provide some "enhanced verification". A former freelancer, bit of a rogue, but effective – almost *too* effective at times, if you get my drift?'

'I think I do,' Gerard said. 'And that sounds perfect.'

CHAPTER FORTY-EIGHT

It couldn't be genuine. No way at all. But clearly it was from somebody who knew about her circumstances – most probably Alex Wilson or one of his colleagues. This was a bluff. Another angle of attack.

What they wanted was for her to panic, Jen realised. She mustn't give them the satisfaction. Charlie was with his dad – she had no reason to doubt that.

But she called Freddie just the same, needing to put her mind at rest, and groaned when it went straight to voicemail. She left a message, asking him to call her right away, and for good measure sent him a text as well, then sat and waited. What were the chances of a prompt reply?

Not great, as it turned out. After a few minutes she sent a second text and a message on WhatsApp, then drove home with frequent apprehensive glances at the phone on the seat beside her.

It was almost one in the afternoon when she reached Henley Gardens. Jolted by the sight of a police car, she realised she hadn't given a thought to Russell Pearce for hours. It was a reminder to stay on her guard, so she was cautious on her approach to the building, and listened carefully for movement on the stairs. She heard a shuffling, wheezing tread, and identified it as Bridie Martin. Jen caught up with her neighbour as she reached the top floor. The old woman was out of breath but excited.

'I've just had to give a statement,' she declared. 'That feller on the corner, murdered his wife?'

Jen swallowed. 'Yes. Isn't it terrible?'

'Well, he was round here Sunday afternoon. I caught him snooping, and he only had the brass neck to claim he was a policeman. He was trying to find out more about you and your, er, bit of trouble. Burglary, he said.' She sniffed. 'Of course, I saw through him right away, and sent him packing. Didn't know then what a lucky escape I'd had.'

'Why didn't you tell me he'd been here?'

Bridie looked uncomfortable. 'I've not really seen you, have I? Besides, I wasn't to know he was a maniac.' A shudder. 'I'm sleeping with a big knife by the bed at the moment, and you ought to do the same.'

Jen agreed that they would keep an eye on each other until Pearce had been caught. As she opened her front door, she thought – *Russell knows about me, he knows about the divorce* – and then: *It couldn't be. . . could it?*

No. Russell Pearce had more important things to worry about than sending malicious emails. He was a fugitive, his face all over the newspapers and TV. But Bridie had made a good point: maybe they'd *both* had a lucky escape.

There was still nothing from Freddie. She rang again, got voicemail and left a message: 'Call me as soon as you can.'

She took a shower and then, still restless, set about making a smoothie from some fruit that was past its best. The minutes slowly passed. She resorted to wading through Facebook, particularly Ella's profile, and then the rest of the girl's social media, hoping for something to confirm that Charlie was safe with his father in Greece. But apart from a few comments added to her friends' posts, Ella hadn't been very active. Too busy enjoying herself, perhaps.

There was one other option. She phoned Gerard on his landline, hoping he might have a number for the villa. No reply. She had a mobile number for him listed on her phone, which she hadn't used for a couple of years, but tried it anyway. Nothing.

'Where the hell are you?' she cried. Then she trawled through her Gmail account and located his email address. Wrote a brief message: *Gerard, I've been trying to contact Freddie and he's not replying. Do you know how I can reach him? Please call me.*

She knew she shouldn't be getting agitated, but after everything that had happened over the past week, it took only the most minuscule of doubts. . . And now there was little she could do but sit and worry, or pace up and down and worry, or maybe go out for a run – and worry.

She went out for a run.

When he received the email, Gerard turned Freddie's phone back on and watched the messages stacking up. Jen was trying frantically to get in touch, which was quite some coincidence. Was she calling to gloat? *I've got him back! Charlie's mine again, suckers!*

Gerard fought the urge to respond. He couldn't bear the idea of Jen getting one over on him. His instinct in such circumstances was always to go on the attack: a show of overwhelming force out of all proportion to the act that had incited his response. He'd done it to a few woolly-headed female journalists over the years – once with some vicious comments about rape that might have ended his career, had he not been able to rely on most of Fleet Street to play it down.

He brooded for a while, then thought of a way to test the water. Using Freddie's phone, he composed a message: *Hey, Jen. Charlie and I are hiking in the Patsos Gorge. Signal not great here but we're having lots of fun. C sends his love x*

He tried to add one of those damn emojis that he'd raged about in more than one column, but the tiny images defeated him. How the hell did you even work out what each one meant?

He was close to hurling the phone across the room when he heard movement. He sent the text, then dropped the phone on his desk just as Freddie shuffled in. With his tousled hair and his cheeks lined from the mattress, he looked like a forlorn little boy, an image that briefly plucked at Gerard's heart. If only they could go back to when Freddie was Charlie's age, he thought; have their time over and do a few things differently. . .

'I'm hoping this is just a bad dream.' Freddie's voice was distorted by the swelling around his mouth; he sounded like he'd had a root canal treatment. 'Who were you texting?'

'Jen.' Gerard saw no advantage in lying about it. 'I want to see what she knows.'

'Did she contact you – I mean me?'

Gerard decided to ignore the question. 'I've got somebody on the case now. He's come recommended from a chap who was once very senior in the security services.'

'And what about the people who were employed to frame Jen? Is that their background?' Without waiting for an answer, he added, 'What if one of them took Charlie?'

'I don't see why they would.'

Freddie sneered. 'The same reasons you claim anyone does anything. Money and kicks.'

'It's unlikely. They're being well remunerated.'

'So what? If these guys specialise in fucking up people's lives, is it really a stretch to think it's a job that attracts psychos?'

Not much Gerard could say to that; Freddie was more perceptive than he had credited. 'I have a lot of faith in this new man to get results. I know it's difficult, but we have to be patient—'

'This is my son!' Freddie shouted. 'And your beloved "Chip", the grandson you're meant to adore!'

'How dare you!' Gerard matched his anger. 'All of this was for *his* benefit, not mine. But one wrong move now and it'll come to light – the conspiracy against Jen – and if that happens, we're ruined. I meant what I said about prison. And you're not immune, believe me.'

'But I haven't done anything.'

'It won't look that way,' he muttered.

Freddie gave a start. 'Why, are you going to frame me as well?'

'Just think on this: if I'm disgraced, I lose my income. And if I lose my income, I'll make *damn* sure you lose yours.'

That, he thought, should be sufficient in terms of a threat. Softening his tone, he said, 'More importantly, we'll both lose Charlie forever.'

'But we've already lost him. Bloody hell, Pa—'

'*No*. I won't give in to that sort of negativity. No one has any reason to hurt him. It's just a matter of time until we find out where he is.'

The phone buzzed. Freddie eyed it, perhaps trying to gauge whether he could make a lunge across the desk.

'You need to cool down,' Gerard warned him. 'Start thinking rationally.'

He picked up the phone. A text from Jen: *Can you call me, please? I have to speak to Charlie. It's urgent.*

This was what he'd feared – replying had only encouraged her. But it had to be a bluff, didn't it? Or a way of opening negotiations.

'What is it?' Freddie asked.

'Nothing.'

Jen hadn't run very far when the text came through. She skidded to a halt on the corner of Sussex Square and read the message quickly, then studied it in more detail.

Freddie and Charlie were out exploring Crete: all well and good. But surely the tone was a little too nonchalant? Wouldn't Freddie have guessed there must be something wrong, or at least wanted to know why she was bombarding him with messages?

Something wasn't right here.

She looked around at the quiet street; a couple of cars and a van rolling past. The outside world made her feel more vulnerable than it had a week ago. She didn't like it.

She jogged back to the flat, running through the possibilities, and decided on a dual course of action. First, a text to Freddie: *Can you call me, please? I have to speak to Charlie. It's urgent.*

If he really was hiking through a wilderness, it might be a while till she heard anything. So her next move was an email to this mysterious bestfriend808: *My son is with his father. This silly tactic isn't going to work.*

To her astonishment, the reply was almost immediate:

Jen, I'm disappointed in you. Haven't you worked out that you can't trust Freddie or his father? They're together right now in London.

This was a lot harder to dismiss than the first email, the tone so casually knowledgeable that it couldn't help but strike a chord. It had an authenticity that Freddie's text was lacking.

But she wasn't quite ready to reply; instead she called Freddie. Voicemail, again. Furious, she sent a text: *Either I speak to Charlie now or I'll go to the police.*

CHAPTER FORTY-NINE

Gerard saw the phone light up and immediately declined the call. Freddie wanted to know why she was trying so hard to reach him. 'Do you think she's heard we're back here?'

'How would she?'

'You tell me. You're the one spying on her.'

Gerard shook his head. 'You drank too much of that brandy.'

'Well, come on. Explain why you're so happy to place all our hope in this one guy we don't even know.' Freddie gave a choking sob. 'If Charlie's missing, we need help from the police, the TV, social media. . .' He shut his eyes, swaying a little in his seat. 'I feel shit. Need some water.'

Gerard went to his aid but Freddie jerked his shoulder away: *Don't touch me*. He got up and tottered out of the room; exaggerating his symptoms, Gerard could see, just like when he was a boy. Pitiful.

It took a few seconds for Freddie to realise that Gerard was just behind him. 'So you don't trust me to go anywhere?'

'I'm worried about that impulsive streak of yours.'

'You are one mean-spirited bastard, do you know that? You've never had any respect for me.'

'Freddie, it's less than three months since that episode with the cocaine and those not-quite-eighteen-year-old girls. I still shudder to think of the favours I had to call in to keep the lid on it.'

In the kitchen, Freddie slurped some water and dribbled the rest of it down his chin. He took more painkillers, then started rooting in the cupboards. 'I need some food. I feel guilty, being hungry at a time like this, but I can't help it.'

'Your motto: "*I can't help it!*"' Gerard mocked his son's whining voice. 'Have a sandwich – don't stuff your face with chocolate.'

'You haven't got any. You're as bad as Jen, with all her healthy regimes.'

'It's in the fridge. And don't liken me to that woman.' Disgusted, Gerard took Freddie's phone from his pocket and saw there was yet another text.

This one chilled him: *Either I speak to Charlie now or I'll go to the police.*

'Shit,' Gerard muttered. 'I need you to talk to Jen.'

'Make your mind up. You said—'

'This is different.' He sighed. 'It's possible she wasn't involved in Charlie's disappearance.'

'I bloody told you that! You never listen.'

'Yeah, well, I don't like the fact she's badgering you. We need to know why – but without giving anything away to her.' Gerard raised an eyebrow. 'Think you can manage that?'

Jen nearly dropped her phone when she saw Freddie's name in the display. She fumbled to connect and lifted it to her ear. 'Thank God. Where are you?'

'I told you, didn't I? We're out for a walk – trekking, I mean, so I might lose the signal at any time.'

'Okay.' There was something odd about his voice; he wasn't forming his words clearly. 'Can I talk to Charlie?'

Freddie made a doubtful humming noise. 'I'm not sure. He's really moody today, I dunno why. I think it's cos he's coming home tomorrow.'

A little dig there, but Jen let it pass. 'Please see if he will. It's important.'

Freddie grunted, but didn't ask why. She heard him call Charlie, and then nothing. He must have the phone clamped to his chest.

Jen frowned. Why would he try to prevent her from hearing anything?

Then he said, 'Sorry, Jen. He just won't. But you'll see him tomorrow, it's not the end of the world.' His voice had thickened with emotion, sounding even stranger than before. And there was a kind of vibration in the background, which subliminally felt wrong for the location she was picturing: rocks and trees, and the chirp of crickets. . .

'Hold the phone out for a second.'

'What? Why?'

'I want to call to him. Even if he tells me to get lost.'

'Bloody hell, Jen,' he grumbled. 'He's more likely to say nothing.' But she sensed the phone being moved away from his body, and she strained to hear a muffled comment, or even just the sound of Charlie breathing.

'That's traffic, the rumbling sound. . .'

'Jen, I'll be home tomorrow—'

'It's city traffic, for God's sake! You're lying to me.' And then, virtually screaming: 'Where's Charlie?'

She made out a brief scuffle, an exclamation from Freddie and then, before the call was disconnected, what might have been the growl of an older, deeper voice.

Gerard.

Had she just heard Gerard?

'You fool!' With Jen's cry still reverberating from the speaker, Gerard snatched the phone and cut the call, and when that wasn't enough to satisfy his rage, he threw it at the wall and saw the cover and battery come flying apart.

'Pa!' Freddie took a step towards the phone but Gerard shoved him into a chair.

'Good old Freddie Fuckitup!' he roared. 'Everything you do, all the silly ambitions – it doesn't matter how much I help out, I give you advice and connections and money galore, and *still* you make a hash of it, every fucking time!'

After that outburst, silence. Freddie sat with his head bowed, gently massaging his jaw, while Gerard reassembled the phone. He had no desire for further contact with Jen, but he needed to monitor what other messages she might send.

He envisaged her going to the cops, in which case he'd have to stow Freddie somewhere safe, then dream up a damn good explanation for Jen's allegations. But his hope was that Hugo's team had left her feeling too frightened to risk being taken for a lunatic.

If she did keep quiet, even for just a matter of hours – maybe a day or two at most – there was a good chance that normality would be restored, and the original plan brought back on track. Prison for Jen, and a new life in Greece for Charlie and his grandpa, and maybe for this miserable waster sitting here. . .

Gerard's sigh prompted a sorrowful look from Freddie. 'So what now?'

'We wait.'

'And I'm your prisoner?'

'If you want to be that melodramatic. Where else would you go? Charlie might come back at any moment.'

'No, he won't. And you're doing nothing to find him.'

'My contact understood the urgency of the situation. And I'm sure the chap he's recommended will be on to it at once.'

Jen knew there was no point trying to speak to Freddie again, or Gerard for that matter. Right now she wouldn't believe a word they told her.

She had to act.

First she sent an email to bestfriend808: *Prove you have Charlie.* She resisted the urge to add all sorts of curses and threats; this was enough.

Then a quick change of clothes: smart jeans and a white tailored shirt, an outfit designed to look respectable – and therefore bolster her credibility – should she need to go to the police.

She'd left the flat and was racing down the stairs when her phone buzzed – but it turned out to be a notification from one of the pressure groups she supported, warning of the damage to bee colonies from neonicotinoids. An issue she felt strongly about, but not the message she wanted right now.

The phone remained silent as she drove to the station. Her heart rate started to settle. She'd called his bluff. This was no more than some miserable little troll, trying to mess with her head.

She was turning into the car park when a reply came in. She swung the Audi into a space, grabbed the phone and saw that the message came with an attachment.

For a second she froze. All manner of hideous images flashed through her mind. Could she bear to look?

She opened the message, scanning the text for ugly or violent language; saw no obvious threats and went to the attachment. Deep breath.

It was a photograph, taken in what was clearly a McDonald's, but beyond that there were no clues as to the location. Charlie had the remains of a Happy Meal on the table in front of him, along with a model of a bright red Porsche 911. The packaging for the toy lay next to the tray of food.

Charlie faced the camera, wearing a slightly uncertain smile. He didn't look truly happy, but nor did he seem particularly scared or upset. Even so, the sight of him caused Jen to groan with pain at their separation. Charlie looked to be unharmed, but was he really in the custody of a stranger?

She wondered if the photo was a fake. There was no way of telling when it had been taken, but Charlie's face was lightly tanned, and he was wearing one of the T-shirts she'd packed for Greece. That pointed to it being recent, and genuine, as opposed to something lifted from social media.

She returned to the message: *Charlie is thrilled with his new car. He's happy that I'm looking after him on your behalf. You need to know the truth about the plot to discredit you. Be at the Jubilee Bridge, on the steps next to Embankment station, at 5 p.m.*

Then a line break, and a final message: *Please don't take this the wrong way – it's not intended as a threat – but going to the police will be truly bad for us both, and a disaster for Charlie.*

'Not intended as a threat.' Jen swallowed. The shock had her reeling but she couldn't afford to lose control now. She shut her eyes, pressed her head back against the seat and took a series of long, slow breaths. This wasn't the time for a kneejerk reaction: she had to think calmly, clearly, and work out what to do next. Whatever was best for Charlie.

But how would she know what that was?

CHAPTER FIFTY

They got lucky with Stemper. He was at his house in Brentwood and had nothing in particular to occupy him at the moment. He'd been all but retired for several years, though always open to offers.

In this case the job was close at hand, and promised to be quick and easy. It was also extremely urgent, which meant top dollar. Stemper had far more money than he knew what to do with, but he derived a particular satisfaction from being lavishly rewarded for work that he would have done for free, for the sheer pleasure of it.

Much like the monarch – for whom he had a great deal of respect, and in whose name, ultimately, he had performed some extremely grisly deeds – Stemper had a choice of residences, placed at strategic locations around the British Isles. Not palaces, in his case, but comfortable boltholes, none of which could be traced to him.

Most were tidy, anonymous bungalows, like this one in Kings Crescent. Brown tiled roof, pale bricks, uPVC windows and a gleaming white garage door. The front garden was paved over, and home to a four-year-old Nissan runabout. Nothing to attract the slightest bit of attention.

He was almost set to leave when the doorbell rang. Mrs Stott, from two doors away. Widowed in her fifties, she was a decade or more his senior, somewhere around seventy now; overweight, a little stooped, but otherwise well-groomed and pleasant-looking. At one time she had considered him a candidate for second husband, or failing that a regular antidote to loneliness. He'd scotched both ideas immediately, but they remained on superficially friendly terms.

A fan of stating the obvious, she declared: 'Ah, you're here! The airline hasn't whisked you away to distant parts.'

'It's just about to,' he said, indicating the briefcase on the floor.

'They work you too hard, Mr Stemper. A man at your time of life should be winding down. . .'

'Smelling the roses?' he suggested, with a knowing smile. 'Now what can I do for you?'

'Oh, it's dear Molly, AWOL again. That cat will be the death of me. Could I ask you to keep an eye out, perhaps check your shed?'

'No trouble at all. I had the mower out this morning and didn't see her, but I'll make absolutely sure before I depart.'

She unfurled a sheet of paper. 'And I've made some posters – not very professional, I'm afraid, but if you wouldn't mind. . .?'

'It will have pride of place in the living room window.'

'Oh, thank you. It's so nice that you actually care.' She gave a disparaging glance at the property next door. 'Some of them round here turn their noses up, and almost seem to think it's funny.'

'Declining standards, Mrs Stott. There isn't the community spirit you saw when I was a boy.'

He soaked up a remark or two in the same vein before easing the door shut on a genial exchange of farewells. He'd been talking pure nonsense: the only 'community' in his boyhood had been the flimsy, ever-changing alliances between a bunch of washed-up comics, shaky-handed magicians and obsolete all-round entertainers like his father, the lot of them scrabbling for the meagre pickings to be found on the variety circuit of the fifties and sixties. Not much appetite for community when a whole way of life is dying before your eyes.

Which wasn't to say he regretted his upbringing: far from it. Many of the skills that were essential to his trade had their origins in his peculiar, painful childhood, not least the ability to adopt an appropriate persona for any given audience. Aging had helped considerably in that respect, too: his bland, grey exterior was like an inexpensive canvas on which a variety of characters could be deftly imprinted.

A few more items to collect, and he was ready to go. He had no need to check the shed, because late last night he'd caught Molly digging in his rose bushes. It had been simple enough to lure the animal into the house, after which he'd strangled it, removed the limbs in the pursuit of scientific enquiry (he regarded himself as a keen amateur surgeon) and buried the remains in a bare patch of earth where he intended, some time next year, to plant more roses.

His interest in the assignment was enhanced by the fact that the first target was familiar to him. They'd never actually spoken, but their career paths had crossed a few times, to the point where Stemper was confident the man would know of him – and of his reputation. When time was of the essence, that offered a considerable advantage.

And so it proved. He'd been given the address of a substantial mock Tudor pile in one of those leafy enclaves that might be in Bucks, or Herts, or Beds: even some of the residents were never quite sure which.

The security was naturally more than adequate, beginning with high locked gates and entry via an intercom. Eschewing a clandestine approach, he rang the buzzer and spoke to a woman who had what he thought was a Vietnamese accent. Stemper supplied his name, and there was a lengthy delay before the gates creaked open.

He drove along a gravel driveway and pulled up at the house. The target waited in the doorway. Hugo Hamilton was taller and thinner than he remembered, but otherwise precisely what Stemper expected. Aged about sixty-five, he wore tan-coloured cavalry twill trousers and a tattersall shirt with a pair of reading glasses poking from the breast pocket. He had thinning red hair slicked back from his brow, and he stood with a rigid military bearing.

As Stemper got out of the car, Hamilton thrust his chest forward, as if to receive a medal. 'I know you, don't I?'

'You may well do.'

A grunt. 'Who sent you?' The question was more cautious than cantankerous. *He remembers me.*

'One of your ops hasn't gone to plan. I think you already appreciate the problem. There was a phone call earlier today.'

'Gerard bloody Lynch? He employed you?'

'Not directly.' Stemper named the man who had recommended his services, and Hamilton looked a lot more perturbed.

'Are you the one involved in. . .?' He referred to a notorious incident in the mid 1980s, the full details of which were known to fewer than a dozen people. Stemper confirmed that he was, and noted the ensuing loss of colour from Hamilton's face.

'I'll tell you now, Mr Stemper, I don't know anything. So whatever your intentions are, you're not going to succeed.'

'Oh, I'm sure you can help far more than you realise.'

'Look, we've done our utmost to fulfil the brief. As I told Gerard, this latest glitch has nothing to do with my people.'

'That's yet to be established beyond doubt.'

'I assure you, no one who works for me is going to kidnap the client's grandson. It's utterly counterproductive.'

'But you were watching the house?'

Hamilton shook his head, even as he admitted to it. 'You'll know as well as anybody, it's purely a matter of covering bases. Gerard has nothing to fear from me.'

Stemper was unmoved. 'Who was it?'

'No idea. I'm hardly likely to get involved on that level, am I?'

'Then who's leading the operation?'

There was a hesitation, and then surrender. 'Chap called Alex Wilson. He was with Five for nearly a decade, perhaps you know him?' When Stemper gave no reaction, he said, 'Not a bad operative, a sort of gifted second-rater.'

'I'll need a full debrief from him.'

'Well, yes, I suppose. . .' Ruefully, Hamilton shook his head. 'What a conniving little prick. Gerard, I mean. Didn't think he could be as vicious as that rancid column makes him appear, but there we are. . .'

'Bad form to misjudge an opponent, old chap,' Stemper said drily, aping the other man's high-born manner.

'He was never classed as an opponent,' Hugo countered. 'I'll bet this kidnapping is completely unrelated, you mark my words. Odd things sometimes happen, you know that. Just in the last few days there's been a murder, scarcely a hundred yards from the daughter-in-law's home.'

'A murder?'

Hamilton noted his consternation, and said cheerfully, 'This is my point. Not everything revolves around the dark master of the diatribe.'

'Tell me what happened.'

'Just a messy domestic: some oddball killed his wife. The police seemed to think he may have been sniffing around Jennifer Cornish. Now he's on the run. Russell Pearce.'

Stemper had heard the name on a news bulletin this morning. He regarded Hamilton with contempt. 'So Pearce showed an interest in your target. He killed his wife, his whereabouts are unknown – and now Cornish's son has gone missing?'

Hamilton blanched. 'Hold on a moment. If you're implying—'
'Call Alex Wilson. I need an urgent meeting.'

CHAPTER FIFTY-ONE

Jen made it onto a train at just after three in the afternoon, opting for a Thameslink service that gave her a choice of stops across London. En route she would have to decide whether to follow the instructions and be at the bridge for five, or first confront Gerard.

Her supposed benefactor had warned her not to involve the police. If Charlie truly was missing – and Jen was still clinging to a possibility that the emails were fake – she didn't think she could abide by that warning. But she also had to consider what she could tell the police – very little of substance, at present – and whether she was likely to be taken seriously.

As the train drew close to Gatwick, it suddenly occurred to her that the whole situation might have been concocted to provoke an overreaction. She would raise the alarm and send the cops rushing round to Gerard's, only for them to find Charlie safe and well, enabling Freddie's lawyers to depict her as hysterical and vindictive. She couldn't risk going to the police until she'd verified the situation with Freddie.

If the messages were genuine, then the demand to meet in London made sense, given that she suspected Freddie was at his dad's house in Bloomsbury. And if Freddie had lied about being in Greece, had he also lied about having Charlie with him? Jen could hardly countenance the idea that Freddie – and Gerard – were aware that Charlie had gone missing, but were attempting to conceal that information from her, and presumably from the police. If true, it was a monstrous betrayal.

Soon afterwards, the train was halted by some sort of issue further along the line. The hold-up lasted ten minutes, and for nearly half an hour after that they limped along at the speed of a horse and cart, through East Croydon and into South London.

Jen sat and stewed, her anxiety gnawing its way deeper into her soul with every passing second. There wasn't enough time to go to Gerard's first and still make it to the rendezvous. If the train carried on at this speed she might not even get there for five o'clock, and then what would happen? The messages hadn't convinced her that Charlie was safe.

Cautiously, as if hedging her bets, she sent one more email: *If you're on my side, tell me who you are and how you got involved in this.*

Her phone lit up almost immediately: a call from an unknown number. It must be him – or *her*, she thought, realising she'd automatically assumed that bestfriend808 was a man.

The voice that greeted her was male, and seemed familiar – or sort of familiar. 'Jen, I'm really sorry. It's a fuck-up – *I*'m a fuck-up – and you should never have—'

'Freddie? Slow down, please. You sound slurred. Are you drunk?'

'Drunk?' He made a noise that might have been a sob. 'Probably, yeah. But that's not why my voice. . . Pa threw something at me, cut my mouth open.' Another explosion of air: definitely a sob. 'He's crazy, Jen. The stuff he's done. . .'

'Where's Charlie? That's all I want to know.'

'I didn't wanna do it, Jen. I'm gonna pay.' Freddie was, for the most part, a cheery soul, but if things were to take a turn for the worse, he could wrap self-pity around him like a comfort blanket. 'I deserve to be punished.'

'Freddie, I need to know if you lied to me. Are you in London?'

'Yes.'

'You came back early, you and Charlie?'

'Mm.'

'What? Is he there with you now? You've got to let me talk to him.'

For a few seconds he sounded too upset to speak; then he blurted out: 'Pa took my phone away. I found this one in a bedroom, but if he catches me. . .'

'What do you mean? You're a grown man. Tell me what's happened. Where is Charlie?' She caught other passengers staring at her, picking up on the strain in her voice.

Freddie continued as if he hadn't heard her: 'He's talking about prison. For both of us. I'm sorry, I'm the worst dad—' She heard him wince, and in the background a door banged open. 'Ah, shit,' he hissed. 'You've got to help, Jen. No cops. You're his only chance—'

And the line went dead.

Stunned, she turned to look out of the window and dimly registered that the train had picked up speed. Freddie's garbled plea seemed to confirm that the emails weren't fake. *Someone had Charlie.*

The thought hit her like a body blow, but at almost twenty to five there was nothing she could do now except head for the bridge. The priority was to get Charlie back safely in her possession, and then involve the police to find out what had happened.

When the train finally pulled into Blackfriars, she had about fifteen minutes to get to the Jubilee Bridges. According to the map on her phone, they were only about a mile away, but in the fine weather the Victoria Embankment was choked with traffic, pedestrians and bikes. Still better than risking the underground at this time of day, she thought.

After a dangerous slalom run along the road, she reached the rendezvous point at a minute to five. There were streams of people on the bridge. As she climbed the steps, her phone buzzed – an email, which told her to cross to the south bank and then wait.

Jen groaned. Was somebody just playing games with her?

Then she considered the timing of the message. Whoever had sent it might be watching her, right now.

She turned in a slow circle, examining the faces of everyone she could see. No one seemed interested in her, and yet she felt her skin crawl, and had a sudden sense of foreboding. *The emails are from Russell Pearce; he's already killed Charlie, and I'm next—*

The vision of that fate was so powerful that her legs nearly gave way. But it spurred her into action; she pushed forward across the bridge, immune to the glorious views on either side but instantly suspicious of anyone who paused to admire them. She kept her phone unlocked, ready to dial 999 at the first indication of trouble. Up here it was busy enough to be safe, but what if the next instruction tried to lure her somewhere quieter?

The adjacent railway bridge was noisy with the clanking, screeching progress of a train. Someone jostled her, bumping shoulders, and she gave a yelp – that could have been Pearce, sneaking in close to plunge a knife into her, before melting away in the crowd. Nowhere was safe.

The Royal Festival Hall loomed ahead, but Jen was only about halfway across the bridge when she received another email: *Turn and come back to Villiers Street.*

She was being taken for a fool. But what choice was there but to go along with it?

Another train rumbled past, braking with an ear-splitting scream. Jen's heart was thudding, causing her to breathe in rapid gasps. She followed a march of commuters along the narrow walkway through Embankment Place and had almost reached the escalators when somebody spoke quietly in her ear: 'Hello, Jen.'

She jumped, at first unable to identify the voice, but in the half second it took to turn and see who had lightly taken hold of her arm, she came up with a name and a face.

It was Dean.

CHAPTER FIFTY-TWO

Alex Wilson agreed to meet Stemper, but insisted on choosing the location. That turned out to be a Costa Coffee in Croydon. An aggravating drive at this time of the day, but he managed to be there ten minutes early.

He bought a bottle of water and found a table that allowed them a measure of privacy. Wilson turned up soon afterwards. He was an unimpressive looking man with lank grey hair, pallid skin and bloodshot eyes. Perhaps emboldened by the public location, his tone was combative from the start.

'Is Hugo bringing you in over my head?'

Stemper acted bemused. 'Why would he do that?'

'Because of the client, wanting the fucking moon on a stick. I've worked my arse off on this case, and just when it's almost done. . .' He tailed off, perhaps detecting Stemper's lack of interest in his tirade.

'I don't work for Hamilton.'

Wilson gave a dubious nod. 'Right.'

'But I do work for your client.' Stemper smiled at the other man's confusion. 'Think of me as a kind of auditor. I'm here to review your operation and determine what's gone wrong.'

'Who says anything's—'

'If I'm here,' Stemper calmly interrupted, 'you can be sure that something needs fixing.'

*

Jen stared at Dean. She was shocked, but also – for a millisecond or two – absurdly relieved. At least it wasn't Russell Pearce.

She craned to look behind him. 'Where's Charlie?'

'He's safe. But he's not here.'

'I thought you'd be bringing him back.' Her voice cracked. 'Where is he? Why have you— ?'

'Hey, hey.' He went to put a comforting arm around her, and she was too disorientated to resist. 'I know how distressing this is, but he's fine, don't worry. My mum's looking after him.'

'Where?'

'She lives in Luton.' He nodded towards the walkway. 'Why don't we find a cafe? I have a lot to tell you.'

He started moving but she pulled free of his grasp, forcing him to turn back. 'How did you get Charlie? He was with his dad.'

'They fobbed him off on a servant, from what Charlie told me. He said Grandpa was nasty to him. He saw me from a window, and I waved.' Dean smiled fondly. 'He's a very bright boy. He suggested a game of hide and seek, which gave him the chance to come outside and say hello.'

'And then you snatched him? There's no way Charlie would willingly go with a stranger.'

'But I'm not a stranger,' Dean said reprovingly. 'He knows me from the Skyway.'

'No, he doesn't. You've been, what, eight or nine times, and Charlie wasn't there.'

'That was the climbing wall. I've been to other parts of the centre, and one day Charlie was in the cafe, on his own, and I chatted to him for a while. I had a game on my phone that he was interested in. Then I saw him a couple of weeks back in Queens Park, when he was there with Lucas. I had my "girlfriend" with me – though I told Charlie she was my sister.'

There was an amused tone to his voice, but to Jen it was a shattering revelation: more proof that she'd failed as a mother

– dragging Charlie to work when childcare wasn't available, neglecting him to the extent that he could form a connection with a stranger without her being aware of it.

'So you've been spying on us? Stalking me and my son?'

'No. Don't make it sound sleazy.' He shivered. 'I admit that I had a small role in this horrible plot against you, but not any longer. I'm on your side now.'

'Who do you work for?'

'*Did*,' he corrected. 'A man called Hugo Hamilton.'

Jen frowned. The name meant nothing to her. 'And what about Alex Wilson? Sam Dhillon?'

Dean was nodding sadly. 'All of us, I'm afraid, recruited to turn your existence into a living hell.'

'But why? Is it Gerard. . .?'

'I'm afraid so. You've defied his wishes for Charlie's future, which in his eyes means you've picked a fight – and he's a man who can't bear to lose anything, ever.'

'So just because he's not getting his own way, he's trying to destroy me?'

'Never mind "trying".' Dean sounded angry on her behalf. 'He's very close to succeeding. But I know how we can stop him.'

In a brusque, resentful tone, Wilson ran through the plot against Jennifer Cornish. The objective was simple enough: to give Freddie Lynch the upper hand in their dispute over custody of their son. But the practicalities of achieving that objective were another matter.

'Do you have any idea how frigging hard it is to manipulate a law-abiding person into committing a crime? We kept laying out the bait, and the bitch kept refusing to take it.'

'Why not just kill her?' Stemper asked. 'It's simple enough to make it look like an accident.'

Wilson seemed to think he was joking, because he chuckled and said, 'There was one day I nearly ran her over by accident – Christ, I wish I'd done it.' He described how she had finally been lured into a scenario that saw her arrested for criminal damage. 'The day it happened, watching everything slip into place, that was a corker.'

'Let's move on to the failings. How exactly did she identify the conspiracy?'

Wilson went bright red, and his knee started juddering against the table. 'That was the client's fault – he was always pushing, wanting more. After the burglary we should have backed right off, but we'd been running multiple streams, you know? One of them was to use sex to trash her reputation.'

'And how would you do that?'

Wilson gave a sly smile, as if he'd detected a prurient interest in Stemper's voice. 'We had two guys working to get close – one a right flash bastard, the other a geek, playing a longer game. Well, all of a sudden she seemed to be interested in the good-looking one, Sam, so we thought, *yes*!' His eyes were shining with excitement. 'The plan was to use a secret camera, get her on film having sex – ideally in a few, uh, *creative* positions – and then stick it up on some amateur porn sites.' He paused to take a breath. 'But there was a backup plan, in case she didn't want to jump straight into bed with him.'

'Rohypnol?'

Wilson scowled. 'Good guess. Only someone said, if we're gonna drug her, why not make it more interesting – go for the full gangbang. As long as we wore masks, we could all get stuck in.' His regretful laugh told Stemper exactly who he meant by 'someone'. 'That was gonna be our exit bonus, except the bitch rumbled us, somehow. Pretended to make a move on Sam, only to go snooping at the hotel where he was staying.'

'I expect seeing him with you didn't help?'

Wilson's shoulders slumped. 'So Hugo told you? Well, he's at fault there, not putting enough people on to it. Had us grafting like navvies, he did.'

Stemper made no comment. 'I'll need to speak to your colleagues. Now, tell me how Russell Pearce entered the picture.'

Momentarily confused, Wilson said, 'The neighbour? I dunno much more than what's been in the news.'

'But he came up on your radar?'

'Only as some perv on the corner, who used to watch her walking past. After that, we kept an eye on him.'

'Who did?'

'Whoever was assigned to it. Mainly Dean, I think.' Wilson had an edge of panic in his voice. 'I admit, we were a bit worried that maybe he'd seen a few comings and goings at the house. But a guy like that, with his own secrets, he wasn't gonna go to the cops or anything, was he?'

'Might have been wise to make sure.'

'That's what Dean said. And yeah, maybe we would've, in time.'

'Who's Dean?'

'The one that was playing the long game. Not that he stood a chance.' He snorted. 'Looks normal enough, but definitely a sandwich short of a picnic, you know?'

Stemper sat forward. 'Where can I find Dean?'

'Er. . .' Wilson scratched his head. 'He's supposed to be in London today, on another case—'

'Watching your client.'

'Nah, I don't think so.'

'Save it. Hamilton's admitted that he covers all the bases.' Stemper gave a thin smile. 'What do you mean, "supposed to be"?'

'Nothing. Just. . . I called him a couple of times, and he's not answering his phone.'

CHAPTER FIFTY-THREE

The cafes in Villiers Street were too busy for Dean's liking, so they found a dark and gloomy pub, the narrow interior so oppressively hot that virtually all its patrons were standing on the pavement outside. Dean encouraged Jen to have a stiff drink, but when she insisted that a Diet Coke was fine, he ordered the same for himself.

The few minutes it took to order and get settled at a table were an agony of frustration. Jen was thrumming with a nervous energy that meant she couldn't sit still. Dean regarded her with an air of exasperation, and said, 'You've got nothing to fear from me. Quite the opposite.'

'How do you expect me to take your word for that? You've kidnapped my son.'

He pouted at her. 'If that was true, I'd hardly be here now, would I?'

'I want Charlie. That's all I care about.'

'I know. Just hear me out, and if you still feel the same, you might as well call the cops and have me arrested.' He held out his arms, the wrists facing upwards as if to receive handcuffs. 'Once I've explained, I think you'll agree that kidnapping Charlie – or hurting you – are absolutely the last things I'd ever do.'

His gaze was earnest, his voice gentle, with a slight accent that she thought might be from the North West, maybe Cheshire. He had a squarish face and wavy brown hair, parted at the side.

His eyes were pale, a greyish blue, and they implored her to believe him.

But Jen wasn't prepared to give in. She crossed her arms and said, 'I have to speak to Charlie. If you can't prove he's safe, I'm not interested in a word you say.'

'There's no need to be like that.' He took out a phone and made a call. While he waited, he ran a forefinger along his upper lip, wiped the sweat onto the leg of his combat trousers and blew out his cheeks. 'Hot in here.'

Jen didn't respond. All that mattered was the call. But Dean tutted, and shook his head. 'Sorry. She's a bit notorious for ignoring the phone, but I'll try again in a minute.' He brightened, still tapping at the screen. 'In the meantime, you'll enjoy this. Look.'

He showed her a video, which seemed to have been taken at the same time as the photo he'd sent earlier. Charlie was delving into his box of French fries, while saying, 'I'm not allowed to have this every week – not with Mum, anyway. Dad's okay about it, but Mum says it's junk.'

Off screen, Dean responded: 'I'm sure that's because your mum cares about your health.'

Charlie nodded with what Jen took to be reluctant acknowledgement, only to embark on a little speech: 'I wish I could be more like her. When I want something that's bad for me, I find it really hard not to have it. But Mum can be strong and go without – it's how she's got to be so fit and she can climb up mountains and walls and stuff, like Spiderman. She's amazing.'

He stopped abruptly, looking slightly bashful; Jen could hear Dean chuckling as the clip came to an end. Quickly she turned away, covered her face with her hands and bit into her bottom lip until it was close to drawing blood.

She'd never known Charlie to express such admiration for her, so to hear it now, in these circumstances, was completely destabilising. She hadn't seen him, held him, kissed him for days, and she felt that loss and longing in every cell of her body.

It would be all too easy to cry her eyes out, but Jen was determined not to succumb. In less than twenty-four hours she was due to be charged for a crime she hadn't committed, and this man across the table was claiming he could help her.

'All right,' she said. 'I want to know how you came to be involved in this.'

'It's a job, that's the simple answer. One I've become more and more ashamed of.' He told her that he'd had a varied career, starting as a police officer in Manchester, then working in the security industry before joining a 'government organisation' – though he turned vague about which department and what, exactly, he did for them. Most recently he'd opted for a more challenging role in the private sector.

'Industrial espionage?'

His eyebrows went up. 'Go on.'

'There's a company in London, called SilverSquare. They're another of your targets, aren't they?'

'You'd make a good detective, Jen.' He conceded that this was indeed among the services that Hamilton's company offered to its clients, and admitted that the job wasn't always easy on the conscience. 'Not something that troubles my colleagues, to be honest.'

'But you're different?'

'I didn't used to be, until you. The doubts started creeping in when our efforts drew a blank, but still we had to keep pushing.'

Jen frowned. 'What do you mean?'

'There were various different things. A few tempters, like a car left with the engine running. You ignored it. Then a handbag with the purse visible – you only noticed it once, and handed it straight in.'

'In the cafe? That was a set-up?'

'Yes. And it proved you were a good person, not easily corrupted.'

'That's what I tried to tell the police,' she said sadly. 'Though you got me in the end, didn't you?'

Nodding awkwardly, he mopped his brow and said, 'We'd spent weeks preparing the ground with Alex, making sure you kept seeing him. It was a nightmare to coordinate.'

'So what was the point of him carrying boxes in and out?'

'So you'd be curious. It's human nature to love a mystery – you see somebody with a big box and you can't help but wonder what's inside. We did dry run after dry run, until we were certain you'd spot the keys falling but wouldn't be able to raise the alarm till he'd gone. Having him collected sped things up a bit, but even then the first attempt failed.'

'The first attempt?' she repeated. 'I don't understand. The loss of the keys was reported to the police, the day before I found them.'

'There was a lot of debate about whether we could risk doing that again. The first time, after you'd walked straight past, Alex had to call the cops – and the Skyway – and tell them he'd found his keys, false alarm, blah blah. We took a chance that the next time round, a week or so later, he'd speak to someone different and no one would think anything of it. And when we saw you popping into work on the Sunday afternoon, it was too good an opportunity to miss.'

'But what if I'd just taken the keys along to a police station, or put them through the letterbox?'

'Then we'd have tried other things instead. From what I heard, the operation had a six-figure budget. All kinds of ideas were bandied about.'

His tone had turned distinctly ominous. Jen's hand trembled as she set her glass down. The scale of the plot against her was difficult to comprehend.

'Putting the broken figurine in the bin – that was to tempt me into stealing it?'

Dean was squirming. 'I'm embarrassed to say this, but I used to admire the thoroughness. Like sprinkling bits of wire and glass over the floor, so forensics would find evidence in the soles of your shoes. The aim is to construct an alternative truth, detail by detail, until the target can no longer distinguish between what's real and what's false.'

'I thought I was going mad,' Jen said. 'I genuinely started to wonder if I was guilty, and had somehow suppressed the memory.'

'That's not uncommon – and it's very much part of the plan. Each little lie nudges the victim closer to madness, collapse, surrender. . .'

'How do you do that to someone?'

She'd made an effort to keep the loathing from her voice, but still Dean flinched. He sat rigidly straight, and wiped more sweat off his lip.

'The fact is, the targets are often extremely unpleasant themselves. They're greedy, sneaky, dishonest, and they've invariably cheated people who are now using us to get back at them. But I recognised that you were different: not a malicious bone in your body. I saw that you're a loving parent, I saw the bonds you form with your customers at work – like that boy with special needs?'

'Oscar.'

'Oscar. The care you take with him, the affection. . .' He sniffed, and looked close to tears. 'I knew I couldn't do it anymore. I couldn't let *them* do it.'

'So why didn't you warn me? Or sabotage their efforts?'

'Because they're very dangerous people. There's this rule – of deniability – that's built into everything we do. But it doesn't mean any of us can just down tools and walk away, let alone try to rebel.' His gaze flicked nervously towards the doorway. 'If they find out I'm betraying them, I'm a dead man.'

*

Dean's initial plan had been more subtle. His boss, Hamilton, always had an insurance policy, which in this case meant trying to dig up some dirt on Gerard. 'We had to watch the house occasionally, so I managed to juggle the schedules to get a few shifts there. I was hoping for an opportunity to go inside and search for something to use against him.'

And then, out of the blue, Freddie and Charlie had turned up.

'Freddie needed money for the taxi, and Gerard was in a steaming temper. I thought then that Charlie might be in danger, so when he saw me and came outside, I acted on instinct and told him I was a friend of yours.' He looked down, shyly, and mumbled, 'Well, a bit more than a friend, that's what I hinted. And he asked if I could take him home.'

Jen's heart ached at that. 'Why didn't you? Just get on a train and come to Brighton?'

'Because, like I say, there's our safety to consider. They're keeping tabs on your movements, you know that? Gerard told Freddie he should lend you his car, because they'd put a GPS tracker on it.'

'You're joking?' It was an automatic response, but she was already remembering what Freddie had said: it had been Gerard's idea to lend her the Audi. And if the same organisation had planted child porn on somebody's computer, fixing a tracking device to a car wouldn't pose much of a problem.

'I'll check when I get home,' she said, wondering if this would call his bluff, but Dean nodded fiercely.

'You should. Lately they've eased off the surveillance, because it was clear you knew about them.'

Jen realised that he'd gone from describing the gang as 'we' to 'they'. She took a sip of her drink, then said, 'You know, I was actually quite relieved when I saw you.'

His eyes lit up. 'Were you?'

'I got it into my head that it might be a neighbour of mine. He's on the run, after killing his wife—'

'Russell Pearce.' Dean spat the name out. 'I saw him once or twice. A total loser.'

'And a psychopath. It scares me to think he'd been coming on to me, pressuring me to go for a drink.'

'I wouldn't have let that happen,' Dean muttered, and then added, 'I knew something wasn't right about him.'

'It's dreadful.' Better to fall back on platitudes than admit to the part she might have played in tipping Pearce over the edge. 'Could we try to phone Charlie again, please?'

Dean looked slightly peeved, but dialled the number. This time someone answered promptly. 'Mum, it's me. I called earlier and you. . . Oh, okay. Don't worry. I'm with Jen here – Charlie's mum. She just wants a word with him, can you. . .?' He paused to listen, then grinned, and clicked his tongue. 'Oh, is he? No, okay. That would be a bit mean. All right, bye.'

Jen had to resist the urge to grab the phone from his hand. 'What?'

'He's asleep. Zonked out, apparently.'

'But it's not even six o'clock!'

'He was in Greece this morning, remember. Different time zone – not to mention all this drama and excitement.'

He was right. Jen's first impulse was to demand that he call again and get his mum to wake Charlie up, but then she imagined how that might upset him. Wasn't it a good thing that he'd managed to fall asleep?

She sensed Dean studying her, and said, 'He's not usually that comfortable with strangers. Are you sure he's all right?'

'He's fine. Good as gold. You saw him on the video, didn't you?'

That gave her an idea. 'Your mum – could she take a picture of him, asleep, and send it to us?'

'I wish!' Dean snorted. 'Her phone doesn't even have a camera. It's one of those clunky ones for old people, with the enormous buttons.' He smiled gently. 'Sorry. But the time will pass quickly enough. It won't be long till you're back with him.'

She only nodded, and looked deep into Dean's eyes. Could she trust this man with Charlie's life? Could she endure a few more hours without absolute proof that her son was safe?

Dean seemed to read her thoughts, leaning forward and gently grasping her hand. Her gaze was still locked on his, and it didn't seem right to pull away.

'Please, Jen. I know how painful this is for you. And if you decide right now to call 999 and let the police take over, I won't try to stop you. But I'm begging you to have faith in me, and let me help you clear your name.'

She pondered for a moment, and retrieved her hand on the pretence that she needed to wipe her eyes. Then she nodded. 'How would we do that?'

The next step, he explained, was to gather evidence. 'I'm afraid it means sending you into the lions' den.' A nervous grin. 'Are you prepared to go to Gerard's and stay there for a while – possibly overnight?'

'Overnight?' She shivered. 'Is that really necessary?'

'It would give us the best chance, by far. But if you don't think—'

'No, no. I can do it, I suppose. But why don't we fetch Charlie, and I could take him with me?'

'Not a good idea,' Dean said gravely. 'Until we have something that incriminates Gerard, it's vital to keep Charlie out of his reach.'

Jen couldn't help but look sceptical. 'They wouldn't hurt Charlie?'

'Don't be so sure. I bet Gerard hasn't reported him missing, has he?'

Jen thought of Freddie's panicked call, and shook her head. 'I don't think so.'

'There you are – that's criminal neglect. Gerard only cares about himself.' He stared at the table for a moment, then spoke quietly. 'As they grow more desperate to break you, so the risks increase. You have to be aware of that.'

'I am. I've already been through—'

'This is worse,' he cut in. 'I didn't want to tell you, but it's something you probably ought to know.' He shifted in his seat. 'Sam Dhillon was trying to seduce you for a very specific purpose. The idea was to slip you a date-rape drug, and a whole group of them were going to. . .' Now blushing, Dean shyly indicated her body. 'Gang rape, basically – it makes me feel sick just thinking about it. They intended to film it and put the footage online. Because of the drug, you wouldn't even know whether you'd been a willing participant, so they'd be able to portray you as a. . . you know?'

'And Gerard knew about this? He approved it?' As she spoke, Jen was thinking back to the conversation on Monday, and the secret obscenity of Gerard's wedding photograph.

'He must have done.' Dean cast a quick, guilty glance around the empty bar. 'The impression I got was that, short of your actual death, nothing was off limits.'

CHAPTER FIFTY-FOUR

After Gerard caught him using a spare phone, Freddie admitted that he'd been speaking to Jen, but only to put her mind to rest. Gerard gave him the benefit of the doubt, though Freddie in this state disgusted him: the boy was a snivelling, snot-faced streak of spinelessness.

And he isn't a 'boy', Gerard had to remind himself. His son was thirty-one. At that age, Gerard had been a strutting prince of the tabloid press, feted by politicians who weren't fit to lick his boots.

There was an Xbox in one of the smaller living rooms, bought for Charlie to use when he visited; after he'd taken a shower to freshen up, Freddie soon lost himself in the meaningless fervour of a racing game. If only he could apply himself so diligently to the real world, Gerard thought. He wanted to feel *proud* of his son, rather than have to change the subject whenever somebody asked after him.

The lad wasn't stupid, as was clear from his comment earlier about the type of people they were dealing with. As he'd said, their job amounted to fucking up lives – which, when it came down to it, wasn't so different from Gerard's own career. Fucking up lives was what he hoped to achieve with every rant about this or that section of society, and he'd always been relaxed about the consequences of what he said, secure in the knowledge that his victims had brought it upon themselves. Losers were losers because they deserved to be: what was so wrong with pointing that out?

As an extreme libertarian, he took the view that it wasn't *what* you did that mattered in life so much as *how* you did it. It could be skimming money from a business or fiddling your taxes: If you get away with it then you're entitled to succeed, simply because you've done it well. Why couldn't Freddie run with that philosophy, grasp the nettle and do something – anything – to make his mark on the world?

Gerard had turned to Hugo Hamilton at the beginning of the year, when his lawyers privately warned him that Freddie was likely to lose the custody battle – and Jen was going to win. Gerard knew that he couldn't accept that. He'd done his best to scupper the mediation process, virtually brainwashing Freddie to take the most belligerent stance possible, but it became clear that a far more unorthodox – and nefarious – approach was necessary.

Jen had to be defeated. Destroyed.

Except here they were, almost in September, and it still hadn't happened.

The afternoon was fading to evening when Hugo called, indignant as ever: 'Poor form, setting that Rottweiler on me. If there's a problem on our part, I would have been happy to resolve it.'

'With the bunch of clowns on your payroll? No, thanks. This time I need some real expertise.'

Gerard expected the other man to huff and puff; instead he said, in a solemn voice, 'I only hope you know what you're doing. Let a creature like that off the leash, and you can't always put him back on.'

The next call came at six thirty, by which time Freddie was locked into a FIFA game. Gerard was tidying up the article for Breitbart when his contact phoned with an update.

'Our chap's making good progress. I've suggested the two of you communicate directly from here on. I hardly need to know the grisly details, after all.'

'This man, Stemper, you're sure he can be trusted?'

'Wouldn't have suggested him otherwise. He's already confirmed that Hamilton was hedging his bets where you were concerned. More importantly, from the workforce there's emerging what you might call a "candidate of interest". Fellow by the name of Dean.'

Gerard heard the doorbell chime, and remembered that he'd sent the housekeeper home. '. . . should know more this evening,' his contact was saying.

'Good. Ask him to update me when he can.' He ended the call and hurried out, just as someone thumped forcefully on the door.

Gerard faltered. Could it be the police?

The thought made him light-headed with shock. Put him in a tight spot and he could usually talk his way out of it. But if Jen had cottoned on that Charlie was missing – or if it transpired that Freddie had admitted it to her – then he was in deep trouble. The boy should be here: he wasn't. End of story.

Unless I can keep them talking, and Freddie has the sense to hide. . .

He was discounting that possibility as he opened the door and found not the police, but Jen herself.

He gaped at her in disbelief. 'What are you doing here?'

'Don't give me any crap. I know Charlie's missing, and I know what you've been up to.'

She pushed past him, shouting for Freddie. 'Have you lost your mind?' Gerard blustered, but it was a weak attempt to regain control.

Then Freddie appeared. In Jen's eyes he must have looked a wreck, because she cried out at the sight of him. Then, to Gerard's dismay, Freddie dropped to his knees and started begging her forgiveness with all the subtlety of a guest on one of those daytime scum shows. Jen spared him a contemptuous glance before marching into Gerard's study as though this were her house, her agenda, her God-given right to take the lead.

With Freddie bumbling after her, Gerard hustled past his son, scowling as Jen dragged a spare chair up to the desk and took out her phone, which she placed on his desk with a little too much care.

'You can switch that off,' he growled.

'Sorry?' She gave a look of incomprehension that he didn't buy for a second.

'I'm not discussing any of this until you switch off your phone. I wasn't born yesterday.'

She gave a scornful sigh, but picked up the phone and held it for him to see as she powered it down. Freddie muttered something about 'craziness' but they both ignored him.

Aware that he had to seize the initiative, Gerard said, 'I've got some good people working to find out who has Charlie. I'm sure we'll have a result very soo—'

'It's a man named Dean. I've just met him, here in London.'

Freddie's eyes widened. 'Did you see Charlie?'

'No. But I'm confident that he's safe – which is why I haven't yet gone to the police. It's not for your sake, so just bear in mind the problems I could have caused you, if I'd been inclined to.'

Gerard sneered; it wasn't difficult to see where she was going with this. But it was Freddie who got in first: 'Who the fuck is Dean? What does he want?'

'More to the point,' Gerard said to Jen, 'what do *you* want?'

'What do you think? Tomorrow I have to attend the police station to be formally charged. I want those charges withdrawn.'

'There's no chance of that, not in less than twenty-four hours.'

'Maybe not, but you can have a damn good try.'

*

Settling back in his seat, Gerard adopted a patrician drawl. 'It's true that I have certain connections, but this is still—'

'I'm not talking about a favour between mates,' she snapped. 'I know you engaged the services of a man named Hugo Hamilton, whose company specialises in spying, and sabotage, and set-ups like the one that was used to frame me.'

She waited for a reaction, but he'd been challenged by far better inquisitors than her, and he simply maintained his trademark supercilious smirk.

'Where did you get all this?' Freddie asked.

'I'm surprised you don't know. Dean was one of the people employed to frame me, only he decided to switch sides and help me instead.'

'I didn't, I swear I didn't have a clue about any of it till today,' Freddie gabbled. 'This Dean – do you trust him?'

'A lot more than I trust your father.' She turned back to Gerard. 'I don't care how it happens – either Hamilton admits the whole thing was a fabrication, or he gets Alex Wilson to confess that he lied about losing his keys and smashed up the artwork himself. But however they do it, they're going to clear my name.'

Gerard wafted a hand, graciously, and said, 'Supposing I can make the charges go away, what happens then?'

'Dean's waiting for confirmation, tomorrow, that I'm okay. When he gets that, I'm going to meet him and Charlie, somewhere in the north of England.'

'Why the north?' Freddie asked.

'For safety.' Jen kept her attention on Gerard. 'He doesn't trust you not to send somebody after him. So I'll be going alone,' she added. 'I'll also be checking my car for a tracking device.'

Gerard snorted, but it was likely that Dean had told her about the GPS tracker on the Audi. He eyed Jen suspiciously. She seemed too sure of herself, almost self-satisfied, and he wondered if there was something she wasn't telling him.

'I don't like the idea of a total stranger taking Charlie to heaven knows where. Didn't you push for more information? Are they going to stay at a relative's, or a hotel, or what?'

'None of your concern.'

'So it's a kidnap?' Freddie broke in. 'I mean, he might say he's acting in your best interests, but you only have his word for it.'

'You've got a bloody nerve,' Jen growled. 'Where was your concern for Charlie when he disappeared? How come you didn't have the guts to call the police, instead of listening to this evil bastard?' She jabbed a finger in Gerard's direction, and it was all he could do not to lunge at her.

Freddie went pale and twisted away, mumbling what might have been an apology. Jen shook her head in disgust.

'For what it's worth,' she said, 'I don't think we could give the police anything that would enable them to trace Dean. And with me currently in the system as a criminal, and you two having failed to report Charlie missing, it's not like any of us would have much credibility, would we?'

'But this guy is looking after Charlie?' Freddie asked. 'You're absolutely sure about that?'

Calmer now, Jen nodded. 'He seemed fine. Dean showed me a video he'd taken, earlier today, in a McDonald's. And he'd bought him a toy car.'

'I'll never forgive myself if something. . .' Freddie gulped, then pointed viciously at Gerard. 'I won't forgive you, either.'

'I'm not admitting to anything here,' Gerard said in his most imperious voice. 'But I'll make some calls, just as soon as you. . .' He shooed them away.

'Get on with it, then.' Jen stood up. 'And once this is behind us, we're going to resume the negotiations over residence.' She turned to Freddie: 'Just the two of us. Your dad and his legal sharks can stay out of it.'

Freddie nodded. 'Fine with me.'

It's not fine, Gerard wanted to scream. But he knew it was better to stay quiet. Bide his time, and hope the good Mr Stemper rode to the rescue.

CHAPTER FIFTY-FIVE

All the time she was talking to them, Jen felt as though she were two people. One the strong and confident woman, the dealmaker, the liar. The other, wrapped up inside, was her true self: guilty, uncertain and boiling with fury. *That* Jen couldn't be allowed to show her face, or else the whole deception would fail.

But it wasn't easy to suppress her disgust, seeing how blatantly Gerard was putting his own career ahead of anything else, including the wellbeing of his grandson. Just being in his presence made her skin crawl. To know that trashing Jen's reputation mattered so much, he was able to countenance the idea of having her drugged and raped.

The confirmation that Gerard and Freddie had failed to report Charlie missing persuaded her that she'd made the right decision in trusting Dean. And although it was torture being away from Charlie, and leaving him in the care of strangers, she had to focus on the long-term goal – to prevent Gerard taking her son out of her life altogether.

On the way here she'd practised a few relaxation techniques, knowing that so much was resting on the next few hours. She had the fear mostly under control, though there were times when the armour almost fell away – as when she got up and moved towards the door, and Gerard called out: 'You left your phone.'

Her whole body seemed to jolt as if electrocuted. Gerard had a malevolent glint in his eye as she picked up the phone, a look that said, *I don't trust you for a second.* Jen offered a thin smile and left the room.

Freddie was waiting for her in the hall, fussing at the plaster on his chin. She wasn't particularly eager to talk to him, but he launched into a heartfelt apology.

'What he was doing to you. . . I'm devastated, Jen. As bad as things have been between us, I *never* wanted this.'

'When did you know about it?'

'Only today, like I said. Our conversation last night really freaked me out. I came back so I could look Pa in the eyes and see if it was true. . .'

'I can't believe you gave in to him, when Charlie disappeared. You could have fought back.'

'I did. I tried.' Freddie's voice was an octave higher than normal. After clearing his throat, he bowed his head. 'No, you're right. I'm sorry, Jen. I feel so ashamed. And I'm gonna make it up to you, any way I can.'

She said nothing. After what she'd heard from Dean, she had prayed that Freddie had known nothing of his father's evil intent, and now, after speaking to them both, she was satisfied that he too had been duped.

'Have you eaten?' he asked. 'I could cook you a meal.'

'Not hungry.'

'I understand that, but it's important. Keeping your strength up, you know.'

He could see behind the armour, Jen realised, though he assumed her pent-up anxiety was centred on Charlie, rather than on her mission here.

'Just coffee or something. Maybe a banana.'

'I'm worried about tomorrow,' he said as they trooped downstairs to the kitchen. 'I don't like the idea of you doing this alone.'

'Dean won't want to see you turn up. He's bound to think you're on Gerard's side.'

She sensed him fuming, and wondered if he was about to challenge her for taking Dean's word over his, or something equally childish. But if that was on his mind he kept it to himself, not speaking again until they were in the Gerard's spacious, handcrafted kitchen.

'At least let me drive you to Brighton in the morning.'

'I was going to get a train back tonight.'

'What's the point? You might as well stay here.'

She paused, glad that Freddie was moving towards the fridge; it gave her a second to get a fix on her reaction; find the correct shade of doubt. 'I don't know if I want to be sleeping in Gerard's house, after what he's done. I can't imagine he wants me here, either.'

'Well, that's tough,' Freddie snorted, just as she'd hoped he would. 'It saves on the cost of a hotel, at least.'

'I dunno, maybe.' She gave it a second, and added, 'I suppose, by staying in London, I'm that much closer to Charlie.'

'Definitely. Please stay, Jen. It's, like, the smallest way of making things up to you. But it's a start, yeah?'

She nodded. 'All right.'

The bitch. Thinking he would simply roll over and capitulate. . .

Gerard made the call to Hamilton, resentful that he had to indulge any of Jen's demands. 'I'm hearing that the problem is someone called Dean.'

'Hearing from Stemper?' Hamilton queried. 'Alex Wilson has just apprised me of their conversation. He says the spotlight was on this neighbour, Russell Pearce. Are you sure that *he* hasn't taken the boy?'

'Don't try and deflect responsibility. What can you tell me about Dean?'

'Not much. He's quite a recent addition, and I have to concede, the reports from his colleagues aren't particularly favourable. Keeps too much to himself, won't always follow orders—'

'What the hell were you playing at, having that kind of man sniffing around my life?'

'Look, I don't recruit from charm school. They're all miscreants, up to a point. Dean, perhaps, rather more than most.'

'How, exactly?' Gerard growled.

'That's what I'm trying to establish. You'll be the first to know, I assure you.'

'I'd better be. Now, the charges against Jen? I might need them dropped.'

He registered a little gulp of surprise. 'Not sure that's feasible—'

'If I say it has to happen, then it happens. Otherwise, the nice Mr Stemper will be paying another visit.'

'Gerard, please. Is this really what you want?'

'Of course it fucking isn't! If your people hadn't botched the job, we wouldn't be having this conversation.'

He stressed that there was no firm decision yet. Despite what he'd said to Jen, Gerard intended to hold out until the last possible moment. If Stemper managed to recover Charlie – and deal with his kidnapper – then Jen would have little in the way of leverage against him. Her talk of a conspiracy would be easy to deny, and the charges against her could proceed.

His next call was to Stemper. The voice that greeted him was more cultured than Gerard had imagined, difficult to place in terms of age, and with a smooth, hypnotic quality that he found oddly unsettling.

Once he'd been brought up to date, Stemper said, 'There are no other clues as to Dean's whereabouts?'

'Just "the North", is all she claims to know. They met here in London earlier today, but I don't think she's aware of his current location.'

'If you have Jen with you now, I could come over and find out for sure?'

Gerard disguised his shock with a laugh. 'Ha! I'd love that, but it probably wouldn't be appropriate. There are other people here.'

'Not too many witnesses, I hope?'

'Oh no, don't worry.' He cleared his throat. 'What about this man, Pearce?'

'I'm following up on that. It does confuse the issue, somewhat.'

He seemed about to add something, but chose to remain silent. Unsure what to make of his reticence, Gerard said, 'I feel that, with the position I'm in now, my options are more limited, and possibly more. . . *extreme*, if you get my drift?'

Stemper made sympathetic noises. 'Either way, I'm sure I can assist.'

In the kitchen Jen chewed down a banana that was about as digestible as cardboard, while Freddie struggled and swore over the settings for the ridiculously expensive coffee machine. It was like going back to their DIY days, Jen thought.

'Instant's fine,' she said. 'If not, don't bother.'

He finally got it working, only to discover a jar of instant coffee seconds later. He made himself a sandwich and they sat in silence for ten minutes, the tension not between them so much as all around them, sucking some of the oxygen out of the room.

'I kind of wish I'd stayed in Greece,' Freddie said at last.

Jen knew what he meant: Charlie would still be with them. But she didn't want to go there, so she said, 'Did Ella come back with you, or is she waiting at your villa?'

'Ella?' His face twitched with surprise. *Here it comes*, she thought.

'I saw a few things on Facebook. Isn't she a bit young for you?'

'She's twenty-two – but she's not my girlfriend.'

'Freddie, there's no need—'

'I'm serious.' He smiled at the expression on her face. 'She came out for a couple of days with a producer I met in Brighton. Quite small-time, but he's worked with good people. I invited him along in the hope that he might be a useful contact.'

'So why wasn't he in any of the pictures?'

'He's married. Told his wife he was in Glasgow, checking out a couple of bands. He and Ella had a huge bust-up when he thought she'd tagged him in something.' He shrugged. 'Don't think he's interested in my music – not that it matters any more, compared to this. . .'

Although she'd been wrong-footed, Jen actually felt a little sorry for him. She checked the time: ten to eight. She tried to visualise Charlie sleeping soundly in a comfortable bed, stood up and said, 'Let's see how your dad's getting on.'

Freddie nodded apprehensively. Halfway up the stairs, he said, 'Don't, uh, don't get your hopes raised too high. Something like this might not be easy to undo.'

'It should never have been done in the first place.'

'I know that. I just mean. . .' Without completing the sentence, Freddie knocked and opened the study door.

Gerard was at his desk, phone in hand. He gave Jen a leering smile. 'I've set things in motion, but it's going to take time.'

'So not before my appointment tomorrow?'

'That's highly unlikely.'

'I'll drive you down,' Freddie confirmed, as if that made up for it. Then, to his father: 'I've said Jen can stay the night.'

'Have you now?' Gerard gave a snort, before muttering under his breath, 'Got your claws back in, have you?'

Jen ignored the comment. 'How does Hamilton intend to get the charges withdrawn?'

'It's up to him. I don't need to know the details.'

He was lying, Jen thought. That's why he'd made them leave the room. Gerard wasn't about to let her off the hook – just as Dean had predicted.

'You know, I can understand your disappointment,' she said, 'especially about the part that Sam Dhillon was meant to play.'

Gerard's face creased with a theatrical display of incomprehension. 'I have no idea what you're talking about.'

'Of course you haven't.' Wearily, she turned to Freddie. 'Can you show me which room I'm having? I think I'll go to bed.'

'This early?' Freddie sounded disappointed, but Jen just nodded.

Gerard was still pretending to be baffled by her reaction. Jen had another last, despairing look around the room and then strode out.

Stay strong, she told herself. *He's lying, and you're going to prove it.*

CHAPTER FIFTY-SIX

After his conversation with Alex Wilson, Stemper fed back what he'd learned so far, along with a recommendation that tracing Dean Geary should be the absolute priority. Shortly afterwards, he received a call direct from the client.

He'd already conducted some swift research into Gerard Lynch, and was expecting a more forceful individual. The man he spoke to sounded apprehensive, out of his depth. He didn't have much to offer in the way of useful information, and Stemper quickly decided to keep his own thoughts to himself for now.

From Hugo Hamilton he obtained, grudgingly, an address for Dean Geary, which turned out to be a poky one-bedroom flat in a new-build development in Uxbridge. It also turned out to be empty. Stemper got inside without too much difficulty, though there were a couple of makeshift booby traps and a hidden camera to deal with.

Predictably, there was nothing in the flat that gave any clue as to his target's whereabouts, nor was there any significant information about his past life. Alex Wilson, however, had divulged that Dean appeared to have just one friend in the world, a man named Nolan who had once, allegedly, been a member of the special forces, but now worked as a security guard at an industrial complex in the Thames valley.

That sounded promising to Stemper.

*

He made use of his own resources to come up with an address: a terraced house in a shabby district of Reading. Wilson had been sceptical about the career in the special forces – his view was that Nolan, much like Dean himself, was something of a fantasist – but Stemper couldn't afford to make that assumption.

Instead he took his time to research, prepare, observe. Having determined that Nolan was home, and seemed to be alone, he went in at a little after two in the morning.

The lock on the back door was simple to overcome. Stemper paused in the kitchen to assess his surroundings. The fittings were poor quality, and the house reeked of beer and onions. He crept up the stairs and into the larger of the two bedrooms. Snoring like a buzz saw, Nolan was a bloated form underneath a thin, bare duvet. A Samsung cardboard box acted as a bedside table, and was home to a crushed can of Foster's and a ten-inch hunting knife.

Stemper approached the bed with a hypodermic needle in one hand and a ball gag in the other. He plunged the needle into the man's arm, and when Nolan went to cry out, Stemper shoved the gag into his mouth and rammed his head down on the pillow.

Nolan flailed and whined and choked, his limbs jerking in panic, but by the time Stemper had fastened the strap that held the gag in place, the drugs were taking effect and Nolan was little more than a mound of sour-smelling blubber.

He hauled off the thin, grubby duvet and rolled the man onto his back, holding his breath as Nolan let rip a long, stuttering fart. He gazed down at the wide eyes and bulging cheeks, the face bright red and running with sweat. Nolan glared back, a look of pure fury that morphed, as he studied his attacker more carefully, into one of absolute terror.

Stemper wore latex gloves, so there was no risk in picking up the man's knife. 'Very accommodating,' he said. 'Saves me using my own.'

Nolan screeched at him, the only sound he could make. His enormous gut quivered as he fought to move. Stemper held up the syringe.

'Ketamine and diazepam. There shouldn't be any permanent effects, though I can't say the same for this.' He stroked the tip of the knife against the whorl of hair around one of the man's nipples. 'You're going to answer some questions, quietly and politely, and then I'll leave, understood?'

Nolan managed a twitch of a nod. Even before the gag came free he was trying to speak. 'Wasn't me, it wasn't, I promise.'

'What wasn't you?'

A little flicker of confusion. 'The mess-up in Coventry – Mike Murray?'

Stemper shook his head. 'I'm here about Dean.'

Nolan looked relieved, but only for a second. Then he groaned, realising he was in no less trouble. 'What?'

'I want everything you know about him.'

'Oh, man. The guy's a bit of a tosser, but he's still a mate. You're asking me to betray him, and I know what you'll do when you find him.'

'In that case, you can probably guess what I'll do if you don't tell me.' Stemper pressed the flat of the blade on Nolan's chest, the tip pointing at the hollow beneath his Adam's apple. 'Your friend Dean has abducted a child. I want to know: where will he go and what will he do?'

CHAPTER FIFTY-SEVEN

At three in the morning Jen woke with the horrific, paralysing certainty that everything she'd been told was a lie. When Dean had rung his mother, she should have demanded to speak to the woman herself, and then insisted on waking Charlie so she could hear his voice and know beyond doubt he was being cared for.

For more than two hours she lay in torment. Calling the police now, in the middle of the night, to give them what could only ever be a confusing, disjointed account of the past week would invariably make things worse, and lead to a long confinement just when she needed to travel to the rendezvous with Charlie.

She'd made her choice; now she had to live with it. Be patient, and trust that her faith in Dean wasn't misplaced.

By morning she felt wrung out, both physically and emotionally, but in daylight some of the worst fears receded, and she was cheered by the prospect of action. A busy day ahead, starting with a vital challenge.

She had to get inside Gerard's study.

She was out of bed before seven. She knew Gerard was an early riser, but hadn't heard any sign that he was up and about. Dressing quickly, she crept from her room on the second floor and descended the stairs, gingerly testing each tread before setting her weight down.

The ground floor was silent, all the doors shut. Jen felt sick at the thought that the study might be locked. She gripped the handle and eased it down, then pushed, expecting resistance, but the door swung open to reveal an empty room.

A memory of last Monday flashed a warning: how Alex Wilson's camera had caught her intruding. But she was past worrying about a hidden camera. Dropping to her hands and knees, she peered under the desk and searched for the device she'd left here yesterday evening.

It was a small black box, not dissimilar to a USB stick. With Freddie close by when she entered the study, she'd had no chance to do anything except set it down by her feet and gently push it under the desk. When she returned after their snack, she'd managed to nudge it with her foot, so that it was concealed by the cables that hung down from Gerard's computer.

The fear of its discovery had haunted what sleep she'd had. In one nightmare Gerard had burst into her room, screaming about the betrayal of his family while he stomped the device into tiny fragments. . .

But the box was still there. She picked it up and stuffed it into her pocket. Dean had assured her that it would capture all conversation within a twenty-foot radius, but she wouldn't know until she gave it for him to analyse, or upload, or whatever it was he had to do.

She reached the doorway and heard a noise from the kitchen on the lower ground floor: the back door was opening. Jen knew she'd never get upstairs without being seen or heard, but there was a cloakroom just across the hall.

Another precious second passed while she closed the study door with the handle rather than pulling it shut, then she darted into the cloakroom and ran the tap. She rinsed her hands, dried them and came out to find Gerard by the stairs, eyeing her with suspicion.

'Morning, Gerard. You don't mind if I put the kettle on, do you? Quick coffee and I'll be out of here.'

He grunted in response, and stood aside to let her pass. Once in the kitchen, she saw a pile of newspapers, an ashtray and a cup on the table on the terrace outside.

He'd been out here the whole time, sitting just below the study window. *Holy shit*, she thought, and hauled in a breath. *Calm. Be calm.*

She could feel his scrutiny, hot and hostile, as she filled the kettle. 'You look very chirpy,' he said.

'I don't feel it.' She thought she must be radiating tension, but perhaps there was also a little more confidence now. 'I'll be chirpy when I hear the charges are withdrawn.'

'I told you, it takes time. Heard any more from Dean?'

'Not yet.'

'How are you contacting him? Do you have a phone number?'

'Just email.'

He snorted. 'Right.'

'It's true. I assume it's because he knows that phones can be traced.'

'And yet he's not a kidnapper, according to you?'

Jen faced him, and said, 'He's worried about what your thugs will do if they find him. That strikes me as a good reason to lie low.'

Gerard harrumphed, then stalked away without denying the accusation that he had people hunting for Dean.

After making coffee, she hurried back to her room and took a shower. With Gerard's taunt about Dean playing on her mind, she sent an email: *How is Charlie? Can I speak to him this morning?*

Freddie knocked soon after. He'd dressed in black jeans and a Radiohead T-shirt. 'What time do you need to get away?'

'Soon as we can go.' She was desperate to begin the sequence of journeys that would see her reunited with Charlie. It was infuriating that she had to return to Brighton first, but she feared the consequences of missing her appointment at the police station. For all she knew, they could put her behind bars if she failed to turn up. 'I could do with going home before I see the police, but I'm fine to get the train.'

'No, I want to take you.' He nodded towards the door. 'And I'm not acting as his spy, if you're worried about that?'

'Not really.' She took a couple of steps closer. The swelling around his mouth had gone down, though there was still an unsightly bruise along his jawline. 'You look exhausted.'

'Didn't get a lot of sleep,' he admitted. 'I wish I knew that Charlie was okay.'

'I'm sure he's fine. I've emailed Dean to find out the latest.'

There was still no reply when they left the house. Fretting over whether to try again, Jen barely registered the fact that Gerard hadn't come out to say farewell.

They were borrowing his Mercedes GLS, which Freddie drove as though he were at Silverstone. The racing style wasn't particularly appropriate for rush-hour traffic in the centre of London, but Jen distracted herself from the fear of an imminent crash by carefully composing another email to Dean. Seesawing between a friendly tone and one that demanded an immediate response, she settled finally on a brief and bland enquiry, then looked up to find they were almost at the M23.

'How fast have you been driving?'

'Quite fast,' he conceded. 'A couple of the bastard cameras got me – oh no, they got Pa! What a shame.'

As he grinned, Jen said, 'He won't mind. Anger to Gerard is like insulin to a diabetic.'

'And he'll get a column out of it. Speed cameras make him furious. And fuel taxes, parking charges, the congestion zone, bendy buses. . .'

'Hm. Whereas child poverty, not so much.'

A heavy silence followed. Freddie had always been touchy where criticism of Gerard was concerned. He could say practically anything about the man, but woe betide Jen if she weighed in.

But now he changed the subject completely. 'After this, what do you reckon's gonna happen?'

'I can't think about anything beyond seeing Charlie. Everything else is a blur at the moment. Irrelevant.'

'Yeah.' A thoughtful pause. 'I like what you said yesterday, about the two of us trying to sort an agreement.'

'Glad to hear that. It really hurt me to believe you'd want to spirit Charlie away to Greece.'

'I was never gonna spirit him away,' he said, defensively. 'But the idea of moving out there sort of made sense. It's not like I have much going on here, do I?'

It isn't just about you. Jen thought better of voicing the rebuke, but she didn't have to. In a morose voice, Freddie said, 'Till yesterday I never realised what a selfish wanker I've been.'

CHAPTER FIFTY-EIGHT

When he heard that Jen had left his Audi at the station car park, Freddie suggested they pick it up before they went to hers. They reached Brighton at around nine thirty. Jen drove the Audi home, with Freddie following. She parked outside the flat, then searched according to Dean's instructions and, sure enough, quickly found the GPS tracker: a chunky black box attached by magnets to the underside of the car.

Freddie groaned. 'This is really shitty. I had no idea.'

'I believe you. But didn't it strike you as odd when he suggested lending me the car?'

'I just thought he was being reasonable, for once in his life.'

He sounded so innocent that Jen couldn't help smiling. 'Oh, Freddie...'

She asked that he stay in the car while she ran inside to change clothes. The silence from Dean was a growing agony. Debating whether to chase him again, she picked up her phone and found that she'd finally had a reply. The message was no more than a mobile phone number and two words: *Call me.*

She stared at the email, wondering why he suddenly wanted to communicate by phone. Had something happened?

She was so nervous, it took her three attempts to tap on the number. She heard the call connect, but first there was only the sound of rapid breathing. Then someone spoke, and it wasn't

Dean, but a small voice, shy and reluctant and perhaps slightly fearful. 'Hello?'

'Charlie?' Jen almost yelled his name. 'It's Mummy. Are you all right?'

Another pause, and a sense that he was listening to instructions. 'Y-yeah,' he said. 'When are you coming?'

'Soon, darling. A bit later today.'

'The man says—' He stopped. 'Dean says we've got to drive a long way.'

'Quite a long way, but I'll be there in a few hours.' A thought struck her. 'Are you worried about being ill in the car?'

Another silence; she could easily picture him shrugging. 'He gave me some medicine.'

'Did he? Well, in that case I'm sure you'll be fine, and it won't be long till I can give you a *huuuge* big hug!'

He snorted, as if stifling a laugh, but then she heard what was unmistakeably a sob. Dean quickly took the phone and said, 'Charlie's okay – aren't you, matey? I gave him Kwells, isn't that right?'

'Uh, yes. Thanks. Where are you?'

'On the move,' he said darkly, as though she was prying into something that didn't concern her. 'I saw your emails but couldn't reply right away. How did it go at Gerard's?'

'Quite well, I think. I got the bug back this morning. It should have caught any phone calls he made last night.'

'Excellent. You've done a good job there.'

'Gerard is still claiming it could take a while to get the charges dropped. I'm due at the police station in about an hour.'

'He's stalling. But it doesn't matter. Even if you're charged, it won't be long before we turn the tables on them. I'll put a copy of the recording on a memory stick, and you're free to take it to the cops – or even keep it for blackmail.'

'I just want a level playing field, a chance to negotiate—'

'That's because you're a decent person, Jen. Unlike Gerard. Was he asking about me?'

'A little bit. He was pushing for details about where you're going, and how we communicate—'

'Isn't that what I said he'd do? He can't be trusted for a second. Which is why we're having to meet so far away.'

'But where, exactly?' She might have sounded a little too exasperated, partly because Dean kept interrupting.

He hesitated, and she could sense the doubt humming through the phone. 'You are alone, aren't you?'

'Yes. I'm back home.'

'Okay. It's Cumbria, close to Lake Windermere.'

She whistled. 'How long will that take?'

'Maybe five or six hours, depending on the traffic. Listen, I'm only talking to you now because I'm on the road. After this call, I'll have to switch the phone off. Hamilton has people who can trace the signal.'

'So how will I find you?'

'Set off for the Lakes. I'll call again, maybe on another phone, at six o'clock, and give you the address. But you *must* come alone.'

'Yes, I know.' Before her nerve failed, she said, 'Last night, Gerard was asking me about Russell Pearce—'

'You don't have to worry about him.'

He said it so dismissively that Jen could only issue an embarrassed little laugh. 'Right now, I'm worried about *everything*.'

'I suppose you are. But don't be – we're nearly there.' He chuckled. 'You and me, Jen, we make a hell of a team.'

She ended the call with the thought that this was just what she'd been craving: a chance to talk to Charlie and make sure he was all right. And yet, out of nowhere came a lurking suspicion that she was being played.

She put together an overnight bag for herself and Charlie, on the basis that they probably wouldn't be home until tomorrow. Then it struck her that tomorrow was Thursday – and Charlie was meant to be at school. One way or another, they'd have to drive back tonight.

That knowledge made it harder to resist Freddie's offer to accompany her. She decided to wait and see how she got on at the police station, though when she agreed to be driven there in the Mercedes, it felt like her mind was made up.

Despite that, she was oddly reluctant to tell Freddie about the phone call, perhaps because she needed time to process it herself. And that couldn't happen until after her appointment with the police.

Freddie dropped her off, and said he'd park in the nearby Asda car park. Her solicitor, Tim Allenby, was waiting on the pavement. He greeted her with a friendly nod, but his demeanour was sombre. 'All set for this?' he asked, gently.

'I suppose so.'

'Try and remember there's still a long way to go.' He described how he'd known clients to feel faint, or vomit, or break down at this stage, though most were just mute with shock. 'Best thing after this is to get right away. Once you're ready to talk, give me a ring and we'll go through it in detail.'

Jen nodded, hoping that wouldn't be necessary, if Gerard played it straight.

Allenby led her into the reception area. The custody suite seemed busier than last week, and their appointment time of eleven o'clock came and went. Too tense to make conversation, Jen sat with her head down, and tried to think about nothing except being reunited with Charlie.

Finally she was met by DS Howard and DC Reed, who took her through to the main room. At the counter, the custody sergeant booked her into the system, ran through the familiar questions and cautioned her again, before reading out the charges.

If she'd been told a couple of weeks ago that this would be happening, Jen might have thought her world had ended. Now, in the midst of so much drama, it felt like just another burden to carry.

She was asked if she had anything to say, and told them, 'No.' She was then released on bail, and informed that she would have to attend a magistrates' court within fourteen days. If her plea was not guilty, the case would be referred to the Crown Court.

With the formalities over, DS Howard offered a neutral smile. 'Do you have time for a quick word?'

Jen felt her stomach flip. Tuesday's road rage incident flashed into her mind: the driver vowing to report her to the police.

She turned to Allenby, who had joined them and was frowning at the detectives. 'A word about what?' he enquired.

'Russell Pearce.' Howard looked grave. 'We've found something that's giving us concern.'

CHAPTER FIFTY-NINE

Allenby took in Jen's expression, and said, 'Perhaps I'll come with you?'

Reed seemed to scowl, but DS Howard said he was welcome. 'We're hoping you can help us,' she told Jen.

The four of them moved to an interview room. As they took their seats, Jen said, 'I take it you haven't found him?'

'Not a single sighting,' Howard admitted. 'He's made no contact with anybody, as far as we can tell. Hasn't touched his bank account or tried to leave the country.'

'That's unusual, isn't it?' Allenby asked.

'Very. With what looks to have been a spontaneous attack, you'd expect a degree of panic, and the killer's attempts to cover his tracks would be quite rudimentary, even chaotic.'

'Instead he's just vanished off the face of the earth,' said Reed. 'Which usually means something else altogether.'

'Suicide?' Jen asked.

'We haven't ruled it out,' Howard said, cryptically. 'You spoke to his wife, Kelly, at about five o'clock on Sunday. Did you see Russell at any time?'

'No. Though I suspect he was in the house.'

'Not even a glimpse, maybe from the window?' Reed asked.

'Nothing at all, sorry.'

Howard: 'So the last time you set eyes on him was, when, Friday?'

'Yes.' Jen glanced uneasily at Allenby. 'Can I ask why?'

Howard pursed her lips. 'We wanted to know if you'd noticed any kind of injury, but Friday's probably too far back.'

Jen went to reply but Allenby coughed, and said, 'I'm going to recommend we terminate this here, unless you can tell us the purpose of this conversation.'

The detectives exchanged a look, before Howard said, 'The forensic examination has revealed blood spatter on the wall and floor in the hallway. It was cleaned up, quite effectively, but the traces still showed up under UV light.'

'And it isn't Kelly's,' Reed explained. 'We're still waiting on DNA, but the assumption is that it's Russell's blood.'

'So they fought, perhaps, before he killed her?' Allenby queried.

Howard nodded. 'Possibly several hours before.'

Reed: 'Which means it might not have been Kelly who inflicted the wound.'

Jen didn't like the sound of that. Neither did her solicitor, who said, 'If my client's under suspicion, this is very irregular—'

'Calm down, Tim.' Howard gave him a tense smile. 'It's an informal chat, nothing more. But you can see our problem? If they fight, and Russell gets hurt, then murders Kelly in retaliation, why does he only clean up his own blood?'

'And why clean it at all if he's about to do a runner?' Reed added.

'On the other hand,' said Howard, 'if he's injured, and then things calm down enough for him – or both of them – to do the cleaning, what is it that sparks the fatal attack on Kelly?'

'I'm sorry,' Jen said. 'I can't explain that, either.'

DS Howard nodded. 'Don't worry, we're not expecting you to have the answer.'

'It's got us stumped,' Reed said. 'We just hoped you might have seen him on Sunday afternoon.'

Again Jen shook her head, but didn't trust herself to speak. Neither of the detectives gave any sense that they were judging her, but surely it had occurred to them – as it was now occurring to her – that Russell's injury may have been a direct consequence of Jen turning up on the doorstep.

'We won't take any more of your time.' DS Howard rose from her seat. This was the moment that Jen might have asked about her own case, but all she could think of was getting out of here and going to meet Charlie.

'Here's hoping you find him,' Allenby told Howard as they were leaving the room.

'I'm sure we will eventually – either alive or dead.'

Once outside, Allenby gripped Jen's hand in both of his. 'Be aware that the full shock doesn't always hit until a few hours later. Is there somebody who can be with you today?'

Jen realised he was referring to the charges against her; she was more preoccupied with what she'd just heard about Pearce.

'I'll be fine.'

'Good. Do you need a lift home, at least?'

'Thanks, but my ex is waiting for me.'

'Your *ex*?' He frowned at her. 'I thought you two were at loggerheads?'

Jen gave a shrug. 'So did I.'

She checked her phone as she walked away. No messages, but it was nearly one in the afternoon. Dean had said he'd call at six, by which time she needed to be three hundred miles north of here.

She found the Mercedes in the bottom corner of the car park at Asda. Freddie got out to greet her, and his face fell. 'They charged you?'

'That was always going to happen.'

'No, I thought Pa. . .' He made an angry growling noise. 'I thought for once he might do the right thing.'

'There's still time.'

As she moved to the passenger side, he said, 'You're gonna let me take you?'

He could tell she was wavering. Dean had insisted, repeatedly, that she must come alone, but that was because he feared Gerard and his associates. If Freddie could be trusted – and Jen, right now, would vouch for him – then surely that stipulation wasn't quite so important?

There and back in a day: it would help to have another driver. . .

'Where is it, anyway?' he asked.

'Cumbria. The Lakes.'

'Oh, jeez.' He nodded towards the fuel station. 'We'd better fill up.'

She nodded, then abruptly dropped out of sight. Freddie yelped, thinking she'd collapsed; he came running round the car and found her examining one of the wheel arches.

'I want to be sure there's no tracker.'

He looked bemused, but helped her to check. While he was getting petrol, Jen tried to work out why she suddenly felt so afraid; almost on the edge of a panic attack.

The bloodstain, cleaned up with bleach. Russell Pearce missing, and Dean's easy confidence as he said, *You don't have to worry about him*. Was she exaggerating, upon recollection, the assurance she'd heard in his voice? A phrase like that was usually a platitude, not something to be analysed for a deeper meaning.

But if it wasn't a platitude. . .

If Dean *knew* that she didn't have to worry about Pearce. . .

And he had Charlie. *He had Charlie.*

CHAPTER SIXTY

Gerard struggled to concentrate on his work, when his mind wanted only to obsess, furiously, over the dangers posed by Dean, Jen, Hugo Hamilton or even by this man Stemper. What he'd envisaged as a small, tight operation had ballooned into something unwieldy and potentially explosive.

Through the morning he texted Freddie a couple of times, but received only curt, grudging replies: *We're in Brighton. Jen's with the police.* Gerard was anticipating a stream of abuse when they charged her, but midday came and went without any word.

He was in the garden, smoking, when Stemper called. A friend of Dean's had given up the information that Dean was an only child, whose mother had died when he was ten. His father, who had never remarried, lived in Carlisle.

'Dean talked about returning to that part of the world. I've traced an address for the father, so Cumbria had better be my next stop – unless you have any objections?'

'Not at all. We're getting closer, then?' Gerard spoke with rather more optimism than he felt. 'Though we, er, we haven't yet discussed what happens when you find him.'

'I'll be guided by you, of course.'

Gerard coughed, plagued by a tickle in his throat. 'Yes, well, recovering my grandson, that's a big priority. But there are a certain number of. . .'

'Loose ends?' Stemper supplied, helpfully.

*

Stemper had known it was coming. Most jobs of this nature reached a stage where the client came to understand that the 'cleanest' solution meant taking things further. It was at the point of no return that Stemper's original fee was liable to multiply; on this occasion he asked for another hundred thousand.

Gerard was stunned, then outraged, then wounded. 'I was assured of your reputation,' he whined. 'I wasn't expecting someone who'd lead me in this far, then try to do me over.'

Stemper let him fall silent, and said, 'You're worried about blackmail. Let me put your mind at rest. I'm a wealthy man, and have zero interest in extorting money from you. There's only one thing liable to endanger our working relationship, and that's if I perceive my services to be insufficiently valued.'

'Well, yes, I wouldn't dream of—'

'My rates aren't up for discussion. That needs to be very clear.'

After a little more bluster, Gerard agreed, and without saying so in explicit terms, they arrived at a mutual understanding that Dean had to be silenced at all costs. Did that objective take precedence over recovering the grandson, unharmed? Gerard weaselled out of a definite answer, but gave Stemper enough leeway to rely on his own judgement.

'My role is to eliminate any threats to your reputation and your liberty, and that's what I'll do,' Stemper told him.

He ended the call and started the car. He had a long drive ahead.

Gerard put the phone down, smarting over the demand for more money – even though it was peanuts in the scheme of things. More importantly, he wasn't a hundred per cent sure what had been agreed.

Upon reflection, he decided he preferred it that way. As a man whose occupation was built on a certain degree of distortion, he knew that *believing* what he said was the crucial first step. Now he merely had to persuade himself that what he'd striven for was the best possible outcome for his family – for himself, Freddie and Charlie – and were anything to go wrong, the consequences were out of his hands.

A minor wobble, perhaps, when Hugo Hamilton's words came floating into his mind: *Let a creature like that off the leash, and you can't always put him back on.*

Well, it was too late now. Accidents, tragedies: they were an unfortunate fact of life. Everyone knew that.

CHAPTER SIXTY-ONE

The journey went smoothly for all of forty minutes, until they reached a notorious stretch of the M25, near Chertsey in Surrey. Then: gridlock.

'Gonna be like this from here till the M40,' Freddie muttered, and he was right. For the next hour they were trapped among thousands of other motorists, all competing to inch forward in a series of stop-starts that made them both half crazy with frustration.

At last they reached the M40, which was running smoothly and allowed Freddie to take the Mercedes up to eighty for a while. Jen finally got her thoughts straight, and was able to reveal that Dean had phoned her this morning, and would be calling later with the address. 'I also spoke to Charlie,' she said.

'What?' Freddie almost lost control of the car. 'Is he all right? What did he say? Are you sure Dean hasn't hurt—'

'Freddie, please. I don't know. He sounded. . . okay.'

'Only "okay"?'

'It was hard to tell. At the time I suppose I was so relieved just to hear him, but now, going over and over it. . .' She shuddered, still struggling – or reluctant – to put it into words. 'I keep trying to imagine what it must be like for him, after all the turmoil of me being arrested, you flying back early from Greece, and then suddenly he's in the care of somebody he doesn't really know – that none of us know – and now they're driving right across the country. . . It must be terrifying.'

'Yeah.' Freddie brooded for a moment. 'Though kids are resilient, you know? And Charlie has your sense of adventure. I bet that's why he made the decision to sneak out and talk to this guy in the first place. And if he's getting McDonald's, and toys bought for him, he might not be as unhappy as you think. . .'

They're superficial treats, Jen thought, but she couldn't say that without touching a nerve. 'Are you sure you're not clutching at straws?'

'Probably – and why not? One way or another, we've got to hold it together till he's back with us.'

'True.' She let out a deep sigh. 'I'm also worried about Russell Pearce.'

'The guy that killed his wife?'

She told him about the bloodstains that the police thought might belong to Russell, an indication that he'd been injured or attacked prior to his wife's murder. Freddie didn't seem to appreciate the significance, even when she recounted what Dean had said: *You don't have to worry about him*. 'To me, that suggests he knows Pearce can't be a danger.'

'What, because Dean's killed him?' Freddie shook his head. 'I'm not gonna buy that, just because of a throwaway phrase.'

Clutching at straws, Jen thought again. Which, as options went, probably beat worrying yourself sick about something that was impossible to determine.

Except that wasn't the only thing bothering her. *I gave him Kwells, isn't that right?* Dean had said about the sickness tablets. Kwells Kids was the brand that Jen used. There was a box in the bathroom.

Did Dean know that because he'd been in her flat? Yesterday he'd strenuously downplayed his part in the operation against her. It might be only a minor thing, but it gave her another reason to doubt he could be trusted completely.

*

More congestion slowed them on the M42, but the M6 toll road offered some respite and they were able to make up a bit of the lost time. They were still behind schedule, but Jen agreed to Freddie's suggestion that they stop to grab some coffees and switch seats, though she had to remind him that she wasn't insured for this car.

'So what? It'll be Pa who has to cough up if there's a problem.'

They pulled into the services at Norton Canes and separated outside the toilets. When Jen emerged from the ladies', there was no sign of Freddie, so she wandered over to the small retail area while checking her phone for messages. Nothing from Dean, but she had an email from her mother: *We should catch up soon – it's been too long. Are you in trouble? Xx*

Jen frowned. The sensible thing would be to ignore the message, but she felt a sudden, primitive desire to hear her mother's voice.

The call took a few seconds to connect, and then rang four, five times: not going to ans—

'Darling, what is it?'

'N-nothing, Mum. I just got your email.'

'Oh, that. I sent it a couple of hours ago, but there can't have been a signal. I wondered if your dad was trying to spook me – he kept insisting you were fine, to the point where I became convinced that you weren't.' She was talking very rapidly, and sounded harried; Jen could hear voices and traffic in the background.

'No, I'm doing okay, honestly.'

'That's a relief, if you're sure? Sorry, darling, but I'm late for a presentation. I'll be home Monday – no, Tuesday, I think – so let's meet up later next week. I'll have time for a real heart to heart, and we'll get to the bottom of whatever it is, even if it's nothing!'

With a jaunty laugh she was gone, leaving Jen feeling more bereft than if they'd never spoken at all. She felt her stomach twisting with negative emotions, and quickly phoned her dad. 'I just spoke to Mum. I think you worried her.'

'I know. I only mentioned that you'd paid a visit, and somehow she deduced that you were in terrible trouble.' He paused. 'How are things now?'

Bad. As bad as they can be. . .

'Fine, thanks.'

'Sure about that?'

'Honestly. I'd better go, I'm in the middle of something. But Mum suggested meeting up next week.'

'Lovely, let's do that – if she doesn't jet off somewhere else. Hey, and send my love to kiddo.'

'I will.' Jen rang off, unsure whether to laugh or cry. *It's only Mum, when she makes the effort, who can see that I'm too proud to ask for help and support – and it's only Dad, who respects my independence more than he should, who can give me that help and support.*

CHAPTER SIXTY-TWO

Gerard couldn't be bothered to cook lunch, so he took a wander to the Carluccio's in the Brunswick Centre and had a seafood linguine. No one bothered him in the restaurant, but on the short walk back he had to sign two autographs and ignore a group of students who yelled from across the street that he was a 'fascist twat'. About par for the course.

Having consumed half a bottle of red wine with the meal, he felt sleepy enough to take a brief nap, and then finished off his column. After despatching it to his agent for a once-over, he returned a call from a TV producer who'd invited him to appear on a panel discussion show about the upcoming American election. The producer, an excitable female who sounded about seventeen, actually laughed when he mentioned the positives they could expect from a Trump presidency.

'Listen, love,' he snarled, 'the world's changing, and I'm giving your crappy little show a chance to be ahead of the curve.'

And then Freddie rang. It was just after three o'clock. 'Thought you'd be here by now. Is the Merc all right?'

'I'm not coming back yet. I'm taking Jen to the Lake District.'

For a moment Gerard couldn't remember if he was supposed to know their destination. 'Why?' he asked carefully.

'To get Charlie back, what do you think?'

'So you know where he is?'

A pause, then Freddie spoke, sounding testy. 'Jen talked to Dean this morning. I only just found out.'

'What did Dean say? Did he tell her where he's going?'

'The guy's not stupid. He knows you're trying to trace him. He's gonna call again later.'

Gerard tried to sound conciliatory, while planting a doubt or two. 'If you weren't present for the conversation, then you can't be sure what was said. Jen might already have the address. Even the name of the town would be very useful. That and his phone number. . .' Gerard could hear Freddie breathing hard, as if struggling to contain his agitation. But was he tempted? 'Please, Freddie—'

'Listen. The police told Jen that the neighbour, Pearce, was injured before he killed his wife. Now she's got it into her head that Dean might have been involved. What do you know about that?'

'Nothing! Why would I?'

'Because it's down to you that Dean came into this in the first place. You've got people hunting for him, and probably looking into his background. If you have any information that could help us. . .'

'I don't. But I'll say again, Freddie, that you should *not* be going anywhere near this man. Get that address for me, and I'll deal with it.'

'Oh yeah? How?'

'You don't need to know that. But we'll get Charlie back, I guarantee.'

Freddie made a scoffing noise. 'You think Jen's gonna trust you for a second after what you've done?'

'I don't give a damn what she thinks, and you shouldn't, either. What else is she keeping from you? She sees you as a useful idiot, and always has. Just get that address – and if she still insists on going it alone, let her take a train or a bus and you come back here.'

'So then I'm *your* useful idiot?'

Gerard thought it wiser not to answer. When Freddie spoke next, his voice was not quieter so much as *smaller*, somehow. Diminished.

'I called you in good faith. I thought Charlie mattered to you.'

'And he does, don't be so fu—'

'*No*. All you care about is covering this up. Protecting yourself. You don't give a shit about any of us.'

He was gone before Gerard could form a credible response.

Jen found Freddie in the queue for coffees. She had the impression he was upset about something, but it wasn't until they'd left the building that he admitted it.

'I just spoke to Pa. I wanted to see if he'd heard anything from these guys who work for him. Instead he kept drilling me about Dean's address. He didn't believe me when I said we don't have it.'

'Was it *you* he didn't believe – or me?'

A snort. 'He thinks you might know more than you're letting on. I'm supposed to wheedle it out of you, then let him take over.'

She absorbed this information slowly. 'And were you tempted to do that?'

A moment's hesitation. 'I'm disappointed you took so long to tell me about speaking to Charlie. But I'd never agree to what he wants.'

'He really thinks we'd just stand by while some other stranger goes for Charlie?'

'It's worse than that. He basically said I should abandon you and come home. And that's. . .' Shaking his head. 'I'm done with him, Jen. Finished.'

With a diplomatic shrug, she said, 'At least you weren't able to give him anything. And I'm sorry – I should have told you sooner, but I didn't know myself what to make of the call.' She briefly laid her hand on his shoulder, the first affectionate contact between them in many, many months.

Freddie acknowledged it with a quick, distracted smile. 'Even if he doesn't have the address, I'm worried. He's planning something, I'm sure of it.'

Gerard deliberated for a short time, then phoned Stemper. When he answered, he was on a speaker, with the rumble of traffic in the background.

'I think Cumbria was a good call, but there's a complication. Jen is heading for the Lake District, and my son is with her.'

'I see.' Stemper sounded unruffled. 'And do they have an address for Dean?'

'Freddie claims they don't, but whether that's just because she hasn't told him. . .'

'I have a good idea where Dean might be. Let's hope I can get there first.'

'You know where he's hiding?' He waited for Stemper to supply the details, but there was only silence. Off-balance, Gerard stammered, 'S-so you don't think it'll be a problem?'

'I hope not, though it would be useful at this point to hear your vision of the ideal outcome.'

Cautiously, Gerard said, 'We're talking on a purely hypothetical basis?'

'Naturally.'

'Well, I'd want Charlie to come out unscathed. And Freddie, I suppose. As for Dean. . . he wouldn't be as fortunate, I think we agreed on that?'

'Absolutely. And Jennifer?'

'Hmm. If a tragedy were to occur, perhaps in such a way that Dean was held responsible. . .?'

Stemper said he could make no promises, though he appreciated the stakes were now very high indeed. Then he warned that the conclusion, when it came, might be 'messy'.

Gerard said, 'I understand.' But as he put the phone down, he wondered if that were true. Had he really just agreed to let matters unfold in a way that could lead to death or serious injury to members of his own family?

He ruminated on that for a while, and decided it was time to recognise that he had, in effect, lost his grandson already. If Jen survived this, she would have his nuts in a vice. Once she'd gained custody on her terms, that would be the last he ever saw of Chip.

Painful, but sometimes you had to harden your heart. Wipe the slate clean and move on.

He turned to his computer and browsed through the cinema listings for the West End. Over the next few hours some form of diversion might be welcome, and a movie was just the thing.

I explicitly told Freddie to dump Jen and come home, he thought. *If he doesn't listen, it's on his head.*

My conscience is clear.

CHAPTER SIXTY-THREE

For an hour or more the motorway unrolled before them, the traffic busy but flowing freely enough for Jen to maintain a speed of seventy to eighty miles per hour.

It still didn't feel fast enough. She was possessed by the grim, apocalyptic certainty that her faith in Dean was misplaced, that something terrible was going to happen to Charlie and it would be her fault, all her fault. . .

She tried to focus on nothing more than driving, and some small talk about music. They were listening to one of Freddie's playlists, and after Jen commented favourably on a bluesy ballad by a Sussex artist called Rag'n'Bone Man, he muted the volume and said, 'Try this.'

Tapping out the beat on his thighs, he began to sing a sweet, soulful love song with a great chorus and a clever little rap that he couldn't quite pull off in conjunction with the main vocal – as he explained, it was designed for two voices.

'You mean *you* wrote that?'

He nodded proudly. 'Finished it in Greece.'

'It's beautiful.' Jen felt glad that she didn't have to exaggerate, as had sometimes been the case in the past. She'd always thought Freddie would do well on one of the TV talent shows – for his looks and charm as much as anything – though she doubted if he'd ever get to the final stages.

Unfortunately Gerard was of the same opinion, and had made it clear that he would withdraw all financial support if Freddie were to apply. Gerard's fear was that anything less than a place in the final would be used to deride him: *Columnist's Son Flops on X Factor*.

As if reading her mind, Freddie said, 'Probably just stick it on YouTube or something. Nowhere else I can go with it.'

'It's a fantastic song. What about offering it to an established artist?'

At first he scowled, then brightened, hummed a few notes from the bridge and murmured, 'It's an idea.'

They cleared the West Midlands and crossed the whole of Cheshire, into Lancashire, and then ran into trouble. Jen had noticed a lot of traffic leaving at the exit for Lancaster. As they rolled past the junction they began to see brake lights flashing up ahead. A moment later the radio broadcast a traffic update: major problems on the M6 northbound near Carnforth, with driver reports of an overturned caravan.

Jen groaned. 'I bet that junction was our last chance to take a detour.'

All three lanes came to a halt, and within two or three minutes the motorway had become a car park. Another fifteen and it was a picnic area. Many of the cars and caravans around them were piled high with luggage: families returning from summer vacations.

Several emergency vehicles eased past on the hard shoulder, and for a minute Jen was sorely tempted to weave through the gaps and follow them. Then a white van tried to do just that, only to be caught by a police car and directed back into the queue.

A second police car slowed, the driver speaking to a motorist who quickly spread the word: probably an hour or so till the breakdown truck could remove the obstruction. Thankfully no one had been hurt.

'Thankfully,' Jen echoed. *Though what if they're wrong? What if something happens to Charlie because I'm not there on time?*

Beside her, Freddie had gone very still. She wondered if he was about to doze off when he suddenly said, 'You know what this reminds me of? When you were in labour.'

'Really?'

'Yeah. All those hours feeling really tense, and knowing so much was on the line – your life, the baby's life – and yet realising that we had to find a way to push it to the back of our minds, at least for some of that time, or else we'd go insane. Was it six, seven hours?'

'Just over nine, thanks.'

'Wow. There you go, then. How the hell did we manage that?'

She thought back, and found herself smiling at some of the daft ways in which Freddie had tried to keep her entertained. 'I think you ended up showing me cat videos on YouTube.'

'God, yeah.' He grimaced. 'So now let's tell ourselves we made it through that, and we'll make it through this.' He reached for her hand and squeezed it. 'Although, I do kind of wish you hadn't told me that stuff about Russell Pearce.'

'You said it didn't mean anything,' she reminded him.

'I know, but I could be wrong.' He gazed at a middle-aged couple standing by the central reservation, eating what looked like sausage rolls. 'Say it was Dean, and he killed Pearce. Why the hell would he do that?'

Because of me. The answer just materialised, without any conscious reasoning. But it felt horribly convincing, Jen thought. It chimed with the lightness of his tone and the way he had looked at her, not just yesterday in London but whenever he'd come to the sports centre. And hadn't he said something else, when she mentioned Pearce's interest in her? *I wouldn't have let that happen.* At the time she hadn't registered how possessive he sounded.

She must have gasped, for Freddie turned to her. 'What?'

'Nothing.' She didn't know anything for sure, so there was no sense in scaring him. In fact, she was already backtracking herself. She didn't want to believe that Dean was capable of a double murder for any reason, let alone that he'd do it simply because those people had crossed Jen's path. . .

Pray I'm wrong, she told herself. *Pray I'm wrong about this, if nothing else.*

By the time they got moving it was twenty to six. The sun was noticeably lower in the sky, filtering through thin streaks of peach and vanilla cloud.

Freddie had suggested he take over the driving again. 'You'll be getting a call soon.'

It was a good point, but Jen didn't spot the flaw until just after six, when her phone started to ring. 'What if he can tell I'm not alone?'

'How would he?'

'I dunno. But sometimes you just get an instinct. . .' While she hesitated, her screen flashed a message: *Missed call.* 'Can we leave at the exit and park somewhere?'

'Sure.' He expanded the map on the satnav screen. 'Looks to be a few minutes away.'

It was a torturous wait. Her phone didn't ring again. The number was different to the one Dean had used earlier, a sign that he was serious about the precautions he was taking. Hardly surprising, if Gerard had people on the hunt.

But how much did either of them – Dean or Gerard – have Charlie's best interests at heart, and how much came down to raw self-preservation?

At last they swung into a slip road. Freddie put his hazard lights on and pulled up on a grass verge covered with wild flowers. Jen got out and dialled the number.

Dean answered immediately. 'Why didn't you pick up?'

'I was driving. I had to find somewhere safe to stop.'

'Are you lying to me? You should be here by now.'

'I'm not. *W*-there was a bad accident on the M6, close to Carnforth. Look it up on the news.' She stopped for a breath, her heart pounding with fear: she'd so nearly said *We* – and was praying he hadn't picked up on it.

'I will do,' he said. He'd gone from irascible to doubtful, even a little panicky.

'I'll try to make up the time. Where do I need to go?'

He said nothing for fifteen, twenty seconds. Then: 'I hope I can trust you, Jen. I said to come alone and I'm not pissing around. I mean it.'

The menace in his voice was unmistakeable. Afraid to antagonise him, she said, 'I know, and I've done what you asked. Is Charlie all right? May I speak to him?'

'Not now. Drive to Bowness and take the lake road south for approximately four and a half miles. You'll find a small parking area where the road cuts away from the lake. Wait there and text me on this number.'

He ended the call. Jen almost collapsed against the car. Freddie opened the window and cried, 'What's happened? Are you okay?'

'I'm fine,' she said. But she wasn't. In that call Dean had revealed a very different side to his character: dark, menacing, vicious. She felt horribly out of her depth, and for a second she wished that DS Howard or DC Reed could have been here alongside her. But that was impossible: she'd made her choices, and there would be no one else coming to the rescue at this late stage.

'I've got the directions,' she said. 'But I need to drive. And we have to be a lot more careful from now on.'

*

For many years Stemper had employed the services of a researcher, an accomplished but blissfully naive woman who accepted that his need for a bewildering variety of information was entirely legitimate. Once again, she had proved her worth. As well as owning a bungalow in Carlisle, Dean Geary's father was listed as the freehold owner of another property, a converted boathouse and former bed-and-breakfast on Lake Windermere. The B&B had ceased trading in 2014, and planning permission had been granted for extensive renovations, designed to return the building to a private dwelling.

Stemper caught the warning of delays in time to get off the M6 and plot an alternative route. He was making good progress when Hugo Hamilton rang with more information about Dean. 'I have to stress that this was deeply buried. I had no inkling when I employed him.'

Stemper wasn't interested in his pleas for mitigation. 'Tell me.'

At the age of twenty-two, while serving as a police constable in Greater Manchester, Dean had fixated on a girl he'd encountered while attending a minor drugs bust. 'She'd broken up with her partner, but wasn't interested in Dean. He had trouble accepting that, and harassed her for months. Eventually his colleagues got involved, and though there were no charges brought, he resigned from the police. Jumped before he was pushed.'

A few weeks later he abducted the girl and held her for several hours, subjecting her to a prolonged sexual assault. 'He told her this was payback for destroying his career, though he was deluded enough to believe there could still be a relationship between them.'

'And this wasn't on record?' Stemper queried.

'By now the girl's family had little confidence in the police. They took matters into their own hands – the father and brother beat seven shades of whatnot out of Dean, and the girl never set eyes on him again. He cleared out and moved to Hereford, where he started working in security.'

'And fantasised about being in the SAS, according to his friend, Nolan.'

'Yes, but that's not the end of the story. Four years later the girl's father failed to come home from the pub one night, and has never been seen since. A year after that, the son, along with his wife and baby, died in a house fire. Both incidents could be unrelated, of course. . .'

'But probably not,' Stemper said. 'I'll bear it in mind.'

He checked the time: almost seven o'clock. Judging that he was about half an hour away, he felt the familiar tingle of anticipation. There were various ways he could bring this to a conclusion, and the one that Dean might have employed himself had much to recommend it.

Fire was good.

CHAPTER SIXTY-FOUR

The attractive town of Bowness-on-Windermere was still choked with traffic at seven in the evening. Jen was sure she'd come here once with her parents, before her sisters were born. The sight of pleasure cruisers lined up at the jetties prompted ancient memories of excitement and vague distress, of Mum scolding her while Dad took a more relaxed view; Jen had a feeling she'd been climbing on a deck rail and nearly fallen overboard.

She'd been to the Lakes a few more times over the years, but usually to the wilder, less populated areas. Here, the huts selling ice cream and the gift shops full of tourist tat were exactly what she used to avoid – at least until she became a parent.

An air of weary elation seemed to hang over the place: how Jen wished she could share that feeling, to be in among the crowds with Charlie, feeding the ducks and geese, then wandering off for pizza and a cheeky vodka. . .

Putting that longing aside, she drove out of town, the road rising and twisting as it followed the contours of the hills beside the lake. Trees grew thickly on both sides of the road, allowing only glimpses of water and the occasional cluster of chalet-style properties by the lake shore.

She kept her speed down, watching the satnav for the turn Dean had described. A motor home rumbled past, followed by a long queue of frustrated drivers. There was a Range Rover on her tail; Jen slowed to a crawl and waved it past, then spotted the car park's entrance, opposite a sharp left-hand bend.

The car park was a rough, uneven patch of earth and gravel, which the surrounding foliage seemed determined to reclaim. It was large enough for thirty or forty cars, though there were fewer than a dozen here this evening. A grassy footpath sloped towards the lake, and a couple of young men were hauling kayaks in that direction. An older man was loading fishing gear into the back of his car, and a middle-aged couple were taking photographs of the trees.

Jen parked in a quiet corner, glanced in the mirror and saw the fisherman staring in her direction. Admiring the Mercedes, perhaps, or wondering how a young woman could afford such an expensive car. She had a flashback to the road rage incident on Monday and shuddered.

She picked up her phone and texted Dean: *I'm here.*

A minute passed, then two. The fisherman got into his car and drove away, and from the rear footwell came a whisper: 'Anybody watching us?'

'I'm not sure,' Jen mumbled.

'It's bloody uncomfortable down here.'

'Tough.' She covered her mouth with her hand. 'There are people around, and lots of places to hide in the trees. You need to stay down.'

Freddie started to grumble again, just as her phone rang.

It was Dean. 'You're alone?'

'Yes.'

'And you weren't followed?'

'No.' She fought the natural tendency to elaborate. If he was watching her now, surely he'd ask why she was driving a Mercedes and not the Audi?

'Okay.' He let out a breath. 'It's quite a way to the house, though it'll be worth it.'

The abrupt switch to a flirtatious tone made her nauseous. He instructed her to follow the path to the shore, then turn left and head along the lake until she reached a barbed-wire fence. She was to climb the hill for approximately a quarter of a mile, where she would find a hiking trail up in the trees.

'Turn right and follow it through a couple of dips. After the second rise, leave the path and head down to the lake. There's a sign warning of forest fires. When you get to that, bear left, through the undergrowth, and you'll see the house about a hundred yards away, sitting on the water. Got that?'

'I think so, but isn't there a way of reaching it from the road?'

'Yes. But I don't want you turning up by car. Oh, and you need to leave your phone behind.'

It's a trap. Jen almost said the words aloud, but that wouldn't have helped. Instead, she asked how long it would take to get there.

'About twenty minutes. It's longer if the ground's wet, so you're lucky there.' She heard him muttering, away from the phone, and then a beautiful voice said, 'Mum? Are you nearly here?'

'Charlie! Yes, I am. Really soon.' All her fears were pushed aside by the flood of relief, the sheer joy at hearing Charlie's voice.

Dean was back: 'He can't wait to see you. And neither can I.'

Jen shivered as the call ended. This was still far from straightforward, much less safe.

She looked around the car park, couldn't see anyone suspicious, but pretended to scratch her top lip as she spoke. 'That was Charlie. He sounds okay. But I've been told to come alone, and leave my phone here.'

'Jen, no. Let me follow you, at least.'

'It's too tricky. The house is on the lake, about twenty minutes' walk from here. There's a road, but he doesn't want me using it.'

Freddie started to say, 'I don't like the sound of—' but Jen knew there was no choice. She opened the door, twisting her upper body to get out, and in the same motion dropped the keys into the rear footwell, where Freddie had been hiding for the past half an hour.

She shut the door and marched towards the path.

Stemper had made only one brief stop for refuelling, at which point he'd gone online to view the property on Google Earth. Satellite images showed that the house was situated on a quiet stretch of the lake, surrounded on the other three sides by dense woodland. The nearest neighbour was half a mile away, one of eight or nine fairly exclusive dwellings served by a narrow access road that had escaped the attention of Google's Street View cameras.

On screen, Stemper had located the place where the access road emerged from the trees and joined the A592. From the main road it looked like nothing more than a farm track. When he reached it, he discovered that the residents must have agreed on further measures to protect their privacy, for there was now a gate across the entrance, and a sign that read, 'PRIVATE'.

But the gate wasn't locked, so he opened it and drove through, and nobody appeared from the gloomy woods to challenge him.

Jen quickly discovered that it was cooler here than in Sussex. She should have got a fleece from the car, but it was too late now. With the sun having dropped behind the hills, the sky overhead was a rich deep blue, and the flat, glassy surface of the lake shone with a pearlescent glow that only served to make the land around it seem darker and more forbidding.

For a moment she was fourteen, and back in Tilgate Forest on that first night as a runaway, her courage ebbing as the shadows lengthened and the temperature fell. She shivered, and thought of the figurine she'd found in Alex Wilson's home: she had to take Elen as her inspiration now, and trust in her ability both to find the hideaway and to know what to do when she got there.

Whether she was right or wrong about his part in Pearce's disappearance, she could no longer avoid thinking about the threat posed by Dean. It was clear that he regarded himself as her saviour – and it didn't take Sherlock Holmes to work out what he was expecting in return.

If it came to it, could she exchange sex for Charlie's safety? The thought turned her stomach, but the answer was so automatic that she hardly needed to pose the question.

To protect Charlie: *anything*.

Within the trees the light was dim, and it took a lot of concentration to follow the path at any speed without tripping over the uneven ground. Fortunately Jen had spent years running on worse terrain than this, and in little more than ten minutes she'd found the final outcrop, which looked down on a lonely lakeside property.

It was a former boathouse with a couple of additions that had turned it into a substantial three-storey home. A light shone from a room on the top floor, which was contained within the roof space. The roof itself was almost a mansard design, flat on top with a short, steep pitch on either side and gables at the front and rear, clad in white weatherboard. On the lower floors, every window in sight was obscured by steel shutters, bolted to the walls. The front door appeared to be equally formidable, designed to deter intruders.

Jen crouched behind a tree and watched for signs of movement. There was a black van parked in front of the house, and a rowing boat tied up at the jetty to the rear. The area around the building had been cleared back to bare earth, though it was strewn with weeds and even a few saplings. A large rusted skip sat close to the house, half filled with rubble and timber.

She was about to move when she heard an engine; she looked over her shoulder but the gradient of the hill made it impossible to see the road. After the vehicle had passed, she made her way cautiously down the slope, not directly to the house but steering to one side, always remaining within the cover of the trees.

She thought of Freddie's concern about her going alone, and almost wished she'd asked him to follow. Being twenty minutes away wouldn't help in an emergency. But perhaps she could reduce the risk in other ways.

For a start, Dean would be expecting her to walk up to the front door and knock.

She had to try something else.

CHAPTER SIXTY-FIVE

Freddie was a coward – he'd admit that to himself, if not to anybody else. But he wasn't the total cop-out that his dad sometimes accused him of being.

So he only fought with his conscience for a minute before sitting up. Wincing, he opened the door and extricated himself from the car. A woman who'd just parked alongside gave him a peculiar look, but he only nodded at her, locked the car and hurried away.

He'd heard snatches of Jen's conversation with Dean and thought he had a good chance of finding the house, providing he could pick up Jen's trail. He ran along the lake and took a left into the trees, only to trip and fall flat on his face.

As he picked himself up, his knee popped, and he yelped with pain. His arm was scratched, a few beads of blood emerging, but the real injury was to his pride. Cursing his clumsiness, he hurried up and along the hill on what he thought was the right course. After taking a turn he wasn't certain about, he changed his mind and was ready to backtrack when he spotted movement: Jen, a long way ahead, just disappearing from sight.

Encouraged, he sped up until he was on the ridge, slowing when he saw the house in the distance, a dark knot against the silvery gleam of the lake. Jen had paused, and was observing the property from a safe distance.

Freddie didn't trust himself not to stumble and make a noise, so he kept still and waited. For a moment, apart from birdsong, there was silence, and then he heard a car approaching from somewhere to his left. It grew louder as it passed, began to fade, then seemed to cut off.

Straining to listen, he thought he heard a door opening, but not the corresponding clunk of it closing. Below him, Jen had glanced round but hadn't seen him. She must have decided it was safe to move, for she set off towards the house, while keeping within the cover of the trees.

Now he was torn. Go after Jen, or check out the car? For a minute he did neither; just watched Jen get further away from him, his insides turning to water every time she was lost from sight behind the trees.

It was a no-brainer, or should have been – stick with Jen – but the car niggled at him. There were clearly very few houses around here, so the chance of someone turning up at the same time. . .

He lost track of his thoughts when he saw Jen burst from the trees in a fast, crouching run. She was heading to one side of the building, rather than the front, probably because the place was sealed up. The only signs of occupation were the van parked outside and a light on the top floor.

Then she vanished again, but only for a second. She was climbing onto a handrail where the jetty was fixed to the house. He stared, uncomprehending, as she stretched to get hold of an ancient-looking drainpipe.

'Oh, shit,' Freddie exhaled in a nervous judder.

She was going to climb.

As she got closer to the building, Jen saw a way she could get in. With the windows sealed by the shutters, the best option was the middle of the three large skylights, which she could see was partially open.

The route to it was far from clear-cut. There was an old cast-iron drainpipe that ought to bear her weight, providing the brackets that anchored it to the wall were still secure. But the next stage – going from the pipe to the roof – was a lot more tricky, and very dangerous.

There certainly weren't any better options, and all her instincts told her that Dean couldn't be taken at face value. Therefore, any small advantage she could gain had to be worth a try. And as a form of climbing, 'buildering', as it was known, had a long and noble history, and wasn't so different to what she did every day at the centre.

That was how she tried to reassure herself as she climbed onto the handrail and reached for the drainpipe. Clutching it with both hands, she jabbed her foot against the corner of the windowsill and let the pipe take some of her weight. It made a dull grinding noise that might have been audible within the house, but she had to hope that Dean would put it down to the natural creaks and groans of an old building.

Gripping the pipe, she tested its strength a little more by slowly leaning back, then planting her feet flat against the wall on either side. It felt pretty sturdy. Most of the brackets looked intact, though she could see one near the top that wasn't as tight to the wall.

As she started to climb, she could feel the pipe straining against the brackets. She prayed it would hold – there was a very hard landing if she fell, with little chance of escaping a broken limb, or worse.

Stay confident, she told herself. *You're good at this.*

And so she was. But at thirty feet up, almost at the top, the bracket came away.

There was a quiet grinding noise, a rusty bolt dropped onto her shoulder and bounced off, and the drainpipe lurched about a foot out from the building. Jen clung on, knowing that panic would only compound her problems. For one long, hideous second she felt sure the sudden added force would blow the next bracket, and then the next, causing the pipe to collapse, but thankfully it held. . . just about.

At least she was close enough now to reach out for the roof: the crux of the climb. Even though the drainpipe had come loose, the thought of letting go filled her with dread. To get over the lip of the roof, there would have to be a second or two when her only purchase would be a one-handed grip on the overhang at the corner of the rear gable. And the act of swinging away from the wall could easily be enough to send the drainpipe crashing to the ground, taking her with it.

She inhaled slowly and willed herself calm. When the bouldering centre had opened, she'd spent a lot of time on pull-ups and other upper body exercises, as well as increasing her finger strength by hangboarding, but in recent months she hadn't been quite so diligent. Did she still have the power and control?

I have to. She braced her feet and shifted a little more weight to her left side, then whipped her right hand out and grabbed the edge of the roof. She tested it, applying more force, and couldn't feel anything working loose. The roof was old but made with slate, a good durable material that wouldn't crumble as readily as clay or concrete tiles.

Then came the toughest part – a lock-off as she let go of the drainpipe and grabbed the roof with her left hand, then let her feet swing to the right, building momentum so that she could sweep them back the other way, at the same time bending her arms at the elbows and rising enough to lift her left foot onto the roof.

The pressure on her fingers, wrists and arms was extraordinary, but she banished the pain by an act of sheer will, refusing to let her nerves speak to her brain. Another huge effort was required to bring the rest of her body over, her mouth wide open in a silent scream and her mind whirring on an incoherent loop – *don't fall don't fail don't fall don't fail* – and then, suddenly, somehow, it was done.

She was up.

Stemper drove the length of the private road, turned round and parked some way short of the property. He took a leather bag from the back seat and put on latex gloves, a long dark coat and a wool cap. An incongruous look for the time of year, but one that concealed any meaningful information about his appearance.

The bag was heavy, and he switched it, gingerly, from hand to hand as he climbed the pothole-ridden tarmac of a narrow driveway, over a rise that gave him the first view of the house. It sat beside the lake on a patch of muddy ground, and seemed to be in the midst of some half-hearted renovation.

The security shutters on the windows were a gratifying sight; perfect for what he had in mind. He crept closer, then froze as he detected movement, high up on the building.

There was somebody on the roof. In the premature dusk of the woods it was difficult to make her out, but definitely a woman.

It seemed Gerard was right. Jennifer Cornish had come to find her son.

CHAPTER SIXTY-SIX

For a moment Jen lay sprawled face down on the sloping roof, still precariously balanced, with a potentially fatal drop just inches away. There weren't any hand or toeholds, so she didn't risk trying to kneel or stand. Instead she stretched out her left arm and leg, then pushed with her right side and shuffled a little further away from the edge.

It was a strange, ungainly form of motion, like trying to move by making snow angels, but on the third go, her left foot bumped over the ridge and landed on the flat central section of the roof. A few seconds later she was in a crouch, looking out over the waters of the lake and then down at the jetty, which seemed very far below.

Aware that the roof space would echo like a drum, she tiptoed along to the open skylight. It was set into the top of the sloping roof, with a hatch that opened like a jaw.

Jen knelt down and peered carefully through the glass. The room below was an enormous junkyard. It seemed to run at least half the length of the building, with several internal walls having been removed. Almost every inch of floor space was piled with furniture, mattresses, bedding, clothes and boxes.

But it also appeared to be unoccupied, which was good news. She studied the skylight and saw that the hinges were at the top. To get in she'd have to descend the slope a little, but at least this time she had the skylight itself to hold for support.

She pulled it open as far as it would go, then stepped onto the slate, both hands still gripping the open window as she positioned herself at the widest point. It didn't open enough for her to step inside easily; she had to bend down, place one foot and then the other over the frame, then wriggle in backwards with her upper body out over the roof and her legs dangling in mid air.

She heard a noise from below, like furniture shifting, but couldn't see anyone. It hardly mattered: she was committed now. Directly beneath her there were a couple of dining chairs and a grubby-looking mattress. Jen swung and dropped onto the mattress, landing heavily but without injury.

She half expected Dean to leap out, and tensed as a cardboard box scraped along the floor. Then a small, pale face popped up, gorgeous brown eyes widening with shock and delight.

Freddie had quickly moved position for a better view of what Jen was doing. It was something he instantly regretted. Watching her climb a three-storey building with no ropes or safety equipment was the most terrifying thing he'd ever witnessed.

It probably only took a few minutes but it felt like an hour, with Freddie frozen rigid the whole time. The slightest noise or movement might disturb her concentration, and the thought of Jen falling to her death because of something he'd done was more than he could bear.

He was hoping and praying and *willing* her to succeed; when she made it to the top he felt nearly as proud as if he'd done it himself. Not that he had any illusions on that score: very few people could do what Jen had just done, and it came as a sobering reminder that marrying her had been probably the best decision he'd ever made, and cheating on her the very worst.

After watching her disappear through the skylight, he punched the air: a brief moment of exultation before the anxiety returned once more. She was inside, but now what?

*

Jen hadn't even got to her feet when Charlie thudded into her. 'It's okay, darling.' She held him as tightly as she could, and promised: 'I'm here now. I won't leave you again.'

Charlie was sobbing, his face pressed to her chest. Jen checked to be sure they were alone. At ground level she could see the room was even more of a tip. Half a dozen radiators and several filthy toilet pans were stacked against one wall, next to a pile of mattresses stained and ragged from years of wear. Mould was growing on the walls and the piles of yellowy bed linen. The room was cold, and stank of decay.

Apart from the skylights, the half dozen windows on three sides of the room were clad with shutters, which were crudely bolted to the wall. There was only one door, made of heavy timber. No sign of Dean, though he must have heard the impact as she'd dropped into the room.

'Where is he? Has he looked after you?'

Charlie didn't answer either question. In a snuffling voice, he said, 'I don't like him, Mummy. I'm scared.'

'There's no need to be.' Jen felt sick, not least because this was a lie. 'Tell me, please, if he's hurt you. . .?'

She was dreading the response, so it was a relief when he shook his head. 'But he's nasty. He pretends to be my friend but he isn't. He made me pretend, too, on the video, or he said. . . he said he'd do things. . .'

'Wh-what things?' she asked, her voice almost breaking.

'Things,' he repeated. 'To you.'

'Charlie, I'm so sorry. I came for you as soon as I could, but he didn't tell me where you were. What about his mum – I hope she was a bit nicer to you?' She forced a smile, but it was met with a blank look. 'Last night. Didn't you sleep. . .?'

She aborted the question, aware that it could make things worse. She felt almost as angry with herself as she did with Dean. At least her decision to sneak into the building had been vindicated – without a chance to hear the truth from Charlie, she might have been suckered into believing yet more lies.

'I want to go.'

'We will. Where is he now, do you know?'

'Cleaning up, he said. When we got here, he had to go out on the lake. To get rid of—' He gulped, as if choking on the words.

'Get rid of what?'

'It was wrapped up in the back of the van. The smell was horrible. He told me it was an animal, to use for the meat, but I don't. . . I don't think it was.'

'What do you mean?'

'It was the shape of a person.'

'Oh, darling. I'm sure it wasn't – and anyway, I'm here now, and I won't let anything happen to you.' A pretty feeble display of bravado, she thought, just as Charlie's gasp alerted her to a sound from outside the room. A bolt rattled back, the door opened and Dean stepped into view.

CHAPTER SIXTY-SEVEN

Stemper watched the woman climb in through a skylight, then waited for Freddie Lynch to show himself. Had he found another way in, or was he watching from somewhere?

When no one appeared, he made the decision to creep down past the left side of the building. Jen's covert entry was likely to take Dean by surprise, and he wanted to exploit this distraction. He checked the back of the house, which had once opened onto the lake. More security shutters covered a set of rear doors.

Perfect. The steel door at the front was the only access point.

Stemper headed back that way and took a crowbar from his bag. Up close he could see that the ground-floor windows had been removed; prising away one corner of the shutter would give him the space he needed to get the incendiaries inside.

They were made to his own design, perfected on the basis of advice he'd received or extracted from sources that included Irish republicans, Chechen rebel fighters and a rogue Libyan scientist. He used jars the size of a coffee mug, designed to shatter easily and release liquid accelerant as well as an inner glass capsule that contained pyrophoric material, in this case tert-Butyllithium.

Fast or slow, it was going to be a noisy job. Since speed was of the essence, he wedged the crowbar between the wall and the shutter and jerked it forward, putting all his weight into a single decisive movement. The bolt on the corner was prised out with a blood-curdling screech, opening a gap just wide enough for his purposes.

He tossed a couple of the incendiaries through the opening, aiming for the area in front of the door. He heard the glass break and the pleasing whump of ignition, then hurried around the right-hand side of the building, intending to repeat the process and ensure the fire spread as quickly as possible. He'd set the bag down when his lizard brain screamed *danger*, a fraction of a second before he felt the vibration of footsteps.

Dean stopped and gaped at her, then looked up at the skylight. 'You came in through the roof?'

'I didn't know if it was safe to knock on the door.' Seeing his displeasure, she added, 'I had no way of knowing who else might be here.'

'Just me.' He nodded at Charlie. 'Us.'

'Okay. That's good.'

He was still suspicious. 'You followed the route I told you? Only I thought I heard a car.'

'I heard that, too. I assume you have neighbours?'

'Not many. That's what I like about it.' He stared at her for a long moment, as if debating whether he could trust her. Then he pressed his hands against his cheeks and let out a long breath. 'I'm sorry if I sounded hostile, but this place is so important to me. My sanctuary.'

Jen took in the squalor and tried to mask her revulsion. 'This is where you live?'

'Not exactly.' He gazed around, pensively, as if seeing it through her eyes. 'There was a bad flood last year, so a lot of stuff had to come up here. Obviously now I'll have to bring my plans forward, but if we both set to work, we can soon get a few of the rooms into shape.'

'You want me to stay here? With Charlie?'

He looked bemused. 'Well, of course. This is where we can all be safe.'

'Dean, I'm not sure—'

'You'll love it, honestly.' He smiled. 'This was my dream, from the moment I saw you at the Skyway. I watched you at work, helping those less fortunate, and knew I had to rescue you from the pain, the injustice of what your father-in-law was planning.' He paused, with an embarrassed glance at Charlie, then said, 'I'd hoped for a bit longer to get everything in place, but as I said, when I saw Charlie looking so unhappy I had to act fast.'

Jen listened in disbelief. She could feel herself trembling but had no idea if it was fear, adrenaline, suppressed rage – or all those things combined.

'Look, Dean. . .' She was nervous about contradicting him, but knew it would be equally dangerous to reinforce his delusions. 'It's really not practical for Charlie and me to hide away up here. I can't break off all contact with my family, my friends, the police.' He was about to interrupt when she quickly added: 'They've been speaking to me about Russell Pearce. I was one of the last people to see his wife before she died. Everyone's looking for him, and if I were to go missing as well. . .'

Shaking his head, Dean sighed. 'You ought to know that Pearce was a horrible pervert. He was a threat to you, Jen. I took care of that threat.'

He said it as if expecting to be thanked. 'Wh-what about his wife?' she asked.

'That had to be done, I'm afraid, to give the police a scenario that stopped them looking elsewhere. And she wasn't a nice woman at all, was she? I was there, on Sunday afternoon. I saw her spitting at you.' He seemed to register her shock and added, in an encouraging tone, 'You don't need to worry, especially now we have Gerard on tape. That'll get the cops off your back, and then we're home and dry.'

He's insane, she realised. Brushing off murder as little more than a minor detail. She understood that there would be no reasoning with him, and nor would he agree to let them leave. Her only option was to take him on and hope that Charlie, at least, was able to get away.

She handed him the recording device, suppressing a shudder as his fingers brushed against hers. 'Can we listen to this, and find out—'

'Oh, we easily have enough to ruin him.' Grinning at her confusion, he said, 'I should have explained – it's got a SIM card. You can dial in and listen through your phone. I already have the recordings on my laptop. Gerard's finished.'

For a moment she was speechless. This meant there had been no need for her to stay overnight at Gerard's: she could have left as soon as the bug was in place, and spent the night with Charlie instead.

She started to protest but the words were lost in a strange rending noise, possibly from outside, that caused Dean to back away and yell at her, furiously: 'Who's that? Who did you bring here?'

Freddie had no idea how Dean would react, but allowing Jen and Charlie to stroll out, unscathed, seemed a remote possibility. It was a hope he clung to for a few minutes, while he tried to figure out what he could do to help. Should he bang on the front door and demand to be let in?

A couple of times he thought he heard movement, maybe from the trees on the other side of the house, but there were birds chirping, and the occasional slap of a wavelet on the lake, so he couldn't be sure. But then came the violent, high-pitched sound of tearing metal. It lasted only a second, the silence returning so abruptly that Freddie began to wonder if he'd imagined it. . .

Until a man strode into view, dressed in a hat and coat that looked totally out of place on a late summer evening. He had a heavy bag, like the sort that doctors carry in old movies. His movements were urgent and precise, and sinister in a way that Freddie couldn't have defined, but one thing was for sure: this guy wasn't here to rescue anyone.

The man stopped at a window close to the jetty. That was when Freddie noticed something curling into the air from the far side of the building. A thin stream of grey smoke.

He'd never moved so fast in his life. He understood in an instant and knew that any hesitation would lead to cowardice – and the lives of Charlie and Jen might rest on his ability to find some courage.

He burst out of the trees, nearly skidded on a patch of wet mud but regained his balance and sprinted towards the man. He had no plan other than to stop him from making the fire any worse, but he wasn't quick enough, or quiet enough.

Sensing his approach, the man dodged to one side, snatching something from his bag. Although he looked to be in late middle age, he was agile, and fast, and clearly used to defending himself. Having lost the element of surprise, Freddie tried to adjust, lashing out with a punch that caught the man on his left shoulder. Grunting, his opponent turned to absorb the blow and brought his right arm up, clutching what looked like a metal bar. Freddie tried to fend it off but the man was too strong, too determined, and he swung the bar and smashed it into the side of Freddie's skull.

Then darkness.

Dean glared at her. 'Are you sure you weren't followed? And you removed the tracker?'

'I-I came in a different car, but I checked it first—'

'Gerard will have people hunting for me, you know that? They'll kill us all to keep this quiet.'

Jen nodded mutely, while praying that Freddie – if he'd come after her and was trying to help – wouldn't make any more noise. Dean glanced at the skylights, then at Charlie, and seemed satisfied that she wouldn't be going anywhere. He hurried out, locking the door behind him.

Jen waited a few seconds, hardly daring to believe that Freddie might be able to liberate them, then tested the door. It was too rigid to break down without making a lot of noise. The same went for the shutters over the windows, and there was no chance of climbing out over the roof when she had Charlie. . .

She heard a disturbance from below – thumps and crashing, and a startled cry from Dean. Charlie jumped, and held her tight. 'I don't like it here, Mummy. I want to go.'

'Me too, darling. We will in a minute.'

But how? She sniffed. Looked around, and heard more shouts and thudding noises from below. If Freddie had come after her, what exactly was he doing?

She sniffed again. What was that?

Something nasty.

Smoke.

CHAPTER SIXTY-EIGHT

There were running footsteps, then Dean unlocked the door. He was red-faced, coughing, and looked distraught. 'They've found us – Gerard, or fucking Hamilton.'

'What?' *So it wasn't Freddie. . .*

'There's a fire.' Dean jabbed a finger towards the floor. 'We can get out, but we have to hurry.'

For a moment she hesitated, then thought: *You can smell the smoke. He's not lying about this.* Without waiting, Dean turned and ran towards a flight of stairs. Jen took Charlie's hand. 'Let's go and see.'

She could feel his reluctance, which grew as they crossed a wide landing and started down the stairs. Just like the top floor, the middle floor had been partially gutted, lath and plaster walls removed to expose the innards of a few tatty bedrooms, like images she'd seen of London homes in the Blitz.

Thick smoke billowed into the stairwell from the ground floor. Dean was already out of sight. Charlie put a hand to his throat and made a choking noise, and Jen recalled something a fireman had once told her: *Don't think of it as smoke, but as toxic gas. Even a few inhalations can be fatal.*

Over the roar of the fire she heard a metallic wrenching sound, and wondered if Dean was trying to remove one of the shutters. Then a gout of flame shot into view, accompanied by a scream that was almost inhuman in its agony.

'Go back up!'

'But Mum—'

'I'll stay in sight – just go. And hold your breath, like you did in the sea with Lucas.'

Covering her nose and mouth, Jen moved towards the bottom flight of stairs. The fire was raging through the whole of the ground floor, and in some places the flames were already creeping into the bedrooms, veils of smoke venting between the bare floorboards.

There was another scream, and Dean staggered into view, collapsing at the foot of the stairs, his hair and clothes alight. Then came a cry from behind her: Jen turned and saw that Charlie had followed, too frightened to be left alone.

There was nothing she could do to help Dean, and no prospect of getting out this way. Saving Charlie was the only thing that mattered. But how?

Stemper gazed at the body, and rebuked himself for not having checked the perimeter more carefully. So this was Freddie Lynch.

After ascertaining that Gerard's son was alive, albeit unconscious, Stemper got back to work, quickly bending the shutter until there was enough space to throw the other incendiaries inside.

As the first one landed, he saw a bright yellow flash and heard a piercing scream. Dean Geary, he hoped; the glass must have smashed at his feet, the chemical igniting upon contact with air.

Stemper lobbed in another for good measure. Probably unnecessary, given the heat and smoke already pouring from the building. There was no chance of anyone getting out of there alive.

It was regrettable, perhaps, that the woman and her son would perish, though a clean conclusion always had its appeal. He was confident that Gerard would come to agree.

Killing Freddie, however, might be a step too far. Stemper knelt to check on his vital signs, then dragged him a little further from the building and placed him in the recovery position.

As he walked briskly back to the car, it occurred to him that the head injury might lead to memory loss. In these circumstances, with no other witnesses, Freddie would be a plausible candidate for the arson attack – and the poor man wouldn't know whether he'd done it or not.

Stemper probably shouldn't have found that amusing, but sometimes you had to smile.

'Go! Go!' Jen urged Charlie up the stairs and raced behind him, coughing and choking from the single breath she'd taken. As they reached the landing, Jen tripped on the final step and fell, her hands slapping against the floor. It was hot to the touch.

Back in the room full of junk, she slammed the door and grabbed a pile of linen, using it to block the gap beneath the door. She embraced Charlie, stroking his hair and murmuring encouragement while she examined the room and tried to work out if they had any chance at all of staying alive.

'We're going to build a tower.'

Charlie regarded her as though she'd gone mad. 'The fire's coming.'

'I know. So we have to be quick.'

He clung to her as she went to move, and though it felt callous to break apart, she knew they might have only a minute or two before the smoke overwhelmed them.

She put the distance from the floor to the skylight at about fourteen feet. The tower had to be at least ten feet high, and stable – so the mattresses might help after all. Standing the chairs with one pair backed up tight to the wall and the other pair facing them, she lifted several of the radiators and piled them onto the seats to add weight and stability. Then she dragged a single mattress over and placed it across the top of the chairs. Added a second mattress and decided she might get away with three.

By now Charlie was helping, both of them sweating from the effort and from the sauna-like warmth in the room. They both kept coughing, and Jen thought the air might be turning slightly murky. As she worked, a horribly disloyal idea came to her: had Freddie caved in at some point, and supplied his father with the address?

No. He couldn't have.

'Looks like *The Cat in the Hat*,' Charlie observed of the tower when it was done, and despite everything Jen found herself smiling.

'You're right. Let's hope it doesn't come crashing down.'

She turned away, searching for perhaps one more object to add to the makeshift climbing frame, and noticed a stepladder resting innocently against the far wall. Cursing her stupidity, she realised that the mattresses had concealed it from view.

In any case, it was an A-frame ladder with only four steps, so nowhere near tall enough to reach the skylight. But could she risk placing it on top of the mattresses?

As she picked it up she heard a loud rumbling noise, and a heavy crash of timber that shook the whole building. Charlie stumbled, almost falling over. Jen guessed that part of the floor below must have collapsed; more smoke was creeping into the room, and the temperature was rising fast.

Either this works, she thought grimly, *or we die*.

CHAPTER SIXTY-NINE

Jen forced herself to take it steady. Too much haste and they would fail.

First she helped Charlie to clamber onto the mattresses, and told him to stay on his hands and knees while she climbed up beside him, bringing the stepladder with her. They were level with a window, and when her elbow bumped against the shutter it burned her skin.

Feeling like a circus clown masquerading as an acrobat, she tried to wedge the stepladder against the wall, wobbling a little as she encouraged Charlie to climb up.

'I don't want to.'

'I know. But you're a good climber – a natural, Nick says.'

He nodded, cheered by this reminder. Praise from Nick seemed to carry twice the weight of anything from his mum, but if it got him up the ladder, who cared? On the top rung he was almost there, and Jen managed to give him the final boost that lifted his upper body out of the skylight.

'It opens more than this,' he said, and released a catch that she hadn't noticed on the way in. Lifting the window higher, he followed her instructions and climbed onto the sloping roof, then used the frame of the skylight to reach the top.

If not for the danger they were in, the idea of sending her young son out on a high roof would have left her catatonic with fear. But there was no other option: if she went out first, she wouldn't be able to reach in and lift him up.

It was a heart-stopping moment when he disappeared from sight, but then came a shout: 'I'm up.'

Jen scrambled after him, terrified that the whole building might collapse and plunge them into the inferno. She grabbed the skylight and kicked for more momentum, causing the stepladder to topple and fall. Desperately scissoring her legs, she wriggled over the rim and onto the slope, thick black smoke billowing all around her.

Charlie was huddled on the flat roof, but bravely leaned forward to help her up. Instead of urging him away from the edge, she understood what this gesture meant, so she took his hand, even though she didn't let him bear any of her weight. 'Thanks, buddy. We're nearly there.'

From down in the room, getting up here had seemed a nearly impossible quest, but at least the urgency had demanded her absolute focus. Now there was the next stage to consider.

She led Charlie along the roof until they were at the edge of the rear gable. With so much smoke pouring from the building, it was impossible to see the trees or the lake, but Jen had a good idea of where the jetty lay, on the right-hand corner.

Having to shout over the roar of destruction, she said, 'Okay, Charlie. Now we're going to jump into the water, still holding hands like this.'

She expected him to baulk at the idea, but he said, 'The fire's going to kill us, isn't it?'

'If we stay up here for much longer, yes.'

'How deep is it?'

Good question, she thought. 'Probably not very. We've got to take a run up and jump out as far as we can, aiming for that corner.' She pointed to the left. 'When we hit the water, try and bend your legs—'

'Like a banana shape,' he said. 'Me and Dad were doing it in the pool. He told me not to tell you, cos it's dangerous.'

Trust Freddie. But Jen nodded. 'I won't say a word.'

Together they retreated four, five paces, then turned, and at her signal they sprinted along the roof and leapt, screaming, into an oblivion of grey smoke.

As she fell, the only thing that mattered was that she didn't lose her grip on Charlie's hand. If this proved to be a tragic miscalculation that killed them both, Jen at least wanted her son to know that she was there with him, at the end.

The drop must have taken only a second or two – she had no concept of time, or of space – but the smoke was clearing and she made out a glimmer of water with just enough time to shout, 'Curl up!'

The lake was a gloriously cold shock to the system, but her instinct on hitting the water was to draw in her arms as well as her legs. She felt Charlie do the same, wrenching his hand from her grasp as she was submerged and the world went dark and murky, and then her feet sank into the silt and her bottom followed, before she managed to push upwards, already flailing desperately to find Charlie. Her head burst above the surface and she sucked in a breath and turned in a full circle and didn't see him; she filled her lungs again and prepared to go back down when there was a splash behind her and Charlie was there, spitting out water and grinning with delight when he registered that she, too, was alive.

She swam to him and they embraced, her feet just about touching the lake bed. They could hear parts of the building collapsing, and turned to see flames shooting from the skylights, smoke pouring from the shuttered windows like steam from a kettle. For the first time, she heard sirens in the distance. *Thank God.*

They waded over to the jetty and then swam beyond it, to avoid the risk of falling debris, coming ashore well away from the house. Jen hoped the emergency services arrived before Charlie got too cold. He insisted he was fine, and more interested in watching the fire. He kept pointing to the roof, marvelling that he had jumped from such a height.

'Lucas won't believe it,' he said. 'You'll tell him, won't you?'

'I certainly will.'

'And Dad. Can we call him later on?'

'He's here. In the car.'

Delighted, Charlie spun to face her. 'I want to see him!'

'We will. We'd better wait till the fire engines get here.'

She looked around, wondering nervously who had set the fire and whether they were still nearby. It seemed that Dean was right: whoever it was had been intent on killing all three of them.

Just as it occurred to her that Freddie must have noticed the smoke by now, something caught her attention. She frowned, squinting at the brightness of the flames. There was a strange dark shape close to the jetty; but it hadn't been there earlier, and didn't look like debris. . .

She jumped up, took a couple of steps, then turned to Charlie. 'Stay there!' she ordered, so harshly that he recoiled.

She raced towards the building. The metal shutters were bulging in the heat, as if they might be about to explode. Dozens of roof slates lay in pieces on the ground. The air here was like a furnace, though it became marginally cooler as she sank to her knees.

The shape, she saw now, was a man lying on his side, with blood on his hair and his face.

Freddie.

She didn't waste time checking for signs of life – the whole building could come down on them at any moment. She grabbed his upper arms and dragged him backwards over the rough ground, not stopping until they were well clear of the house and Charlie was beside her, asking who it was and then working it out himself.

'Daddy!'

'He's all right,' Jen said, because the last thing Charlie needed was yet more trauma, but she also prayed that the words wouldn't come back to haunt her.

Right now she had no idea whether Freddie was dead or alive.

EPILOGUE

September had been, for the most part, an Indian summer, and Jen and Charlie had regularly gone to the beach after school. A couple of times Nick had joined them, and on one occasion – coincidentally, Jen hoped – they had bumped into her solicitor, Tim Allenby.

Too many men interfering in my life, and the only one I want or need is Charlie. Jen had a distant memory of that sentiment, in the days before she knew what real problems were.

Charlie had started school on the Monday, missing the first two days, but so had three of his classmates. Like them, he blamed the absence on a foreign holiday. It meant Jen had to endure the school's disapproval, but this was preferable to a lot of inquisitive questions about what had really happened. Charlie's fear was that if any of the teachers were aware of the truth, they would treat him differently, leading to problems when the other kids invariably picked up on it.

Jen was intensely concerned about the psychological impact of the ordeal, but Charlie seemed remarkably unaffected. After two or three sessions with a counsellor, arranged in conjunction with the police interviews, Jen was told to trust her judgment as a mother. If Charlie was behaving normally and seemed fine, then he probably was.

It turned out that Dean had treated Charlie reasonably well, though the boy had never truly believed his claim to be close to

Jen. 'But he knew lots of stuff about you, so I thought I must be wrong.'

There was one blatant lie that Dean had told Jen. On Tuesday evening, before they drove north, Charlie hadn't stayed with Dean's mother – the woman had died when Dean was a child. In fact, Charlie had almost certainly been given a sleeping tablet, crushed up and added to a bottle of juice, and left to sleep in the back of the van while Dean met up with Jen. By then he'd guessed they would be hunting for him, so it wasn't safe to stay at the flat he rented in Uxbridge.

Jen was horrified that Charlie had spent hours lying beside what he himself suspected was a dead body, though fortunately he'd woken the next morning in the front seat of the van, feeling sick and disorientated. It was possible that he hadn't been fully aware of his surroundings during the night, and Jen prayed that the memory was lost forever.

The body of Russell Pearce had been recovered from the lake two days after the fire. Cause of death was a single stab wound to the neck, consistent with the blood spatter found in the hall. The detectives now believed that Kelly Pearce had gone for a walk on Sunday evening, at which point Dean had entered the house and murdered Russell, then cleaned up and waited for her return. The frenzied manner of her killing was nothing more than an attempt to create the impression of domestic rage.

'Everything suggests that Dean was very cool, very sly and deliberate in his acts,' DI Booth had told her. 'Even if we find no evidence of it, I'm convinced he'll have committed similar crimes in the past.'

Despite this, the police were still initially dubious about Jen's claim that the kidnap was linked to a conspiracy. On the morning after the fire, Alex Wilson had given a statement retracting his earlier allegations against Jen, apparently muddying the waters just enough to avoid prosecution for wasting police time. At that stage she was still in Cumbria, receiving treatment for smoke inhalation and shock.

By the time she spoke to the Sussex detectives, Wilson had disappeared. Subsequent enquiries revealed that he and Sam Dhillon had used false identities, leading to a dead end which DS Howard agreed was regrettable. 'But surely the important thing is that the charges are being dropped, and you and Charlie are okay.'

True enough, Jen couldn't really deny that. But then there was Gerard.

'You're frowning.'

Jen took what she thought might be her final swim of the season on the second Tuesday of October. Charlie was at school, which made her feel a bit guilty about going to the beach, but the sea had taken on a sudden chill, so she had to make the most of it.

'I was thinking about Gerard,' she said. 'And I don't like thinking about Gerard.'

She was lying on her back, eyes shut, towel wrapped tightly around her. It was a day of slate-grey skies and almost no wind: pleasantly warm until you plunged into cold water.

Recalling the jump into the lake, she shivered. It still haunted her, all the not-quite tragedies of that terrible day. Like finding Freddie, and moving him only a couple of minutes before a section of the roof came crashing down on the spot where he'd been lying.

'Don't blame you,' he said now. 'I'm thinking about him less and less each day.'

She opened her eyes and watched him towelling off, briskly rubbing his head but avoiding the area above his left ear. The hair was growing back nicely where he'd had stitches, but that part of his skull was still tender. He'd regained consciousness in the ambulance, and spent a week in hospital, undergoing a battery of tests before the doctors concluded, tentatively, that there should be no permanent damage.

Jen hoped they were right. Freddie had struggled a little with his balance and coordination for a few weeks, and there were times when his choice of a particular word seemed to take him by surprise, as if it had sprung from some disordered part of his mind.

'Have you heard anything more from him?' she asked.

'Not since last week. He was talking up the villa, but I don't think he likes it there. He didn't have a single good thing to say about the Greeks.'

'And did you see that article in the *Sun*?'

'Yeah. If Trump wins next month, he's gonna move to the US.' Freddie snorted. 'Well, good riddance.'

'Except it would mean Trump wins.'

'Shit. Yeah.'

They lay together in silence for a couple of minutes. They were just down from Hove Lawns, and had the entire beach to themselves – if you didn't count a few disgruntled seagulls, prowling over the stones and squawking their displeasure.

Jen's first statement to the police had included everything she could give them about Gerard's part in the plot to send her to prison. At that point Freddie was incapacitated, but when interviewed later in the week he was able to confirm much of her account.

As a result, Gerard was arrested and questioned at length. Ignoring the advice of his expensive lawyer to say nothing, he stridently denied every one of the allegations against him, and left the investigating officers in no doubt that he would raise hell if they brought what he termed 'a wrongful prosecution'.

At the same time, he must have called in any number of favours, because apart from a nervous little dig in the *Guardian*, the entire news media failed to report on his arrest. 'Straight out of the Jimmy Savile playbook,' was how Freddie described it.

Without any solid evidence, the police had no option but to release him. The same was true of Hugo Hamilton, who was just as emphatic in denying his involvement. Contact between the two men could not be established – Freddie suspected Gerard had been using an anonymous mobile phone, which he would have ditched well before his arrest.

The only piece of worthwhile evidence was the recording that Dean had allegedly transferred to his laptop. But the computer, along with the recording device and several phones, had been vaporised by the fire.

Exactly as Gerard had planned it? That was what Jen suspected, but she would probably never know for sure.

Gerard's only concession to his guilt was to declare that he was giving up his column to begin a life of semi-retirement at his new villa in Greece. That announcement was followed by the news that he and Deborah were divorcing.

Jen had made it clear to Freddie that she vehemently opposed contact between Gerard and his grandson, at least until Charlie was old enough to be told some of the background, whereupon he could decide for himself. In the meantime, her fears that Charlie might be hurt by the silence appeared to be unfounded. He hadn't once asked to see his granddad.

Freddie's attitude towards Gerard was, if anything, even more negative than hers. He was certain that his father had used his friends in high places to avoid what should have been a long prison sentence.

But the great advantage of Gerard's absence meant that he was no longer interfering in their lives. That had enabled Jen and Freddie to work out a sensible arrangement for Charlie – one that gave him the stable routine he would need to do well at school while also allowing for plenty of leisure time with each of his parents. An agreement that had once seemed impossible had been reached in a matter of hours.

Jen's own parents had been a great help in picking up the slack. Charlie had spent several weekends in Surrey, and on one occasion Jen and Freddie had both joined them for a Sunday lunch. Jen hadn't said too much to her mum, despite her vow to strengthen the relationship, but there was talk of a spa weekend – just the two of them – in the near future.

When Jen sat up and checked the time, Freddie cleared his throat and said, 'I, uh, I've got some news.'

'Oh?'

'I've met someone. Lauren. Early days, but. . .' He was grinning broadly.

'You think it could be serious?'

He nodded. 'She's a teacher – and she's only suggested I should get into it, too. Teaching music.' He seemed to flinch, perhaps expecting Jen to pour scorn on the idea. But she nodded with genuine enthusiasm.

'I think that's brilliant. You're great at communicating your love of music – and you're really good with kids.'

'Am I?' He blinked a few times. 'Thank you.'

They hugged, a little awkwardly, and then he asked about her love life. Anything on the horizon?

'No. And that's fine with me just now.' Since returning to work, Nick had made a few advances, all of which she had gently rebuffed. Having listened to her instincts, she'd decided that he wasn't right for her.

'So, er, about Lauren,' Freddie said as he pulled on his jeans. 'I'll see her a couple more times, and then I wondered about introducing her to Charlie. You okay with that?'

Jen nodded. 'Completely okay.'

*

There were one or two other bright spots. She'd recently had a message of thanks from Jonathan Oldroyd at SilverSquare. The police had investigated the material planted on their computer and confirmed that no charges would be brought against the creative director. The takeover deal was proceeding smoothly, and off the record Oldroyd had learned that the image of the mysterious female employee had been passed to MI5 for further investigation.

The road-rage incident at Brighton Marina had continued to worry her for a while, but she'd heard nothing more about it. On balance, she no longer felt it was connected to the wider conspiracy; as Freddie put it: 'Just a couple of con artists who changed their minds when you went psycho on them.'

Far more significant mysteries remained unsolved. Despite his grisly record of murder and a host of other crimes, Jen knew that Dean had virtually sacrificed himself in order to save her and Charlie. If he'd simply fled the building at the first sign of a fire, he would no doubt have survived. Instead, he'd run back upstairs and unlocked the door, urging them to follow him out. His final act had been a selfless one, and perhaps, in a small way, that should count for how he was remembered. Certainly Jen preferred to focus on that rather than on whatever fate he'd planned for her, or how he might have reacted to her inevitable rejection.

But the issue that plagued her most was the identity of the man who had started the fire, and almost killed Freddie. That he'd been working for Gerard was beyond doubt – in her mind, and Freddie's, too – but they knew they would never be able to prove it.

In a final confrontation before he left for Greece, Gerard had insisted to Freddie that he had no idea who the man was, and that on no account had he employed anybody to do them harm.

'He nearly killed your grandson, and you don't care that he's going to get away with it,' Freddie had said, to which Gerard merely shrugged.

'A madman like Dean was bound to have enemies. Perhaps this arsonist had no idea anyone else was in there?'

Jen didn't believe that. Neither did Freddie. What they had to hope, Freddie had told her, was that the man was merely a professional. As terrible as that sounded, at least it meant he had no further reason to intrude on their lives. 'Better a hitman, or whatever he is, than a sociopath with a grudge.'

Jen agreed. She didn't tell him about the nightmares, where this malevolent figure suddenly appeared to finish the job. She guessed it was a natural consequence of a near miss, and in time no doubt the fears would subside to a manageable level, even if they didn't fade entirely.

'Actually,' she said, 'I've got a request of my own.'

They'd bought coffees at the open-air cafe on the promenade, and were sharing a Kit Kat. Freddie was smirking at a text he'd just received: from Lauren, presumably.

'Oh?' he said.

'Next summer, I've been wondering about escaping to Kenya for five or six weeks. I ran it past Nick and he's okay with me taking the time off. A girl I used to work with is doing safaris out there. She said I'd be welcome to help out, and combine that with a bit of travelling, maybe get into the mountains.'

While he considered it, Freddie pouted. 'And you'd be taking Charlie?'

'If he wants to come.' She swallowed nervously. 'I hope he will.'

Freddie nodded, and his expression relaxed. 'He'll love it.'

'You don't mind?'

'No way. It'll be an amazing experience – just what he needs, after this.' He leaned over and kissed her cheek. 'Just what you need, too. An adventure.'

Jen smiled, raising her coffee in a toast. 'An adventure,' she agreed.

AUTHOR LETTER

Firstly, if you're reading this, I hope it means that you have read and enjoyed the novel. If you haven't, please be aware that this letter contains references to the story that might be considered spoilers.

My previous book, *All Fall Down*, featured a large cast of characters and multiple viewpoints, so by contrast I wanted this one to focus on a smaller group of people. After mulling over several ideas, one in particular grabbed my attention – that of a law-abiding person doing something that appears to be risky or wrong, and then paying a heavy price. An image came into my head of a set of keys falling to the ground, and my protagonist picking them up and being faced with a decision: what to do with them?

It's easy to forget that our attitudes to risk vary greatly from person to person, and I had a lot of fun placing my main character in a situation where her actions were likely to divide opinion. Some readers will no doubt be thinking, as she enters the house, 'Why on earth are you doing this?' while others will feel that it's a perfectly reasonable choice to make. Only later does it become clear that Jen's free will wasn't quite so free, after all.

Each Little Lie is a story about manipulation, and deceit, and what seems to have become a horribly topical theme: the use of power and money to tilt, in secret, an apparently level playing field. An era where it has become acceptable and even celebrated for the rich to bully the poor, for the strong to bully the weak. Of course, I must stress that the character of Gerard Lynch isn't based on any real person, but he is inspired by the many newspaper columnists and TV pundits of this type: men and women who enjoy a life of extraordinary wealth and privilege and yet seem to be consumed with fury that the world isn't quite unfair or cruel enough. Sadly, such individuals rarely have to face the consequences of their words, a fact which is duly reflected in the ending of this book.

Thankfully, most of the novel is seen through the eyes of a much nicer and more decent human being. From the very beginning I knew that my main character would be a woman, my first female protagonist since Julia in *Skin and Bones*. With that book, I found it quite daunting at first (in my experience female writers capture the male psyche a little better than the other way round, perhaps because we men are such simple creatures!) but I'm glad to say that Jen sprang to life in an instant, and it was always a thrill to follow her quest for the truth.

I only hope that you felt the same – and if you did, I'd be very grateful if you would consider leaving a review at the site of your choice. I'd also love to hear from you via social media: see the links below. And if you would like to keep up-to-date with all my latest releases, just sign up at the following link. Your email address will never be shared and you can unsubscribe at any time.

www.bookouture.com/tom-bale

Thanks,
Tom

www.tombale.net

ACKNOWLEDGEMENTS

As ever, I'm very grateful to my editor, Keshini Naidoo, for helping to make this book as good as it can possibly be. Huge thanks also to Oliver Rhodes, Kim Nash and the whole team at Bookouture for the amazing job they do in bringing these books to the attention of readers.

I'd like to thank my agent, Camilla Wray, and everyone at Darley Anderson, particularly Mary Darby, Emma Winter and Rosanna Bellingham.

For help with research I'm deeply indebted to Jenny Dunn, though I'd like to stress that any errors or liberties taken for the sake of a fast-paced story are entirely my responsibility. Thanks also to Dan Rosling, Demetra Saltmarsh and Renee White.

Much of this book was written in various cafes, one of which – at Hove museum – has an off-stage role in the story, and has now sadly closed. I worked on four or five different novels in that cafe and will always be grateful for the warm welcome and continuing friendship from its manager and staff, especially Kirstie Sutton, Julia Mckernan, Bridget Moore and Rosa Steele.

Thanks to my fabulous Bookouture buddies who are now too numerous to name, and similarly I want to say thank you to the extraordinary army of bloggers, tweeters and reviewers who have helped to spread the word with such lovely comments and reviews on Amazon, Twitter, Facebook, Goodreads and elsewhere. I feel honoured to have such support.

Lastly, thanks as ever to my family and friends, and most of all to Niki – it's not easy living with someone who spends a lot of his time in another world entirely, so thank you for putting up with me.

Lightning Source UK Ltd.
Milton Keynes UK
UKHW02f0506161217
314558UK00004B/270/P